GALLOWAY'S GOSPEL

Also by Sam Rebelein

Edenville

STORY COLLECTION
The Poorly Made and Other Things

GALLOWAY'S GOSPEL

A Novel

Sam Rebelein

WILLIAM MORROW

An Imprint of HarperCollins*Publishers*

hc.com

FIRST EDITION

Designed by Leah Carlson-Stanisic
Wave pattern ©marukopum/shutterstock.com
Map by Leah Carlson-Stanisic using art by Atipathique, Adobe Stock Images

Library of Congress Cataloging-in-Publication Data

Names: Rebelein, Sam author
Title: Galloway's gospel : a novel / Sam Rebelein.
Description: First edition. | New York, NY : William Morrow, an imprint of
  HarperCollins Publishers, 2025. | Identifiers: LCCN 2025012346 | ISBN
  9780063423954 hardcover | ISBN 9780063423961 paperback | ISBN
  9780063423992 ebook
Subjects: LCGFT: Fiction | Horror fiction | Novels
Classification: LCC PS3618.E3355 G35 2025 | DDC 813/.6—dc23/eng/20250527
LC record available at https://lccn.loc.gov/2025012346

ISBN 978-0-06-342395-4

Printed in the United States of America

25 26 27 28 29 LBC 5 4 3 2 1

For Rachels everywhere

Teenagers scare the livin' shit out of me.

—"TEENAGERS," My Chemical Romance

MAP OF
RENFIELD & BRADDOCK

RENFIELD COUNTY

BRADDOCK COUNTY

The Billowhills

▲ Boldiven Lodge

▲ Mount Slake

Crumdugger
State Forest

Shembelwoods

Bent River

▲ Bartrick Prison

• Slake Hill

Billows Road

County Road 7

▲ Dome Lab

• Lillian Art
School

• Edenville

• Leaden Hollow

• Lillian

• Tinker's Falls

Bartrick Lake

• Bent

• Furrowkill
(Branson College)

• Bartrick Mill

Nettle River

▲ Bent Asylum

N

Deep Shembels

▲ Burnskidde Tunnel

W   E

S

Billowhills

Clate River

Bent River

to the Taconic

GENESIS

Addekkea

After Lawrence Renfield was hanged on March 3, 1935, for the murder of his family, his heart continued to beat. It filled the small white room they hanged him in with an echoing *thump*. The four men there stood still for a long time, listening to the creak of the rope and the beat. *Thump-thump*. A regular sixty-five bpm. *Thump-thump*. His body was still; his neck had snapped; by all accounts he was dead. But they could not declare him so, when still the room boomed with the beating of Lawrence Renfield's heart.

The prison doctor checked Lawrence's pulse. Nothing. After three long minutes of waiting, the doctor took Lawrence's body to the morgue in Bartrick Regional. All the way there, it continued to *thump*. He conducted an autopsy, exsanguinating the body, removing the stomach and kidneys and spleen, and placing each cold, still sac on a metal shelf. The doctor unraveled Lawrence's intestines and unstoppered his brain from its seat in his skull. The doctor cracked apart the ribs and peeled out the lungs, and there sat Lawrence's murderous heart, beating all the while. *Thump-thump*. Contracting and shivering, *thump-thump*.

The doctor watched it as he worked. He knew it sensed his hands, rooting around, and his tools, clipping and slicing . . . When he was finished with everything else, when he could delay it no longer, he cut out the heart from Lawrence Renfield's chest. He lifted it, still beating, in his hands.

The doctor was not a religious man, but he feared God all the same. How could he not? Just look at what God was making now.

"The Warden, the Sheriff, the Doctor, and the Priest," Carter Moone, from his 1947 collection, *Things I've Seen Above the Mist: An Oral History of Renfield*

RENFIELD COUNTY, OCTOBER 2019

Here is a car in the rain. From inside its thin metal shell, hear thick drops splatter against the roof like buckshot. Look outside at the wide expanse of woods at night: sharp pine, lit blue-green by lightning. Branches dancing in the roar of the storm. The hungry grumble of thunder on the horizon. The mist creeping through the undergrowth, groping blindly toward the car with long gray tendrils.

The car sits at the mouth of a gravel service road, next to the jaw of a tunnel through the belly of a hill. The car is as still as a rabbit, frightened stone-stiff. Out here, in the storm in the dark in the woods—even the cars feel watched.

An alarm. Out there in the cold. A wailing, bad-weather drone.

Movement in the trees. Twigs snapping underfoot. A silent strobe of lightning. A glimpse of shoulders shoving their way through the barbed branches of the pines. Thunder growls as a man throws himself against the side of the car. Drenched, clutching something tight to his chest. Hair in his eyes. He leans against the side of the sedan as he digs in his pocket for the keys. His pants are so soaked he can barely yank them out.

"Fuck you," through gritted teeth. "Come on . . ."

Finally, he scrabbles the keys loose and unlocks the car. He throws himself inside and slams the door, catches his breath, head back against the seat, eyes closed. Panting. Dripping. He throws his eyes open, shoots out a hand, slams the door lock down. He sighs, head back on the seat again. Breathing deep. Holding the bundle to his chest.

A small lump of gray cloth.

Big fuckup, he scolds himself. *Big stupid fuckup. Freakin amateur hour over here.*

He looks up at the rearview, still panting, still clutching that bundle to his chest. He shakes his head at himself. *You know better than that, Mark. You were almost a liability tonight, buddy. Come on.*

Mark moves his head side to side, analyzing his face in the dim reflection of the mirror. He smears his long black hair back with both hands, probes at his right ear with his fingertips.

There's a very special hearing aid lodged deep in the canal there. He's still worried he'll damage it someday in the rain, or the shower. But the man who'd crafted this hearing aid had assured him: it was practically impossible to break.

This hearing aid is made of brass. It whirs and clicks, and the teeny titanium wires strung deep within Mark's eardrum all vibrate at frequencies the normal ear cannot hear. The instruments inside—little tubes of glass and mechanical ticking gears—are all so small, so delicately wired into the structure of Mark's brain, that he can't tell where *he* ends and the augment begins. The implant is so strong, in fact, that sometimes when he's home alone, he hears whispers and cannot place where they are coming from.

Something shrieks. *That* he can place. The high-pitched scream stretches the springs in Mark's augmented ear, sending a metal vibrating *zing* through his jaw. He tilts his head so he can locate the sound. Far overhead. Swooping through the storm. He can't hear it with his normal ear at all, so the thing is still far away.

But he can hear it coming closer.

Mark jams the key into the ignition and roars the engine to life. His headlights blast against the wall of weeping pine. He cradles the small cloth bundle in his lap as he throws the car into reverse. The tires spin uselessly, vomiting gravel. The car wobbles but doesn't move, stuck in a rut.

The thing in the storm has heard the engine. It shrieks again, diving down, cutting through lightning.

Mark eases off the throttle, gently nudges the car out of the rut, and finally, he feels the tires grip. He rolls back, nice and steady, staring out the back windshield at the red wash of the taillights, the mouth of the tunnel. He manages to get the car back onto the road, whirls it around, throws it into drive, and guns it toward the tunnel—just as the large dark shape bursts out of the clouds, swoops down and *scrrrapes* three long gashes into the windshield. It circles back, dives again, screaming in the rain, ripping into the side of Mark's car, just before he roars away into the tunnel.

The tunnel is dark and littered with chunks of old debris. Mark dodges them, swerving left and right. "Jesus, shhhit!" The engine roars loud in both ears. He takes a breath, slows. Glances over his shoulder. The thing hasn't followed him. He can hear it, shrieking away into the thunder.

Excellent. But *fuck*, his *car*. Sure, the car is a pain in the ass. If it'd been a newer model, he could've just booped it unlocked instead of scrabbling for the key. But this was his grandmother's Oldsmobile. Bench seats, warm leather interior, sharp blue paint job . . . Mark adores this car. It even smells like her Pall Malls. But now it has gashes in its side, its windshield, *fuck*.

Light up ahead. Mark eases off the gas, relieved. *You are fuckin lucky, you dumb idiot. You desperate, cocky—*

The car starts shuddering. Making a limp flopping noise.

He tilts his head. Listens.

It's the tire. When that thing clipped the side of his car, it popped his tire. *Fuuuck.*

He shakes his head at himself again. *So stupid, Mark. Really shouldn't have been in Burnskidde at all. And you definitely shouldn't have tried to save her.*

He cradles the bundle in his lap ever tighter as the car rattles into the lights of town.

The town of Bent hugs the river on both sides. It is a place of faded brick and concrete, where most of the buildings are smeared with black from the Great Fire of 1953.

This diner on the corner of Anchor Street is no exception. Above its crusty smogged exterior, neon fish jump in an eternal, buzzing arc over a neon river (*eent-eent-eent, eent-eent-eent*).

Mark pulls his car into the lot and parks at its edge, against a shoulder-high retaining wall of rock, holding back the woods. He hunches his shoulders against the rain as he gets out and hip-checks the door shut. He peers down at the wounded tire. Kicks it.

It is magnificently flat. The tear in it is spectacular. If *he'd* been gouged like that instead of the car, he'd be spurting on the way to dying right now.

He clutches the bundle to his chest as he runs up the three concrete steps to the diner door. Inside, it's all red linoleum. Bright, harsh lighting. Walls covered in fish trophies, curved and gasping. *From the largest swordfish to the smallest bass, we all curl up and gasp in the end, am I right?* he asks a salmon as he passes.

He shakes out his coat and gives a nod to the waitress (name tag: *Diane*) as he slides into a white pleather booth.

Diane is a middle-aged woman who'd been spending her customerless shift scrolling happily through Facebook on her phone. She grumbles over to Mark. "You're dripping everywhere."

"Sorry," he says. "Could I get a cuppa coffee?"

Diane narrows her eyes. "You look like you been runnin."

"Yeah." Mark laughs, smears his hair out of his face. "I have."

"You in trouble?"

"No. I left it behind."

"Where'd you leave it?"

Mark stares at her for a beat.

"Behind," he says. "I hope."

"It's been a quiet shift," Diane warns.

"I'll keep it quiet, I swear."

"Mmm. Just coffee?"

"Yeah. Thank you."

He cranes his neck around to watch her go, making sure she's all the way gone. Then, and only then, does he unwrap the bundle in his lap.

From the damp gray cloth, he unrolls a small gray book. The soft felt of its cover is stained by several hands' worth of grease, patters of coffee, smudges of blue ink. It is a well-loved little volume, its edges beginning to yellow. Mark runs his hands over the cover. The leaves are thick, the full text only a hundred and fifty pages or so. A short volume for something so powerful.

He can *feel* the love in this text. Can feel how many people have turned to these pages in need, in pain, in loneliness.

On the cover, there's a stencil drawing of a woman holding her hands palms up. Her eyes are blank white as she gazes into the sky. Fog billows out of her eyes, spooling in her hands. Surrounding her are many monstrous faces. Fanged, tusked, hairy, snarling. If the black penciled lines were shaded in, this could easily be a stained-glass depiction of a monster-saint, surrounded by her flock.

Gently, he folds open the book, runs his hand down the title page. The paper is soft. It sighs under his fingers. In bold, black type, gothic and regal, the title page reads:

The Gray Book, as retold by Rachel Galloway

2ND PRINTING

Addekkean Press

Mark stares at the text for a moment before feeling someone at his side. He jerks his head and is startled by the waitress. "Jesus!"

She holds his coffee out at arm's length. "Careful. It's hot."

"Oh. Thank you." Mark cradles the book in his lap again and accepts the small white mug with both hands.

"You can pay for that, right?" Diane asks.

"The cash is gonna be soggy, but yeah."

She grunts again, glares at him for another moment, then leaves him alone.

He doesn't take it personally. She's probably seen all *kinds* of weird people pass through here. He can only imagine the shit she's experienced, as a night-shift waitress in Renfield County.

God, this place. Renfield County. And Burnskidde . . . *man*.

Burnskidde, though it is technically in Renfield County, is actually the only town that lies outside the wall of the Billowhills, a crescent-shaped offshoot of the Catskills that surrounds old, deep-forested Renfield Valley. The Burnskidde Tunnel is the only road from the valley into Burnskidde. Well, into Burnskidde from *any* direction. But in the fall of 2009, that tunnel collapsed, sealing the town off from the rest of the valley and, effectively, the world.

It remained that way for an entire decade.

But two nights ago, Mark was on patrol, and he realized as he passed the tunnel that he could *hear* the other side with his augmented ear. Someone—or something—had unclogged the tunnel at last.

Man. He should've just left it alone.

He sips at the coffee, and it burns his tongue. Typical diner fare, served fuck-you hot in a fuck-you tiny mug. He lets the mug cool on the table, and goes back to the book. Flips to the beginning. Stares at the title of the first chapter: "The Addekkean Journals."

He's already read this book. Already knows what it's about: A lost American colony from the seventeenth century called—Addekkea. A place that, according to this little gray book, has been forgotten by history. Is that possible? Surely, that . . . isn't possible. As far as Mark knows, there was no Addekkean colony. People still obsess over Roanoke; people would *know* about this. Wouldn't they? There'd be *some* documentation. This book cannot be the sole surviving evidence of Addekkea's existence.

So then why is it presenting Addekkea as truth?

He doesn't know. Doesn't know *how* this all started. But he knows that whatever happened in Burnskidde ten years ago, whatever made them close that tunnel, it led to *this*. A false history and a faith that, as far as he's concerned, should not exist. A faith that's given rise to "miracles" that made his blood run cold. "Miracles" that are chasing him even now.

Mark gently closes the book. He spies the waitress in the corner, eyeballing him, bobbing her foot. Poor Diane. He wants to give her money, tell her to find someplace better to go, far away from Renfield County. But he only has seventeen dollars. And he's never left Renfield in his life.

He shoves the book away across the table and wipes his hands on his still-dripping coat. He needs to report this. He doesn't have a cellphone for the same reason he has the analog car—all those electronics are just too much noise. He needs to hoof it to the closest outpost *now* and file a report about his fuckup. Maybe if he runs, he can make it, but he needs to tell someone tonight. They have less than a week to stop what's coming.

He looks out the window. Lotta night out there. And if he tilts his head just right, lets the gears in his ear sing and chime, he can still hear the shrieking call of that thing, searching for him in the shadows, searching for the book. Coming closer.

He plucks a napkin out of the dispenser, a pen out of his pocket, and scribbles out a note.

He hesitates. Then adds a final line:

I tried to save her. Save somebody. Sorry.

He stares at the note for a moment. Then wraps the book in the cloth, downs his coffee in one wincing gulp, and slides out of the booth.

Diane straightens as he approaches the counter. He holds out the bundle. "Would you mind holding this? If I can't come back, someone else will come for it."

Diane sneers at him. "What is this?"

Mark digs in his back pocket and comes up with a dented stone coin. "Here." He puts the book on the counter and claps the coin down next to it.

Diane tenses at the sight of the coin. She stares at it, then flicks her eyes up at Mark. "You workin tonight?"

"I work every night," he says, exhausted. "Look, if I stay here, you could get hurt. But my car's stuck, so I gotta go on foot. Now, my hopes ain't high, I gotta be honest. So I'm leaving this with *you*." He puts a hand on the book. "If I don't make it, hopefully this will." He puts a finger on the stone coin and slides it toward her. "My code word is *canal*. If anyone asks. Okay?"

She puts her hands on her hips. Narrows her eyes at him and snarls the name, "The Renfield County Guard. Yeahh, I know your outfit. Called you guys on my ex-brother-in-law when I figured out: He wasn't Darren. Just some *thing* pretending to be Darren."

"Yeah, that kind of thing happens a lot. Listen—"

"Two of you assholes came in, shot up my whole damn house! Some guards."

"Did they stop fake Darren?"

Diane fidgets. "Well . . . sure, but—"

"Look, that sounds like some of the new guys. They think they're hot shit. They get the coin and the gun, and they . . . Ma'am, I've been in the Guard for over fifteen years. You can *trust* me. Please."

Diane picks up the coin and drops it, letting it clatter on the counter. "Fine. I'll hold your stupid book." She snorts. "Ma'am."

Mark nods, relieved. "Thank you." He takes his sodden seventeen dollars out of his wallet. "Keep that."

Diane purses her lips, accepts the cash. Mumbling, she says, "Thanks. I . . . I get spooked."

"Don't worry. I get it." Mark opens the door, and the bell above it chimes. He turns back, smiles at her. "I'm always spooked."

Back outside, he runs through the rain to the Oldsmobile. He opens the passenger's side door, leans in, pops open the glove compartment. The gun in there is fully loaded. He checks the mag just to be sure, then slams the car door shut and stands for a moment in the rain.

The nearest County Guard outpost is three miles away. Three miles of night, rain, and open sky. Maybe he can make it. Or maybe this is yet another fuckup in a long line of recent fuckups. He shouldn't have tried to save her. Shouldn't have neglected to pack a spare tire. Shouldn't have even followed his ear to Burnskidde in the first place.

Mark bends low to the ground in a runner's stance. Bobs on his knees. He can do this. He can make it.

He cocks his head so his augmented ear can sing to him better. He can still hear the thing soaring over the Billowhills, moving slower than he'd initially thought, farther away.

Good. In fact, he laughs a little, he's so relieved. A minute ago, he'd thought it sounded much closer, practically next door. Maybe the ear needs tuning or something. He wonders if . . .

Something hisses behind him. Slowly, he turns.

From the shadows atop the steep granite wall at the edge of the lot, two yellow eyes glint down at him. The mouth below these eyes bares its fangs. It growls, deep in its belly. Revving like an engine.

"Shhhit." Mark whirls around, gun arcing toward those glittering yellow eyes, just as something slams into him from behind. It moves so hard, so fast, that Mark feels something important in his back *snap* as he flies forward, face smashing into gravel. Its hard buckshot crunches into his teeth, his chin, his cheeks. He wheezes, his fingers twitch, and he realizes he'll never move again. Nothing left to do now except watch what happens to his body from deep within his skull.

He watches as shapes converge over him. Shrieking, swooping low, hoisting his body into the air. Claws press against his flesh, poking into his ribs, massaging his stomach. His cracked spine screams in pain. Then they're pulling. Hard, fast, in opposite directions, snapping bones, yanking him apart piece by piece. His ankles are twisted off, his wrists wrenched loose. So many hands. Swarming him. Twisting and tearing, just *tossing* Mark's body in scattered pieces into the puddles around the lot. He's awake for all of it, screaming inside his skull, as his body grows smaller and smaller.

Finally, they drop what's left of him. More gravel digs into his ragged stumps. One of them lands on top of his torso and digs its fingers into Mark's head, probing his nostrils and his gums. It turns his head so it can scream directly into Mark's augmented ear. It screams so loud, so shrieking high—*"HAAA!"*— that all the little brass gears and wires quiver until they snap, until his inner ear bursts in a sharp *crunch* of machinery. Mark's brain shakes like a snow globe rattled by a toddler, and what's left of his body spasms as his skull explodes outward, bloody gray matter and metal bits flying into the gravel under the car.

Then the beasts begin to feed. Slurping and grunting happily, jostling each other, chattering and shrieking with delight as they stuff themselves full.

Mark's final shivering thought, as his life pulses out into the puddles of Renfield rain spreading across the lot, is that this was a colossal fuckup indeed. *I tried to save her. I tried . . .*

WHEELS WITHIN WHEELS

The Gray Book

The mere idea of colonies is madness. To push across an ocean—to suffer rats, disease, and the sickening solitude of the sea. To arrive at last in a whirlwind of cruelty and infection. To eradicate ecosystems, raze forests, to crack apart the very earth for pleasure. To murder and violate every single inhabitant of this "new world"—and then, to rewrite that history entirely, weaving new mythologies of men shaking hands across a cultural divide. Giving thanks, breaking bread . . . What utter, narcissistic brutality.

Thus, when famine, illness, and raiders tore into the great colony of Addekkea, a number of the colonists recognized: *This is what we deserve. We deserve to perish, covered in oozing boils and cracking wounds, plundered and ravaged by knifemen. We deserve to starve in this place we mutilated to make our own.*

Not all of the colonists felt this way, of course. But Addekkea was a place of scholars and freethinkers, and many of them recognized divine karma when it sat upon their chest and breathed sulfurous steam into their eyes. *I will die here,* they thought, gazing up at the face of Death. *And I deserve to.*

In the winter, Addekkea almost lost itself, as many such colonies did, devastated by cold and strange germs. In the thaw of spring, there were precious few Addekkeans left.

So it was that they turned to the way of the beasts.

The beasts were merciful. Miraculous. They nursed Addekkea back to health—to even *greater* health than the colony had enjoyed before.

But the beasts demanded payment. Gifts of blood. Of flesh. The beasts, though a boon, were not without consequence. And in their desperation, their gratitude, the Addekkeans were more than willing to comply.

We deserve this, they told themselves as they sang. *We maimed this land. Now—it maims us in return.*

"The Addekkean Journals"
Rachel Galloway, the Gray Book

BURNSKIDDE, SEPTEMBER 2009

No Roads Out

Walk through the halls of Burnskidde High.

The walls are painted blue, littered with flyers for clubs, sports, plays. Here's a mural of handprints, signed by the Class of 1994. Think of it as a memorial. Courtney Edwards, Kevin Fetterman . . . Angst-addled ghosts in the bricks.

The floors are white cracked tile, smeared by decades of sneakers and gum. Breathe in: The air is a poisonous mélange of sweat, Axe, rubber, and Victoria's Secret Pink. Look out the windows: a gray raining day in the school courtyards.

They built Burnskidde High with two courtyards, so that wherever you are in the building, you always have a window. The yards themselves are never open. They are filled with dying trees. The courtyards' only purpose is so students can see the sun. Around them, the school is shaped like an 8 made of bricks, or like infinity—an accurate depiction of the beautiful, dramatic, zitty, greasy eternity of high school.

Rachel Galloway looked through one of these windows as she floated along toward eighth period. The dead trees of the courtyard always looked so grateful for rain. It matched their mood. The same way Fall Out Boy was really matching Rachel's mood right now. She'd had "Sugar, We're Goin Down" on repeat for about a week and a half. Songs were a dollar each on iTunes, or free if you went on thepiratebay.org, which Rachel often did. But she really wanted to support Fall Out Boy, and just one dollar off Mom's debit card would go unnoticed.

Besides, this was such a perfect bus-ride-in-the-morning song. Crisp and bitter, but hopeful somehow, at its very core. As she rode the cold meat beast each morning, she'd look out at the sun peering through the trees, knowing that the day itself did not want to be awake yet either. She'd rest her forehead against the cool window glass, breathing in the stale rubber bus-smell, and she'd doze for a few minutes at a time, before she had to restart "Sugar, We're Goin Down" on her iPod Nano.

On this particular Wednesday afternoon in late September, Rachel wore her blackest hoodie, her most appropriately shredded jeans, and her little skeleton bear earrings from Hot Topic. She was bittersweetly glum today, feeling very old for a sixteen-year-old, like her best years were already behind her, already wasted. Like there were things her body wanted to do, ways it wanted to bend and stretch and run, but she didn't know how to give it these things. She gave it Oreos in her room while rewatching *Arrested Development* on her little box tv.

When she'd started working at the Pancake Planet a year ago (her first job ever), her arms and shoulders had hardened with new muscle. Carrying plates and clearing tables, hauling up boxes from the Planet's grisly, cobwebbed, pipe-clanging basement. She admired these muscles in the bathroom mirror during breaks. The lighting in the Planet's bathroom was better than the lighting at home, ironically. Even though it lit up her loose stomach; her short neck; her thin and perpetually, maddeningly greasy curly brown hair; the small hill-ranges of acne across her forehead and chin—the Planet bathroom mirror *also* lit up the slender-ish curvature of her arms, the strong blue veins in her hands. She adored her arms and hands. She thought they were her best feature. They felt human and normal. The rest of her did not. In fact, she kinda hated having a body. Bodies were so smelly and demanding.

She'd rather be mist.

She drifted into history class, wrapped her noodly white earbuds around her iPod, and stuffed it into her hoodie pocket. She slid into her seat and turned to the girl sitting next to her, held up her fist. "Sup, loser."

While Rachel Galloway was short and sturdy, Emma Dring looked healthy and athletic, though Rachel knew she'd never run a mile in her life. She could belch the alphabet, but that doesn't count as athletics.

Emma had said many times that her boobs were too small, she was too gangly, her blond hair lay too flat along her skull. Rachel—whose hair was a wild and curling beast she could never tame into anything other than greasy braids—didn't understand Emma's anxieties. She had that secret best-friend loathing for Emma. Just wanted to shake her and yell in her face, "You're fucking beautiful and talented and I *love* you, you stupid idiot! Shut up! Jake Mendez is an asshole for not going out with you!"

They'd been friends a very long time.

Emma fist-bumped her. "Sup, idiot."

"Galloway." Mr. Tolley stood glaring by the chalkboard at the front of the room. His khakis were stained by yogurt and yellow chalk, per usual. He referred to all his students by their last name, as a display of what he called "mutual respect." "You're late again, Galloway."

"I'm sorry," said Galloway, in her best pleasing-an-adult voice. "My last class is all the way at the other end of the school. Remember? I timed it? I can't make it in less than five minutes."

Mr. Tolley narrowed his eyes at her. Rapped a chunk of chalk against his knuckles. "Mmm. Annoying but acceptable."

"That's what I strive for, sir."

"Mmm." Tolley frowned at her for another moment, then took a deep breath and announced to the class, "Well! Get excited, everyone. I am assigning you—a project."

The class groaned. Troy Pittner (of the "large helmet of brown hair, freckles, silver chain, and cargo shorts" species) started flipping his pencil round his thumb tip. "Maaan. Way to go, Galloway."

"Boooo," said Jake Mendez behind him. Jake of the "spiky black hair and polo shirts" Mendezes.

Galloway put up her hands. "What'd I do?"

Emma whispered, "He gave us that quiz last week because you were late."

"Okay, homework is not my fault," Galloway whispered back. "The school is too damn big."

"This project," Tolley went on, "will consist of a presentation on the colonial unit we've been working on thus far. The topic will be up to you, pending my approval, of course. So prepare yourselves! To discuss such *thrilling* topics as the intricacies of the French and Indian War, the complexities of the Stamp Act, and beyond. I'll get into the specifics near the end of the period, but first! More notes. Notebooks open." He began to scrawl furiously on the board. "Ohh, the joys of being a Son of Liberty . . ."

Everyone grumbled as they flipped open their notebooks.

Galloway sighed. It was so warm and dreamy in here, in the older section of the school. The radiators clanged dangerously loud and hot. A kid fainted once from the heat, in this very room!

Galloway was naturally good at taking tests and bullshitting essays, so she often allowed her mind to drift, riding the thermals far from Tolley's droning voice. Just doodling away in the margins of her gray marbled notebook.

Today, she found herself sketching a little pig. A cute little cartoon pig with a mouthful of food, munchin on something good (Galloway was starving). After a moment's consideration, she added a stick-figure Mr. Tolley, getting his arm munched clean off. The pig chewed happily as Mr. Tolley wept little stick-figure tears, his torn arm weeping blood. *Try to write "Pop Quiz" on the board now, asshole.*

The pig looked so cute and content, Galloway just *had* to turn her notebook to Emma. Emma frowned at it as she deciphered what it was, then stifled a laugh.

They were lucky Tolley's back was turned. He'd caught her doodling in class five times already. Once, she'd been working on a rabbit in a leather coat, finger-gunning and winking, and Tolley had held it up to everybody. "What is this? Why is this in your notes? How is this related to Thomas Paine?" Jake Mendez and Troy Pittner, homecoming kings in the making, had winked and finger-gunned at her all week.

Today, she'd gotten off easy. Before Tolley even turned around, she had her notebook back on her desk, pretending to take diligent notes. Brow furrowed, all *Oohh*, nodding along, very studious. This forced Emma to stifle another laugh. She mouthed, *Stop.*

Galloway left her alone. She fantasized about cartoon pigs bursting into the classroom and devouring Tolley whole. The kids would cheer, and the pigs would smile and wave their hooves. They'd put on some ridiculous pop music, like Black Eyed Peas, and everyone would dance. And one of the monsters would poop out Tolley's stupid yogurt-stained khakis, and flowers would sprout from them, and it would suddenly be summer, and everyone would be happy. In fact, the pigs would eat *all* of the teachers, and their poop would be like magical fertilizer. The trees in the courtyards of Burnskidde High would bloom once more, and the children and monsters would dance upon the bodies of the dead.

Fun!

She began to imagine a beautiful village, not unlike Burnskidde, where these pigs were welcomed, even revered. A colony up in the hills, where they celebrated intelligence rather than brawn. Maybe, like, a place founded by academics escaping persecution in the Old World, with its own academy, its own government. A whole self-sustaining community, rich with life. So self-sufficient that they built walls around their colony, to keep outsiders from marring their peaceful, scholarly existence.

She found herself falling in love with this imaginary colony, its tall walls and its magic pigs.

And it wasn't long before Galloway's class notes were subsumed by this cute-but-slightly-creepy world.

HE NEVER SPOKE IN CLASS. HE HAD GROWN ACCUSTOMED TO BEING a shadow, adrift in the sea of bodies filling the high school so effortlessly. All of them laughing, running, making out. By comparison, this boy felt powerless, like he wasn't even there. Sometimes, he pretended no one could see him at all. No one could see him watching Rachel Galloway. Tracing his eye down her ear, down her neck to her black-nailed hands, scribbling and erasing and swiping at eraser chaff. Oh, to be the gray marbled notebook beneath those beautiful hands.

This boy wanted to know her.

"SEE?" EMMA TURNED HER LAPTOP TO GALLOWAY.

Galloway lifted her head from her hands and frowned at the screen. A black-and-white sketch of a woman with sharp dark hair, surrounded by tree branches. From the branches hung jars filled with eyeballs, centipedes, a human foot, etc. The only pop of color was her red eyes.

"What am I . . . looking at? Right now?" Galloway asked.

"*That's* the Horridge Hill Botanist," said Emma, swiveling the laptop back to face her. She leaned over the bar and flicked her eyes around the screen. "This is a police sketch they did in '98, based on testimony from Ariel Young. The Botanist supposedly lives in the swamp behind Horridge Park. In the shadow of Horridge Hill," she added with a spooky flair.

"The police gave her red eyes?" Galloway asked. "Or was that the internet?" She rested her chin on her hand again. Her attention wandered back to her latest pig sketch. This one was pooping and smiling, just like its predecessors earlier today. From its cheery little poop piles sprang little daisies, because that was the only flower Galloway knew how to draw. A ring of stick figures stood around the pooping pig, mouths open, musical notes floating to the top of the page. She imagined they were caroling. Maybe the pooping pig was like their Christmas.

"According to the *Bent News*," said Emma, reading off her laptop, "Ariel Young went missing from Horridge Park on August 9, 1998. She returned three days later with *no* memory of what had happened to her, except that she got lost in the woods and a 'kind old lady in a shack showed her the way back home.' Oooh. Police combed the park but found no evidence of the kind old lady or her alleged shack. Mmm. Despite providing testimony that led to this infamous police sketch and a wild goose chase throughout Horridge Park, Ariel seemed 'happier than usual,' and started making new friends at what her parents called 'an alarming rate.' Ahh. The Youngs grew concerned that something had happened to Ariel that made her 'not herself' while she was missing. Which is, like, typical Renfield, right?"

"Right," Galloway murmured, not paying attention.

The story of the Horridge Hill Botanist was not unique. The entirety of Renfield County was a black hole of supernatural and criminal activity. Throughout the entire zip code, people went missing, lost their minds, received phone calls from dead relatives at two a.m., and worse. It was just something Galloway, Emma, and everyone else in Burnskidde had grown up with. Everyone in Renfield County had a story. Especially in Burnskidde, Renfield's farthest downriver town, the victim of all the county's supernatural runoff. A sewer of unexplainable misfortunes.

The one commonality between all these stories was Lawrence Renfield. Everyone knew *this* one: In 1927, farmer and family man Lawrence Renfield killed his wife and children without warning, rampaging through his house with a shotgun. No one knows why he did it, but that's not the strangest part. When he was finished, Lawrence drew a giant stick figure on the barn wall in his son's blood. According to local legend, that bloodied wall was torn apart, its pieces scattered throughout the county, and everything that bloodywood touches turns evil. There could be pieces of it anywhere—in your home, your office, a park bench . . .

Even worse, the blood of Lawrence's family soaked into the earth of their farm and, again, according to local legend, seeded a curse that spread across the entire valley. Thus, everything in Renfield has been touched by pain and terror, ever since December 1927, when old Lawrence Renfield sent his family to heaven.

That was the old nursery rhyme. *On this you can bet: This place knows / your every secret.* Galloway could recite the entire rhyme by heart. Chanting it on the playground, pouncing on each other, tickling hard, "Tell us your secrets! Tell us your secrets!" A fun way to find out who had a crush on who, and to make light of the shadow under which they'd all been born.

Emma was still reading: "Now, upon seeing this police sketch and pictures of the shack, Leigh Young, Ariel's father, recalled an old story *he'd* heard back when *he* was a kid. In 1965, twenty-year-old Nic Donnelly vanished for three days while on winter break from Edenville College. He returned with a similar story, plus a 'sunnier disposition' and 'an almost uncanny ability to make new friends,' which was bizarre because he was totally introverted before then. In both cases, victims reported seeing a woman in a shack in the woods. And *both* stories bear similarities to the urban legend about a woman known only as: the Botanist.

"Now, according to somewhat vague clippings from the *Slitter Standard*, Edenville College's student newspaper, the Botanist was a biology professor at E.C. back in the 1940s. Apparently, in summer 1947, the entire E.C. biology department lost their minds. Spent too much time around Renfield plants, I guess. The infamous Edenville Butcher was part of that crew as well. Anyway, the Botanist moved out into the woods to conduct secretive experiments on children, 'perhaps using them for fertilizer and replacing them with nearly identical plant copies, like something out of Grimms' fairy tales,' says the *Standard*. See?" Emma slapped the bar excitedly. "Right there!"

"You're really this upset your parents joined an adult bowling league?" Galloway asked.

Emma started ticking off on her fingers: "A: They have never mentioned bowling ever before in my life. B: They're *always* laughing together now. What's so funny, Jeff? What's so funny, Darlene?"

"Maybe they're upset you don't call them Mom and Dad."

"Uh, C: They weren't *this* happy a year ago. Last year, they were watching tv in separate rooms. Now they're playing Scrabble together and *bowling*? No."

Galloway sighed, not looking up from her doodles. "Soo this old lady lives in a swamp shack, snags anyone who comes near, and releases them back into the wild as happier people? Geez, Em, that's terrifying."

"She replaces them with *plant*-people," Emma huffed. "Rach, these are all the same stories, across decades of cases. There are others I didn't even read."

"What are you reading this off of?"

"Tumblr," said Emma. "Why?"

They were standing at the bar of the Pancake Planet, on the southern edge of town. The Planet was a Renfield-based chain, and this particular branch was a squat building marked by a giant, bright pink *PP*, buzzing like a neon beacon into the night, on a pole at the edge of the parking lot. The booth benches were a sticky plastic orange. The laminated menus were wide and filled with pictures. The Planet was silent most weekday nights, except the occasional family and the small gangs of young adults rolling through on their way home from football practice or play rehearsal or whatever. Laughing and blowing straw wrappers at each other, tying knots in cherry stems with their tongues.

Galloway envied them. The way they owned their bodies, instead of simply inhabiting them.

Tonight, the Planet was empty except for two middle-aged men staring at each other in a corner booth. Emma was hunched over her laptop at the bar, and Galloway was sitting next to her, doing homework. Okay, it wasn't homework *per se*, she was just sketching more pigs pooping flowers. But the stick-figure people seemed stoked about it, and it made her happy.

Greg came out of the cellar carrying a box of syrups. He passed behind Emma, limping slightly, and read the screen over her shoulder. He dropped the box on the bar and snorted. "Is it Fringe Conspiracy Friday again already?"

"She's still got a bug up her butt about your parents," said Galloway, giving her little pig a cute, curly tail.

Greg Dring was nineteen. He'd gotten both Emma and Galloway their jobs at the Planet last fall. He was a wiry guy, with a silver earring and a patchy beard.

"You still think they were kidnapped and turned into plant-people?" he asked, unpacking his box.

"I think the pattern is there," said Emma defensively. "The Botanist is connected to at least five similar cases."

"Yeah, but they're not real cases," said Greg, making neat rows of syrup bottles. "Emma, this is just like when you freaked out about those five-legged rats. They weren't following you around. And none of those people"—he nodded at her laptop—"*actually* went missing. They were lost for a few days, and when they came back, they were excited to be alive. Big deal. Mom and Dad are happy to be alive. I don't know why this is so upsetting."

From the pass-through window behind Emma, above a grill full of frying eggs and potatoes, Dominic the cook shouted, "You guys talkin about the Botanist again? She steals people from their beds."

Emma pointed at him and smirked at Greg. "See?"

"Our parents didn't go *missing*, dumbass," said Greg. "They're fine."

"You can't tell me they haven't been weird," said Emma. "A whole year, they've been acting like cheery cheery pod-people. Ever since they went missing on that hike for a few hours last July. *On* Horridge Hill!"

"I wish my mom was a pod-people," said Dom. "Maybe then she'd chill out." He put up a steaming plate of eggs, dinged the bell. "Egg o'clock."

Dominic Zambrano was a big dude, often sweaty. He was Greg's age, and they'd been friends for as long as Emma and Galloway had been friends, so working at the Planet felt like working with family. He had long dark hair and strong hands. Galloway wished she could feel as strong as he surely felt with those hands.

"I like Jeff and Darlene," she said, sliding off her stool and taking the plate of eggs. "I think they're nice."

"Too nice," said Emma. "This is . . . Are you even listening? God, this psycho-witch in the woods is gonna replace the entire world with pod-people and no one is even gonna care!"

"Why, though?" Dom asked. "Like, what does she want from us?"

"World domination, dude," said Greg. "Aren't you listening? God!"

Galloway carried the eggs to the men in the corner. Over her shoulder, she dimly registered someone else coming into the restaurant.

She returned to the bar to find Greg putting syrup bottles under the counter, limping a bit as he said, "*I* think they were hypnotized. You remember that dude who showed up on the roof of the school last year, right before first period? Waving a handful of silver stopwatches around, all drenched in blood?"

"Oh hell yeah," said Dom, leaning through the window. "Absolutely. Officer Wilson went up there and the dude just vanished? Everybody within a half-mile radius lost two *hours*."

"We were there, doofus," said Emma.

"I loved it," said Galloway. "I was supposed to have a math final that morning. Instead, I woke up on the gym floor halfway through third period. Our teacher just gave everybody A's."

Greg shrugged. "Maybe Stopwatch Man had a test he wanted to skip, too. Anyway, I bet that's what happened to Mom and Dad. Somebody zapped em."

"While we were hiking?" Emma asked. "Look, you don't know cuz *you* didn't want to go hiking that day, but we got separated, and when I found em again, hours later, they were all smiles. I'm telling you, it was the Botanist."

"I don't know, Stopwatch Man's reach is far and wide," said Dom. "My uncle says everything in Renfield is true until you can prove otherwise."

"Then *this* is true," Emma whined, pointing at her laptop.

"Is this really our life?" Galloway sighed. "We're so surrounded by superstitious bullshit that we can't tell what's real anymore?"

Dom thrust his spatula into the air and started chanting, "No roads out!"

Greg took up the cry. "No roads out! No roads out!"

This was an old Renfield saying, that there are no roads out of the county. There are two, literally speaking, but it's a metaphor. The county's influence is pervasive and permanent. There is no escaping its entanglements. Emma rolled her eyes and returned to her laptop. Greg and Dom let the chant die out, then fist-bumped each other and went back to what they were doing. Galloway went back to her . . .

"The fuck," she said, looking around. "Where's my notebook?"

They all frowned at the empty space on the bar where the gray marbled notebook had lain.

"Woow, thanks, guys," said Galloway.

"Maybe Stopwatch Man took it," said Greg.

"Oh shit," said Dom. "*That* dude took it." He pointed his spatula at the other end of the bar.

There sat a tall, silent boy. He ran his fingertips over the surface of the notebook, lips parted in awe.

"Who is that?" Galloway hissed. "You let him take my book?"

"Oh my god, he's in our class," said Emma. "He's in Mr. Tolley's."

"Well, who is he?"

"I dunno."

"He must've swiped it when you had those eggs," said Dom.

"And you let him?!"

Dom shrugged. "We were talking. I didn't know."

"He likes your sketches," said Greg. He leaned against the bar and rolled his ankle. "Aw, look, he's smiling."

The boy grinned to himself as he cracked open the notebook and ran his hands over its pages.

"Ew," said Galloway. She looked at Emma. "I have to go say something, right?"

Emma shrugged.

She turned to Greg and Dom. "What do I say?"

The boys shrugged.

"Jesus. I am *so* happy to have such a supportive friend group."

"Just wait until your parents are abducted by a madwoman and replaced with lobotomized plant-clones," Emma sighed. "Then see what kind of support you get."

"No roads out," Dom chanted. "No roads out."

Galloway grumbled and prepared herself to approach. As she began to march toward the boy, she heard Emma say behind her, "So what's up with your foot?"

"What foot?" said Greg.

"You're, like, limping and rolling your foot. What happened to you?"

"Nothing, fuck off," Greg grumbled, his voice fading out of Galloway's earshot.

She raked her fingers through her hair and felt fresh grease under her fingernails. *Just great.* She hated having genes. She wanted to claw them out of her skin. Tear off her dad's bad hair, her grandmother's dry skin. Sometimes she couldn't even breathe right, thinking about all that DNA being *in* her. She wanted out. Out of this body, this life, this town, this greasy fucking bullshit fucking hair, *strike me dead, oh my god . . .*

"Heyyy," she said. She waved her hand awkwardly in a big arc. "Um . . . can I help you?"

He swiveled on the barstool. He had wide brown eyes, warm and inviting, like rich earth. He had light brown skin, from an Irish father and an Indian mother, though Galloway didn't know this. He wore an old black leather trench coat, over a black T-shirt featuring Heath Ledger's Joker holding a playing card. He was also, under his long shining black hair, sort of, almost . . . cute. If he slicked his hair back and ooh, yeah, if he had a lip ring? Then he'd *really* be cute. So, actually, he didn't seem that creepy up close. Just . . . lonely.

"Oh," he said. His voice was soft, light as a feather. "I'm sorry. Can I sit here?"

"Y . . . eah. I mean, you can sit anywhere. But . . ."

"Can I have a Chicken Caesar Belgian Waffle? I've been craving one."

Even hearing the phrase "Chicken Caesar Belgian Waffle" was enough to curl Galloway's nose in revulsion. The Planet served a wide variety of hideous food, and she would sometimes gag while sniffing her clothes after a shift.

But she smiled and said, "Sure thing. Um. You know that's my notebook."

"Oh. I'm sorry."

"It's okay. I just don't . . . usually share my notes." She eyed the cartoonish pooping pigs. So stupid, he must think she's so stupid.

"I like your drawings," he said. "These pigs are really cute."

"Oh. Thank you." Galloway smiled. She fidgeted, then stuck out her hand. "I'm Rachel."

He smiled as he shook it. His hand was stronger than expected. Calloused. "Francis."

"Cool, nice to meet you. Can I have that back, though?"

"Oh, sure." Francis slid the book across the bar. "Sorry again."

"Thank youuu," she said as she hugged the gray marbled cover to her chest, relieved to have it back. "I'll get your waffle." She began to shuffle away.

"Thank *you*," he said. "Hey, are those real?"

Galloway paused. Turned. "Is what real?"

"The pigs," said Francis, eyes wide and earnest. "Is that something you've actually seen around here?"

"Oh." She laughed. "Just . . . in my head."

"Really?" He leaned forward. "Like a vision?"

"Uhh. I guess."

"Wow." Francis nodded, impressed. "You're really special."

She scoffed. "Yeah. I was actually *in* the 'special' class in second grade because I couldn't sit still in the 'normal' class? It was not my favorite. So, I'm not special. But thank you." She turned away again.

And again, he called her back: "Why do people sing to them?"

"The . . . pigs?"

"Yeah," said Francis. "They look so grateful for them."

Oh god, this is gonna sound so stupid. "Well, the pigs have magic . . . poop . . . fertilizer. Everything they eat turns into flowers and crops and stuff."

"Even Mr. Tolley's arm?"

Galloway laughed. "Yeah, *especially* arms. The pigs love arms." She stepped closer. "I was thinking they have this special enzyme in their gut that . . . This is stupid, I'm sorry. I never share my doodles. It's just dumb stuff I fantasize about on the bus and—"

"No, no, I asked," said Francis. "And they're not doodles. They're good. It's *art*. I want to know." He smiled again. Warm and sincere.

She stared at him. She'd been drawing her whole life, but no one seemed to care. Mom rarely commented on her art. Dad always said she was good, distractedly. Neither of those opinions counted anyway. And Galloway's twin younger brothers, Teddy and Bobby, they never gave a shit about *anything* she did. They were eight.

So to have a *boy* say something kind about her work—to have him show interest—was huge. Very new. And very strange.

She shifted uncomfortably in his spotlight for a moment before she allowed herself to continue explaining this bizarre flight of fancy she'd been nursing since eighth period: "Well, *I* think they have a special enzyme in their gut that makes them capable of turning any organic matter into any *other* organic matter. Like, they could eat someone's arm and shit out a bunch of pumpkin seeds."

"How is that possible?" Francis asked. "I know anything in Renfield is possible, but . . ."

"Well, that's what these guys want to know." She pointed to the smiling people. "The pigs couldn't explain it to them, obviously, and the local scientists couldn't explain it. They were forced to believe it was a . . . miracle."

"A miracle," Francis repeated. "Wow. So they pray to the pigs? In . . . in song? To thank them for the flowers and food?"

"Yeah, they call the pigs out of the woods through song, the pigs eat a little bit of arm, and they poop out fresh crops. The pigs get to eat, the villagers get to eat, and Mr. Tolley can't write on the chalkboard anymore. It's a triple win."

"Yeah." Francis stared past her, into the corner. He sounded almost sad. "Sounds beautiful."

"It is. Here." Galloway opened her notebook, started flipping through it. "Sorry if this is, like, too much? But I've been working on some sketches of the village where they live. It's a big colony, actually, full of super smart people. They're all atheists. But like a lot of colonies, these people fell on hard times. They got sick, they ran out of food. They got raided by these people in the north called knifemen, who sewed needles and blades into their skin."

"Whoa," said Francis.

"Yeah, over the course of a single winter, the colonists were almost completely wiped out. The only people who survived were the ones who sang to the pigs. They saved the colony from total collapse, and the pig-faith became their, like, national religion. See?" She found the page she was looking for. She held up a big sketch of a colony with tall towers and walls and people standing around singing to half a dozen pigs, while the pigs all shat daisies in a field together, beaming proudly. Some of the people had missing limbs, but they all *seemed* happy. They sang and danced despite their wounds.

"I always think that's crazy," said Galloway. "When smart people lose their minds. When they get obsessed with a religion like that. But it saved them, so."

"You drew all this?" Francis asked, leaning forward to see the penciled colony more closely. Its walls surrounded and partially overlapped her old notes on the Revolutionary War.

"I was super bored," said Galloway. "I don't really give a shit about America."

"But you saw this," he said. "In your vision."

"Well, yeah, I made it up."

"Off something you saw in your *head*."

She laughed. "Why, where do you see things?"

"I don't see things," said Francis. "I mean, I imagine things, but I don't have visions like *that*."

"Okay, but this wasn't a . . ." Galloway struggled. An awkward laugh cracked through her. "I was just *bored*."

"It's so fascinating how when you're bored, the mind opens itself up to possibilities," said Francis.

Galloway was about to say something else when Dom called out behind her, "Nine o'clock! Kitchen's closed."

"Oh shit, your waffle," said Galloway.

But Francis was already standing, hands in the pockets of his coat. "That's okay, I should get home anyway. My mom gets worried. She's a nurse, though, so she sees *lots* of stuff that makes her worry. If I come back sometime, can you tell me more?"

Galloway jerked her head back. "More about the poo-pigs?"

"All of it. I want to know exactly how the pigs helped. If they can help Burnskidde."

"Burnskidde needs help?"

"It's almost winter," said Francis matter-of-factly. "Who knows when *we* might have a winter like those colonists. Disease, starvation. Knifepeople."

"I mean, we're probably okay on starvation," said Galloway. "We've got enough food in the Planet to last us. Fingers crossed about those knifepeople, though," she added sardonically. "But yeah, I'd be happy to talk more about the pigs. If they could save us all from dying, that'd be *great*."

"Cool," said Francis brightly. He grinned. "I'll come back soon. It was nice to meet you, Rachel. See you in class."

"Same, Francis. I'll see ya."

He slumped quickly out of the Planet. She watched him through the window as he retrieved a bike from the small bike stand out front.

Emma appeared at her side. "What did he say? Are you engaged?"

"He was really sweet, actually," said Galloway. "He asked about my drawings."

"Ooh."

"He, like, thought they were real. Like I was drawing real animals."

"Rach, we live in Renfield. You could draw a unicorn man holding a chainsaw in his hooves and I'd believe he was real. Plus, maybe they *are* real. Maybe we *do* have magic pigs in these woods. Maybe Renfield's in your heeead." Emma waggled her fingers spookily.

"Stop." Galloway shoved her. She watched Francis hop on his bike and pedal away. He vanished from the pink glow of the Planet sign, into the dark.

Emma wandered away, rolling her eyes. But Galloway lingered for another moment. Someone had treated her like she was real. Like her mind was an actual place, capable of creating change in this world, of actually adding to it. No one had ever made her feel that way before.

She hugged her notebook close to her chest. Suddenly, she couldn't wait to draw more. To share more with Francis. She had a strange and powerful imagination. She'd even come up with a name for her imaginary colony. A nonsense word that meant nothing. But it was a calm place to turn her mind to, when Tolley monologued on and on.

She called this place: Addekkea.

FRANCIS BIKED ALL THE WAY UP TO THE NORTH SIDE OF BURNSKIDDE, shadowed by the spine of the Billowhills. He was alone on the streets, except for the occasional car whizzing past. Even if everyone were out tonight, Burnskidde was only home to about five thousand people, and the streets would still feel relatively empty.

It was a misty, cool evening. Francis swerved his bike back and forth under the streetlights, grinning, breathing deep the cool fall air.

He'd talked to a *girl* tonight. The cute girl from class. She'd spoken to him, and he'd felt her warm hand, and she'd given him a brilliant idea he was very excited about. He smiled and biked with his eyes closed, feeling alive.

He biked under the clear stars, past the strip mall with the pizza joint and the nail salon, the video store and the deli. He biked past the nicer neighborhoods, large houses with mother-in-law apartments atop big sweeping hills, with playsets and treehouses and trampolines. He biked past Miner Memorial Square.

This is a mining town, founded around the Burnskidde Unconsolidated Salt Mine in the late 1800s. The recession did not hit hard here. Everybody needs salt, granite, and sand. Mine pride runs deep— Memorial Square is the first thing you see when you come down out of the Burnskidde Tunnel. Here, a large marble statue of three men in hardhats, dedicated to the brave souls who died in The Big Accident of 1968, Renfield's most infamous mining disaster.

Francis biked past this statue to the library. He used to *love* the library. He biked past without even looking at it, then past the large brick prison of Burnskidde High. The tennis courts, the big blue dome that housed the theater, the football field with their mascot, Prospector Percy, painted over the turf, his cliché pickax over one shoulder.

Francis had never been much for sports.

He biked past the old church, the two-screen movie theater, the neighborhood of miserable-looking modular homes where he lived. He biked past it all, and wished that instead of its squat brick and barbed wire, Burnskidde was something . . . better. A glorious city instead of a decaying one. A beautiful colony like the one Rachel had drawn, instead of this dying old mine town. He hated it here. He hated Burnskidde.

He biked up to the old entrance of the mine. The Burnskidde Mining Corporation had moved on from this particular shaft, leaving most of their equipment behind and many of the tunnels unexplored. Agonizingly bored last summer, Francis had taken it upon himself to explore these tunnels. He'd even found, to his great surprise and delight, that the old mine hoist was still operational. Then he'd discovered something else. Something very, very cool . . .

He hopped off his bike and kicked the stand up, leaving it in the gravel lot outside the wide maw of the mine. Cold dark engulfed him when he stepped inside. Graffiti lined the walls. People had parties here sometimes, or so he'd heard. He didn't do parties. He'd bet no one who came here for the parties knew the mines like he did. No one had spent countless hours exploring by themselves. Endless. Deep. The kind of focus you can only achieve when you have little family and zero friends.

He took the old key out of his pocket and unlocked the cage door of the elevator. The hinges screamed with rust as he rolled the door back. The cage bobbed as he stepped onto the hoist. He tried not to think about the shaft stretching down into the earth below, straight down for thousands of feet of absolute black. He turned the key in the elevator, pressed Down. It began to crank and grind, then it *whooshed* him down into the earth, fast. Two hundred feet a minute. Down, down. His eardrums filled with cotton, and he worked his jaw, trying to pop them. Down, down . . .

For every three hundred feet down you go, the temperature goes up by four degrees. Francis was two thousand feet deep when the hoist came to a halt. Sweating now. Breathing hard the thick briny air of the salt mine's forgotten avenues.

He took a small flashlight from his pocket and glided through the tunnels. He turned left and right, then left again. Deeper and deeper. Picking his way around old signs: WARNING! ABANDONED SHAFT! STAY OUT, STAY SMART. Francis had explored it all. He'd even unclogged a couple tunnels himself, hefting rocks by hand. Opening avenues that had been forsaken since before he'd been born.

He kept walking, swiping sweat off his forehead, until he was deep enough to hear it. Soft at first, vibrating the stone pressing in on him from all sides. *Thrum . . . thrum . . .*

As he went farther, the sound grew louder. Became a regular thrumming, a low pulse. *Thrum-thrum . . . thrum-thrum . . .*

He smiled wider and wider as he drew closer to the sound. *Thrum-thrum. Thrum-thrum.* Grinning by the time he came into the central chamber.

Pulses of light lit his face from below. *Thrum-thrum. Thrum-thrum. Thrum-thrum.*

He knelt. He licked his lips. And he whispered, "I have a wish now."

BARTRICK MILL, OCTOBER 2019
Durwood & Oake

"I'm just sayin it's a shame," said Bruce around a mouthful of choco-late. "Imagine you're in the cartoon. Okay? You *are* Inspector Gadget. You wake up, and your name is different? Everybody's referring to you by this nickname coined during this insane traumatic experience you've had. That's terrible! Isn't that the thing, he's in a freak accident and they say what the hell, let's fill him with gadgets? It's been a while since I've seen the show."

"They put a bubble-blower in his finger," said Durwood around a mouthful of Skittles. "That's canon. Doesn't sound very traumatic. I bet he was thrilled to be Inspector Gadget."

"They also laminated his hat to his skull," said Bruce. He ripped off another huge chunk of his king-sized 3 Musketeers. "I wouldn't be ec-static about having to wear a fuckin fedora all the time."

Durwood wagged her head. "Yeahh. Spose not."

Durwood and Oake were parked on a dark suburban street. A har-vest wind whipped shapes around the night outside, dancing dead leaves across pools of streetlight. The house they were watching was dim, ex-cept for a single light in the living room. Durwood watched that light religiously, rarely blinking.

She ran a fingernail down the scar along her forearm. The web of soft, numb scar tissue that the Tattooist had molded into the shape of a hawk. A beautiful piece of art, branded over the night she almost died.

"So what was his name before they filled him with gadgets?" Bruce asked. "Inspector Pete?"

Durwood snorted a laugh. She swallowed a gummy wad of Skittle. "Is this you working up to asking if you can call me Inspector Gadget?"

"If anything, I want to be Inspector Gadget," said Bruce. He held up his own gift from the Tattooist: a heron, wings outstretched, etched in shining pink scar tissue along his arm. "Hell, we could *both* be Gadget."

Durwood grunted and poured more Skittles into her palm. Bruce monologued as she shot her head back to munch on four of them at once: "I just wonder how you refill it all. Does another part of his hand pop out so you can put more bubbles in? I mean, you gotta oil that propeller hat. You gotta *reload*, ya know?" He took another king-sized bite of Musketeer. Chewing thoughtfully, "I don't know. Just makes me sad. They tore that poor bastard apart."

"Maybe it's a metaphor," said Durwood, chewing. "Maybe it's, like . . . all trauma reloads itself? Your painful memories have endless ammunition?"

"Okay, Professor. I wasn't trying to make a *point*, I'm just saying you can't apply logic to cartoons."

"Sure." Durwood nodded. "You ever seen those videos where people analyze episodes of *SpongeBob*? There's strong evidence to suggest Mrs. Puff was a hardened criminal."

Bruce chewed. "Was she the squirrel?"

Headlights swung down the street. Durwood and Oake stiffened, watching as a car pulled up in front of the dim house.

"Food's here," said Durwood. She tossed a final Skittle in her mouth, then crumpled the bag in both hands. "You ready?"

Bruce inspected his candy bar. He had about two big bites left, but he shoved it all in his mouth. "Les boogie."

They climbed out of Bruce's sedan and hustled to reach the other car just as the two people inside were getting out. The male couple in their mid-forties froze half-in, half-out of the car as Durwood and Oake jogged up to them.

"Can . . . we help you?" asked the driver, deer in headlights.

Durwood and Oake came to a stop before the car and caught their breath. They held up their twin stone coins, and Durwood introduced them: "Durwood and Oake, sirs. We're with the Renfield County Guard."

The driver's eyes widened.

The passenger jerked his head back, frowning. "The hell is that?"

The driver asked, "Are . . . are you working tonight?"

"Evan, who's the County Guard?" asked the passenger.

"Fraid so," said Bruce as they pocketed their coins. He sucked chocolate off his teeth and glanced up at the house. "You might wanna mosey."

"Okay," said the driver, voice rising as he moved back into the car. "Yeah, okay. Uh, thank you. Thank you! Evan, get in the car."

"Who's the County Guard?" the passenger asked again. "Evan?"

"Good luck," said the driver quickly. "Evan, get in the car!"

Both men ducked back into the car. Its engine roared and its tires squealed as they drove away.

Durwood and Oake glanced at each other.

"Both of their names were Evan?" Durwood asked.

"That's sweet," said Bruce.

"I hate it."

Bruce Oake was fifty and broad, where Rachel Durwood was thirty and wiry. Together, they looked like backwoods cops, with their twin plaid shirts and their badges made of rock. Durwood's plaid was purple and black, tucked into black jeans. Bruce wore classic lumberjack red, untucked over his beer gut.

Durwood had never had a definitive style of clothing. Since joining the Guard, she had happily adopted Bruce's flannel-forward wardrobe, with slight variations. Her stone coin, however, looked just like his. A smooth circle curved like a worry stone, with Gothic black letters burned into its face. The coin was pure Billowhill limestone, blessed by priests out of Braddock. She rubbed it between her fingers as she and Bruce walked up the driveway to the dim house.

A two-story colonial covered in vines. Three wooden steps up to the door, creaking badly underfoot.

Durwood rang the doorbell. As they waited for someone to answer, she turned and said, "The squirrel was Sandy."

Bruce smacked his lips. "What."

"In *SpongeBob*. Sandy was the squirrel. Mrs. Puff was the driving instructor."

"Right." Bruce nodded. "Wait, the squirrel could drive?"

"Dude."

A light above them came on, and shapes swam behind the frosted glass in the door. Durwood straightened as someone unlocked the door from within.

A middle-aged woman in mom jeans, a pink baseball cap, and a floral sweater opened the door with a very wide smile that fell very quickly when she saw who was there.

"Hello," she said, confused. She peered around Durwood's shoulder. "Are you . . . with the Evans?"

Durwood and Oake held up their stone coins again.

"Durwood and Oake, ma'am," said Durwood. "We're with the County Guard."

A man in a blue baseball cap and a bright yellow sweater came jauntily into view, carrying two ice-tinkling tumblers. "Fee fi fo fum, I hear there are Evans in need of some . . . rum . . ." His smile faded fast, too, when he saw the people outside in their matching plaid. "Evans, you look different."

Durwood and Oake flashed their coins for the third time. Durwood sighed. "Durwood and Oake, sir, we're with the Renfield County Guard. We sent the Evans home."

"Ohh." The man frowned deeper. "You're those damn vigilantes. I hear you people don't even report to the police."

Durwood and Oake glanced at each other. They'd heard this song before.

"Vigilantes" was only semi-accurate. They did not report to the police, nor did they entangle themselves with any other governmental agency. But the Guard *had* cooperated with the County Sheriff's Department on countless cases throughout the years, and town police departments across the county frequently turned over cases to them in times of need.

However, the R.C.G. switchboard was notoriously slow at responding to civilian calls. Sometimes, it took weeks for operators to relay messages to on-duty partnerships or lone senior agents.

Bruce had been a lone agent for years, until this random girl smashed her car into a tree in his front yard. He'd found Durwood sprawled across the dash, covered in whiskey-stink vomit, her right arm punched through the windshield, thorned with glass. Bruce learned later that this poor girl had just lost her mother *and* brother to "suicide by bloodywood," which was Guard parlance for "dying while in possession of Renfield barnwood." In other words, they had either ended their lives of their own volition, or the madness of this cursed valley had driven them to it. It was frustratingly impossible to say which was the truth.

Most Guards found their way into service like this. They smashed headfirst into rock bottom, lost everything to the whims of Renfield's delirium, and awoke with the incurable itch to fight its machine in any way they could. Many of them also passed through the offices of the Tattooist on their way into the field. He had been an actual tattooist once, with a small shop in the Mill. But ever since entering the Guard's employ, he had become something of a machinist/surgeon. His talent was the ability to stitch damaged flesh into elaborate shapes. Through no more magic than a simple operation, he reknit Renfield scars into something beautiful, powerful. Like a hawk with outstretched talons, instead of the ugly, pale splotch of a drunk-driving windshield-scar.

Durwood had been a textbook recruit, and Bruce had been more than happy to sponsor her, to take her under his wing (no pun intended), because he'd been no older than her when he nearly scraped off his entire arm in a motorcycle accident. High out of his mind, driving home from his son's funeral. The Tattooist had carved a heron into his mangled arm because "herons fly better than motorcycles."

"We're an independent organization," he said diplomatically to the man with the two glasses of rum.

"You mean communists," said the man.

"Well." Bruce wagged his head.

"Sir, would you mind if we came in?" Durwood asked. "We heard there was a disturbance in the neighborhood, and—"

"You don't have authority to just *come* in." The man held his drinks against his chest like Durwood might try to take them. "You're not cops."

"Ohh, ignore Albert." The woman smiled and scratched at the top of her head, moving her pink hat up and down. "We were the ones who called in the disturbance."

"We were?" Albert was alarmed.

"*I* was," said the woman. "Please, come in. Or, no. Look." She pointed to the spot in the road where the Evans' car had been. "People have been parking right there and disappearing. Car and all. *That's* the spot I was talking about on the switchboard. People come over for dinner, they park, and then we don't hear from them. Something is happening on this street." She raised her eyebrows theatrically.

"For heaven's sake," said Albert behind her. "Audrey, you're causing trouble."

"It isn't trouble," said the woman. "It's *good*. Come in, come in."

The entryway was narrow and low-ceilinged. Durwood was short, only five foot three. Bruce was just over a foot taller, and had to bow his head to keep from scraping it against the popcorn ceiling as they stepped inside.

Audrey glanced around outside, then shut the door, locked it, and turned to face them. She scratched at the side of her head, just under the brim of her pink hat. "Can I get you anything?"

"No, thank you," said Durwood.

The woman looked at Bruce. He shook his head.

"No rum?" Albert asked, rattling the glasses.

"Twenty years sober," said Bruce.

"Ahh." Albert laughed awkwardly, then turned and whispered a series of hissing syllables at Audrey. Audrey whispered back, and Durwood caught only the phrase *plain sight*.

"How long have these disappearances been happening?" Durwood asked.

"About six months," said Audrey. "Four different couples, up in smoke."

"And you didn't think to stop inviting people over?" Bruce asked.

"Sometimes it isn't even our fault! We had a mailman vanish in that spot over the summer. I don't know *what's* happening."

"I'm surprised no one else has called it in," said Albert.

"Well, not everybody loves the switchboard," Durwood said pointedly. She made a show of looking around the hall. Its walls were covered in faded photos of children in braces. A redheaded bowl-cut boy with an ice-cream-smeared grin, beaming at the camera. A sweaty teen girl with a volleyball cocked against her hip, laughing with her eyes shut. "These your kids?"

"Laura and Joshy," said Audrey. "Where are my manners. *I'm* Audrey Arthate and this is my husband, Albert."

Albert Arthate muttered under his breath as he carried the two glasses into the kitchen. Durwood heard him dumping ice and rum into the sink.

"Nice to meet you," she called after him.

"Thank you so much for coming," said Audrey, adjusting her pink hat. "This is truly the saddest thing. Anything you can do to help."

"It's the stupidest thing," said Albert, coming back into the room.

Bruce cleared his throat. "Mr. Arthate, where are your kids tonight?"

Albert scratched the side of his head, thinking. "Laura's off at a volleyball thing in Braddock. Uh . . ."

"Joshy's staying the night at a friend's house," said Audrey. "Up in Lillian."

"Gotcha," said Durwood. "Well, would you mind if we took a look around?"

"You don't think there's something *in* our house, do you?" Audrey asked.

"Don't know yet," said Bruce.

"Well," said Albert, "second floor's this way." He nodded up at some stairs. "And there's a basement through the kitchen."

"Kids' rooms upstairs?" asked Bruce.

"Here, I'll show you," said Audrey.

"I'll take you up on that basement," said Durwood.

Albert extended an arm, gesturing toward the kitchen.

Durwood and Oake nodded to each other as they headed into separate parts of the Arthate house. Their hands hovered near their waistbands, inches away from their guns.

BRUCE HAD TO DUCK UNDER ANOTHER CEILING TO GET UP THE STEPS to the second floor. When he lifted his head and felt his boots hit carpet, he found himself at the end of a short hall containing several darkened doorways. Lining the walls, more faded photographs of children wearing braces.

"This is Albert's den," said Audrey, pointing into a room.

Bruce leaned into the doorway and flicked on the light. Desk, computer. Large brown armchair in the corner.

"Very cozy," said Bruce.

"He's writing a book," said Audrey.

"Nice."

"It's about ducks."

"Can't beat ducks."

"And here's the master bedroom, the bathroom . . ." Audrey showed him around the entire second floor, Bruce flicking on lights in her wake. It was always a good idea to have as many lights on as possible in situations like this.

"So that's it," said Audrey, shrugging. She frowned and scratched the side of her head. "What kind of thing are you looking for?"

Bruce moved in a slow circle about the hall, leaning into rooms and frowning at furniture.

"Well, Mrs. Arthate," he sighed, "since just about anything is possible in Renfield County, we look for just about anything . . . out of the ordinary . . ." He trailed off.

The bed in the guest room was exactly the same as in the master bedroom. Same sheets, same quilt, same headboard.

He pointed at one of the pictures on the wall. An identical twin to the picture downstairs: sweaty teenage Laura, holding a volleyball against her hip, laughing with her eyes closed. "Laura and Joshy don't have a lotta good hair days, huh?"

"I spose not." Audrey laughed. "Rug."

"Sorry?"

"Oh." Audrey laughed again and waved a hand. "Nothing." She coughed and said, "Do you need anything else up here?"

Bruce looked through the doorway of the den at the brown armchair. He looked through the doorway of the guest room, at the armchair's doppelgänger.

"Not yet," he said.

As they padded back down the steps, Audrey asked, "Do you really think this all has something to do with our house, Mr. Oake?"

"Well, ma'am, it certainly ain't caused by ducks."

THERE WERE GAPS BETWEEN THE BASEMENT STAIRS. DURWOOD walked down them with her head bent, waiting for hands or knives to slice out at her ankles from the dark. Albert walked a few steps in front of her. When he reached the bottom, he vanished for a moment around the corner. Then an overhead fluorescent flickered on, revealing a stone floor, cracking stone walls, and the cobwebbed debris of an abandoned rec room. Wilted beanbag chair, sunken black couch, box television, scattered free weights. Bad vibes.

Durwood automatically put a fingertip to the small puckered wound in the base of her palm. It had healed like an old piercing. Around it curled the talons of her scar-tissue hawk, soaring across her wrist.

Albert Arthate watched her take in the unfinished basement. He rubbed the side of his hatted head, shifting the blue hat like he was massaging his scalp with its edge.

There was a metal door in one wall. Durwood rattled the rusty doorknob. It wouldn't open. She gave Albert a pointed look.

"That's always been locked," he said. "We moved in about . . . fifteen years ago? It was open then, just more storage space. But we never used it and it rusted over." He shrugged.

"Fifteen years . . . Huh." Durwood pointed to a rug several feet away. A random brown rug in the middle of an otherwise-unused section of the basement. "What about that?"

Albert shrugged again. "Rug."

She nodded, looking around. "Okay. Correct me if I'm wrong, but from the way the house is oriented, it seems like the part of the street where people go missing is right above that room." She pointed at the rusted door.

"Sure," said Albert.

"And the cars. You know, there are records of things in the woods scrapping cars for parts? Building their own machines?"

"Really."

"If one was trying to get rid of a car, one could easily drop it off somewhere along County Road 7. Somewhere that doesn't get a lot of light. And the woods would take it from there." Durwood turned and stood facing Albert, pressing the small round hole in her palm. "Ya know, one of your neighbors says you've been going out for a lot of nighttime drives, Albert. In different cars. She also says that you only moved in a *year* ago. That this house was abandoned before then."

Albert laughed, scratching his head. "Okay. I don't . . . And who are *they*? Are you investigating them?"

"Not yet." Durwood smiled, then jerked her chin at Albert's hat. "Would you mind . . . taking off your hat, Mr. Arthate?"

"My hat," said Albert.

"Yeah, would you mind taking it off? Just for a second."

Albert hesitated. Then took a step closer, bent the top of his head, and removed his hat.

Underneath, the skin was pale and bloodless. His thin, dark hair was sweaty and matted to his scalp. The wet flesh of the scalp itself was filled with hundreds of small, pulsating holes. They opened slowly, glistening in his skull, dilating like the hungry mouths of countless baby worms, burrowed deep within his brain.

"Oooh," said Durwood, hand moving around her waist toward the back of her jeans. "Yeahhh, I'm gonna have to—"

Albert headbutted her, cracking her under the chin and sending her stumbling back. Her teeth snapped, her jaw buzzed. She whipped her hand behind her back and pulled the revolver out of her waistband, "Anglers! Bruce, anglers!"

Albert hissed and grabbed the sodden beanbag chair in both hands. She fired, punching a bullet into the stone wall behind him, just as he chucked the bag at her. She threw up both hands, shoving it out of the way, and in the split second she was defending herself, she couldn't see, Albert flew across the room, eyes rolling, teeth chattering fast, like an insect, charging at her, he was on her, on top of her, and—

When a cat wants to extend their claws, they contract a particular tendon in their paw and the tension pops that claw into the air. Similarly, the Tattooist had woven a slim metal barb into the muscle beneath Durwood's hawk-scar. He never *just* worked on the scar tissue. No, he always left a gift of metal behind. Mark's special hearing aid, for example, or the plate of titanium embedded in the flesh of Bruce's arm. In Durwood's case, she could flex the tendons in her forearm and that slim metal barb would shoot out of the earring-hole in the heel of her hand. A slender six-inch spike of iron-titanium alloy, hidden in her flesh. The wound on her hand had healed in such a way that she never hurt herself when her talon was extended. It always slid out perfectly, with a soft, dry *shlick*.

She jerked her wrist, springing her talon into the air, just as Albert's chattering teeth fell onto her hand. She punched the spike up into his mouth. It popped straight through the back of his head with a wet *crunch*. He clanged his teeth on the metal, sliding down. His wide and empty eyes rolled back, and he didn't even seem to notice he'd been staked, he just gnashed at the metal and slid forward toward her hand.

She tried to shake him off. "Go away, go away!"

Upstairs, in the living room, Bruce heard Durwood shout, but couldn't make out the words. At the exact moment Albert was flying at Durwood, Audrey threw her head back, hissed, and chattered her teeth toward Bruce as she flew across the floor.

"Oh fuck!" He threw up his heron arm and she chomped down, teeth crunching into his augment so hard she dented the slab of metal. He yelped in pain, "God*damn*!" Then drew his revolver and fired it point-blank into Audrey's temple. She gasped, and her skull spurted black slime as she fell to the floor.

In the same instant, Albert gargled and slid off Durwood's spike, vomiting slime over her sneakers.

Their bodies began to flop. Their arms danced against the floor and their mouths wheezed open and shut.

Something in the house—roared. The walls trembled.

Durwood stomped to the rusted locked door and kicked at it. It dented but didn't open. She kicked again and felt the frame give a little.

Upstairs, Bruce slammed shoulder-first into a wall as the floor shifted and trembled underneath him. Pictures of Laura and Joshy clattered off the walls, revealing jet-black flesh beneath.

"Rachel!" he called as he stumbled down the hall. The floorboards split apart and became teeth, chomping at his ankles as he tripped, barely holding himself upright. "Rachel, sound off!"

"I'm fine!" she shouted. "Still *kicking*." She kicked the rusted door a final time, and it burst inward, revealing a black throat of a room. She took out her cellphone and held up the flashlight.

Dozens of bodies, mummified in cocoons of black silk. They lined the floor, stuck to the walls, the ceiling. The threads of each sack not only wove around the bodies, but *through*. Each one was riddled with the same hives of puckered wet holes that lined the Arthates' scalps, as if every pore on their body had been widened, straws inserted, and their insides sucked out clean, replaced by black wires. The threads of each cocoon wove into arms and out of chests, through necks and out of eye sockets, into ears and out of noses, into thighs and out of groins. But she could still see their faces. Could see how they'd screamed.

She snapped a quick picture with her phone for her field report. As she turned away, the house roared again. The bodies twitched, threads vibrating. Some of the ceiling bodies flopped to the floor. The threads through their bones hoisted them up, brought them wobbling to their feet, knees bent, hundreds of strings suspending them from the ceilings and walls.

"No thank you." Durwood reached into the room and pulled the door shut again, just as one of the thread-things gargled and swung its mouth toward her. She felt it bang its head against the door from the other side.

She ran to the random brown rug, knelt, and whipped it back. Beneath was a wide, ragged hole, smashed through the stone floor into the ground below. Down in the hole, a glowing, throbbing mass. Pulsing pink and yellow.

Bodies banged against the door behind her as she pointed her revolver straight down and fired directly into the mass. The house screeched, and the mass throbbed brighter, faster.

Smash, bodies crashing into the rusted door, bending the metal outward. *SMASH!*

Durwood cocked her revolver, pressed it into the mass, and fired again, nearly breaking her wrist as the gun kicked back. The house roared, and the rusted door exploded outward, flying across the room and smashing into the box television, exploding sparks as bodies tumbled into the basement, puppeteered by the thousand black strings weaving back into the room behind them. They moaned and wavered, stumbling toward Durwood.

Bruce jumped down to the bottom of the stairs.

"Kill faster!" he cried.

She spun around. "Bruce, behind you!"

He turned and saw the threaded corpses advancing fast. He gasped, stumbled back, fell. He sat on the floor, wide-eyed, as one of them loomed over him. It opened its mouth wide, black threads crawling inside, stitched between its teeth, webbing its empty eye sockets.

Its head burst, its entire body flipped sideways. Bruce whipped his head toward Durwood as she turned her gun back to the mass in the floor.

"Alright, asshole," she said through gritted teeth. She buried her talon inside the mass. The house screamed as she dug, shoving her fist down, talon spearing into its glowing flesh. "Eat this."

The house roared in answer, and she fired the gun twice, fast, so deep inside the mass she only heard two dull thumps. The house shrieked and the mass plunged away from Durwood, shlicking off her hand, yanking her forward so she fell onto her stomach and stared directly down into the hole as the mass burrowed into the earth away from her. Threads whipped free from their cocooned bodies. Corpses dropped like cut marionettes, tumbling in a heap on top of Bruce, all over the floor. Threads tore out of the walls like wires ripping free, whipping down into the hole in the floor in a swirling madness. Durwood lay on her stomach with her hands clamped over her head until it was over, until she was left staring into the dirt where that goddamn *thing* had escaped from her, diving deep, badly wounded but still alive.

She spat into the hole. She hated it when things got away.

She rolled over onto her back and caught her breath, staring up at the ceiling. She licked her lips. "Oake? You still with me?"

No answer.

She lifted her head. "Oake?"

He was holding a thumb up in the air, breathing hard. His heron arm was trembling and misshapen.

"She bit my augment," he said. "Bent it. I didn't know it *could* be bent."

Durwood grunted to her feet. "As long as it's not broken." She limped over to him and held out her hand. "Come on." She pulled him to his feet.

"You knew what it was before I did," he said.

"I just put the pieces together," said Durwood. "I guessed *that* was the stomach where it was digesting everybody." She waved at the cocoon-room. "And the hats, the sweaters . . . I figured they'd be holed. See?" She lifted the edge of Albert's sleeve, revealing countless little pinpricks along his arms, matching those in his head. They no longer expanded and contracted, tasting the air. Everything in the Arthate house was still now.

"That's a lot of pieces to put together," said Bruce.

"There's only one other case of an angler-house in our files," said Durwood, cleaning slime off her talon. "Back in '82. I remember because it's so unique. Swallowed an entire house with its little silk threads, then camouflaged itself. Camouflage wasn't perfect, though. Certain pieces repeated. Pictures on the walls . . ."

"Furniture," Bruce added.

She nodded. "Exactly. In 1982, the angler took over the residents of its chosen house slowly. Used subsonic psychic waves or some shit to burrow into them over the course of three weeks. Starts as a headache; buncha little dents in your scalp. Then it bites down, and it's all weeping, pus-crusted sores. All over your head, your entire body. As the house keeps drilling into your brain, the pressure on your skull is . . . Well, you lose your mind. And the house becomes not a building, but a body. A skin. You're not you anymore. Just a lure for more food."

"Shit way to go," said Bruce.

"Yeah. No fun."

"So Albert and Audrey were real people?"

"They all were. Look." Durwood put a foot on one of the corpses and nudged it over. There lay Laura, without her volleyball or her smile. Squishy and hollow, and full of tiny holes. "It drew them all in. Sucked em dry. I bet if we dug into photos of everyone reported missing around here, we'd recognize all four Arthates."

"Damn . . ." Bruce snorted. "Man, how do you remember all this? From one file?"

Durwood flexed her talon back into her arm. "I like to read."

Upstairs, the house looked as if it had been abandoned for a long time. The walls were bare and peeling, dust bunnies everywhere. The camouflage was all gone, and the house was no more than an empty ruin. In fact, that had been Durwood's first clue as to what kind of creature this was: According to the neighbors, this house had been empty for years before the Arthates recently, suddenly appeared. She'd had a hunch before they'd arrived, but hadn't mentioned it, just in case. She hated being wrong.

She sighed into the passenger's seat of the car. Bruce collapsed into the driver's seat and sighed with her.

"I'll call a burn crew here; they can ID the bodies and clean everything up," he said.

"Great."

"You okay?"

She nodded. "Peachy. Pissed it got away."

"Yeah," said Bruce, putting the car in drive and the Arthate house in their rearview. "Yeahh, that always bites . . ."

The drive home was silent. When they arrived at Durwood's apartment, she got out, slammed the door, and leaned into the open window. "You should get Vic to look at your arm. It shouldn't have bent so easily."

"Maybe the house was stronger than we thought," said Bruce.

"Maybe." But she didn't want to admit that. "Breakfast tomorrow? Do our field report, get some hashbrowns?"

"Sounds like a dream."

She stared at him. "*Are* you okay?"

He nodded. "Yeah." Staring blankly through the windshield.

Durwood had only been a Guard for a year, and already, she felt hollowed out. She couldn't imagine the weight Bruce must carry, after twenty-three years.

"Alright," she said. "Have a good night, man."

He put the car in drive. Didn't look at her. Said simply, "You, too, Gadget."

And he was gone.

THE LAST CALM MOMENT OF RACHEL DURWOOD'S LIFE:

Lying in the dark, feeling herself throb, understanding that she was still alive somehow, but adrift in a dark sea outside of time. She could see the blood pulse through her limbs like fireflies. *Hush*, a soft rush of light, moving through her being. *Hush*, telling her she was safe, it was alright. She had *not* been too drunk to drive last night after all. She had not punched her car through a guardrail and plummeted down an embankment into a birch clump. She had not thrown out her hand and felt her wrist slice through the broken windshield. Had not cracked her skull on the steering wheel and vomited pure bourbon and Mountain Dew into her lap. *Hush*, her car had reached its destination. *Hush*, this void was her destination. She wasn't a waste of life after all. Wasn't the same idiot who'd climbed into her car at three a.m., soda and liquor bubbling inside her otherwise empty stomach. That wasn't her. No. *Hush* . . .

She smiled to herself in the blackness. Fingers twitching against the endless sea.

Then she became aware of a voice. Hoarse, with a slight, wet wheeze. Like a doctor intrigued by her case, reading her chart, muttering to himself, "Mmm, Durwood, eh? Very Renfield name, must be old blood. AB-positive, speaking of blood. Mm, very nice . . . Wound to the right forearm, let's see . . . Yes, good skin, this Durwood blood. Firm but"—*sniff*—"pliable. Ooh, a nice manglement. I do love a *fresh* manglement. Lots of loose muscle here, wound opened pretty . . . Oh-hoo-hoo, opened pretty *wide*! Tendons torn, so *bend*able now . . . Yeeesss, I see. Yes, lots of new room in here. Lots of room for *metal*."

The freshly mangled Durwood this voice was muttering about—she realized suddenly it was her. *She* was Durwood. She was alive. She *had* totaled her car and fucked up her wrist and puked all over herself. She *was* being probed by cold, clammy fingers.

With an electric jolt, she threw open her eyes and yanked her hands against her chest. "Whaddafffugg."

The face hunched by her side had a broken nose and sharp teeth. Paper-white skin and bloodshot eyes. It snarled and pulled its own hands back protectively against its chest. It rose to its feet, towering very tall and thin over Durwood, in a long black cloak. It *appeared* to be a man, but it acted like a startled cat, a wide-eyed Nosferatu. It hissed at her, "Heee!"

"Vic." A man appeared behind the hissing thing. Middle-aged, broad, and dressed in plaid. The thing glared at him. The man jerked his head away from Durwood, toward an open door. "You're scaring her. Be patient."

Vic wrung his hands and muttered to himself as he sulked out of the room. He kept his eyes glued to Durwood until he was gone.

The man in plaid stepped forward. "Sorry about him. That's Victor Stropp. Used to be a tattooist. More of a . . . an eccentric sawbones now. I know this seems hard to believe, but you're gonna be real grateful for him in a few hours."

Indeed, later that day, Durwood would find herself in a dentist's chair in the Tattooist's office, in the headquarters of the County Guard. There, Victor Stropp, the Tattooist, would fuss over her, carving into her fresh wound and sliding metal inside, filling the chasm of her heart with iron. She would rise from that chair with the hawk stretched over her wrist, its beak screeching angrily, its talons outstretched toward her palm. Despite his gothic outward appearance, the Tattooist had an innate understanding of people. He knew what kinds of birds they were in their hearts.

But right now, Durwood was still twitchy, shivering. She blinked around at the hospital room. "Which one am I in?"

"Bartrick Regional," said the man.

Durwood nodded. This was a relief. Renfield has two hospitals: Bartrick Regional and Mount Slake Medical. You do *not* want to wake up in Mount Slake.

"Okay, and who are you?" she asked.

"Oh, I'm Bruce." He smiled. "And I know this seems hard to believe, too, but . . . I'm gonna be your new best friend. Trust me."

And something in the way he said that—Durwood's obstinance cracked. Suddenly, she *did* trust him. She trusted him so bad she wanted to bury her face in his chest and sob until she fell back asleep. She didn't know this man yet at all. But she knew she'd follow him to the ends of the earth.

THAT WAS A YEAR AGO. RIGHT AFTER SHE'D LOST HER MOTHER AND her brother, Tom. Bruce had been there. Had shown her how to fight. Except, even after a full *year* of fighting, she struggled to feel like she was making a difference. She hadn't saved her family. Hadn't saved Laura or Joshy. She hadn't saved *any*body, except maybe the Evans earlier tonight. But still.

She stood in her living room, staring out the window at the Bent River. It glittered under the moon, peaceful as it curved away toward the hills. She stood picking at her lip between her fingernails, digging into herself just a little. She felt slippery, uneasy, and alone, the way we all do when something in our life has changed irrevocably, in a small but significant way that we cannot easily articulate.

After a while, she went into the kitchen and made herself a drink.

BURNSKIDDE, OCTOBER 2009

The Owl and the Deer

Galloway sat on her bedroom rug, her back against the bookshelf next to her bed. She dug her fingers into the rug's comforting depths as she scribbled more Addekkean sketches in her notebook. Jimmy Eat World trilled through her earbuds.

She was supposed to be working on Tolley's colonial history project, but she, uh . . . wasn't doing that. Instead, she was drawing new monsters to keep her pigs company. Early drafts of bat-like beasts and ravens who could read minds.

She drew contentedly for a while before someone tapped on the top of her head. She jumped, and looked up to see her mother, Nicole, standing over her.

"Boo," said Nicole.

"Jesus, I could've punched you," said Galloway.

"Ohh." Nicole straightened her blazer. She worked in real estate, and was often as clinically clean as the model homes she showed. "What if I'd been your little brothers? You wouldn't punch a minor."

"I've punched both of those minors multiple times," said Galloway.

Her twin eight-year-old brothers, Teddy and Bobby, were the bane of her existence, a fact they relished. All the Nerf darts, Oreos stuffed with toothpaste, tripwires of floss in the hallway . . . Yeah, she'd punched them once or twice.

"Fair enough." Nicole cracked her neck. She was a tall, thin woman, and Galloway resented her for passing along *none* of her genes. Galloway was all Keith, wide and creative. He'd been an AV kid back in the day, while Nicole had been a champion pole-vaulter. Her picture *still* sat in a trophy case in the hallway outside Galloway's chem class. Galloway did not love this.

She popped an earbud out of her ear. "So what? What's up?"

Nicole held up five bright, red-painted nails. "Five minutes and we're going to Eddie Spaghetti's."

Galloway groaned. "Why?"

"Because your brother picked it. Be ready." Nicole tried to back out of the room.

"You approved this?" Galloway asked. "You *want* to eat at Eddie's? Because you're the adult here, Nicole, you have the final say."

"Ew, don't call me Nicole. And I'm very happy with Edward Spaghetti. He has that minestrone soup I like. And their *bread*." She rolled her eyes. "Don't be a grump, come on." She clapped her hands, did a little chant. "Bread, bread."

"I'm not a grump, Eddie is *gross*. He always hits on you. In front of Dad!"

"Well, he hits on Dad, too. He's an equal opportunity creep."

Galloway waved her hands around, appalled. "How are you not hearing yourself right now?"

"Oh, come on," said Nicole, closing the door. "Eddie's is good. You *like* Eddie's. What was it, you had your eighth birthday there."

"Tenth. And that was the day Willy Neglani tried to kiss me, then threw up spaghetti all over my dress, so yeah, I love Eddie Spaghetti's. It's my favorite."

Eddie Neglani was a thick-armed, gregarious man of questionable Eastern European heritage. He was as tall and wide as a grizzly, with gorilla arms. How he had arrived in Burnskidde, or why his life dream was to open an Italian restaurant, was beyond Galloway's comprehension. Worse, he had an idiot brute of a son, Willy, who had short, spiky blond hair and bulldog jowls.

"Can't we just go to the Burrito Bunker?" Galloway asked. "I know you love their nachos. We—"

Nicole's eyes went wide. She clung to the door with both hands.

"Rachel, I've been trying to be courteous, but I am *barely* holding it right now. I have been home for forty-five seconds, and I am going to pee my pants if I don't go to the bathroom as soon as possible. So *please* get ready to go, and next week's family dinner is your choice, so we can go wherever your little heart desires. Mmkay?" She smiled super wide. "Yum, yum! Spaghetti! You'll love it."

She almost succeeded in closing the door, but not before the family Maltese darted in and leapt upon Galloway's notebook.

Galloway normally loved Doofus. He was just a lil white floof of a guy! But he was rolling around on her sketches.

"Doofus!" she cried.

"See, Doofus loves spaghetti, too," said Nicole, shutting the door at last.

Galloway scooped up Doofus and carried him down the hall to her dad's den, a small room covered in papers and framed pictures of the Galloway kids.

"Mom says we're going to Eddie Spaghetti's," said Galloway as Doofus nibbled at her fingers.

Keith put his pen down and smiled behind his mustache. "Awesome. I love their bread."

"Daddy, we ate there last week," said Galloway matter-of-factly. As she'd grown older, she'd evolved from whining to stating her point very clearly. This never worked on Nicole, who was immune to all breeds of bullshit, but it sometimes worked on Keith.

"Hmm, this is true," he said, frowning. "But last week was Teddy's choice."

"Daddy, the twins are in cahoots. Bobby only chooses what Teddy wants because Teddy gives him his allowance. Bobby doesn't understand *money*, he just likes the attention. He's gonna have, like, two hundred dollars saved up at this rate. He could buy his own iPod. At eight!"

Keith sighed. "These are strong points, Rach. But"—he threw up his hands—"Family Night is all about choices and compromise. We go out once a week, and every week we take turns choosing dinner. That's the rule. Sorry, my hands are tied."

"They're literally not, though. If anything, it should be Nicole's choice because *she* makes dinner the other six nights a week."

"Alright, first of all, her name is Mom."

"Oh my gooood."

"Secondly, did you ask her where *she* wanted to eat?"

Through gritted teeth, Galloway said, "No."

Keith smiled and stood up, stretching his back, slapping his belly. "Well, I know she likes their soup, so."

Galloway let out a groan that lasted through the car ride and the entire meal at Eddie's. Halfway through, Eddie Neglani himself sauntered up to their table and clapped Keith Galloway so hard on both shoulders that Keith winced in pain.

"Everyone is lookin so *beau*tiful tonight," said Eddie Neglani, in his unplaceable Bela Lugosi–esque accent. The several silver chains dangling over his hairy chest sparkled in the candlelight. "Nothing makes a person look so lovely as a mouthfulla spaghetti." He laughed and squeezed Keith's shoulders.

Teddy thwacked Galloway's arm with a breadstick. He cackled.

She snatched the bread out of his hand and crumbled it between her fists. "That's gonna be your face, you little accident."

"Uh oh." Eddie Neglani laughed. "Somebody's spaghetti isn't sitting right."

"She's just grumpy today," Nicole cooed. "Everything's lovely, thank you."

"Not as lov-e-ly as *you*," said Eddie. He squeezed Keith's shoulders again, fingers kneading. "Ooh. Such muscles. Ha ha!"

"Thanks." Keith winced.

Bobby blew the paper wrapping off his straw, hitting Galloway in the eye. The twins laughed in stereo. Eddie laughed with them. Keith chuckled nervously. Nicole was hiding her mouth behind her spoon, chewing as she said, "This soup gets better every week, I swear."

Galloway stared dourly into her lap. Her mind drifted elsewhere, to a place filled with *smart* people who lived a fantastical way of life. A place that she controlled.

Addekkea.

❧

PROSPECTOR PERCY BURST THROUGH THE DOUBLE DOORS OF THE gymnasium. His giant head wobbled violently as he cocked a fist on his hip, slung his large foam pickax over his shoulder, and beamed his foam teeth at the crowd. The kids in the stands lost their minds, stomping their feet, clapping their hands. Prospector Percy put a hand to his ear and waved it to the ceiling, so everyone cheered louder, deafening, horrible. Percy danced on the polished maple floor as, from the speakers all around the gym, Black Eyed Peas sang on about how tonight was gonna be a good, good night.

Percy, in his signature blue shirt and overalls, danced into the throng of teenagers shaking sparkly pom-poms, flinging their hips this way and that, in their short sparkly skirts. Boys in blue jerseys stood to the side, clapping to the beat, pumping their hands. The cheerleaders whipped their hair around.

Burnskidde High was very proud of its young meat.

It was a blue and yellow school. All the banners on the walls were large sheets of blue cloth stenciled with yellow lettering. The one directly over Galloway's head: REGIONAL CHAMPIONS, 2007. The principal, a squinty man named Dr. Eric, had an endless collection of blue and yellow ties.

The cheerleaders danced and threw each other into the air. Percy ogled them, so the crowd felt okay ogling them, too. Teachers stood along the walls, looking glum and old. Some of them mouthed along to the song, bopping slightly. But Mr. Tolley had his hands in the pockets of his chalk-stained khakis, shoulders hunched.

Galloway wondered what he'd been like in high school. Hadn't *he* ever doodled in class?

She'd donned, for this special homecoming pep rally, her finest anti-establishment garb. Her hair was in pigtails secured by big black beads with cat skulls on them. She was wearing her baggy *Invader Zim* hoodie, black and loose and very effective at hiding her untoned body. She wore ripped black jeans over fishnets, a new purchase from her last trip to Hot Topic that she sort of regretted now because they were *far* too tight. She sat hunched, legs tight to her body, feeling totally enmeshed. Why did she do this to herself? All over her body, buttons and cables and wires. Tightening around her back, her waist, her boobs . . . Arcade Fire was right, her body *was* a cage.

"I Gotta Feeling" woohoo-ed its way to completion over the speakers, and everyone cheered. Dr. Eric took his place behind the podium, smiling his squinty, toothy smile. His hair was a solid gray sheet combed badly over his red face. He wore wire-framed glasses, was broad-shouldered, had played football for Burnskidde himself back in the day.

"Wow," he said into the microphone. He laughed and clapped for the cheerleaders again. "Aha ha. Okay. Wow! Wasn't that *great?* Let's give another hand to our Prospector gals. Yeah!"

The crowd cheered. The cheerleaders beamed and shook their pom-poms. Dr. Eric smiled at them, squinting so hard his eyes were invisible.

Like most young fans of the macabre, Galloway found great comfort in the terror it was possible to inflict upon these shining happy people, these people who were thin and had good hand-eye coordination. In horror movies, they were so easily reduced to screaming, sobbing liabilities, too stupid to escape the woods without getting cleaved in two (or was it *clove?*). Galloway loved horror movies because they helped her foresee the cruel demise of the spotlit people she resented. If only some smiling little pigs could march in here and start munching off arms . . .

Emma (who had as much distaste for this shaking, sparkling gospel of flesh as Galloway did) nudged her. "Lookit."

Case in point: Ashleigh Hunt was shaking her pom-poms in the front row of the cheer squad, closest to the bleachers. Legs long and tan. Smiling brilliantly. Eyes wide and blue. Naturally red hair halfway down her back.

"Geez," said Galloway.

"Look at Jake."

Jake Mendez stood with the rest of the varsity football team, eyes running up and down Ashleigh's body as he bit his lip.

"Five bucks they've had sex already," said Emma.

"No way," said Galloway. "She goes to church."

They locked eyes and snorted laughter.

Ashleigh had been cool once. She and Emma and Galloway used to have sleepovers. Threw popcorn at each other, made lizards out of beads, talked about boys. Then Ashleigh got her braces off, started running track, tried out for the *cheer* squad—and started going out with Jake Mendez. That had officially sealed it. She knew about Emma's crush but dated Jake anyway? Wow.

They hadn't spoken since. Galloway had once walked all the way around the school, in the opposite direction of where she'd needed to go, because she'd seen Ashleigh coming down the hallway.

Ashleigh's new popularity and confidence didn't feel accessible to Galloway. It felt impossible in a country soaked in the ideologies of Miramax Films, *Shallow Hal*, and *Family Guy* to be "big-boned" and beautiful. You could only be big-boned and bitter.

"Her left leg is longer than her right," said Galloway, pointing. "See? I wonder if she knows."

"Well, I hope to see you all at the game tonight," said Dr. Eric, squinting out at them through his thick glasses. "I'll be there for sure. Can't wait to see our boys bring home the trophy for the sixth year in a row. Those Bent High Whalers think they can best us, but wait until they get the ax!"

Jake Mendez cupped his hands around his mouth and shouted, "Go Prospectors!"

Percy waved his pickax in the air, causing everyone to cheer and clap. Dr. Eric gave his smarmy laugh. "Aha ha. Aha ha. Wow."

Galloway wondered how many people an Addekkean pig could chew through before Officer Wilson, the school safety officer, shot it down. She imagined the pig launching itself at Dr. Eric, crunching into his throat with its big tusks, snorffling deep into his esophagus, chewing up a big spurting hunk of meat and shredded tubes.

She looked around for Francis but couldn't see him.

"By the way, the plant-people want you to come over tomorrow," said Emma. "For dinner. If you want."

"What are they serving?"

"Ziti."

"You gotta be kidding me. I *just* had spaghetti."

"That's another thing. Have you noticed they never serve vegetables now? It's all this red meat. Ziti with meat sauce."

"Are there, like, spores in the sauce?"

"Just hamburger."

"Ooh boy, somebody's *gotta* stop this Botanist. Homemade pasta and no spinach, oh my god."

Before Emma could respond, Dr. Eric was announcing the end of the pep rally. The girls suddenly found themselves in a crush of bodies rushing to the buses, eager to go home.

"Text me!" Emma called as they were pressed in opposite directions, toward opposite buses.

"I'll remember youuu," Galloway called back, reaching dramatically over the crowd.

When she turned to see where she was going, Galloway found herself facing Ashleigh Hunt. Ashleigh gaped at her, frozen in the same awkward panic as Galloway. She seemed sad, alone outside the gym, without her new pack. Her blue and yellow bows drooped. Her outfit seemed less sparkly.

"Hey," she said.

"Hey," said Galloway quickly.

"Heyyy!" Jake Mendez swept through the crowd, hooking an arm around Ashleigh's neck and reeling her away out of sight. Galloway was swept along amidst a pack of boys throwing wet paper towels back and forth.

How many pigs would it take to devour Ashleigh Hunt in her entirety?

ON THE BUS RIDE HOME, SHE RETURNED TO HER SMALL, COMFORT- able bubble. "Transatlanticism" on her iPod, notebook open on her lap, the brilliant clear wash of the first week of October outside. Skies deep blue and puffy-clouded, leaves just beginning to lava-lamp into new colors.

She felt like her monsters needed a bit more muscle. A little more agency. They should fly, for sure. All week, she'd been sketching these bats. Large gargoyle-esque beings with human faces. They swooped and snarled over the graphite towers of Addekkea, soaring across the college-ruled pages. The V's of gothic black ravens flitted between them. She imagined the birds had a psychic language all their own. *You're flying so high*, they praised each other telepathically. *Great form!*

She scratched small aphorisms in the margins of these sketches. Big, angular letters several layers deep, bleeding through the pages. *FLESH TO EARTH. MAN TO BEAST.* She wanted it to look crazy, like the journals they found in that guy's apartment in *Se7en*.

She imagined leaving the notebook somewhere and letting whoever found it think it was all real. The *real* delusional ravings of a madman. But that would be a lot of work, to fill this entire book just to leave it in the school library or whatever. She'd never know the impact it would have. What if a janitor threw it away without even looking at it? It could become an internet legend, like *Blair Witch* or *Cloverfield*, or it could become trash.

Francis wouldn't think it was trash.

She felt a little light-headed, thinking of him. She drew people offering their arms to pigs with a smile. She drew pigs shitting out those arms into patches of pumpkins and apple trees. The rush of this art made her giddy, the same way the *Saw* movies made her happy when she downloaded them onto her laptop and watched them secretly in her room. Jigsaw loathed his rusty, broken world, and she felt like she could relate, living in this nowhere salt-mine town.

But the pigs were giving rise to a beautiful, natural world. Look at these people standing around, laughing with their bleeding stumps.

She figured this world of hers needed some kind of organizing principle. A major deity they prayed to. Who governed all the pigs and psychic ravens and gargoyle-bats? Maybe, like, a god-beast. The biggest beast of them all.

She started sketching something huge. So huge, in fact, his face spread off the page. He towered over the walls of Addekkea, stomping around on four colossal, elephantine legs. His mammoth body was shrouded in long, matted icy-white hair, and she imagined that the skin beneath this hair was a deep blue. His big saurian snout was the size of a bus. He lumbered through the woods, and he was so tall that you could never see all of him at once. She imagined that his breath was thick, white fog. Not frightening, but cool and refreshing. A balm that could cure all ills. In fact, it was the balm Addekkea had been praying for! Yes, when they hit desperate times, Addekkea sang to the beasts until their god-king arrived. His breath cured the colony of all disease, and blew away the knifemen, the nonbelievers, leaving behind nothing but a glorious, pale peace. A pure white blanket of safety and calm.

She paused, massaging her hand. She considered her god-creature, several stories tall, barfing fog from his vast snout. After a moment, she dug her black Sharpie into the page:

THE FOGMONGER COMETH.

She smiled. Francis would love that.

THE FIRST TWO HOURS OF GALLOWAY'S SHIFT WERE PARTICULARLY slow. She listened to Dom and Greg argue about who would win in a fight: Batman or Rorschach. Then at about ten o'clock, the door clanged open. She looked up from her latest sketch (a whole swarm of gargoyle-bats) and saw a group of familiar faces. Prospectors coming to eat after the homecoming game, Jake and Ashleigh among them.

"Hey, sick." Jake snapped a finger gun. "Galloway. I didn't know you worked here."

"Yep," said Galloway limply. Behind her, Emma slid into hiding in the kitchen. "How was the game?"

Ashleigh was silent, Jake's arm draped heavily across her shoulders. He threw up his hands. "Lost. Plus, get this. Somebody took Dear!"

"Oh no," said Galloway, genuinely saddened. "What happened?"

"Don't know," said Jake. "Bad omen, though. You know the story, right? The night before The Big Accident of 1968, Percy McManus dreamed about a deer standing in the mine, shaking his head at him. Next day, Percy didn't go into work—*bam!* Big Accident. He lived! Now ..."

"Yeah, yeah, every year we rent a deer as a good luck charm for homecoming," Galloway recited. "I know." She was bummed to hear the deer went missing, but she didn't care *that* much. The deer was just an excuse for everyone to pose in cute outfits by the bleachers. The deer was well trained; it hardly ever bolted at the camera flash. "Are you sure it didn't just run off?"

"Who knows?" Jake shrugged. "Anything's possible. Whatever. Kinda lame, but it's all good. Them's the breaks, right?"

"Them's the breaks" was a Renfield aphorism popular among people like Jake, who found it difficult to work up the energy to mourn any particular macabre occurrence, as there were so many of them. It was often shorthand for, *If I think about it too hard, I'll probably scream.*

Jake finger-gunned at a corner booth. "Cool if we take that one?"

"Sure," said Galloway.

"Sick." Jake led his crew to the booth, where Ashleigh sat diligently at his side.

In the kitchen, Emma was frowning through the corner of the window.

"I don't want to serve them," Galloway whispered.

"*I* don't want to serve them," Emma replied.

"Yeah, but I'm . . ."

"Waiting for someone?" Emma finished for her. "He didn't even say when he'd be here, just that he *might* come back."

"He'll come," said Galloway.

"You know, we had PE together in eighth grade, and he sneezed so hard he puked."

"I thought you didn't know him."

"I don't. I just remember he sneezed so hard he puked and then I laughed so hard I cried."

"Uh, yello?" Jake called over. "Can we get a plate of the chili cheese English muffins?"

"Sure," sighed Galloway.

"Sick," said Jake.

A few minutes later, just as she was putting down the plate and scurrying away from the table, Francis shuffled through the door. *Ohmygod.* She floofed at her hair, trying to give it some semblance of life. As he smiled and walked closer, Galloway noticed just how raggedy his yellow

Vans were. Torn and covered in white dust. He popped a hand out of his pocket and waved.

"Hey," she said as cheerfully as possible. "I . . . didn't see you at the pep rally."

"Oh, yeah, I don't pep." He looked at the pack of Prospectors in the corner, tearing into sodden chunks of bread. Ashleigh was laughing and spooling hot cheese into her mouth with the rest of them. "Are you busy?"

"No, no," said Galloway quickly. "Can I get you anything?" She snapped a finger gun at him, immediately feeling stupid for copying Jake. "Chicken Caesar Belgian Waffle?"

Francis brightened. "You remembered."

"Of course. Have a seat anywhere you want."

She called the order back to Dom, who gave her a thumbs-up.

Greg limped by with a pallet of clean glasses. "Your boyfriend's back."

"Yes, thank you, Greg. Why are you limping?"

"I'm not, fuck off."

"Okay, geez." She started to walk away, then froze when she saw where Francis was sitting: the booth right next to the Prospectors, literally back-to-back with Jake and Ashleigh.

Why would he do that?

Jake was craning over his seat. "Tolley's class, right?"

"Yes," said Francis, in his airy feather-voice.

"He suuucks," said Jake.

"Yeah," said Francis. His eyes caught Galloway's. She thought she heard him calling silently for help.

She took a breath, scraped her notebook off the bar, and approached.

"Hey," she said. She jerked her head to the bar. "You wanna sit over there?"

"Oh, I like it here," said Francis. "Did you draw something new?"

"Ooh," said Jake. "What'd you draw?"

"Leave her alone," said Ashleigh meekly.

Francis turned in his seat. "Rachel has visions. She sees things in the woods."

"I don't . . ." Galloway shook her head. "That's not true."

"What kind of stuff do you see?" Jake asked, snapping his fingers and popping his fist against his other hand. *Snap-pop. Snap-pop.*

Galloway winced. "Just . . . creatures."

"No shit?" said Jake. "I've seen shit in the woods behind our house for sure. This one time, I saw a racoon eating itself from the paws up." He pretended to gnaw on Ashleigh's hand. She laughed and batted him away.

Galloway clutched her notebook protectively to her chest. "Cool. Well, this isn't like that. I didn't see these things outside my house or anything, I just—"

"She saw them in her head," said Francis.

"No, no. I *imagined* them."

"You sure?" asked Jake, eyes glinting. "My mom says sometimes when you think you're imagining something, it's really just Renfield fucking with you."

"I'm not . . . Can we sit somewhere else?" Galloway asked Francis.

"No, come on, I want to see your drawings," said Jake. "For real. My cousin Chelsea sees shit in her head that she thinks is made up, but it isn't." He turned to Ashleigh. "I told you about her, right? Chelsea? She sees things in her head all the time. She says there's more crazy shit around here than we even *know* about."

Galloway tried to regain hold of the narrative. "I didn't *see* these creatures. I was in class and I just—"

"Does Chelsea know about the poo-pigs?" Francis asked.

"The what?" Jake snorted.

"No, nobody knows about the poo-pigs," said Galloway. "I was just—"

"Show him the pigs," said Francis.

"Yeah," said Jake. "C'mon, show me!"

They looked at her expectantly. Five tall kids crammed into a booth.

She sighed. "Fine." And turned her notebook to show them: "These are the poo-pigs. They're friendly. If you offer your body to them, they'll eat it and turn it into magic fertilizer. It's good for the whole community. It's, like, good for global warming, too."

"You saw these around here?" Jake asked, squinting at the page.

"They're from a place I made up," she said. "An old colony called

Addekkea." She showed them her sketch of the colony. "See? It used to be up in the hills, about four hundred years ago, but it doesn't exist anymore." She looked up from her book, and realized everyone was listening now. Even Greg, across the restaurant, sitting on a barstool and massaging his foot.

She flipped ahead to her drawing of the humungous beast-god: the Fogmonger. "See, they all prayed to this big guy, the Fogmonger? His breath is, like, magic fog. It cures sickness, starvation . . . But he only blesses you if you believe in him enough. If you pray to him and his disciples the pigs. And the bats! See?" She showed them her sketches of the gargoyle-bats.

Francis leaned in and read some of her psycho Sharpie scrawl. "'Flesh to earth.' That's what they all say when they feed the pigs?"

"Mmhmm," said Galloway, nodding. "They're really excited about it, see?" She pointed to the smiling, limbless people.

"These are really good," said Ashleigh.

"Thank you." Galloway didn't look at her.

"Yeah, these are great," said Jake. "Damn, you're, like, actually talented."

"You don't have to sound so surprised," she muttered.

"So this Fogmonger's, like, the king of the monsters," Jake clarified.

"Yeah, see, there's Renfield monsters and then there's these," said Galloway. "*These* guys are something different. They're part of an ooold faith. Older than Christianity."

"Shit, my mom wouldn't like this." Jake laughed. "She'd be like, 'Burn that book!' This is a whole religion?"

Galloway nodded again. She was sweating a little, hoping they wouldn't all burst into laughter at her stupid drawings. But at the same time, she was suddenly bathed in a spotlight she didn't hate. "Yeah, this is a whole thing. The Addekkeans knew about this old faith, but they never really followed it. Then they fell on hard times, and the only people who survived were the ones who had been singing and praying to the woods. They asked for help, the Fogmonger heard them, and he sent out his beasts, the pigs and the bats. They healed the colony."

"Sick," said Ashleigh.

"The beasts saved them," said Francis, lost in her art. "Saved them all . . ."

"Shit, I want to meet a bunch of magic pigs and go to fog-heaven," said Jake.

"That's great," said Galloway, "because he's set to return anytime. When he hears his song sung enough, he'll come back and offer us a . . . a foggy salvation. A reprieve! From Renfield at last. But we have to earn it. It could take, like, a decade of singing and feeding the beasts."

"2019." Jake whistled. "Damn! That's, like, *Blade Runner* times! We gonna be wearing hover-sneakers and shit, damn."

"It's sooner than you think," said Galloway.

"Wow," said Francis. "The promise of a reprieve from Renfield." He was still staring at her notebook, his eyes moving endlessly, drinking in her work. She tucked her mouth behind her notebook so they couldn't see her beaming.

"Soo," said one of the other kids, "everyone who's good gets to go to fog-heaven but everybody else just melts?"

"Yep," said Galloway, imagining Ashleigh melting. "You have to . . . have faith in the fog in order to be blessed."

Francis seemed like he was in the midst of some intense personal journey. He repeated this slowly: "Have faith in the fog."

"Mmhmm," said Galloway. "Have faith that the Fogmonger will return and breathe blessings on us all. Big old . . . fog breath. Good . . . stuff." She was running out of things to say. She was enjoying herself, but her improv skills were running dry.

Only, they seemed so rapt. Francis especially.

"So, the Fogmonger could save Burnskidde?" he asked, looking up at her. "No more Renfield curse?"

"No more missing deer?" Jake threw in.

Galloway smiled. "If we have faith, yeah."

"Have faith in the fog," said Francis again, as if a great revelation had just occurred to him.

"Have faith in the fog," she repeated, hypnotized somehow by these words she'd just made up. They sounded so solid, so real, now that she'd spoken them aloud.

"Well, I have faith in the check whenever you get a chance," said Jake.

"Oh. Sure." She shut her notebook, breaking the spell.

As she was punching buttons on the register, Ashleigh approached her with the same wide-eyed, fake-shy Bambi look she'd worn in the hallway earlier. Galloway pretended not to see her until she asked, "You really believe that's real?"

"What, the register?"

Ashleigh's Bambi facade dropped. "No, asshole. All that stuff about the Fogmonger."

Galloway opened her mouth. Closed it. Watched Ashleigh blink earnestly.

She shrugged. "Why not? Jake's right, people see weird shit around here all the time. I guess I just never thought of it that way."

"I know you've always liked to draw." Ashleigh took a step forward, as if simply expressing this intimate memory of Galloway somehow made them close again. "I know that's the kind of stuff you'd . . . make up."

Galloway put her hands on her hips. "Well, what if I'm like Jake's cousin Chelsea? Maybe I *can* see shit, Ashleigh."

Ashleigh pursed her lips. "I don't . . . I feel like you're fucking with Jake and that other kid. I feel like you're still mad at me."

Galloway jerked her head back. "I didn't think of *you* at all. I was talking to Francis. He was excited about the idea of helping Burnskidde. Your boyfriend clearly doesn't give a shit, but them's the breaks, I guess."

Ashleigh looked wounded. "Okay."

"Okay," said Galloway. "So, believe whatever *you* want to believe, but I'm really starting to think I am special. Maybe the Fogmonger *is* coming back someday and I can see it." She shrugged smugly. "Who knows."

Ashleigh tried to read her face. Couldn't. She said tersely, "I guess we'll see."

"I see you owe me fifteen bucks," said Galloway.

Ashleigh flicked a twenty at her. "Keep it."

Galloway glared at Ashleigh's back as the Prospectors all stumbled out of the Planet in a tight-knit throng.

"Thank you for the waffle," said Francis, suddenly standing next to her with his own twenty outstretched. "It was salty."

"Thanks for listening to my dumb stories," said Galloway.

"I don't think they're dumb. I think they're important. Everyone else seemed to think so, too."

"I guess so." Galloway gave him a lopsided smile.

He smiled back. "You're cooler than you think, Rachel."

She snorted, looked away, blushed and hated herself for it. "Okay. Thanks. You're cool, too."

"Thanks, but your pigs and bats? Your Fogmonger? They're *powerful*. You wait. They'll be grateful you showed them the way." His gaze was so intense, but so inviting. Intensely inviting. She couldn't look at him for long.

"Well, I gotta close up," she said awkwardly. "Good night. Thanks for stopping by."

"You, too. And?" He finger-gunned at her. "Have faith in the fog."

She smiled hard. "Have faith in the fog, Francis."

She watched him bike away, feeling warm and light.

Emma slid up behind her.

"Francis, you're *so* cool," Emma joked.

"Shut up."

"Hey, you should do your Tolley project on Addekkea. He'd love it!"

"Emma. It's *imaginary*. Come on."

Emma shrugged. "So? Lots of history is made up."

"You think the Crusades were fake?"

"No, but, like . . . The way they tell it in the textbook isn't true. Like, the textbook itself isn't history. It's just written by some guy. You're just some guy, why can't you write history?"

"Because I don't *know* history. That's why I'm in this class. I can't just make stuff up."

"What if you didn't?" Emma's eyes took on a mischievous gleam. "What if Francis is right? What if this is all legit stuff? Renfield's fulla stories."

"And I just happened to 'imagine' one in class?"

"Why not?" Emma clapped her hands. "Do it, do it! Addekkea project! It'll be fun."

"Ughh. What if Tolley fails me?"

"He . . . won't. I mean, hey." Emma punched her shoulder. "Have faith in the fog, right?"

ABBY'S ANIMAL RENTALS OWNED THREE TRAINED DEER, AMONG A coterie of farm animals who could hit their marks, lizards docile enough for birthday parties, and over two hundred trick-performing rats. The doe Abby had brought to the Burnskidde homecoming game that night in early October 2009 was named, aptly, Dear.

Dear's disappearance was a tragedy, to be sure, but not a rare one. In many parts of Renfield County, missing-pet posters wallpaper the bulletin boards and telephone poles, several layers deep. Years ago, there had been a young girl named Rachel Durwood, whose mother forbade her from having a dog for this very reason.

Abby was enjoying the final minutes of the game as Dear wandered beneath the bleachers of Burnskidde High's football field. She snorffled at a half-eaten bag of Fritos, pawing and gnawing at it as humanfeet pounded above her in a metallic artillery-fire roar.

She was not alone. From the trees beyond the field, a barred owl watched from above. It was a cool, calm night in Burnskidde. The owl felt safe and content.

Dear sniffed at a patch of grass. She began to nibble, then suddenly, the grass shot up into her nostrils and *grabbed* her. It held tight as she yelped and flailed. The grass grew deep, up, up toward her brain. It cracked through the membrane of Dear's skull and wormed out through her ears, down her neck, pulling her down, down. It buried her head in the dirt, smothering her. Her back legs kicked madly, frantically, then went still as her entire body was engulfed by earth.

The owl was still as the deer struggled. It waited for the night to quiet again. Some time passed before it swooped down upon a mouse, and the owl, too, screamed as it was sucked underground.

The people in the stands heard none of this, as they chanted and cheered and booed the Bent High Whalers. They did not hear the dirt begin to writhe. They did not see the strange shapes pushing their way out of the soil. A swollen-bellied thing, low to the ground, teeth twisted into tusks. A thing with great, leathery wings beating at the air. They snarled and howled as they clawed their way up into the night. They were starving, impatient. Eagerly awaiting their call to feed.

BENT, OCTOBER 2019
Diner Debrief

The first time she walked into the Shelter, Durwood knew she would sink into her work as a Guard with her entire heart. It was her usual M.O. to sink into things with nothing less than her entire soul, no matter how many times in her life she had been taught the hard way not to do so. Relationships, household projects, pets—she'd run the gamut of letting one specific thing eat all of her time and energy for several months before deserting it altogether. This was another thing Tom had hated about her. She would shower him with older-sibling affection for an entire season, even sleeping on his couch just to wake up near him. Then she'd vanish, sucked into the next big thing that made her feel alive and worthwhile.

The Shelter of the Renfield County Guard was no exception. It was located beneath Bartrick Regional Hospital. When Durwood woke up there after her accident, Bruce took her down in the elevator, turned a special key to make it go down one extra floor, and ushered her out into the nicest space she had ever seen. Burgundy carpet, faux-wood paneling. Fake wood! Genius! No Renfield influence here. The air hummed with sage, eucalyptus, palo santo, and moss.

Altogether, the Shelter felt like the operating center of a tech start-up, complete with Ping-Pong tables and a café that sent up waves of the freshest, darkest coffee scent Durwood had ever smelled. Signs pointed to SHOWERS, ARCHIVE, BRIEFING ROOMS, SHOOTING RANGE,

CURSED STORAGE. Immediately before her was a circular reception-ist's desk populated by three people in headsets, answering phones. A brass plate on the desk identified this as the SWITCHBOARD.

"Does the hospital know about this?" Durwood asked, itching the fresh bandages on her arm.

"Oh yeah," said Bruce behind her.

"Do they . . . pay for it?"

"Other way around. The Guard's founders had stock in Mither Lumber & Co., Pancake Planet, and a few other local endeavors that have done well. Our donations to Bartrick Regional are very generous.

"Now, the outer doors are protected by a lock that'll only open for your specific key. Every inch of this place has been blessed, and it's secured by several layers of steel and concrete. Look." He pointed to a room filled with warm lamps, big chairs, and people drinking beer. "That's the Decompress Lounge. They probably all worked cases last night, need to blow off some steam. Get rid of some cursed energy. Beer's a good way to do that, but candy'll do the trick as well. I *always* eat candy before a job. Big chocolate guy myself."

Durwood watched them all laughing. Her chest felt hollow and sore, like the reverberating *boom* after a firework.

"Look up," said Bruce.

She did.

Hanging from the ceiling was a massive sculpture, carved of white marble, glowing in the lamplight from below. A huge creature with wings that stretched over the entire room. It had a man wrapped up in its pointed tail. The man was firing a rifle into its wide, snarling jaw. A plume of immortalized smoke bloomed from the muzzle of the rifle, and the double rows of fangs in the creature's snout roared in answer. It had wide blank eyes and fantastic feathery wings. On its back stood a woman with a spear, the sharp point aimed at the back of the creature's hairy skull.

"The first call the County Guard ever received," said Bruce. "*That* is Ezra Dixon and Muriel Gnash. During World War II, Muriel was a nurse in the European theater. Ezra was a marine in the Pacific. When they came home, they formed a platonic partnership. Wanted to keep fighting the good fight, but in the Renfield theater." Bruce shook his head at the memorial in awe. "Tinker's Devil. Haunted the woods around the Falls for years before Ezra and Muriel managed to crash it into a limestone outcropping, crack its skull against the rock. And to commemorate that day"—he dug into his pocket—"we all carry a piece of limestone from the Billowhills with us." He removed a small stone coin from his pocket and dropped it into Durwood's hand. It was carved with the letters *R.A.D.* in bold, regal black.

"Aw," she said. "Rad."

Bruce laughed. "It's you. Rachel Avery Durwood?"

"Oh shit." She analyzed the coin more closely. It was beautiful. It was *hers*. "Wow."

"Just made it this morning," he said. "Figured you'd want one."

"I don't get it," she said. "Why . . . Why. Why are you showing me this?"

"Because we have bikes you can use," said Bruce. "Rumor is your car's totaled and your license is suspended. But also because I had a hunch you'd like *them*." He jerked his chin up at the Devil. Ezra Dixon, carved in marble, bearded and furious. Muriel Gnash's hair wild about her face for eternity.

"They were warriors," said Bruce gently. "Instead of allowing the valley to feed on their pain and anger, they fed their *hope* instead. Are you angry?" he asked, as a man who had been angry for so long it had exhausted him.

Durwood curled her fingers about the coin. So many memories of growing up in Renfield flashed before her mind.

"Yes," she said. "Yeah, I'm . . . I'm fuckin pissed."

Bruce nodded. "Yeah. *That's* why I'm showing you this. Now, c'mon. I'll reintroduce you to Vic. Like I said, you'll be grateful for him. I mean." He ran a hand over his heron arm. "I certainly was."

IN A BOOTH WITH HER BACK TO THE WALL, DURWOOD SAT STARING far off into space. Her thumb ran in dry circles over the shining pink wings of her hawk-scar, feeling the small talon-slit in the heel of her hand.

This diner had a bizarre fishing theme that Durwood did not appreciate. Many wide-eyed fish gaped at her from the walls, reflected and multiplied in the diner's many mirrors.

Her eyes hung in the middle distance. A looping reel of film flickered behind her eyes:

Tom Durwood on a slab. Arm sliced open. Flaps of cold, colorless flesh like deli meats. He'd been found slumped over his kitchen table, his hand hamburgered like he'd been searching for something inside. Digging farther up his arm, pulling and plucking and unraveling until he simply couldn't do it anymore.

Mom on a slab. Wrists sliced deep, all the way up to the elbow.

Both of them had dug into themselves, looking for . . . what? For the Renfield under their skin?

Durwood found herself scraping a fingernail along the numb scar tissue of her arm. She made herself stop. Looked around for something else to distract her.

Her eyes landed on the television bolted to the opposite wall. Local news was running coverage of the fire again. She'd seen it before, the footage of the flames. Multiple times. She watched again now, just to have something to do:

"It's been seven weeks since the tragic fire at Edenville College," came the melodramatic voiceover, narrating stale B-roll of the E.F.D. spraying water along Edenville's brick-walled halls, "and still, the loss of several faculty members has cast a pall over the entire campus. Investigators are still searching for what might have caused the sudden blaze, but at *this* point, we may never know."

Bruce slid into the booth with a sigh. "Alright. Burn crew says they ashed the Arthate house. Tried tracking the angler underground, but no dice. Only thing they could tell was—"

"It fled south," Durwood finished for him.

"How'd you guess?"

Durwood nodded, eyes still on the tv. "It fled south back in '82, too. It was down in Bent then. Whoever wrote the field report at the time figured it'd gone south into Burnskidde. Or, more specifically, it retreated *back* to Burnskidde."

"Gonna be hard to follow it there now," Bruce observed.

Durwood grunted.

The collapse of the Burnskidde Tunnel, in late November 2009, was one of Renfield's more infamous unsolved mysteries. Was it on purpose, was it an accident? Not only were dozens of people stranded on this side of the tunnel, with no way to reach their loved ones in Burnskidde and no answers, but the event also put a sizable dent in construction costs for the rest of the county. Burnskidde Mining Company's entire clientele was forced to seek rock and salt farther out, from Leaden Hollow and Bleatsfield. But them's the breaks.

"So that's the interesting thing," said Durwood. "In '82, they *were* able to trace the house's path underground all the way down to Horridge Hill."

"What would an underground squid-thing be doing under Horridge Hill?" Bruce asked.

"It's not a squid-thing," said Durwood. She dug into the back pocket of her jeans. "Lab crew at the time caught a sample of it, ran some tests. Turns out . . . it's a plant."

She exhumed a crumpled picture from her pocket. She'd printed it that morning. A black-and-white sketch of a woman with sharp dark hair, surrounded by tree branches. From the branches hung jars filled with eyeballs, centipedes, a human foot. Her red eyes were the only color.

"The Horridge Hill Botanist," said Durwood, smoothing the picture flat on the table. "The house retreated all the way into *her* territory. To this day, no one's ever found her, but the angler-house fits her M.O. perfectly. Mutant plant poses as real people in order to lure other people in and eat *them*, too? She's been doin it for decades." She pulled out other pictures—bleached headshots of smiling people. "Ariel Young, 1998. Nic Donnelly, 1965. All of them went missing for three days around Horridge Hill and came back more social than before. Eerily social. Just like the Arthates. Only difference is, the angler-house is a larger, less-refined experiment than these others. Maybe when she figured out she only needed *people* and not a whole camouflaged Venus flyhouse, she cut the angler loose. I mean, its camouflage did have a problem glitching, right? The repeating furniture, the fact that they both said *rug* at the same time.

It's not a perfect organism. By comparison, Ariel Young never glitched. Maybe the Botanist perfected her process. Maybe—"

"Aw, come on, these are all convoluted conspiracy theories." Bruce waved his hand in the air, like the idea stank. "Ariel Young never lured her dad in and turned *him* into plants."

"That we know of."

"You know what people sound like when they talk about this?" Bruce asked. "I've known only three people who have believed in the Botanist in my life. Rach, it sounds insane. There's no tangible evidence about her plot for a human-plant hybrid . . . apocalypse, or whatever the fuck. Our file on her is razor-thin."

"What if this house is evidence?" asked Durwood. "What if she's been working in secret this whole time? Growing power, hidden in Burnskidde? Look, our file on the 'Edenville College Biology Department Incident of 1947' *is* admittedly slim."

"I hate that you memorized that whole name."

"But the manifesto she carved into her desk before she left the college is crystal clear. We fucked it up here! Paper mills, pollution. She wants to return the entire valley to the plants. It's a nice idea, she just has a . . . bad way of going about it."

Bruce scoffed. "Rachel. The Botanist is a ghost. Just like the rest of Burnskidde. That tunnel's been closed for years. The angler-house was nothing more than a stray dog. I bet Audrey called herself in because she was *tired*. Monsters do that sometimes, ya know? Stopwatch Man? In 2012, he committed suicide by Guard, too. Sometimes you just . . . get tired."

He probed gently at his misshapen heron.

Durwood folded her hands on the table. "Bruce, are you okay?"

He sighed, shook his head. "I feel like . . ."

The waitress appeared at their table with mugs of coffee.

"Thanks," said Bruce. "Can I get three eggs over easy and a medium rare burger? Plus a double helping of potatoes and sourdough toast. Thank you."

"A grapefruit," said Durwood, handing over her menu. It was such a large spiral-bound sheaf of blue plastic, the waitress had to use both hands to accept it. She cast a suspicious glance between Durwood and Oake before stalking off to get their food.

"Listen," said Durwood, leaning forward. "It doesn't mean anything. That you choked."

"It's not just the choke. Although that *would* be enough." Bruce didn't meet her eye. "I've been doin this a long time. I *know* the seasons and I know when the seasons are different. This last season has been different."

"Well . . . every new job I get, people are like, 'Oh, it's *never* this way.' My first year as a sub, everyone was all stressed about the budget. 'Oooh we're not gonna have any textbooks.' But after worrying about the textbooks for four years, I was finally like, 'Wait, they say this every year.'"

"I don't say this every year," said Bruce. "I didn't even say this last month."

"You did, you said the lake-bugs really took it out of you."

"Yeah." Bruce's eyes only grew more distant. "Lake-bugs was . . . a bad one."

One of their last jobs had been investigating the recent influx of insectoid squid-things crawling out of Bartrick Lake. They kept showing up outside people's houses and screeching in a wet, horrible tone. It had taken Durwood and Oake two weeks to figure out that these things had once been human children, pulled and warped and rebranded by the cold pressure of the bottom of the lake. They'd all just wanted to go home.

Durwood leaned deep over the table. "Can I reiterate that I was a *substitute* teacher before I got this job? I was . . . floating through air. You brought me back. At a time when I easily could have dissolved. You can't bail on Durwood and Oake." It came out a bit harsher than she meant it, so she bit her lip to stop anything else from coming out.

Bruce absorbed this barb without slinging any malice back at her. He simply nodded and said, "Yeahh, I know. But I don't know how much longer I can do the gig. I'm sorry."

She sneered. "The *gig*? I thought this was a sworn duty. Who *are* you? You—Oh, Jesus, that was fast."

The waitress appeared with two plates, one significantly larger than the other. They waited in awkward silence as she placed the plates before them. When it looked like she was leaving, Durwood started to speak again, taking a big breath in because she wanted to say *a lot*, but then the woman turned back and asked, "You guys talkin about Burnskidde?"

Durwood and Oake blinked at her.

"Why?" Bruce asked.

The waitress fidgeted. "You, uh . . . workin today?"

"Might be," said Durwood, turning casually on her bench, putting her talon-arm within stabbing distance of the waitress's abdomen. Just in case.

"You here for that book? That guy?"

Durwood and Oake glanced at each other.

"I think we are now," said Durwood. "What book?"

"I'll be right back." The waitress went away.

"I'm not working this," said Bruce softly. "I'm sorry. Whatever it is, I . . . need a break, at least."

"Come on, man," Durwood whispered. "You're gonna leave me alone with some random book?"

The waitress reappeared carrying a small bundle in both hands, holding it away from herself like it was contagious. She placed it carefully on the table, then, out of a pocket in her apron, pulled a stone coin. "He left me this. Said his code word was *canal*."

As she dropped it on the table, Durwood and Oake shot each other another look.

All Guards memorized their colleagues' code words. You never knew when someone might, for example, whisper *revenant* to you in the grocery store, and you had to drop what you were doing to fight a pack of monsters.

Canal was easily identifiable. Mark Wend was a kindred spirit. He'd lost a sister to "suicide by bloodywood" years ago. When Durwood first joined the Guard, Mark had helped show her the ropes. He was a dick who cheated at ping-pong, but a good guy overall.

Durwood took the coin and turned it over. The convex side of every coin was engraved *R.C.G.*, the letters curling around each other, royal and unbreakable. On the concave side, each one bore the initials of its holder. Sure enough, this was Mark Wend's: *M.I.W.*

"He gave this to you?" Durwood asked, putting the coin on the table between them so Bruce could inspect it himself.

He didn't. Just kept his hands folded in his lap.

"Seemed like he was runnin from somethin," said the waitress. "All upset and drenched."

"When was this?" Durwood asked. Parting from your coin was very serious.

"Bout a week ago," said the waitress. "I kept waiting for someone to come by and get it. I . . . I was gonna call, but . . ." She gave Durwood a pained look.

"You didn't want to get mixed up in something. I get it." Durwood glanced again at Bruce, who was gazing down at his dented arm. "Did he say anything else about the book?"

The waitress shook her head. "I didn't even look at it myself, just kept it wrapped up."

"And did he say where he was going?"

"No." Annoyed that Durwood might even suggest such a thing. "I mean, he didn't *go* anywhere. Or if he did, he left his damn car."

Durwood narrowed her eyes. "Left it where?"

"FOUND IT AT THE END OF MY SHIFT," DIANE THE WAITRESS EX-plained as they crunched over the gravel of the parking lot together. "Just sittin here in the rain."

Mark's Oldsmobile sat at the border of the lot, against a stone retaining wall at the edge of the woods.

Durwood ran a hand over the flattened tire, then strode over and felt the claw marks in the windshield. She opened the driver's door, leaned into the car, and peered around inside. "Ohmygod!" A chipmunk shot out of the open doorway and chattered away. Durwood put a hand to her heart and laughed, looking at Bruce.

He was gazing up at a bird in the sky, riding thermals high over the trees.

"Haven't touched it," said Diane. "Nobody has." She untucked a Nox-boro from behind her ear. They were the only brand of cigarette available in Renfield, and allegedly had the power to relieve the user of the curse's effects for a short duration. No one knew from whence this wives' tale originated, and Durwood didn't care. She'd always hated their taste. Grainy mudwater and blueberry pancakes. Earthy, cloying yuck. Diane stuck the cigarette between her lips and fished a Bic out of her apron pocket.

"You tell anybody else about this?" Durwood asked.

Diane glared at her, blowing smoke out the corner of her mouth. "Like you said. I didn't want to get involved in anything." She sucked deep on her Noxboro. "No roads out, and all."

Bruce grunted. Offered nothing else.

"You mentioned Burnskidde," said Durwood asked. "Did he say anything about that, or . . . ?"

"Oh. Shit." Diane dug into her apron again. "Sorry. Here." She held a napkin out to Durwood, who plucked it from her hand and flapped it open. She recognized Mark's cramped scrawl:

Burnskidde: CULTWATCH
Mass suicide event HIGHLY LIKELY 10/30/19
"Miracles" an indoctrination technique?
i.e., THE RENFIELDS ARE ALIVE

I tried to save her. Save somebody. Sorry.

Durwood looked up at Diane. "Was there anything else with this?"

Diane held up her hands. "Just that book." She went on as Durwood ducked back inside the car, searching the glovebox, under the seats. "Ya know, lately my friend Cora's been sayin something bad is comin. She usually has an eye for these things. Storms, car accidents . . . If somethin's happening again in Burnskidde, I'd read this as a very bad sign."

Durwood gave up on the car and showed Bruce the note. He frowned at it, then sighed, shook his head, and sauntered away to finish his breakfast.

"Cultwatch sounds like a serious claim," Diane observed.

"It's, like, the most serious," said Durwood, fiddling with Mark's coin.

The angler-house, Mark missing, *cultwatch* . . . Something was happening on the other side of Burnskidde Tunnel. She could feel it. Actually, she could *feel* something grind under her shoe. She lifted her sneaker and saw tiny bits of metal glittering in the gravel under the clouded sun.

So. Something was happening on the other side of Burnskidde Tunnel, and that something had crushed Mark Wend's ear right where she was standing.

She swallowed and gave Diane a tight smile. "Thank you for your help. I'll have someone clear that car away for you."

Diane nodded. "Course. Hope you find your friend." She stomped out her Noxboro. "By the way, is that real? About the Renfields . . . bein alive?"

"To be honest, Diane? I don't know. But Mark has a habit of never lying."

When she slid back into the booth, Bruce was already halfway through his meal. He said nothing, so she ate in silence, too. The Guard's social protocol was strict about giving your partner space when they needed it.

That was the thing about working the Guard: The world never got brighter, you just got a better understanding of how dark it could be. You only ever gathered bad experiences, like a boat cutting through still water, a great tumultuous wake building forever behind you. Dragging an ever-growing hoard of memory and dust.

But their social protocols were one of the main reasons Durwood found great comfort in the Guard. She wanted badly to find the right thing to say to make this moment better, but she was strictly forbidden, by etiquette alone, from saying anything at all. That was good for her. The practice of silence.

She stared at the crumpled napkin on the table between them as she ate. Bruce was absorbed in his food, but she kept staring at Mark's note, digging her spoon into her grapefruit without looking.

Burnskidde: CULTWATCH.

Mass suicide event.

THE RENFIELDS ARE ALIVE . . .

Mark was dead. No one was ever missing. She knew that. But he had tried to save someone. *I tried to save her.* Who?

Durwood's insides yawned. She felt the beginning of that teeth-grinding need. That feeling of *I have to know*.

There was a great new gravity pulling her toward Burnskidde. Toward someone whom she still might be able to save.

BURNSKIDDE, OCTOBER 2009

First Chorus

"Thanks for having me over, Mrs. Dring," said Galloway.

"Oh my god, our pleasure!" chirped Mrs. Dring. She took a steaming scoopful of ziti and spattered it onto Galloway's plate. Galloway sniffed at it, trying hard not to grimace. It had only been two days since the latest Galloway pilgrimage to Eddie Spaghetti's, and the memory of Eddie's sauce still burned in her gut.

All four Drings were seated at the table around her. Their dining room was in a small corner of the Dring home, covered in navy blue wallpaper, with lace-curtained windows looking out onto a night-blackened backyard. The home was dominated by a grandfather clock in the living room, ticking grandly, chiming zealously every hour.

Over the last year, Mrs. Dring had completely redecorated the house, imbuing it with a Rockwellian, overly manicured vibe. Stiff wooden furniture, quaint wallpaper, and heavily posed photographs of the family, all of them grinning painfully in matching sweaters. Emma wasn't exactly sure what the pod-people had to gain from turning her home into a Stepford-esque burrow, but she found the new atmosphere deeply claustrophobic.

At Galloway's side, Emma's eyes tracked the spoon as her mother dug into the large Fiestaware bowl for a second heap of pasta. Mrs. Dring chirped on, "It is *so* nice to have you over, Rachel. Ever since Dear went missing, I've been worried about people going outside."

"Yeah, it's . . . scary times," said Galloway, gaping at the steaming pasta.

"But also," Mrs. Dring went on, "Greg rarely has friends over, and Emmy *never* has friends over, so—"

"Mom," Emma protested. "Rachel comes over all the time."

"I have friends over," said Greg, mouth full of garlic bread. He nodded at Dom. "Look."

Dom also had a mouth full of garlic bread. He held a fist to his lips, trying to be polite. "Great bread, Mrs. Dring. And your new perfume smells really good, too."

"Dominic, you're too handsome to waste those compliments on *me*," said Mrs. Dring, blushing. She was not an unattractive woman, with short hair and bright eyes, and she accepted Dom's frequent compliments with lightly flirtatious deflections. Even now, she smiled to herself as she concentrated on the wobbling threads of cheese clinging to the ziti as it rose, rose, wobbling, out of the bowl.

Galloway tensed, waiting for the tendons of cheese to snap.

"It's just nice to have people over for dinner, that's all," said Mrs. Dring, wrinkling her nose at Galloway as she spattered another heap of cheesy noodles onto the poor girl's plate.

"I do enjoy having company," said Mr. Dring. He was a large, heavy-breathing man who voted Republican. A bulldog of a guy, with a leisurely, grim way of speaking. He sat slumped at the head of the table, cleaning his glasses with a small bottle of spray and a handkerchief. His bald head looked very red against the blue wallpaper. "Company means more room for conversation. Did you know . . ."

"Oh my god." Emma buried her face in her hands.

"They did a study recently," said Mr. Dring. "Video games . . . don't actually make people more violent. Did you know that? In fact, Gregory, you'll like this." He reseated his glasses on his nose, sniffed. "They apparently teach problem-solving and *pattern* recognition. They don't rot the brain at all."

"Well, I don't like video games, of course," said Mrs. Dring confidentially as she dug into the bowl of pasta once more.

"I don't like video games, either," said Galloway. "And actually, that's enough past—"

"I still think they fail to teach you social skills," said Mrs. Dring, unraveling another beating heart of noodles, sauce, and cheese. "I've heard your brother play *Halo*, with the green man? He says the nastiest things online."

"Mom, Rachel and I don't play video games," said Emma tersely. "And she said that's enough pa—"

"Video games are against their religion," said Greg.

"What religion is that?" asked Mr. Dring, folding his handkerchief and smoothing it down beside his placemat. He did this in a mechanical way, every evening, moving his hands very precisely.

Greg shrugged in Emma's direction. "I don't know, you said you were praying to the woods or something."

Emma jerked her head back, frowning. "Why would I pray to the woods?"

"Because of her pig things." Greg pointed his garlic bread at Galloway.

"Ohhh!" Emma slapped Galloway's arm. "Oh, oh, that's right! Your pigs are gonna save the town!"

"Which pigs are those?" Mr. Dring asked.

"The poo-pigs," said Emma.

Mr. Dring widened his eyes. Dubiously, he repeated, "The poo . . . pigs? What are those?"

"They grow crops," said Emma. "They have a special enzyme in their gut that allows them to digest meat and turn it into, like, whatever you want. You make a wish and let them eat your hand, and they poop out flowers. And if we pray to them enough, their king will bless us. No more Renfield curse, no more *Botanist*." She eyed them to see if they had anything to say about "no more Botanist."

Mrs. Dring paused her ziti scooping and frowned. "Where did you hear about these pigs, honey?"

"Uhh." Galloway glanced at Emma. "I . . . saw them. In visions?"

Emma gave her a thumbs-up.

"She has sketches of a whole colony," said Dom. "Ad-uh-kia."

"Uh-deh-kia," Galloway corrected him. "Addekkea."

"Fun," said Mrs. Dring. "So, is this a club you're starting? Like a . . . drawing . . . club?"

"She has followers," said Greg. "This guy Francis, these other kids."

"Woow," said Mrs. Dring, impressed. She dug back into the bowl. "Oh, you're such a good artist."

"I *loved* that painting you had in the school art show last year," said Mr. Dring. "Like a young Edward Hopper. *Twins at Daybreak in the Car.* I still can't believe it came in second place to that other girl."

"I only drew my little brothers at McDonald's," said Galloway. "Really, that's enough pa—"

"Mom!" Emma shouted. "Stop giving her ziti!"

Mrs. Dring blinked and looked around. No one else had food on their plates except Galloway.

"Ohh. Is that enough, dear?" asked Mrs. Dring, wielding a mountain of steaming noodles. Insane, that she could even hold the plate in one hand.

"That's great, Mrs. Dring," said Galloway as the woman placed this burden of a plate before her. "Thank you . . . so much."

"Alright, well, everyone else can help themselves," said Mrs. Dring, putting down the bowl and sitting at the table with a sigh.

Emma reached for the bowl, scowling as Galloway stabbed a bit of ziti onto her fork. She didn't even make a dent in the mountain before her. She chewed slowly.

"Mmm," she said with effort. "So good."

Mr. Dring reached for the spoon. "So, Rachel, you had a vision, you say? I had a vision the day Emma was born. A spirit *told* me to call her Emma. Isn't that interesting?" He smiled at Emma, who glared at him. "I think lots of Renfielders have visions. It's very common. But . . ." He turned, frowning, to Galloway. "Tell me more about these pigs."

"SORRY MY MOM TRIED TO DROWN YOU IN ZITI," SAID EMMA. "YOU *don't* have to take it home with you."

"Thank god," said Galloway, on her back with her arm slung over her eyes. "I'm so full of noodles. I am noodles."

Emma lay on her bed with her head flopped backward so she could gaze upside down at Galloway on the floor. She had, in her room, one of those small robotic dogs that acted as a speaker. He waved his head as he played Paramore for them, blinking different colors on Emma's desk.

"You spose there was fertilizer in it?" Galloway asked.

"Stop."

Galloway laughed.

Emma was quiet for a moment, then rolled over and propped herself up on her elbows. "Okay, for real, though, can I tell you something weird?"

"Do you have to?" Galloway felt a great emotional burden coming her way.

"I was on Tumblr again," said Emma, rolling her eyes as Galloway groaned. "I know, I know. But there are actually a *lot* of posts about Horridge Hill. There's this one . . ."

Why couldn't Emma see she was feeding her own obsession through the internet? The fucking internet, what a joke. Everyone out of their minds, screaming into the void. It was just a mirror dimension. An artificial hell.

"Anyway, the point is," said Emma, "if we cut my parents open, I bet they'd bleed green. Leigh Young thought the same thing. He poked his daughter Ariel with a pin when she came back from the woods and *she* bled green."

"What? He cut his own daughter?"

"To prove a point, yeah. Now he's posting this stuff online, helping form this map . . ."

"Wait, what did he do after she bled green? Did he, like, report her?"

"He thought about it. But he said he'd rather have a plant-daughter than no daughter at all, so he just kept her. She's in college now."

"Oh my god, well, what is the point," Galloway sighed. "Why make a whole plant-person if they're just gonna do regular people stuff?"

"These were *trial* runs, Rach," said Emma. "To see if her pod-people could exist in the wild."

"Emma, we are not cutting open your parents to see if they bleed green. That's insane."

Emma scoffed. "More insane than pigs who poop flowers?"

"They don't *poop* the flowers. They poop the stuff that *grows* the flowers. And it's not the same. How many times do I have to say I made that up?"

"What if you didn't?" Emma threw up her hands. "What if it's all true? Anything's possible."

"Okay, but *this* is not possible," said Galloway. "This is imaginary."

Emma looked haunted. Scared. "We live in Renfield, Rach. You never know."

"I do know. Addekkea isn't real. I. Made. It. Up."

Emma paused, then shook her head slowly. "I just don't believe that. There are lots of things in these woods. It's not hard to believe that maybe you think you made this up, but you actually saw something."

"Oh my god." Galloway couldn't believe this was happening.

"Like false memories!" said Emma. "People have those all the time! Plus," she singsonged, "Francis believes in youuu."

"Stop."

"Handsome Francis likes the pigs and bats."

"Stop! Look." Galloway stood up, pasta sloshing in her gut. "I'm not having false memories. And your parents are fine. *Don't* cut them. I gotta go. I have to work on Tolley's project."

"Okay." Emma frowned. "Are you mad at me?"

"No."

"Do you think I'm crazy?"

"No! I'm just really full of pasta, and I want to go lie down. I'll see you tomorrow, okay?"

Emma looked unsure.

Galloway cupped her face in her hands and said, as gently as she could, "You're human. We're all human. Don't worry about it." She squeezed. "Okay?"

Emma said through her smushed cheeks, "I have faith in the fog that that's true."

Galloway stared at her.

"Okay," she said, patting Emma's cheeks.

DESPITE HER BEST INTENTIONS, GALLOWAY COULDN'T FOCUS ON finding a topic for Tolley's looming colonial history project. Instead, she found herself scribbling new and strange designs, adding pieces of mythology to her Addekkean lore. For a moment, as she was drawing more gargoyle-bat creatures, she felt a vague panic. At some point, this project would actually be due. She couldn't just hand in a bookful of sketches. Tolley would kill her.

Then it struck her: Emma was right. There were already people who thought this was true. Ashleigh, Jake, Francis . . . Emma, clearly. If she could keep this going, maybe she wouldn't have to think up a topic after all. Maybe she could bullshit this the whole way through. Plus, these sketches were opening doors. The popular kids had listened to her. A *boy* liked her work. That was better than winning the stupid school art contest, right?

She sat back, considering her notebook. Dozens of creatures seemed to shift across its pages, snarling in the dim light of Galloway's bedside lamp.

Aw, what the hell, she smirked. *Maybe I did see these.*

"SO THESE GUYS," SAID GALLOWAY, HOLDING UP HER HANDY-DANDY gray marbled notebook, "are called gluttonbats."

Greg and Dom leaned in. Dom laughed. "Ohh, sick."

"Do they eat babies?" Greg asked.

"Ew, Greg," said Emma.

"They do not," said Galloway. "They only eat the sick and the elderly. The healthy may offer pieces of themselves to the pigs. Good flesh for good earth. But if you're, like, sick or ailing in any way? Then the gluttonbats take you. They can't digest bad meat, but their bile has near-magical properties, just like the pigs. It transforms even partially digested flesh into fresh living tissue. So wherever they puke, little animals grow. Like goats and stuff. Grow . . . out of the puke." Galloway was suddenly worried this sounded irreparably dumb.

"Like Uruk-hai," said Dom. "That's dope."

"Yes!" *Okay, thank god.* "I mean, they'll eat anything. Hence the name gluttonbat."

"I wanna grow sheep," said Dom. "That'd be sick."

At the back of the group, Francis said softly, "Man to beast."

They turned to him. He stared at the notebook. There, flying against blue college-ruled lines, were several bats with pointed wings and long barbed tails of black bone. They swirled in the air and screamed with gargoyle faces, half-human, half-brute. They had short legs trailing behind them, long curling claws. Underneath them, the words *MAN TO BEAST*.

"Flesh to earth," said Francis. "Man to beast."

"And have faith in the fog," said Galloway proudly. "Those were the three main sayings of the Addekkeans after they took to the way of the beasts."

"After they got attacked by knife-dudes, right?" Greg asked, itching at the foot he'd been limping on, for reasons he still hadn't explained. "And they were starving and sick and covered in boils?"

"Greg, ew," Emma whined.

"No, he's right," said Galloway. She started flipping through her notebook. She'd been busy, filling it with pithy aphorisms and teachings. It was fraying at the edges, loose in its binding.

Her commandments ranged from the simple to the bizarrely specific, things she'd come up with just to make herself laugh. For instance, Book I, Verse 12 was "Offer the pigs thy hand first. They envy our thumbs and will devour them gladly if given the chance. But do not anger them during your offering!"

"Noodles are forbidden in Addekkea," read Book II, Verse 17. "They anger the Fogmonger and hurt his tummy."

At last, she flipped to the sketch she'd made of Addekkea on the brink. She had imagined piles of diseased corpses, buried under snowdrifts. She'd imagined hellish knifemen riding into the colony from the north, astride great bears and elk, needles dug into their arms as weapons; members of some other colony that had lost its mind during the same terrible winter. She'd imagined the surviving Addekkeans weeping in the midst of all this despair. Reaching for the sky, singing for a reprieve—and she'd imagined the Fogmonger looming out of the blizzards, in answer to their call.

She'd imagined all of this, and she had rendered it in breathtaking colored pencil across two entire pages.

The other kids leaned in, breathless, as she revealed this apocalyptic mural. "See," she said, "the way of the beasts was a lost faith that some scholar in the Addekkean Academy discovered in their archives. An old scroll detailing the benefits of praying to the ancient beasts in the woods. Sure enough, the *only* plants and animals that didn't rot that winter were the ones born of pigs and bats, and the only people who survived were the ones who had eaten those special plants and animals, whether they knew it or not. So all the survivors started to sing. They sang all spring, and all summer, and when the harvest came, the Fogmonger blessed them with his breath. That was how they survived."

"Wow." Francis nodded, open-mouthed. "Fascinating."

They were gathered in the basement of the Pancake Planet. Galloway, Emma, Dom, Greg, and Francis. The basement was white-painted cinder block and cold metal shelves, filled with boxes of condiments and "food." Cobwebs and old peels of paint hung low from the rusted pipes along the ceiling. A perfectly clandestine bunker, at the bottom of an eerie set of stone stairs.

"Alright, I got another question," said Greg. "I'm sure you guys have noticed this, but I have this thing on my foot."

"No shit, you've been limping for weeks," said Emma.

"Yeah, I didn't want to say anything," said Greg. "But . . . can I show you?"

"No," said Emma.

"Yes," said Francis firmly. "This is supposed to be a place of support and healing. We're hearing *gospel* right now." He pointed to Galloway's book. "You can share anything, Gregory."

"Thanks, man," said Greg. He started to untie his shoe. "So, I got this a couple weeks ago. Stubbed my toe on our porch, and it . . . It started growing weird? Here."

He slid off his shoe and carefully rolled his sock up over his foot, wincing. He held it out for them all to see.

The nail on his big toe had curled up, away from its bed. It seemed as if it had been crowded out of its home by a second nail, curling up underneath. In fact, there were several toenails growing out of the same bed, curling up and around each other in a perfect keratin spiral.

"Dude, what the fuck," said Dom. "Eww! You gotta pull that out, bro."

"I have," said Greg. "I grow a new one every day. I was . . . starting to wonder if we had some bloodywood on our porch."

"I've always wondered that!" Emma gasped. "I *always* get splinters on that porch. I told you it was barnwood! Nobody ever believes me."

"So would the gluttonbats take this?" he asked Galloway. "Would they be able to turn it into good meat?"

Galloway studied the foot, trying not to gag, then nodded. "Yeah. They'd take it. Any unhealthy flesh, if the pigs can't eat it, the bats will. Either way, your cells are reborn as resources for the colony."

Dom laughed. "Ha ha! You're gonna be puke, dude! That's fuckin hilarious."

"Yeah, but my cells could come back as a cow and kick your ass," said Greg.

"Ohh, that's true. Cows kick hard, yo."

"You're making fun of it," Francis snapped, drawing the air out of the room. "She's explaining a powerful system of beliefs—something that could benefit *you* directly—and you're making fun of it."

"I . . . I'm sorry," said Dom. "I just got excited."

"It's okay," said Galloway. "It is actually a really cool system. The colony became totally self-sufficient after everyone gave themselves to the beasts. When someone was terminally ill or super old, they gave themselves back to the community through the bats."

"Like a symbiotic relationship," said Francis.

"Yes! And the more they gave themselves, the more the beasts trusted the Addekkeans. Finally, the beasts trusted them enough to call the Fogmonger a second time, and he blessed them *again*. This time, he restored all the limbs people had given to the beasts, and graced them with renewed strength, letting them live longer, healthier lives within the fog."

"Aw," said Emma. "I wanna live in Fog Town." Then she and Francis asked at the same time, "How do we summon him?"

"Jinx," she said, and Francis stifled a grin.

"They have a song," said Galloway. "It's what everyone sings when they're feeding the pigs. See?" She flipped back to her very first sketch of people singing around a pig. "When they're offering themselves, they always sing. When they sang enough, the Fogmonger finally came back for them."

"How's it go?" Greg asked.

"Sing!" Dom called. "Sing!"

Galloway could *not* sing, and even if she could, she certainly would not have done so in front of people. But she *had* thought about this. She figured a big beast breathing fog would probably enjoy a long, low whale-note, like "Oooooohh." So that's exactly what she did, bellowing and feeling absurdly dumb, until Francis echoed back, "Oooooohh."

And then, to her surprise, they *all* did it. They threw back their heads and sang, "Oooooohh!" The entire basement filled with the low bellowing note of the Fogmonger's song. "Oooooohh!" Galloway took up the cry as well, singing with them until she laughed with pure glee. Something she had created was coming to life. "Oooooohh!" She worried someone upstairs might hear them, but the Planet didn't open for dinner for another few minutes, and even then, the basement was secluded enough that customers wouldn't catch their song even if they tried. "Oooooohh!"

SOMEWHERE OUT IN THE DARK, IN THE DIRT, SOMETHING DID HEAR. Something deep in the ground vibrated in tune with their voices. Something reached up through the underbrush of the woods and snatched up more meat. The owl and the deer were not enough.

It took a pregnant doe. It took a family of possums. It took a raccoon and a stray cat and another owl, a hawk, a goose. It mashed them together and mangled their bones into new configurations. Like clay, it squeezed and rolled and remade them underground, then birthed them back up into the night with new, raw skin. It took, and took, and still, it knew it would need more.

More, more. It needed more.

The thumping underground sent pulses throughout the neighborhoods of Burnskidde. Reaching, searching, stretching. It licked at the underbellies of basements, and coiled about the pipes beneath homes. Tasting, seeking. Until it felt the vibrations of tiny running feet. Little six-year-old sneakers dashing about a backyard. Uninhibited. Unaware.

Nathan Brenner was flying his Iron Man action figure around in swooping figure-eights. His father watched from the window above the kitchen sink, smiling. Wishing Nathan's mother were still alive to see this.

He went to the bathroom, and Nathan Brenner was left unsupervised for the last time.

Running, he tripped and fell forward onto the ground, smacking his chin hard. Dazed, he turned and tried to see what he had tripped upon. But the ground held his foot fast. It seemed like he'd managed to lodge his sneaker in some kind of hole or burrow. He pulled. His foot was . . . remarkably stuck. He cried and beat at the ground, tried to claw away the dirt around his ankle. But the dirt did not budge. In fact, the dirt *pulled*. The dirt pulled the boy under as he struggled and cried, and it bent his head far up, his mouth gasping panicked breaths as he was dragged down, down, into the ground. "Daddy!" he cried, just before his mouth was stuffed with earth. He raked his teeth along rocks buried deep, as he screamed silent into the dark, dragged into a place where he was wrapped in fine pulsing threads, beating bright painful light over his body, into his tear ducts, up his nostrils, deep inside his ears. *Thrum-thrum. Thrum-thrum.*

It held him there as he wriggled, suffocating and blind. *Thrum-thrum.* Pulsing, tightening around his flesh, until his flesh went cold. Then the tendrils about his body flickered, sending yellow light rippling across Nathan's corpse. *Thrum-thrum.* It illuminated him from within. It tightened about his body. Squeezing, grinding, compressing him into fossil, then cracking that fossil into chunks, into a fine crumbling stone that could easily be crushed into powder, and the powder blasted into vapor. This, it would use as poison. Necrotic red flesh, weaponized and waiting.

By the time his father returned to the window, Nathan Brenner had been pulverized off the face of the earth.

And even so—it needed more.

"FRANCIS, YOU'VE GOT A GREAT VOICE," SAID EMMA.

"Yeah, dude," said Dom. "Way to ooh."

Francis blushed and shuffled his feet coyly. "I was in choir in middle school."

Greg fist-bumped Galloway on his way out of the basement. "That was dope. I wish I could draw that good."

"Thanks, Greg." She smiled at him.

Dom chased Greg up the stairs and clutched his shoulders from behind. "You're gonna be poop!"

Francis watched them. He looked grim, an affect only aided by his Nine Inch Nails shirt. "They were laughing at you."

"They were laughing *with* her," said Emma. "We were all having fun. Wasn't the point to learn and lighten up?" She glanced at Galloway, clearly relieved that Galloway had come around on believing in the fog.

"The point is to save people," said Francis. "To give people something they can hope for. 'Have faith in the fog' is about the *future*. It means you should trust in the unknown that's coming toward you. Anything could happen. Anything could be in the fog. Just have faith that it's *good*. That's not funny, that's hope."

"Aw," said Emma.

Galloway found herself surprisingly touched by this display of emotion as well. She put a hand to her heart. "That's exactly right, Francis." She gave him a peace sign and said cheerfully, "Have faith in the fog."

Francis smiled and said, "You, too. Flesh to earth."

"And man to beast," said Galloway and Emma together.

"Jinx," said Emma.

They all laughed.

"Well, good night. Thanks for the hope." Francis smiled at Galloway again, then disappeared up the stairs.

Emma elbowed Galloway's side. "Alright, he's sweet. I take back what I said about him puking on himself."

"That was nice what he said about hope."

"Right?" Emma glanced up the stairs and lowered her voice. "You think Greg's foot is gonna be okay?"

Galloway grimaced. "I don't know."

"I mean, if it isn't, we can feed it to the gluttonbats. Right?"

Galloway hesitated. Maybe she should drop all this. Something in the far-back of her mind told her it was a bad idea. This would all spiral out of control before long.

But whenever she shared her sketches, everyone was looking at her. Why give that up? She could keep this going until Tolley's project was due, at least. Right?

She said none of this. Said only, with conviction, "Right."

LILLIAN, OCTOBER 2019

The Renfield Tomb

Durwood was biking upward. Sweat rolled down her sides, trickling down her back, as she pedaled faster and faster. It was a dismal, overcast day, but she was panting as her bike zoomed under the grand black iron archway of Bottomland Cemetery.

Bottomland resides, ironically, atop a hill just northwest of Lillian. Durwood did not find this irony amusing as her bike wobbled up the long, cobbled drive.

At Bottomland's peak, there is a beautiful view of the Bent River, majestic and undying, as all great rivers are. Here, too, you can see Bartrick Bridge, the red metal structure that leads to Lillian's oldest, nicest homes.

Bottomland is Renfield's ritziest graveyard, filled with Renfield's higher class, the Lillian elite. But even they are not exempt from Renfield's saddest and most peculiar tradition: the give-up plot. Plots in which families and loved ones bury coffins filled with memorabilia of the long-missing.

In high school, Durwood had been friends with a guy who went missing for over a year before his parents eventually declared him Gone. He was the first person Renfield took from her, and she could still remember the time capsule of his casket: Pictures, shirts he'd owned, his football helmet, a DVD of *Fellowship of the Ring*, and more. Into this mix, Durwood had thrown the one bit of memory she'd kept from their friendship: a receipt from the Pancake Planet in Bartrick Mill.

She found herself scanning the graves as she worked at the pedals, throttling her handlebars. She wondered how many headstones marked actual bodies, and how many marked nothing but trash.

She pedaled ever faster as Mark's note clanged in her mind like funeral bells:

Burnskidde: CULTWATCH
Mass suicide event HIGHLY LIKELY 10/30/19
"Miracles" an indoctrination technique?
i.e., THE RENFIELDS ARE ALIVE

I tried to save her. Save somebody. Sorry.

That date was only four days away. What the hell was happening in Burnskidde? What had Mark stumbled across? Who had killed him, and why?

The Guard's archives held precious little information regarding Burnskidde's infamous isolation. On November 26, 2009, residents in the valley reported hearing/feeling a massive explosion, which they later assumed was either a controlled collapse of the Burnskidde Tunnel or something much more serious. Either way, the county sheriff's office was disinclined to investigate. As far as they were concerned, their jurisdiction now ended at the Billowhills.

To Durwood's surprise, Mark Wend had been the reporting Guard in '09. He'd never mentioned it to her, but, according to his files, he had personally visited the site of the Burnskidde Tunnel collapse several times over the last decade. He'd put his mechanical ear to the rock and reported singing. Several voices, singing one low note, over and over again. For ten years, he filed bimonthly reports in which he reported no change in the tunnel, and no change in the chorus beyond.

Durwood guessed it was on one of these routine visits that Mark discovered the tunnel was suddenly open. Presumably, he'd gone in to investigate, and . . . what? Discovered a famously dead family? Is that why they'd sealed themselves away? To keep the Renfield resurrection a secret? But then why *re*open the tunnel?

She had far more questions than answers. Durwood hated questions. And she'd be goddamned if she let *questions* get away with taking another loved one from her.

Finally, she kicked her stand and left the bike on a patch of gravel in front of the mausoleum at Bottomland's peak. Her legs trembled and almost gave out on her as she stood, arched her back. To her credit, she had lost weight since she'd been forced to bike everywhere, and she was quite proud of her calves. Still, it had been a two-hour ride from her apartment.

"Fucking Jesus Christ," she panted, hands on knees. "Oh my god, Mary Mother . . . Whew. Okay." She sniffed, stood. Swaggered toward the mausoleum, dripping sweat. The large white tank looked imposing and frigid cold. Her skin tightened at the mere thought of going inside.

Sitting in a metal folding chair, just outside the mausoleum's bright marble maw, sat a wizened old man with large calloused hands. He was neckless, stout and square, with a shock of white hair. As Durwood approached, he rose wobbily from his chair.

"Hello," he said cheerfully. He held up a thick finger. "Just one?"

"Yessir," said Durwood. "Good weather for graveyards."

"It's never bad weather for a graveyard. Five dollars."

Durwood pulled out her stone coin. "How much is this worth?"

The man's face fell. He got that look most people get. That scared-stiff, *I didn't know I needed guarding* look. "Oh . . . Are you working today?"

"Just investigating," she said, pocketing the coin. "I only have a twenty. I don't need change if you help me out."

He brightened. "You're the first one in today. I'm Frank." He held out his hand.

"Rachel." She shook it. Coarse and very cold. "How long you worked here, Frank?"

He turned, leading her into the mausoleum. "Oh, only two or three years. Maybe four . . ."

"See anything out of the ordinary in your time?" she asked, walking along behind him. Around her, the high white walls closed in. The air was heavy. The marble sapped the color out of the bouquets left in sconces. The names lining the halls were meaningless jumbles of letters, designating meaningless piles of bones.

"Not particularly," said Frank. "We had an infestation of those five-legged rats one winter. Couldn't do anything to get rid of them until we brought in a priest from the Mill."

"And what'd he do?"

"Threw holy water on them. They boiled! Ha! The *screams* they made." He shivered theatrically. "Quite the time, that was. '73, I think."

Durwood narrowed her eyes. "Right. Anything odd happen to the family, though?"

"Noo, they've been fine," said Frank, his voice getting misty. "Quieter and quieter as time goes on, actually."

He led her deeper into the halls of marble shelves. Corpses stacked nine feet high on either side. She could hear nothing but Frank's voice, and his shoes, and every so often, at the very periphery of her hearing: a murmur, a whisper of fabric, a sigh, as the bodies around her turned over in their sleep. She wondered what Mark might hear in a place like this. What whispers would his ear pick up?

Frank turned a corner, moving out of sight beyond the wide expanse of blinding marble. Durwood was alone, and her heart turned inside out. Frank's voice lilted back to her through the cold hall, nostalgic and melancholy, "They don't even weep at Christmastime anymore . . ."

She lunged around the corner, and Frank was right there, waiting patiently. A dim stone room lay behind him. Glacial air breathed out from within, bathing her sweaty skin in ice.

"Have you visited them before?" Frank asked.

"Almost once, when I was a kid," she said, staring into the room. "My dad brought me and my brother, right before he ditched us for D.C. My little brother got scared so I ended up waiting in the car with him. I've . . . never been back." She held out a sweaty bill. "Here's your twenty."

"Oh, Ms. Durwood," he said, smiling. "I remember you. So little back then. But already so angry."

He turned and flipped a switch. A fixture overhead blinked on, and a pure white bath of light filled the room. It revealed stone floor, stone walls, vaulted ceiling—and five glass coffins lining the perimeter of the tomb. The coffins ranged in size from full-length adult to miniature child-boxes.

Durwood stepped forward and peered into these five Sleeping Beauty sarcophagi. Frank slipped the bill out of her hand as she passed, and pocketed it with a smile.

The Renfields lay under crystalline glass, on beds of wilted flowers. Their hands were all crossed peacefully over their chests. The image would have been sweet, had they not all rotted through. Their corpse grins leered, gritting cracked teeth forever, eye sockets hollow. Plaques beneath them gave their names: *Adelaide*, the corpse without a face. *Henry*, the eight-year-old. His hands slumped into the hole where his sternum used to be. *May*, the sixteen-year-old, somehow the most whole of the group, except for the woodchips still embedded in her bones. And poor *Robert*, mangled and exsanguinated. Not much left of him at all. He had been four when his father shot him in the back and squeezed him dry for barn wall paint.

"Initially," Frank narrated, as Durwood hovered her hands above the glass, feeling the cold breathing against her palms, "they were laid to rest in a plot with a fine view of the lake. But when the rot took hold in the summer of 1928, they were exhumed, blessed by every priest Bottomland could find, and never allowed to touch the soil again. I don't know how much of that you knew."

"I knew," said Durwood, nodding at the corpses as if to say, *I know you*. She held a hand over May, imagining what it would have been like if her dad had gone around the house with a shotgun, instead of calling her mom "a psycho cunt" and moving away to Washington. If he had, there would have been a brief period in time when either Tom was dead and she was still alive, or vice versa. The *thought* of that. Hearing your brother boomed out of existence, and up the stairs comes Daddy, breaking the shotgun and sliding in a fresh shell for *you* . . .

"Where's the baby?" she asked.

"There wasn't anything left of her to bury," Frank sighed.

Durwood grunted, staring into May's empty eyes. The dried flowers round her skull. "Do you ever feel like they're radioactive? I know even their old furniture can be . . . unhealthy."

"Ms. Durwood," Frank said gently, "the glass has been blessed, the crypt has been blessed—the entire *grounds* have been blessed. I've never felt any energy in here except for them. And *they* . . . Well, they're not restless. Not angry. Simply lost. Melancholy. Confused."

"Confused about what?"

"Well, they don't have the full story. For them, Papa suddenly just . . . didn't like them anymore. They don't know there's a whole legend about why he did it. A whole *series* of legends. You and I are privileged to know that."

"Right," Durwood murmured. "So they wouldn't have any motivation to . . . walk around again."

"I can't see why," said Frank sadly. "I think they're content to simply lie together. This is, by and large, a peaceful place, Ms. Durwood. We don't get a lot of stories around the tomb. Other parts of the cemetery, sure. People claw their way out every now and then. You hear giggling late at night. The full moon is always a real show." He chuckled. "But in *here*, they're just . . . here."

"And you don't have Lawrence's ashes here, do you?"

"Scattered to the winds," said Frank. He rubbed his chest. "Do you know the story about his heart?"

"I've read the Moone version," said Durwood. "The . . . what's it called. 'The Warden, the Sheriff . . .'?"

"'The Doctor, and the Priest,'" Frank filled in for her.

"Yeah, that one. Moone writes that, despite official reports to the contrary, Lawrence was never actually declared dead because his heart never really stopped."

Frank nodded. "Moone's is an accurate retelling. The heart wasn't even charred after they stuck him in the crematorium."

"But did it actually grant wishes? Moone is explicit about the heart granting wishes to whoever holds it and asks nicely. But that's fiction."

Frank chuckled. "I assure you, it's not. Yes, it granted wishes, in a way. It always exacted a price, though. After Lawrence was hanged, Sheriff Rook wished he could consult his mother on the Renfield massacre. She'd died years ago, and he missed talking through complex cases with her. He claims he was looking right at that heart when he wished his mother could still talk to him. Next thing he knew, I was giving him a call from the cemetery, telling him his mother had woken up! Too bad she came back *bad*, and I had to put her back under, but . . . Anyway, that's what I told Moone. So I can personally attest to the version he wrote."

"Back in 1935," said Durwood.

Frank blinked. "Hm?"

"*You* talked to Sheriff Rook back in 1935."

"Oh!" He chuckled. "Not me, no. I meant I, er . . . whoever had my role at the time."

"Good save, Frank." Durwood sighed. "Alright. And no one knows where the heart is now?"

"Buried," said Frank. "Lost on purpose."

"Yeah, after the heart Monkey's Paw-ed its way through half a dozen people, Rook hid it deep and killed himself alongside it so no one would ever find it. Right? I've seen the note Rook left his wife. Lillian has it in their museum."

"Yes." Frank frowned. "Why are you asking all this? If you don't mind."

Durwood thought for a moment, staring at May Renfield. Finally, she settled on an answer. "Just trying to save someone. That's all."

Frank nodded. His eyes fell on May as well. "It's funny, you know, that people fear the dead. I think it's because we know bodies still have stories to tell. Stories that don't always make it into the Shelter archives." He gave her a knowing wink. "But these stories can be fascinating, if you listen. For instance, did you know your mother loved you very much?"

Durwood's heart stopped. She tipped forward, caught herself on May's coffin. "What, um . . . Did she . . . How do you know that?" She glared at him.

Frank offered a sad smile. "I'm the undertaker, Ms. Durwood. I *know* bodies. And I know that no matter what else may have been true about her, your mother adored you. I know she had regrets."

Durwood's whole body ached. Her heart burst, burst, burst in her chest. She did not take her eyes off Frank.

He kept smiling. "Do you have any other questions?"

Durwood looked away. She sucked a deep, grounding breath through her nostrils. She had *lots* of questions.

If these Renfields had been secure behind blessed glass for decades, how could they be alive? Had Mark really stumbled across a miracle in Burnskidde, or was the county playing tricks on him?

She let out her breath. "No. Thank you, Frank." She stuck out her hand.

He shook it. "So nice to meet you, Ms. Durwood."

Only then did she realize she'd introduced herself as Rachel.

She yanked her hand away. "Take me back outside."

AS SHE CLIMBED ONTO HER BIKE, FRANK WAVED TO HER. HE KEPT waving to her as she pedaled away down the hill, away from the cold mausoleum, away beneath the grand black metal gates that read, in curling iron letters, *Thank you for visiting Bottomland. See you again soon.*

THE ARCHIVE OF THE R.C.G. SHELTER WAS A SEEMINGLY ENDLESS catalog of every oddity seen in Renfield since the beginning of the curse in 1928, dating all the way back to the yellow hand-signed field reports of Muriel Gnash. A musty maze of green metal filing cabinets, far underground. More cabinets and boxes than Durwood could count.

In the summer before she'd joined the Guard, she had spent weeks poring over old newspaper clippings, photographs, census records— anything that might explain her mother's sudden death. Had this place warped Mom's mind? Was it warping Durwood's and she didn't even know it? What *was* Renfield's curse, exactly? But she never quite figured it out.

After a particularly long night of drinking and writing down everything she'd discovered, Durwood piled all her notes into a cardboard box, strapped it into the passenger's seat, and set off to find more answers, right before she slammed headfirst into a tree. Thank god that tree had belonged to Bruce. She might have spiraled all the way down if not for him.

As soon as she beheld the scope of the archive, Durwood donated her one measly box anonymously to the Edenville Library and never looked back.

In many ways, this was all she'd ever wanted. To sit alone in a dim room, researching by candlelight.

She lay on the floor of her bedroom on her stomach, gazing at the waterlogged book Mark had left behind. On its cover, the corona of monstrous faces haloing a young woman with fog rolling out of her eyes.

Durwood stared at the book like she was making a silent deal with it. *Don't totally fuck me up here, okay?*

She took a grounding breath, then reached out and peeled open the book.

The Gray Book, as retold by Rachel Galloway

2ND PRINTING

Addekkean Press

Durwood's brain fuzzed for a moment. It is an old Renfielder belief that one should always trust odd coincidences. There are forces of great evil in the world, but if there were evil forces only, wouldn't everything be rotten? The fact that you're still breathing is evidence of something working in your favor. So something positive *had to* be calling to Rachel Durwood, because here was another Rachel. Perhaps it was a good omen. Perhaps not. Either way, she couldn't shake the feeling that she was exactly where she was intended to be.

She flipped through an array of prophecies and stories, fables and prayers, all of them about a place she'd never heard of: Addekkea. She read about the lost colony's mystical pigs and gluttonbats, its psychic ravens, and the horrors it faced one winter at the hands of famine, disease, and raiders. She read, of course, about the song of the Fogmonger.

She picked at the corner of her mouth, frowning as she read on, never moving from the floor. She had always preferred the hard security of floors to the soft wooshiness of furniture. Floors were sturdy. Chairs and beds could always give.

She remained on the floor, reading until she came across a folded sheet of paper stuck between the pages. "Hello," she said, carefully untucking it from its hiding spot. It was yellow parchment, folded into quarters. She had never actually held parchment before, and worried it might crumble. It looked ancient, or perhaps homemade, perhaps both. She unfolded it slowly. In purple ink, handwritten:

I don't know when I started to remember things I've never done. When I unearthed these memories of a life I've never led. But when you found us, Mark, I knew I had a chance to share this with the outworld. This proof that All–Speaker lies. I want to record for you all that I remember that isn't mine.

I remember blue banners. I remember dancing. I remember the feasts, and being afraid. I remember when things got bad. Everyone losing their minds. I remember feeling sad, watching it happen. Feeling like there was nothing I could do.

Maybe everyone is someone else, it's not just me. Maybe everything is wrong. When the Fogmonger comes back—not if, but WHEN—I don't think he'll be what he seems either. I think he'll be worse.

Durwood turned the parchment over. Only one side had writing on it. She sat pinching the corner of her mouth, staring at the note. Then she set it aside and bent the covers of the book all the way back, fanning out the pages. She put her chin to the thin carpet so she was eye level with the book. She could see the thicker bits of parchment stuck between them. Maybe a dozen or so notes from whoever this was.

I tried to save her . . .

She began picking the notes out of the book and unfolding them one at a time. Whereas the book itself told the story of Old Addekkea, these notes outlined the story of Burnskidde. Each one read like blank verse. Single-line remembrances about the town's end days. They were all vague: *I remember Horridge Park. I remember Burnskidde High . . .*

Durwood formed a neat little stack of notes at her side, then propped herself up on her elbows and set to reading the book front to back. She read until the birds heralded the dawn, picking absently at her lip until the corner of her mouth stung. Her face hurt, greased and throbbing, but she'd known this would happen. Once she started working a case, she never stopped. Not even to sleep. Not until she knew what was happening in Burnskidde now, and who was left to save.

BURNSKIDDE, OCTOBER 2009

An Overture for Fog

"Alright, everyone," Mr. Tolley announced. His room smelled of hot plastic, lit only by the overhead projector, displaying their project rubric on the board. "Recall that I *warned* you you'd be peer reviewing each other's project drafts today. I expect most of you haven't even begun yet." He glanced at Jake Mendez, who was drawing a Cool S on his desk. "So, let's consider this a brainstorming period. I'm going to have you sit with a partner to discuss some of your . . . I'm sure, *breathtaking* ideas. Listen for your names, please, like adults. Emma Dring? You'll be with Jacob Mendez."

Emma shot Galloway a look, mouthing, *No fucking way*.

"Rachel Galloway?" Tolley went on. "You'll be with Ashleigh Hunt."

Galloway and Emma shot each other another look. Galloway scratched her neck to gaze over her shoulder at Ashleigh in the corner of the room. She was silently gathering her things to move desks, jaw tight.

Galloway barely heard Tolley call Francis's name. "Aaand you'll be with Troy Pittner. Okay, if any of you need me to repeat that or have any issues with the person I've chosen for you, please let me know and I will endeavor to *pretend* to care. You may move your desks now."

"Oh my god," Emma whispered, rolling her eyes. "Freaking great. How's that zit on my chin?"

"Awesome, can't see it."

"Okay." Emma held her binder to her chest and began marching toward Jake. "Here I go."

Ashleigh and Emma passed each other without acknowledgment. Ashleigh slid into Emma's seat, reopened her binder, and offered a tight "Hey."

Galloway eyed her cautiously. "Hello."

Ashleigh uncapped her pen and started writing down what Tolley had on the board.

Galloway scoffed. "What, are you mad at me now?"

Ashleigh blinked at her. "No."

"Then why are you being weird?"

"I'm not, I'm taking notes."

Galloway scoffed harder. "Look, I don't want to be awkward with you. You're the one who moved on *and* started dating Emma's all-time crush." She lowered her voice, eyeing Emma across the room, laughing ebulliently at something Jake had said.

"Well, I didn't think it mattered, because you guys weren't even talking to me anymore," said Ashleigh.

"Because you were always on your phone when we were hanging out. Texting guys who didn't give a shit about you back when you had braces."

"Well, maybe if you focused more on art than boys, you'd be an award-winning artist now, too, but." Ashleigh shrugged.

"And what are *you* ladies working on?" Tolley asked, appearing suddenly before them.

Galloway flicked her hair out of her face and said, "I'm doing a project on Addekkea."

Ashleigh whipped her head up and squinted at her.

"And what is that?" Tolley asked. "A perfume?"

"It's an old colony," said Galloway confidently. "I heard about it on the Discovery Channel." She felt more versed in improvisation after her experiences preaching at the Planet. The lie came effortlessly: "I thought it sounded interesting, so I found this old book in the library about colonies that vanished in the early days of the country. Like Roanoke and Fort Caroline."

"What's Fort Caroline?" asked Ashleigh. "You make that one up, too?"

"It was a short-lived colony in Florida," said Mr. Tolley, eyes narrow, chalk whacking against his knuckles. "I believe it was a French settlement ultimately destroyed by the Spanish. Addekkea is new to me, however."

"It was nearby," said Galloway. "Just a few miles north of Renfield."

Ashleigh stared at her, lips pursed. Mr. Tolley stared, too, chalk thwack-thwack-thwacking. "And what is this text, exactly? The one you 'found' in the library."

"Well . . . it's . . ." Oof, she hadn't been ready for this one. "It's . . . based on a journal they found in the colony ruins in . . . the early 1700s." She gathered steam. "It talks about how they prayed to the creatures in the woods. A whole lost faith centered around beasts."

Tolley *hmm*ed at her. "And what did you say this book was called?"

"A . . . *Record of Lost American Colonies*," said Galloway, holding firm.

"And what was this *faith* called?"

"The way of the beasts. Here, I took a lot of notes." She opened her gray notebook and held it out to Tolley. He stopped whacking his chalk against his knuckles and took the notebook in both hands. He flipped through it, frowning. Galloway cocked a fuck-you eyebrow at Ashleigh.

"You sketched all these?" he asked. "From the book?"

Galloway nodded.

Tolley frowned as he continued flipping pages. "And what's the event you're analyzing, precisely? The colony's vanishing?"

Galloway nodded again. "Yeah, the journals they left behind aren't perfectly clear, but when they fell on hard times, they supposedly prayed to the beasts of the woods for clean food, and the beasts provided. In fact, they offered themselves to the beasts for so long that the *king* of the beasts came and blessed them with renewed prosperity. Or . . . so the story goes. The colony was totally abandoned when it was discovered."

"Their god was made of fog," called Francis from across the room. Galloway looked over at him. He smiled at her, his brown eyes piercing hers.

How long had he been listening? Wait, now *everyone* was listening. The room was entirely silent.

"They had faith in the fog," said Francis, in his strange airy voice. "They *all* had faith in the fog. It saved them."

Mr. Tolley turned to Francis. "Did you also see this on *tv*?" He sneered the word *tv*.

"She told me," said Francis. "And them." He pointed to Jake and Emma.

"Yeahhh, Rachel told a lot of us at the Pancake Planet," said Emma slowly.

"You talkin about the pigs?" Jake asked.

Emma nodded.

"Those pigs are legit, Mr. T," Jake said helpfully. "Rachel didn't make them up."

Tolley gave them all another "Hmm."

A tense beat throbbed throughout the room.

"Well." Tolley snapped the notebook shut. "If this is a *real* historical event and you have a primary source to back it up, then fine. You may do your report on . . . Addekkea. I've never heard of it, but the sea of history *is* as vast and ultimately unexplored as any literal ocean. Time's waves are gentle but pervasive, and much more is washed away than recorded." He held the book out to her. "Good luck."

Relief flooded Galloway's nerves. She took the gray book reverently, like it was now validated as a magical, powerful text.

"Thanks, Mr. Tolley," she murmured. Then, she pulled the coup de grâce. She turned to Ashleigh and asked, innocently, "What is *your* project on, Ashleigh?"

"I . . . don't know yet," said Ashleigh.

"Best figure that out soon, Hunt," said Tolley, peering down at her with disappointment. "Galloway here is certainly lapping you."

"Yes, Mr. Tolley," Ashleigh muttered.

"You know, there are a number of dead faiths out there," said Mr. Tolley, returning his gaze to Galloway. "I look forward to hearing a *detailed* report about the rise and fall of this one."

"This one isn't dead," Francis called over again. "It was for a while, but Rachel's resurrecting it."

Tolley looked at Galloway. "Oh?"

She floundered. "I . . . guess." Then a flash of an idea. "Actually, yeah. I could do a presentation for my project. Instead of an essay? I can lead everyone through a typical Addekkean, uh . . . beast-calling ceremony. A ritual reenactment." Anything to not write a fucking essay.

"Hmm," said Mr. Tolley.

"We could make it a party," Emma blurted. "Like a potluck! For the whole class!"

"Hmm."

"Yo, that's a dope idea," said Jake.

"That is a great idea," said Francis. "Rachel can teach everyone the Fogmonger's song."

"Totally!" Emma chirped. She gave Galloway a thumbs-up.

Wow, at this rate, Galloway might actually be able to bullshit her entire project.

"Hmm," said Tolley once more. He glared at her, considering. "Perhaps."

There was a variety of murmuring. Some excitement, some hesitation, some snickering about how dumb this all sounded, or "How come *she* doesn't have to write an essay?"

"You should all come," said Francis, to the entire class. "Hear the gospel of the fog. It's really inspiring." He smiled at Galloway and she had to duck her head to not blush.

Emma nodded. "Definitely. I'll get my mom to help plan it. *Everybody's* invited," she said at Jake. "I'll send out the details on Facebook. We'll have snacks."

"Have faith in the fog!" Jake cried. Troy Pittner laughed.

"Fine, fine," said Tolley. "Thank you, Dring, for planning what promises to be an . . . enjoyable class outing. *Perhaps* I will allow it to count toward Galloway's grade as well. Let's get back to our projects now, people! Hunt, looking at you."

The chatter in the room moved on. Ashleigh leaned across her desk and whispered, "Thanks for shoving me under the bus."

Galloway beamed. "Well, maybe if you focused more on class instead of boys, you'd be an A-student now, too, but." She shrugged.

Ashleigh simmered in silence for the rest of class, while Galloway drew on. Pigs and bats and psychic ravens, oh my.

THE IDEA CAME TOGETHER MUCH FASTER THAN SHE EXPECTED. BY the following afternoon, a Facebook event had already been set up, people had been notified, and the wheels were deep in motion. This was largely thanks to Emma, though Francis was eager to help. Galloway felt a pang of jealousy, lurking in their group text as Emma and Francis sent Tolley jokes back and forth. Francis was also more willing to listen to Emma's rants about the Botanist. He'd even dug up an old *Bent News* article about one of the Botanist's lesser-known experiments, the angler-house. *That's one plant we won't have to worry about anymore when the fog comes,* he wrote. This elicited a :) from Emma and a groan from Galloway.

Meanwhile, Mrs. Dring was delighted to help organize an evening of music, food, and prayer.

"You know the pod-people *love* a party," said Emma at lunch. She was eating from a cup of peaches. "Jeff and Darlene are so stoked you're doing this. Even if it's just for a grade. They looove community events."

"Tolley might not even buy it," Galloway grumbled.

They were sitting in the corner of the jungle gym of a cafeteria. Prospector Percy was painted in brilliant cartoon colors on the wall, grinning with his pickax. The plastic stools along the long gray tables were a cheery blue and yellow. A pack of Axe-drenched, cargo-short-clad boys were having a Yoplait fight two tables over.

Galloway picked at her spaghetti. "This isn't even food. It's, like, canned paste and wheat powder squeezed into tubes through a goddamn, fuckin . . . Play-Doh toy, *fuck*."

"I thought you liked spaghetti."

"I've just had pasta, like, four times this month. Ya know, my dad says this is the same company that serves Bartrick Prison."

Emma swallowed a thready bit of peach. "Well. I don't know what all you're planning for your sermon."

"My what?"

"Your sermon," Emma repeated, like this was obvious. "I've seen you give two of them now in the Planet. What would *you* call it?"

Galloway hesitated.

"Anyway," Emma went on, "don't know what you're planning to say, but my dad wants to hear about the knifemen. He's big on antique weapons. And that's a Jeff thing for sure, not a plant-dad thing? He's owned that Civil War gun for years."

"You told them about the knifemen?"

"Sure. Why not? It's an inspirational story. The Addekkeans were doomed, but a devout few survived. What's not to love?"

Uneasiness stirred in Galloway's gut. She couldn't get in trouble for this, could she? For lying about a religious ceremony?

She shook her head. "I don't know, man. If we're getting, like, adults involved . . ."

"It's just my parents. Plus, worse comes to worst, everyone just goes home disappointed if the beasts don't show. But it's still—"

"Show?" Galloway echoed.

"But it'll still be fun! It's like your own little Bible study. We can eat, drink, and be merry, just like the Addekkeans once did. Then we all sing the Fogmonger's song and do a dance at the edge of the woods. It's *fun*, Rach."

"You think this can prove if your parents have been Botanisted, don't you?"

"I mean . . ." Emma chewed. "If the pigs *do* come and don't want to eat my parents, doesn't that mean they're bad flesh?"

"Duuude. You can't make your parents offer themselves. They have to *want* to get eaten."

Emma shrugged, like this was no big obstacle.

The P.A. system warbled to life. Dr. Eric's smarmy voice came over the loudspeakers: "Hello, Prospectors. It's 12:35 on Tuesday. Today is a C Day. Hope everyone is enjoying your lunch, or P.E., depending on your C Day schedule, aha ha. Here is your daily aphorism: 'You can kill a man, but you can't kill an idea.' Medgar Evers."

Galloway hated the image of Dr. Eric's squinty toothy smile whispering aphorisms into the mic in his office. Every day, he'd make his little announcement and then strike his singing bowl into the mic, sending a horrible vibrating *gong* throughout the building. When the gong died down and the building stopped shaking, Dr. Eric—with degrees in philosophy and childhood education—would whisper into the mic very gently, *too* gently, "Have a burden-free day, Burnskidde."

God, he pissed her off. Everything bugged her. Dr. Eric, this shitty spaghetti . . .

Suddenly, Francis was standing before them. "Hey."

Emma brightened. "Hi, Francis! We were just talking about our event."

"Oh cool." He smiled. "I hope this isn't all embarrassing for you," he said to Galloway. "I didn't mean to put you on the spot. I know it's *your* vision. I'm just excited to share it."

"No, not at all," said Galloway, stunned. "You're all good."

"Personally, and I know I've said this before, but I think this is a really great thing you're starting," said Francis. "People will be stoked to be a part of it. Not just for Tolley's class, but because of what it could mean for the town. This community *needs* something to bring us together."

Emma nodded seriously. "Absolutely."

"Are we . . . not together?" Galloway asked. "I mean, it's not a community event, it's just for class." She laughed nervously.

"It's a tense time," said Francis. "It's a recession, it's almost 2010 . . . New-decade energy, ya know? And there have been more disappearances lately. Here."

He reached into his black leather trench coat and took out a flyer. Galloway found herself blinking down at the smiling ghostly face of Nathan Brenner. MISSING since Thursday.

"Plucked out of his own backyard," said Francis. "You believe that?"

Galloway did not believe it. Despite the regularity of the macabre in Burnskidde, missing children were always a gut punch. There had been three during her lifetime: a middle schooler several years ago, a toddler snatched from the playground when Galloway was ten, and a third she couldn't even remember. Little Nathan Brenner made four.

"I've been poking around some of the neighborhood watch forums," said Francis. "There are people who think it could be the Botanist."

Emma slapped the table. "Yes."

"But if he doesn't come back in the next few days, that breaks her M.O.," said Francis. "Which means it could be something *else*. Something worse."

"Well," Galloway started uneasily. "One missing kid isn't . . . I mean, I don't want to be a dick, but it's just one missing kid."

Emma and Francis gaped at her.

"Rach, it's not just one," said Emma. "Haven't you been watching the news?" She nodded at the tv bolted to the wall behind them. It was always on, always tuned to the local news, perhaps in an attempt to educate the youth about current events, even if by osmosis. Galloway watched it every so often, but she'd never seen anyone else pay it any mind. What sixteen-year-old watches the news? Even now, it was just some boring bull about the recent Oktoberfest in Miner Memorial Square.

But Emma was grave when she said, "Three kids went missing last week. Other stuff is happening, too. Missing pets, missing animals. Dear! Also, the annual deer cull was supposed to start last week, but guess what? No deer."

"The police haven't even tried to look into this," said Francis. "You know Chief of Police Pittner? He says there's nothing he *can* do. They have no evidence, no witnesses. Zero leads. As far as he's concerned, Nathan Brenner is just another missing deer."

Galloway had heard this before. Her own father was not a fan of Chief Pittner. Most adults she knew, in fact, found him to be gruff and ineffectual. When that toddler had been snatched from the playground years ago, Pittner had ordered a half-hearted search party for a single day, then shrugged on live tv and said, "Them's the breaks."

"I guess I've been wrapped up in my art lately," said Galloway, staring at Nathan Brenner's picture. "I hadn't noticed . . ."

She could hear her heart beating in her ears. The MISSING poster shivered in her hands.

"Well, point being," Emma said brightly. "My parents are hoping this might distract people from the missing-kid situation and some of the . . . ya know, growing tensions among Burnskidde's adult bowling league.

Some of my mom's new friends have seen Nathan Brenner's dad putting these posters up around our neighborhood. Here, look at this."

She pulled out her phone and opened YouTube. A video titled "BURNSKIDDE IS DOOMED?" One of many that Seth Brenner had posted since his son had gone missing.

"Hello, my name is Seth Brenner," he said to the camera. He had wire-framed glasses. He was balding, and his shirt looked unwashed. He looked altogether unwell. A Noxboro bobbed in the corner of his mouth. "My son, Nathan, has been missing for eight days. I've been reevaluating some of the evidence regarding my son's case, and I want to revise my previous statement about the Botanist's involvement. At this point, we've broken her usual pattern of behavior. For the first three days, I hoped Nathan would return, but I'm forced now to believe that she is, in fact, a red herring. Something *else* is taking things in Burnskidde. Woodland creatures, our beloved Dear, our *children*. If you look at these maps . . ."

"But *you* can give people hope," said Francis. He put a hand on Galloway's shoulder. It was warm, and she felt her body melt slightly. "Not just a couple people in a basement, but lots of good flesh for good earth. Imagine how many voices *you* could get"—he squeezed her shoulder—"to sing for the Fogmonger. I bet if we got people like Seth Brenner to sing with us? The Fogmonger would answer for sure." He beamed. "Aren't you excited? To change the very *earth* of Burnskidde from something cursed into something miraculous?"

Galloway felt a little nauseous. "Totally."

"Me too. Have faith in the fog! I'll see ya later."

She watched him walk away.

"Are you gonna eat that?" Emma pointed her fork at Galloway's spaghetti.

ON THE BUS RIDE HOME, GALLOWAY FLIPPED THROUGH THE PAGES of her notebook, MCR at full volume on her iPod, the Fogmonger roaring in her heart, monstrous and powerful. Just like she wanted to be.

But for the rest of the day, she continued to worry. She worried through dinner, lost in the idea that somehow, *somehow*, she had caused all this recent weirdness. She was so lost in worry that she didn't even hear her mother.

"Sorry, what?" she asked.

"I *said*, you excited for your party this weekend?" Nicole repeated. "Hey, no Nerfing over dinner."

The twins whined as they lowered their Nerf revolvers. Under the table, Teddy fired a foam dart into Bobby's groin. Bobby groaned and they both laughed.

"It's not a party," said Galloway. "It's, like, for class."

"But the twins can come, right?" Keith asked.

"What? No! I'm not babysitting."

"Babysit *this*," said Teddy, firing a dart at Galloway's head. It clocked her right above the eye.

She leaned over to grab it, but Doofus already had it between his teeth. He gave it a couple of chomps, then spat it out, personally offended by the fact that it wasn't a treat.

Galloway scooped the dart off the floor and flicked it at Teddy. "I'm gonna shove the next one so far up your nose, your thoughts are gonna be Nerf."

"Nerf *this*," said Bobby, shooting her above the other eye. Both twins cackled with glee.

"Ya hear that, honey?" said Keith, cutting into his meatloaf. "She said she'd babysit. We should go to the movies."

"Ohh, I want to see that new Gerard Butler movie," said Nicole.

"*Don't* go to the movies," said Galloway. "It's just gonna be me and the rest of Tolley's class. The twins will be bored!"

"Darlene said it was going to be like a show?" said Nicole. "You're doing a special . . . art show? They won't be bored for *that*."

"It's not a show," said Galloway. "It's for class."

Nicole didn't hear her. "Darlene is so excited you're showing off more of your art. She says you based it all on this true story she's never even heard of. That's *really* cool, Rach."

"I feel like I haven't seen you draw in a long time," said Keith. Doofus put his front paws on Keith's lap, tongue lolling out the side of his mouth, eyes glued to the meatloaf on Keith's plate. Keith shooed him away. "Off, buddy."

"Well, I didn't expect to be sharing it like this," said Galloway. "Like, this is just sort of . . . happening. Really, don't go. It's not a big deal."

"Alright, we'll watch Gerard Butler at home," said Nicole, waving a hand. "I'm just thrilled you're doing something with people other than Emma. Not that we don't love Emma, but it's good to have a . . . variety of friends."

"We'll come to the next one," said Keith. "Hey, Bobby, you're gonna give him heartburn. Stop it."

Bobby was scraping meatloaf and potato off his plate and feeding it to Doofus, who inhaled every scrap without chewing.

"Do dogs get heartburn?" Teddy asked.

"I'm sure they must," said Nicole. "Isn't that right, Doofy?"

Doofus panted and grinned at her, licking potato off his snout.

"Ya know, your mom is right," said Keith. "It's exciting to see you putting more of your stuff out there. I still think you were robbed at the art show last year."

"Dad, can we not?" Galloway moaned.

"Who could possibly beat *Twins at Daybreak in the Car*? I mean, come on!"

"It was really good, sweetie," said Nicole. "Like a young Edward Hopper. I still hang it in some of the houses I show."

"I have a copy pinned to the wall of my office," said Keith.

"Oh my god, I wanna die," said Galloway, stabbing at her food.

"Die!" cried Teddy, shooting her in the eye.

THE BASEMENT OF THE DRING HOUSE. A HALF-HEARTED REC ROOM, starring a sunken couch and a cracked leather armchair, plus some randomly dumped rugs and pillows in a ring around a box television. Not cozy, but soundproof, which is all teens really want.

Tolley had encouraged them to meet with their peer reviewers outside of school. Under that pretense, Emma, Galloway, Jake, Francis, Ashleigh, and Troy Pittner sat on the floor of the basement, watching Brenner chatter from his own basement rec room on Emma's laptop. Brenner pointed wildly to maps of Burnskidde threaded through with red wire. He chain-smoked through the entire video, cigarettes bobbing wildly.

"Lotta white noise out there, kids," said Brenner. "Lotta red herrings. But if you know where to look, you can put the pieces together. That's why I smoke all these Noxboros. You gotta keep the mind"—he tapped his temple rapidly several times—"clear."

"It's so sad," said Ashleigh. "He's, like, an adult. And he's losing his mind."

Emma paused the video. Seth Brenner stared at them from the screen, sucking his cigarette down past the filter.

"This is what Rachel's project is really about," said Emma. "Helping people not to feel this way anymore."

"I feel bad, guys," said Troy. "Chief Dad saw these videos, too. I know. And he's not doing *any*thing."

"No one's blaming you," said Emma. She glanced at the title to Seth's video ("PITTNER WAKE UP") and gently shut her laptop. "If I had to take the blame for all my parents' dumbassery, I'd never get over it. Right, guys?"

The others nodded.

"Thanks, man," said Troy, smiling and picking at the rug.

"That's why I wanted you to come," said Francis, putting a hand on Troy's shoulder. "To see the alternative to our parents' feeble acceptance of Renfield's curse. To hear the song of hope."

"What song?" Ashleigh asked.

"It wasn't just cuz I'm your peer review partner?" said Troy.

"Troy, this *is* the peer review," said Emma.

"What *song*?" Ashleigh asked.

"The Fogmonger's song," said Emma. "That's how we call to him. And his beasts."

Ashleigh fidgeted. "We're not actually . . . calling to beasts, are we?"

"Don't worry, babe." Jake put an arm around her shoulders. "It's gonna be dope."

"Rachel will teach you," said Francis, putting a hand on Galloway's knee. Sparks shot up her leg, shocking her entire body into stillness. Icy panic tightened around her ribs as he looked at her.

"Do it," he said softly. "Sing them the song. They should all learn it, if they're going to be members of the chorus."

"We should get tattoos or something," said Jake.

"When we give ourselves to the beasts," said Francis, holding Galloway's gaze hypnotically, "the marks of their teeth will be tattoo enough."

"Totally," whispered Galloway.

A tense beat of silence. Emma was open-mouthed, darting her eyes between Francis and Galloway. So badly, the world wanted them to lean toward each other. Right here, in Emma's basement. Galloway could feel it. She thought her heart was going to pound right through her chest.

Troy leaned forward, breaking the tension. "Soo were you gonna sing, or like . . . ?"

"Yes," she said, blushing. "Sorry. Um. Yes. The Fogmonger's song . . . goes like this."

From low in her belly, she felt the single powerful note roll forth. From the very core of her, a deep truth rumbled out: the fact that she never wanted to hide or be mist at all. She wanted people to *look* at her. To recognize her mind, her heart, as special, powerful things. She wasn't singing, she was purging—bellowing out a yearning so buried she'd hardly known it was there, but it filled the entire basement when she sang, "Ooooooohh."

Emma joined her. Then Francis, and Jake, and Troy. Ashleigh was last, not quite committing, not quite opening her mouth all the way. But she *did* sing. In the end, they all sang. "Ooooooohh." And as they did, they all looked at her.

Look at them looking at her. Look at *her* in the spotlight. She was in charge. No stupid adults or popular skinny kids. Just her. Singing a song for a god she'd created. "Ooooooohh."

And there was Ashleigh Hunt, looking scared, singing right along with her.

"Ooooooohh," they sang, sound vibrating through the basement into the ground. "Ooooooohh." Music billowing into the earth, where something beneath the Dring basement heard—and answered.

Vibrations pulsed through the soil all over Burnskidde. Shadowy things spread their wings, screaming into flight, swooping low over the neighborhoods. They swept up mailboxes, yanking them off posts and flying away without breaking pace. They ripped up strips of chain-link fence and tore scraps off cars in junkyards. They screeched over town, beating at the crisp October air with their wide, moon-blotting wings, nothing more than dark shadows in the stars.

Where it could, where the pavement was not too thick, the veiny pulsing ground sucked entire cars into itself, squeezing them and cracking them in half, shattering glass, then sealing up the ground behind, leaving nothing more than a few sparkling shards and a small rift in the asphalt.

It took streetlamps and stop signs and everything else that it could melt and repurpose in the mantle of the earth. It had been asked specifically to listen, and to create whatever it heard. It would mold these things happily, in the kiln of the ground.

But it would demand things in return, when the time was right.

It wanted specific things as well.

BARTRICK MILL, OCTOBER 2019

Cultchaser

The cold slice of the moon across the Bent River. The woods, the hills, the endless woods. And the stars: dim promises of possibly better worlds, far from this godforsaken place. This home of hers. This Renfield County.

Durwood sat on the edge of the Bartrick Regional Hospital roof. She straddled the roof edge, dangling one leg over the abyss. She turned Mark's napkin over and over in her hand, reading the note again by moonlight.

It was a still night; the sound of her breathing was loud. She gazed out over the carpet of trees filling the Deep Shembels. She could see the southern edge of the lake, glittering under the moon. She took a deep breath of autumn.

"It's beautiful," said Bruce behind her. "People forget that. I forget it."

"I forget it all the time," said Durwood. She folded the napkin and stuck it in the breast pocket of her plaid shirt. She'd gone with a rich forest green today.

Bruce sat next to her with a sigh. He looked out over the valley. "You check on the Renfields?"

"Doornails," she said, swinging her leg. "Everyone accounted for. Except Lawrence, of course."

"They could be dummies," Bruce pointed out. "Someone took the bodies, revived em and replaced em?"

"I don't think the undertaker would let that happen on his watch."

"Okay, what if Mark misunderstood? Or the note is a trick?"

"Mark can hear into people's *brains*. He doesn't like lying. He doesn't lie, and he wouldn't let anyone lie for him."

"You know," Bruce laughed, "he only said that to get a rise outta you. He can't *hear* your brain."

Durwood gave a light shrug. "Still." Then her face broke. She swallowed a thick lump. "He died, Bruce. Trying to save somebody." Her breath hitched badly. She sniffed, blinked up at the moon. "Fuck. I can't believe he's just gone."

"He's only missing," said Bruce.

"No, I saw those give-up plots today," said Durwood, desperately losing the battle against a hot downpour of tears. "I got so fucking mad. I—I think of all those people and I just want to . . . I want to find just *one* person. Stop *one* bad thing."

"I know. I remember feeling that way." Bruce looked out over the valley again. He sighed, long and deep. "I turned in my coin."

A small sob burst out of Durwood's throat. "Please don't leave me. We *just* got another job."

"We didn't. If you'd filed that note like you were supposed to, the switchboard would have processed it and assigned it themselves. It could go to someone else."

"This *event*"—she flapped the napkin at him—"is in three days. The switchboard takes that long sometimes just to process calls."

"Not everyone is your burden, Gadget."

"He was our *friend*."

"I know," said Bruce gently.

Durwood sniffed, kicking her heel against the roof.

"Look, cultwatch is a serious accusation," said Bruce. "I've only seen one of those before. I think there have only ever *been* two or three."

"Two." Durwood sniffed. "The Alpha Bent in '86 and the Clate River Crew in '98. The Crew all drowned themselves."

"I was there, smartass. That was one of my first jobs. The Clate River Crew was . . ." He went away for a second. Shook his head. "If this is legit, Mark was calling in a Code fuckin Red."

"Right before he vanished. Before our *friend* vanished."

Bruce reached out and put a hand on her knee, gently stopping her leg from kicking. He met her eye. "You do not have to follow this. You do not have to save every single person."

They looked at each other. Durwood felt pinned and twitchy. "Then what am I supposed to do? I have to help."

"Getting yourself killed by a cult of salt miners wouldn't be helping."

"Well, neither is fucking quitting." She looked away.

Bruce let this sit for a moment before he said, "You know the rules. When you choke . . . you're done."

This was a well-respected superstition in the Guard. Bruce had known a guy in '03 who refused to quit when *he* choked. Just a bad day, that was all. He could've taken down that antlered coyote by himself, he just got rattled.

But the very next job he did—fighting that cave-thing in the Falls? Bruce remembered it all too well. The way that thing had torn him apart . . .

Bruce would not be swayed.

"God." Durwood dug the heels of her hands into her eyes. She wanted so badly for him to keep caring for her. Wanted him to, like, make her soup. She wanted *anyone* to make her soup.

The edge of her hawk-scar rubbed into her cheek. She didn't feel like a hawk right now. She felt dangerously close to crying.

"Please don't go," she murmured.

"I'm sorry, Gadget," he said. "You can call me anytime. Okay? Just because I'm leaving the Guard doesn't mean I'm leaving you."

"Yeah." She rubbed her chest. Sniffed, looked away. "Yeah. Right." Cleared her throat. "Look. I'll . . . check out Burnskidde tomorrow and I'll call you. Just a look-see."

Bruce sighed. "Well, I was never gonna stop you anyway, so fine. But be smart. The Clate River Crew almost fucked me up for good. You can't go charging in there demanding to know where the Botanist is, or what the suicide event is, or why Burnskidde closed themselves off."

"But those are all the things I really want to know."

"Then be *smart* about it. Stay overnight there if you can, see what the night's like. See what the morning is like. Breathe it in, don't just kick the door down and start stabbing and shooting."

"I do love stabbing and shooting."

He laughed a little. "Just . . . be smart. Please."

"Okay." She sighed and looked up at the moon.

Over its pale face flew a heron, dark and grand, wings beating against the night air in silence.

They watched it go by.

It was the best omen Renfield could have sent them.

"I'll be careful," she said.

"I didn't say be careful. I said be smart."

"Sure," said Durwood, smiling. "I'll be that, too."

IT'S DIFFICULT TO KNOW WHEN WE ACTUALLY MAKE BIG DECISIONS because most life choices belong to the homunculus buried deep inside our mind. The little child perpetually sobbing or giggling or starving, who drives our heart from a secret place we rarely notice, even after years of self-reflection.

Durwood's inner child was a perpetually screaming girl covered in marker. When she was eight, she'd loved drawing on herself. It drove her mother crazy. They'd get all ready to go somewhere, then little Rachel would trace the bones in her hand in bright green marker. Ohh, the scrubbing sessions at the sink. The things her mother said to her through gritted teeth. To be fair, little Rachel had only ever done this to spite her mother. It was an ongoing battle.

She lay in bed tracing the lines of the scarred hawk along her arm, and she knew nothing Bruce could have said tonight would have deterred her from going to Burnskidde. Even if Mark was nothing more than pieces in a swamp, she had to see it. Had to try.

She had always been a stubborn little asshole.

In the morning, she packed her go-bag (basic medkit, phone charger, clothes, trail mix, etc.), and pedaled back to the hospital. She took the elevator down to the Shelter, turning the key she'd kept on a chain around her neck for a year now. She went to the armory to collect her gun. Stocked up on iron bullets, fist-bumped the woman working the receptionist's desk.

"Big trip?" the woman asked, lifting her headset off one ear.

"Hope so," said Durwood, slinging her black duffel bag over one shoulder. She felt a surge of excitement knowing she'd be getting answers soon. *I remember the singing. I tried to save her* . . . Somehow these notes were connected. Somehow.

She was grateful Bruce had not returned to say goodbye, or to try talking her out of going again. But on her way out of the Shelter, she did run into another friendly face, come to see her off: The Tattooist was wringing his pale hands by the elevator. He gave her a fanged grin and hissed, "I hear you're doing something dangerous."

"Yeah, I hear that, too. You want a souvenir?"

Vic hissed again, in what she thought was a laugh. "You won't have time for souvenirs. Any cult worth its salt will try to *turn* you."

"Well, then I won't do that."

He smiled, sick and gray, leering at her as the elevator doors closed between them. "Good luck, Cultchaser . . ."

His laughter echoed through her heart as she pedaled away from the hospital, through the Mill, down into Bent, and down toward the Burnskidde Tunnel.

She paused, panting, outside its maw.

The tunnel pulled at her. A black hole.

She paused. Then kicked into gear again.

"Alright," she said, pedaling. "Be smart, Rachel. Be smart."

She pedaled away into the icy dark.

She kept expecting to run face-first into a giant pile of rubble. She pedaled and pedaled, dodging rocks, pushing harder, grinding her teeth, *come on, asshole, kill me, fuckin kill me*, daring the tunnel to dead-end and slam her into rock. She pedaled faster, faster. Nothing but shadows and dank cold. And then:

The tunnel opened up, spat her out into daylight.

She braked, coming to a sweaty stop.

Here was the small patch of gravel where Mark had parked his car. Here was the wall of pine that had trembled as shadows pursued him through the storm.

She craned her neck back and looked up at the hill whose bowels she'd just biked through. The hillside around the tunnel had been sheared away. She could see where the lighter rock beneath the surface layer had been exposed in whatever explosion had collapsed the tunnel ten years ago. She could see the large, sharp dent, and the pile of rubble that had been cleared away to the side.

"Interesting," she muttered.

But the broken hill wasn't as interesting as the wall of vegetation blocking the road. Thirty feet ahead, vines twisted over the blacktop. Grass and flowers pushed up through cracks in the pavement. A curtain of willow branches completely cut off her view of the other side. It was all abundantly, alluringly green.

A rustling of feathers overhead. Durwood looked up again and caught sight of a large black bird cawing as it flew out of sight, in the direction of Burnskidde. If she had to guess, it'd be alerting them to her presence. They'd be expecting her now.

Durwood took a breath. "Alright. Here goes nothin."

She swung her leg off the bike and walked it toward the branches. She slid into their embrace, letting them glide over her face, her hands. She walked stiffly, half expecting the branches to tighten around her at any second.

But they didn't. They licked over her body, tasting her. Welcoming her. As she walked deeper, the sunlight darkened, then grew again. Brilliant golden light trickled through from the other side as she stepped carefully over twisting vines, chaotic brambles, thorny shrubs. All of it pulling at her, snagging on her, whispering over her skin. The sound of her pushing through the foliage was so loud that at first, she did not hear the voices. She paused, cocked her head.

Singing. The bright sound of a faraway chorus awaiting her.

She pressed on. Kept her head bent, her eyes forward, as the voices grew louder and louder. She didn't hesitate, not even for a moment, as she pushed closer and closer to the glorious joy of countless people singing just for her.

BURNSKIDDE, OCTOBER 2009

Greg's Leg

Thunder rattled the glassware in the chemistry lab cabinets. Lightning strobed the classrooms. Dark trees roiled in the courtyards outside. Burnskidde High was a lost ship, rocking in the onslaught of wind and rain.

In the midst of this gothic day, Dr. Eric's sleazy voice unfurled from the PA system: "It is a sad morning, Prospectors. Our beloved town experienced a streak of widespread vandalism and terror last night. I've spoken with our school safety officer, Officer Wilson, and he assures me that the police are doing everything in their power to catch the individuals behind these crimes. For now, please avoid rumor-milling, and keep your valuables locked tight. And let's have a moment of silence for our most recently missing friend."

In a dizzying moment of coincidence (or fate), the news on the tv in the cafeteria displayed Abby Fetterman's picture at the same moment Dr. Eric said her name. The woman was laughing as a monkey wrapped itself about her shoulders.

"Abby Fetterman," said Dr. Eric, "was a pillar of the . . . *is* a pillar of the Burnskidde community. Abby's Animal Rentals gave us our Dear every homecoming game for the last ten years. No one can understand why she or our beloved Dear were taken this month. But, as with the others who have recently gone missing, if you have *any* information regarding this situation, please speak to Safety Officer Wilson. Thank you. Have a safe day, Burnskidde."

Emma was staring at the tv. Dozens of thefts in one night, plus a kidnapping. Mailboxes missing, cars stolen. Apparently, the culprits even jacked a police cruiser. The thief must have tinkered with the cameras at the precinct as well, because the footage simply blinked, and the cruiser wasn't there anymore.

"We're looking into tightening our security systems and deploying more officers around the lot," Chief Pittner told a field reporter. "Right now, we, uh . . . we don't have a lot of information."

Emma snorted. "Typical Pittner. See? This is what Francis and I were talking about."

"He does seem like kind of a loser," Galloway agreed. Onscreen, Chief Pittner was literally scratching his head.

"Somebody leaked footage online," said Emma. "You can see the cruiser getting sucked *right* into the ground, and then the ground seals up after it. There's a big crack in the parking lot where the car used to be. That's what they're not telling us. They're more stumped than Chief *Dick*ner is letting on. Don't tell Troy I said that, but it's true."

"Where do you think the cars went?" Galloway asked.

"Something underground is eating them, maybe. Maybe the same thing that swallowed Nathan Brenner right out of his backyard. Do you . . . know anything?" Emma leaned in close.

"How would I know?"

"Because you know things now," said Emma.

Galloway just gaped at her.

IT WAS EASY TO SHRUG OFF EMMA'S CONCERN. SHE WAS ALWAYS catastrophizing. But in Tolley's class, things felt much more real.

On Facebook, Emma had invited everyone to a gathering in Horridge Park. "A traditional Addekkean beast-calling. For Tolley's class!" read the invite. Jake was spreading the word about the Fogmonger's song. Now, Troy and several other kids kept glancing at Galloway and whispering.

"You hear about all the thefts?" Ashleigh asked.

"Of course," said Galloway. "And before you ask, I don't *know* anything."

"But what're the chances?" Ashleigh leaned over her desk to whisper. "What're the chances that we were talking about protecting ourselves against bad stuff, and then the *same* night, this happens?"

"Ashleigh, just because the events correlate, it doesn't imply a cause and effect."

Ashleigh screwed up her face. "Okay, don't get all pre-calc at me."

Jake knelt by the side of Galloway's desk. "Hey, is it true?"

"What?" Galloway asked.

"About the twenty-sixth. People are saying the Fogmonger is coming on November twenty-sixth."

"Really?" Ashleigh's eyes were wide with wonder.

Galloway felt like she was being pulled along on some ride she couldn't remember boarding. "Who . . . who's saying that?"

Jake shrugged. "I dunno. I heard it from Troy."

"Mendez," Tolley called out. "Back to your seat."

"We'll talk later," said Jake, knocking on her desk like this was a done deal. He returned to his seat, and Galloway stared across the room at Troy Pittner.

"Is that true?" Ashleigh asked.

Galloway's voice was far away. "I . . . guess so."

She cornered Troy after class to ask where he'd heard this rumor about the twenty-sixth.

"I don't know," he said. "I heard it from Francis; he said he heard it on the bus."

SHE CAUGHT FRANCIS IN THE HALL. GRABBED HIS ARM AND PULLED him over to one side of the stream of bodies. She started to speak, then some douchebag shoved her out of the way to get at his locker, so she pulled Francis into the corner.

"What's happening?" she asked.

He smiled. His eyes were electric. "I should ask you."

"I didn't take all those cars and mailboxes, Francis. I didn't take Abby's Animal fuckin Rentals. Do you . . ." She looked around. "Did you *do* something? Are you telling people this rumor about November twenty-sixth?"

He frowned. "Why would I . . . What do you mean?"

"I mean, what are you telling people about the Fogmonger?"

He laughed a little, held her shoulders. "Nothing. I saw this thing on-line about numerology and how people predict certain big events. There's a prediction set for Burnskidde on the twenty-sixth. Did you know that?"

"There is?"

"Mmhmm. And it only makes sense that *this* is what they were talking about. Right?"

Galloway faltered. She didn't know what to say.

He laughed again. "Have faith in the fog, Rach. Things are happening!"

Galloway nodded violently and backed away from him. "Okay. Alright. Well, I'll . . . see you at the thing tomorrow."

Francis smiled again. "I can't wait. I have faith in the fog that it'll be a really fun time."

MERE DAYS AGO, ADDEKKEA HAD EXISTED ONLY WITHIN GALLOWAY'S mind. Now, this story was worth thirty percent of her semester's final grade.

She felt outside herself, floating through some dream of a different life, as she sat at the bar of the Planet.

The Planet was a nightmare in the rain. Its pink neon sign took on a garish, ghoulish glow. The interior lights looked painfully artificial, as if the building didn't even exist, but was only a murky mirage to lure strag-glers inside, safe from the storm.

There were no customers, so the Planet crew sat at their usual spots at the bar. Greg had his shoe off and was rolling the sock down over his ankle carefully. He winced anytime it caught on his infected toe. "At this rate, it's only a matter of time before really important shit goes missing, too. Not just cars and deer."

"Uhh, Nathan Brenner was important," said Emma, arms crossed. "Abby Fetterman? *She* was important."

"Yeah, but, like . . . if the entire movie theater goes missing, then we'll *really* be screwed."

"We'll probably be fine," said Dom. "All this stuff will even out. It always does, right, Rach?"

Galloway looked up. "Huh? Oh. Yeah. I don't know." She looked back at Greg's sock as he rolled it slowly, gingerly, off his foot. "We just need to . . . keep singing."

"Right," said Emma, biting a nail.

"Good thing we got the party tomorrow," said Greg. "Really build the chorus before it's too late."

"Don't keep *talking* about it, man," said Dom. "My mom says you draw bad energy to yourself even talking about bad shit."

"Dominic, we're balls deep in bad shit," said Greg. "The woman who lives across from us just had her entire tool shed stolen. Ahh." He finally wriggled the sock off his toe, "*There* we go," and revealed an appendage that looked frostbitten and withered. The veins coming out of this toe were blackened and sunken, as if something had dried out the arteries in his foot and crisped them from within, burning straight through to the surface of his skin. Tiny black cracks spiderwebbed up his ankle, across his calf.

"Oh my god!" Emma jumped up. "Greg, what the fuck?"

"Jesus, dude," said Dom, standing back with his hands up, like Greg was contagious.

"How long ago was that?" Emma asked. "When you stubbed your toe?"

"Couple weeks," said Greg. He grimaced. "Looks super gross, doesn't it?"

"It *looks* like you need eighteen doctors yesterday," said Emma.

Greg waved her off. "It's Renfield stuff, what are doctors gonna do?"

"Honestly, probably amputate at this point," said Galloway.

Emma punched Greg's shoulder. "Why didn't you tell me about this?"

"It wasn't really bad until a couple of days ago," he whined. "I thought it was just gonna be that toenail thing, and I was like, *Well, I can live with that.* But hey, it's all good. Dom and I have an idea."

"Does it smell?" Dom asked. "Lemme smell it."

"Oh, get in there, dude. It doesn't smell at all."

"*What* is your freaking idea?" Emma demanded.

"Okay, so." Greg spread his hands for effect. "As long as you guys are calling beasts for class tomorrow, we figured *we* would offer ourselves."

"We're gonna offer ourselves!" Dom echoed, grinning. "Greg can offer his foot, see if the gluttonbats want it. I mean, he's sickly, right? We can see if they puke up some little critters."

"I will be wishing to become a little lamb," said Greg. "It's not my wish, it's my foot's wish. I asked. My foot has always wanted to be a lamb." He wriggled his toes and winced. "Ouch."

"I want to see if the pigs will take my hand," said Dom. He slapped his forearm. "See if they like Zambrano rare. I'm wishin to be raspberries."

"This is literally the most insane thing I've ever heard," said Emma. "You guys can't do this. Right . . . Rachel?" Her voice faltered as she looked at Galloway.

Galloway didn't know what to say. They were talking about this with the kind of half-serious madness boys often get when they talk about, like, what weapon they'd choose in a zombie apocalypse. It became more real the more they talked about it. More violent. What if something *did* show up and ate Greg and Dom? Could they send Galloway to jail for that? No . . . Right?

She licked her lips and spoke slowly. "If Burnskidde really is in danger, then I guess . . . we're gonna have to try it sooner or later."

Everyone started chattering excitedly at once. She was silent, wondering if this had been her absolute final chance to put her foot down and demand everyone stop.

If it was, she watched it sail by without a word.

HORRIDGE PARK. SEAS OF GREEN GRASS, SOCCER FIELDS, BASEBALL fields, picnic tables by the stream. The Galloways used to picnic here every Sunday. The Drings used to hike through the trails in the woods behind Horridge Hill, that big lump overlooking the park. Those are the trails the Botanist supposedly haunts.

James Horridge was one of the original founders of the Burnskidde Mining Company in 1892. He helped found the town along with Horace Burnskidde, then built himself an estate at the top of Horridge Hill, a mansion at the edge of the woods with enough room for James, his wife, and their one daughter, who famously threw herself off the roof in 1931, when the Renfield curse finally trickled through the boundaries of Burnskidde. The Horridge house has been empty ever since, except for daily tours. It is a claustrophobic, labyrinthine building, but Francis had always coveted its scope. Its sheer number of rooms.

To book one of Horridge's picnic areas after dark, you do need a special permit from the park office. Francis had acquired this permit by making a special case for a religious group he called the Fogmonger's Chorus. Galloway had not been directly in front of him to ask what they should call themselves, "So I hope that's okay," he said to her, wriggling a tiki torch into the ground. "I think it has a nice ring to it."

"No, it's great," said Galloway. "Thank you."

He stood up and smiled at her. He looked so handsome, so suited to this weather. Dead leaves rasping through the harvest wind. Long black trench coat. Jack Skellington T-shirt.

"You ready?" he asked.

"Absolutely," she said.

She moved fluidly between all the people setting up. Jake and Troy helping with the tiki torches, Emma stringing up paper bats between them. It wasn't a Halloween party per se, but Galloway figured the beasts might enjoy some representation.

The Drings were the only adults there aside from Mr. Tolley. Mrs. Dring had brought two picnic tables' worth of food, all wrapped up in large bowls, and Mr. Dring was chatting amicably with Mr. Tolley. He was under the impression that this was a performance of some kind, and he didn't want to miss it if Greg was involved.

"So rarely does he get involved," Mr. Dring confided in Tolley.

"I recall," said Tolley. "He sat in the back row for an entire year and never *once* raised his hand . . ."

As Galloway came up to her, Mrs. Dring was peeling the plastic wrap off a bowl of potato salad that she'd dyed orange and black, because "why the Hell-oween not."

Galloway gazed down at the tables laden with Halloween-colored treats. Her classmates were already picking at them, chatting peacefully in little clusters throughout the clearing. The energy was light and expectant, with the slight eerie underchill that accompanies everything in October.

"Thanks for helping set this all up, Mrs. Dring," said Galloway.

"Oh, of course, dear," she said. "I'm really excited to hear your talk. I hope you get a good grade. But of course you will; you're so smart." She frowned, then stopped fussing with the table, put a hand on Galloway's arm. "Sweetie, can I ask you something?"

"Sure."

"Is something going on with Em? She seems so unfriendly lately."

"Oh. I . . . think she's just stressed about school," said Galloway. She tried to slide away from Darlene's hand.

But it tightened, clamping her in place.

"I just can't shake the feeling that she's mad at me," said Mrs. Dring, furrowing her brow. "I thought tonight would give us a chance to chat, but she's been dodging me all *day*. She hasn't seemed off to you? This last year or so?"

Galloway glanced around the park, sending out psychic signals for help. Anybody, *help*.

"I don't know, Mrs. Dring," she said. "Lots of people seem stressed lately. With all the missing kids and stuff . . ."

Mrs. Dring leaned closer, furrowing her brow deeper. "Can you ask her for me? What's bothering her?"

"I will," said Galloway, wincing. "Absolutely."

Mrs. Dring's face cracked into a smile. "Thank you, dear. I see why the other kids all listen to you. You've got that humble charisma."

"Thank you. You're hurting me."

Mrs. Dring looked down at her hand, saw it clawed around Galloway's wrist—and released her.

Galloway fled the snack table. She stood apart from the crowd, surveying them. Tolley's *entire* eighth-period class had showed up. Kids she didn't even know! They stood around with pumpkin-shaped paper plates, digging into Mrs. Dring's food.

What was she thinking? *Why did I agree to this? This is so stupid, I shouldn't be—*

"This potato salad is exquisite," said someone behind her.

She turned. Mr. Tolley was methodically scraping salad off his plate.

"But if you think that affects your grade," he added, "you're sorely . . . not mistaken, actually. It's really quite good."

"Mr. Tolley, is it too late to call this off?" she said breathlessly, before she even realized she was saying it. "I'll write my essay on Fort Caroline or something instead."

He frowned at her. "Why?"

"I just . . . I don't want anyone to get hurt."

"If the *poo*-pigs show up and start eating us, you mean?"

"Yes?"

He nodded and picked at the salad on his plate. "Ohh, Galloway. Here's the thing. I am not a fool. I understand I seem quite ponderous and oafish to you."

"I like your class," she said unconvincingly.

"Mmhmm. Fact is, I was quite the little bullshitter myself when I was your age." He gave her an unprecedented, knowing smile. "And I'm impressed with your ability thus far. Truth is, I'm curious to see how you stick this landing, and to be honest, it would appear that something larger than our class project is at work here as well. People are frightened. Parents, colleagues, my neighbors—they're all tired of bowing to Renfield's influence. They don't want more people to go missing. And perhaps it's all coincidence, perhaps not, but the fact remains that *you* seem to be at the intersection of several simultaneous twists of fate. If history has taught us anything, it's that God doesn't work in mysterious ways, Rachel. God is a mad beast with an endless supply of toys and an ever-crueler imagination. And I, for one, am curious to see what He does tonight." He slid a large chunk of potato in his mouth. "Aren't you?"

She was stunned. She backed away from him and collided with someone else. She yipped and turned around once more—to see Francis. She
relaxed. He put a hand on her shoulder. "You're so nervous."

"Yeah, I guess so. I've never, like, performed like this."

"It's heavy, spreading the word. But I believe in you. *They'll* believe
you."

She licked her lips. "But why? I mean, why do *you* believe it's not just
bullshit?"

"Well, I appreciate the simplicity of it," he said. He sounded so much
older than he was. The oldest soul. "My dad used to drag us to Mass,
but I never understood it. I never felt like God listened to me. Any of
us. You know, environment necessitates faith. Especially an environment
like Renfield. These people are easily compelled, Rachel. Look at them."
He nodded at the crowd. "They *want* to be led. They want something
concrete. We all find comfort in knowing that something guides us, even
if that something is terrifying, beastly. It's why so many of us stay in abu-
sive relationships far longer than we should. At least *someone* is in control
of our lives. My mom said that to me once, just before she left my dad."
He sighed. "You can't help what you believe. But you *can* listen." He
squeezed her shoulder. "I listen. I hear you guiding us. And I have faith
in the fog."

"Thank you." She smiled at him. "Mr. Tolley did tell us the best leaders don't want to be leaders."

"Exactly." Francis smiled back. He was standing so close to her. He
squeezed her shoulder again. "Break a leg." And he retreated, leaving
her alone.

She took a breath and clapped her hands. "Alright, everyone! Hi!
Hello."

Gradually, the clearing went quiet. Everyone's eyes on her.

She stood in the center of the circle of tiki torches, everyone standing
in a half ring around her. The Drings held each other proudly in the back
of the crowd, next to a very dubious Tolley munching potatoes.

Here goes nothin. Galloway cleared her throat. "Thank you all for coming here tonight. Um. This project started two weeks ago as something
for class, but it's actually grown into something kind of cool. So I just

wanted to share a bit of the Gray Book with everybody. Not just for my presentation, but also because . . . This book has been really important to me, and I know I've made it important to Francis and a few others as well. And it seems that this story might be even more important than I thought, because . . . Well, because we live in a place where stories like this *are* important. So." She cleared her throat again. Opened her notebook. "This is the gospel of the fog."

It was slow and sweaty at first. She was more nervous than she thought. But she gained steam as she showed them her pictures. Told them the history she'd written. The prosperity of Addekkea, then its near-demise. She told them about the way of the beasts, and how those beasts brought life back to Addekkea's walls. She told them about the gluttonbats, the psychic ravens who relayed messages throughout Addekkea, and of course, the Fogmonger. She told them all of it.

When it was done, they stared at her. Glanced at each other. Faces flickering, unreadable in the firelight. She got an excited patter of applause from Mrs. Dring. Tolley was wiping his hands on his pants.

"Okay so, uh, *now* we conclude with the three Addekkean aphorisms," said Galloway. "Good flesh for good earth: a reminder to eat healthy, to keep the body fit for the pigs. Good men for good beasts: a reminder to live a full life, so that even when your flesh is sour, the gluttonbats will accept your offering. And have faith in the fog: Believe that one day, if we honor the beasts enough, their king, the Fogmonger, will return."

She closed her book. Stared at them. They all stared back.

What do I say now?

"I'll lead us in the echoing of the affirmations," said Francis, stepping up next to her. She fell back, grateful to let him lead for a moment.

"Everyone, repeat after me," said Francis. "Good flesh for good earth."

And to Galloway's immense surprise, they did, they all repeated it after him. The entire class, Greg and Dom, and even the Drings: "Good flesh for good earth."

"Good men for good beasts," said Francis.

"Good men for good beasts."

"And have faith in the fog."

"Have faith in the fog," they all said. Some of the classmates chuckled.

Not out of malice but awkwardness. This was a silly, fun thing they were saying, wasn't it?

"It's not a joke!" Francis snapped. "This is a real thing you just got to hear. A real *faith*. And you're laughing?"

Silence. Unease rippled through the crowd.

Galloway stared at him, heart banging against her lungs. She caught Ashleigh's eye. Emma's. Dom's eye, and Greg's. Suddenly, they all looked spooked.

Francis was right: They were Renfielders. New things happened all the time here. New, dark things. If there was light to be had, they would follow it, no questions asked.

She spoke up, "Look, this is . . . I know we all feel something bad is coming. And . . . I think it is." She licked her lips. "But . . . we can sing to the beasts to survive it. If we obey their ways, they will protect us through the coming Revelation." *Holy shit, that sounded awesome. Where did that come from?* And it was such a surge of adrenaline to boldly make this claim that she called out in reverent glee, buzzing from a high only recognizable to those who have secretly longed to be onstage, "Not long from tonight, Burnskidde will fall unless we sing. Sing to survive. Sing the Fogmonger's song." She turned her gaze to the stars and held out both hands as she sang a long, low note: "Oooooohh."

Francis joined her, thrusting out his hands and singing, "Oooooohh."

Ashleigh and Emma joined in. Some sang ironically. Greg and Dom sang into each other's mouths. But some of the others looked downright scared.

"Oooooohh." Over and over, and with each repetition, Galloway's confidence grew. "Oooooohh." The park was still and silent around them. The entire night was listening to Galloway's chorus.

At last, she paused, waited for them to pause with her. "Now that you all know the song, we proceed to the offering." She turned to Dom and Greg. "You guys ready?"

The boys looked at each other. Nodded.

She didn't know what she was feeling. Part of her wanted so badly for this to be real. So badly, she wanted her life to be fantastical. But at the same time, she wanted this to fail miserably. She wanted them all to leave, disappointed but safe. She didn't want to call *anything* out of the woods. Not at all.

Still, she said nothing. She watched Dom help Greg lower himself to the ground. His bare legs stretched out in front of him, pants rolled up, facing the woods: a solid barrier of brambles. Thorned vines knit so tightly against a wall of trees that she could see nothing on the other side.

The Drings stood close, Jeff's arm around his wife. They watched with quiet smiles.

The park was dead silent. A boy Galloway didn't know leaned over to his friend and whispered, "This seems like a load of barnacles." The friend snickered.

Greg looked up at Galloway. "How do we start?"

Galloway hesitated—and again, Francis stepped forward, arms held out toward the trees. "Beasts of the woods!" he cried. "We offer you this flesh. Good flesh for good earth. And ill flesh, in exchange for fresh life. Man to beast. Please! Accept our offerings." He sucked in a great breath, and sang. "Oooooohhh."

Greg joined him. "Oooooohhh."

"Beasts of the woods!" Dom cried into the trees. "I offer you my flesh." He rolled up his sleeve and thrust out his arm, underskin up. Soft, tender, veiny. "My arm. My thumb. I offer you my blood and bone. Beasts of the woods, I offer myself to you. Feed, and feed us in return." He took a deep breath. "Oooooohhh."

Again, everyone else joined in. They sang one low note, over and over. "Oooooohhh."

It went on and on.

It went on so long, Tolley checked his watch. The "load of barnacles" boy fake-coughed for more laughs.

But then. At last. A rustling in the undergrowth.

It silenced them mid-*ooh*. Everyone held their breath as something shook the wall of brambles from the other side.

Then the wall—parted.

Out of the shadows came lumbering, slow, a large and pale hog, low to the ground. It had great tusks in its lower jaw, curved and cracked and old. Its skin was a mottled pale blue, veiny and water-bloated. It had a wide gut, stubby legs, a short hairy-poofed tail. The rest of it was utterly bald. Its abnormally intelligent eyes blinked as it snorffled out of the vines, moving its snout back and forth. It oinked as it approached Dom, breath steaming.

Dom remained frozen, kneeling on the ground, arm outstretched, breathing fast.

Everyone stood absolutely still.

What . . . the fuck, thought Galloway. The pig had come. The thing she'd made up was now standing right in front of her.

Dom laughed, whispered, "Holy shit." He adjusted his position on the ground, steadying himself and keeping his bare arm outstretched as the hog sauntered closer, closer. Warm, wet dog stench wafted off its hide. It sniffed at Dom's arm, giant tusks brushing against his flesh.

No one even breathed.

"It likes you, dude," Greg whispered.

"Sh-should I try to pet it?" Dom asked. "Do I sing again? W-what does it want me to—"

It turned its head sharply, smacking its jaw upon Dom's arm. Blood spurted out around its snout. Galloway heard the *crunch* of bone.

Everyone gasped. Dom screamed and fell back on instinct, but the hog held fast. It jerked its head back. Strings and cords and spurting tubes of things snapped and stretched as it chewed, ripping, flicking its tail. Dom screamed so loud his voice cracked and warbled. The hog had taken a massive dent out of his forearm. His eyes were wide and terrified as he stared at the wound. He cried, "Oh my god!" just as the hog took another *crunch* out of his elbow, the sound wet and grinding as it chewed. The great molars behind those tusks ground and ground, blood and chunks dripping off the edges of its snout in great slobbering drags. Dom screamed on and on as the hog wrenched his arm off at the elbow. Galloway watched Dom's hand disappear down the snout as the hog threw back its head and gobbled up Dom's fingers. Greedily, happily, snorting and smiling to itself, sending hot blasts of sulfurous steam into the sky.

"Holy shit, dude!" Greg cried, half laughing, half gagging. "Look at your fucking ar—"

Something yanked Greg's leg into the trees. It screeched a high, piercing sound that made Galloway smack her hands over her ears and squeeze her eyes shut, but she could hear the *snapping* as something wrenched Greg's foot back and forth, back and forth, hard, until the foot cracked off at the ankle and was scuttled away into the woods.

Trembling, Greg pulled his leg back into the light. Flaps of flesh, jagged bone, strings of muscle, dark and dripping in the torchlight.

Greg stared at his twisted, ragged stump.

Then screamed.

The crowd burst into a whirlwind of activity. The Drings ran to Greg as he went into shock, shuddering and sweating on the ground, his remaining limbs flailing. Mr. Dring was whipping off his belt. Mrs. Dring was yanking her cardigan off and wrapping it around Greg's shredded leg. The eggshell-colored cashmere turned very red very fast.

Dom was screaming, digging his remaining fingers into the shorn arteries of his stump, trying to clamp down on the bleeding, blood trickling audibly into the grass. As soon as he had his belt cinched tight about Greg's leg, Mr. Dring was ripping off Dom's belt. "Son, I'm gonna need this."

Galloway was numb in the center of it all as the Drings carried the bleeding boys back to their car. Through the chaos, she caught Tolley's eye. He stood dumbfounded, fork frozen halfway between his mouth and plate.

A gust of wind blew by Galloway, sending her hair into her face. She blinked, and realized the wind was Francis, marching past her to the nearest tiki torch. He yanked it out of the dirt and thrust it into the sky. "Oooooohhh! Ooooooohhh!" He marched toward the woods. Galloway's classmates were dry-heaving, crying, scattering to their cars. But when they saw Francis, some of them hesitated.

"Come!" he called. "I saw them! The gluttonbat, the poo-pig! The beasts lead us to prosperity! Good flesh for good earth." Yelling over his shoulder as he marched, flame bobbing over his head. "We have to see where it goes! We have to *sing*! Ooooooohhh. Come! Ooooooohhh."

Greg Dring was in the back of the car, head cradled in Mrs. Dring's lap. She blubbered at him as she smoothed the hair off his sweat-soaked forehead. Dom sat next to them, head lolling on the seat, Greg's remaining leg in his lap.

"Dude," said Greg hoarsely, holding up his fist for Dom to bump.

Dom help up his stump in response, and Greg groaned.

Mr. Dring was behind the wheel, roaring the engine to life. He rolled down his window. "Emma, get in!"

Emma was caught halfway between them and Francis. She bit her lip. Then turned toward the woods. Took a huge breath and sang, "Oooooohhh!" She took up a torch and marched after Francis. "Oooooohhh!"

"Emma!" Mrs. Dring cried, rolling down her window, too.

Mr. Dring threw the car into drive, tires spewing grass, "We have to go!"

Mrs. Dring leaned out the window as they sped away, yelling, "Emma!"

And they were gone.

Jake and Troy marched after Emma, singing loud, and suddenly, Ashleigh was handing a torch to Galloway. She looked scared. She sang in a trembling, horrified voice as she turned away. "Oooooohhh."

Numb, Galloway followed. She followed these people following her. A long procession, actually—eighteen kids, she counted. Less than a third of Tolley's class had fled.

Francis crashed through the wall of brambles, shoving branches out of his way, moving fast. They sang as they stumbled after him, nearly blind in the dark and crazed with adrenaline. They sang louder and louder the farther they ventured into the woods, and all the while, Galloway thought, *This is insane, this is insane. I'm going to get everyone killed.* Branches whipping across her face, roots catching at her feet.

They burst into a moonlit clearing. There was the hog, smiling proudly before a pile of steaming, stinking brown pulp. Fresh and hot. When it saw them, it oinked happily. The chorus spread out around the clearing, singing, glancing at each other, following Francis's lead as he laughed and gesticulated at the poop. People gagged, put their hands to their mouths. Emma was crying a little in awe.

Finally, the hog turned slowly to Galloway, took several steps toward her. Everyone stopped singing. The creature looked up at her. And knelt. Dipped its snout to the ground in a deep bow. Then rose, and wandered away, back into the night.

Somewhere overhead, screams sliced through the clouds.

"What does it mean?"

Galloway looked up. Everyone was looking at her. Ashleigh was blinking away terrified tears.

"What does it mean?" she whispered again. "Rach, tell us what this means."

Galloway swallowed. She stared at the bloody shadow on the ground where the hog had just shit and walked away.

"I guess," she said, "it means I was right."

"Of course you were," said Francis. He beamed. "Of course. I had faith in the fog that you would be."

GREG AND DOM WERE PLACED IN SEPARATE ROOMS IN BARTRICK RE-gional, on separate floors. In the morning, they awoke at almost the exact same instant, and they both demanded to know, "Did it grow? Did anything grow?"

Doctors were concerned, of course. They had questions. They frowned at the parents. The authorities were similarly concerned, though no charges were pressed. No one seemed to be doing anything without consent. Greg and Dom weren't even interested in talking to Chief Pittner when he showed up at the hospital. "This doesn't involve you," they said. All they wanted to know was, "Did anything grow? In the *poop*, did anything grow?"

And indeed, it had.

Overnight, the fertilizer in the clearing had blossomed into a rich bouquet of beautiful wildflowers, spices, and a heavy vine of raspberries, brilliant like beads of blood. Just as Dom had asked for.

Someone must have planted the seeds beforehand. The entire thing must have been orchestrated. Surely, it was a setup. That's what Chief Pittner believed, as he frowned down at the blooming earth with his hands on his hips. *Surely, this is some teen prank bullshit.*

The fact that Greg and Dom simply beamed and said they were proud to have given good flesh for good earth, every time he asked them—that didn't help his case.

"MA, THEY'RE *HELPING*," SAID DOM. HE WAS SITTING ON THE COUCH in their living room. Thunder grumbled hungrily in the distance. He held up the bowl of raspberries in his remaining hand. "Look, it's food. It's a miracle."

"It's the devil," said Mrs. Zambrano, clutching Dom's little brother, Tomas, to her side. She was a stout woman with huge earrings. "As long as you're worshipping it, you cannot sleep under my roof."

"Oh my god, Ma."

"How are you gonna cook?" she cried. "How are you gonna drive a car? You can't make these kinds of choices so young."

"Mama, people can do lots of things with one hand. Please."

At that moment, something slammed into the roof of the Zambrano home. Dom shot off the couch. He looked up at the dining room chandelier, swinging violently. He rushed to the side door, his mother screaming behind him.

He slid open the glass door and stopped. Something was on the roof directly above him. He could hear it murmuring to itself in a chittering animal growl. He'd have to step under it if he went outside.

He leaned out and listened. The thing hoarked, hawked. He could picture it rolling its back like a retching cat. He heard the glistening wet bloom of a mass rising from its throat, uncoiling from between its fangs.

The mass dropped. Fell *splat* straight down to the lawn inches away from Dom's face. The thing on the roof breathed heavily, saliva dripping, sulfurous steam billowing out.

Dom leaned out farther, in awe, trying to catch just a glimpse.

The thing screeched and launched itself off the roof, beating at the night air with vast leathery wings, *whoomp, whoomp, whoomp* . . .

Dom ran outside and watched it soar away. It let out one last distant shriek, like a boiling kettle and a screaming infant, together in a blender. Then it disappeared.

Dom's mother screamed at him in Spanish from inside the house. Tomas wailed, tears streaming down his cheeks. Dom felt the cool grass on his bare feet, felt it whisper over his toes, as if the ground itself were greeting him, welcoming him, drawing him closer to the steaming thing in the yard. As he stepped toward it, the mound—moved. It shifted and squirmed and let out a small mewling bleat.

"Dominic!" his mother bawled. "Dominic!"

Dom knelt and stared into the mound as it continued to mew and writhe. His first thought was, *Holy shit, Greg's foot is still alive*. But then he leaned closer, put out his hand, pulled apart the thin membrane of mucous. He saw its head pop out. Saw its mouth open wide, bleating blindly at the sky.

"Oh my god," he whispered.

His mother was dialing 911 on her pink Razr when Dom stepped back inside. "Ma."

She looked up. Cradled in the nook of his arm and a half, Dominic Zambrano held a small, wet, newborn lamb. He gazed at his mother, holding this miracle to his chest. "Mama . . . we've been blessed."

FIRES WITHIN FIRES

The Yellow Book

It was on this day that Rachel Galloway, the original All-Speaker, threw herself on the mercy of the hills.

"Spare them," she cried. "Those who live in that cursed valley have not yet had the grace to hear our song. They do not deserve to rot at your breath, O Fogmonger. We thank you for breathing your blessings unto us this day. But please, grant one more boon: I give myself in Renfield's stead. I may die, but please, spare the rest of the valley! Give them time to join our chorus."

The Billowhills heard her, and knew her as a child of the earth—a follower of the way of beasts, the way of the woods. Thus, the Billowhills granted her wish, crumbling the tunnel from within, so that none may pass into or out of this land. So taken were the hills by this sacrifice, in fact, that they bestowed a special gift upon the people of Burnskidde. A miracle to match all miracles. But this miracle required warm flesh as a spark, for the crucible of the mines under Burnskidde had long cooled.

So it was that All-Speaker Urquhart gave his good eye in exchange for this miracle. He was allowed to live as the hills crumbled over the tunnel and smothered All-Speaker Galloway.

All-Speaker Urquhart emerged from the mines with his new miracle in tow, and one shorn eye. Galloway had granted him the right to spread her word, her commandments, and her stories, and the first of these commandments, spaketh Urquhart, was thus: "Give yourselves to the fog! Have faith that when the Monger returns, he will restore all that was offered."

This was the end of the nonbelievers, and the beginning of a new and clearer age.

"The Fall of Old Burnskidde"
F. Urquhart, the Yellow Book

NEW ADDEKKEA, OCTOBER 2019

Cultwatch

The Clate River Crew was a fairly basic polygamy cult, as far as polygamy cults go.

In the mid-1990s, a man named Barnaby Wroth managed to convince a shocking number of people that his "seed" contained a cure for Renfield County's curse. He gathered three hundred people to himself and instructed them to build a community in the swamps far south along the Clate River. In theory, this was Wroth's chosen land, but it was also far from the eyes of the law. Here, Wroth preached unwavering obedience, claiming that a day would come when his "Wrothies" would all be tested. A Judgment Day, to cull the wheat from the chaff. His acolytes, terrified of this future vision, prayed ever harder.

In December 1998, one of Wroth's wives managed to escape and contact the authorities. In the mere two hours she was gone, Wroth declared that Judgment Day had come at last.

Imagine the officers who first saw that hut-village deep in the swamps, where no one was recorded to be living. Imagine the scene in the bog. The boxes sunk into the muck with large stones. All the little bodies inside, clutched in their mothers' arms, bloated by the mud. Imagine the empty bottles floating on the surface, chained to those boxes, bobbing like headstones. Hundreds of them. *So your soul can float upward to heaven*, Wroth drawled as he tossed another box into the bog and chugged another bottle of bourbon.

Imagine what it's like to be told God wants you drowned. Waiting for your turn, all the coffins lined up along the bank. Imagine Wroth hammering the nails into that final coffin, then slipping away into the woods, never to be seen again.

No wonder Bruce didn't want to work another cultwatch. Witnessing all those bottles bobbing, the bodies in their boxes below . . . Durwood could see how that would change you.

She understood a few things about cults, simply by reading up on the Crew and others like it. Cults required consequences, for one, but it was necessary that their rules be somewhat fluid. If they had a deadline, it should be nebulous enough to activate at any given time. But most importantly, cults needed to be self-sufficient and isolated, or at least able to impose strict control over the flow of information and media, so that indoctrination could be as complete as possible. Some of the crueler orthodoxies out there cannot survive in the presence of tv.

Knowing all this, Durwood expected whatever awaited her in Burnskidde to be a heavily brainwashed community. Whoever was in charge, they'd had a solid decade to entrench their values here.

But she didn't expect them to look so . . . cheery.

When the curtains of the willow finally parted, they opened onto dozens of people standing in a half circle in Miner Memorial Square, around the tall marble statue of three men in hard hats. Life bloomed in uncanny abundance here as well. The statue was ensnared in morning glories and moonflowers, so that it blossomed at all times of day. Beyond the square was what looked like an abandoned strip mall, bleached by the sun, missing windows and store names, but alive with trellises laden with rainbows. Hummingbirds and butterflies flitted to and fro. Everywhere, things grew around the shell of the town. The lampposts, the cracks in the pavement. The road was broken and uneven underfoot, jiggling Durwood's bike in her hands as she walked it closer to the choir of smiling people, full of joy, with grins stretched wide across their jaws. They held their hands out to her, palms up, like sirens drawing her into the sea, singing one long continuous note, "Oooooohhh."

Except, not all of them had hands *to* hold up. Most of these people were . . . missing things. Hands, feet, both. Some had large dents in their shoulders, their arms withered from the lack of muscle and tissue at the joint. Others had dents in their legs, their ears. Their clothes looked handmade, not badly done or worn, just simple. Home-woven shirts and undyed jeans. Leather shoes without buckles or laces. These clothes hung asymmetrically, their woolen sweaters and leather jackets crooked against their bodies. Their pant legs fell inward, or were rolled up to reveal missing feet.

But they all sang so joyfully.

Between two ivy-choked streetlamps with cracking paint, they had hung a banner. The letters were painted in a dark purplish smear across yellow fabric. Durwood would later learn that their paints were all made from bugs, berries, and roots. The fabric was an old banner celebrating Burnskidde High's football team. Now, it read, WELCOME TO NEW ADDEKKEA.

Durwood stopped at the edge of the square, trapped between the wall of green behind her and the smiling faces, the outstretched hands and stumps. Singing, bellowing, "Oooooohhh."

She wasn't sure what to do. She stood, tense, waiting for something else to happen.

Then, out from the press of dented bodies stepped a man. He was young, not even thirty. He had dark hair swept back in a handsome wave. It curled up at the edges on the nape of his neck. He wore a shining monocle over one eye which reflected the sun at every angle, so she could never see what it was looking at. The other eye was a rich mahogany. He wore a robe that swept down to the ground in glacial blue folds. Frigid, refined, and reminiscent of morning fog. On his shoulder sat a raven. Its claws dug into the man's shoulder. Its beak tilted this way and that as it analyzed Durwood head to toe.

The man in the blue robe fixed his eye on her and smiled. He lifted a hand, and all the shining happy people in their homemade leather, wool, and cotton stopped singing.

"Welcome," he said. His voice was cool and smooth, like he was in awe of everything all the time. "I am so happy to have you here."

Durwood glanced around the crowd. Everybody smiled. Nobody moved. The banner flapped in the breeze.

"You were expecting me," said Durwood, remaining as still as possible.

"Not you specifically, but *some*one," said the man. He chuckled. The raven on his shoulder squawked and ruffled its feathers. "You're only the second guest we've ever had. We've been so eager. It is a momentous day." He looked around at the people behind him. They nodded in agreement.

He went on: "I'm guessing you know one side of this story, or you wouldn't have come. *Our* side is that a man stumbled into our community, unannounced and completely unexpected. He was . . . confused by what he saw here." He frowned. Some of the others shook their heads mournfully. "He left in such a hurry, we couldn't explain our customs to him properly. So I thought it best to organize a greeting for whoever came after, whether it was him or . . . someone even *less* open-minded." His raven cawed, shifting its weight between its claws.

"Ah," said Durwood. She punted the kickstand of her bike and finally let go of it. She felt like she might need her hands free. "Well, consider my mind open. The man you mentioned. His name Mark?"

"It is," said the man robed in fog.

"Then you guess correctly. He's a friend. We both work for the County Guard."

Murmurs. People glancing at each other.

The monocled man frowned again. "We don't know what that is."

"They're like police," said a middle-aged woman in the front of the crowd. She was missing half of her lower lip. The other half was pulled taut over her gums, and Durwood could see her teeth as she breathed through her mouth. Her dark hair was stringy and unwashed. There were dents in her sweater along the arms, and she was missing an ear. Altogether, she looked unwell. Or maybe these missing pieces meant she was holier than everyone else. She certainly sounded righteous when she said, "The Guard has no jurisdiction here. They're knifepeople. Outworlders who sew metal in their skin."

More murmurs throughout the crowd. People stepped back. Durwood stiffened, angling out her wrist, ready to fight.

"Be good, Isabella," said the monocled man calmly, putting up a hand. "She is our guest."

Durwood raised her voice, addressing everyone. "I don't intend to cause trouble. Mark was on a routine patrol when he disappeared. He left behind evidence that suggests he was here, and your story seems to corroborate that. I'm just following up. That's it. I don't mean anybody any harm, and I'm certainly not a . . . knifeperson." Carefully, she laid her hands flat against her thighs, concealing the talon-hole in her hand.

"Where was he last seen?" the monocled man asked. "Our mutual friend."

"Well, that's what I want to know."

"Aha!" The man shook his head jovially. "That's what *we* want to know. I was so hoping that was him Victoria spied coming through the tunnel." He stroked his raven's head. "But I'm sorry, we didn't know *anything* had happened to him."

"Right," said Durwood. "Well, did anyone see him leave, ah . . ." She squinted at the banner. "New Addekkea?"

The man smiled. He enunciated the name correctly, "*Uh-deh-kia.* And no, Mark absconded in the middle of the night. Listen, we have nothing to hide. We are a peaceful people. We simply have different ways."

Durwood gave a tight smile. "Of course." She cleared her throat and pointed over her shoulder. "If you weren't expecting visitors before, why'd you open the tunnel?"

"Ahh, yes," said the monocled man slowly, smiling the blissful drugged smile of the devout. His raven seemed to smile, too. "So that we could be open to share our blessing with the valley. He's due in three days' time, and we are *very* eager to breathe deep his blessing."

A cold wind shivered through Durwood's bones. Mark's note whispered in her mind. *Mass suicide event highly likely* . . . "And what blessing is that, exactly?"

"The fog," said the man, and a rasping, breathless anticipation breezed over the crowd, like wind through dead corn. *The fog* . . .

The dented woman with the bad lip stepped forward. "What's your name, Guard?"

"Rachel," said Durwood.

The crowd chuckled.

"What an unbelievably good omen," said the monocled man. "You're in excellent company. Rachel *gave* us our gospel. In fact, many of our children are named after her in homage." He pointed to a little girl, about eight. "That's Rachel. Another Rachel over there. And *this* is Rachel Anne. She just turned ten, she'll be offering herself tomorrow night."

A little girl with blond pigtails smiled nervously at Durwood. "I want to see that I have good flesh." Behind her, her mother patted her shoulder lovingly with a thumbless hand.

Durwood's skin buzzed. She had read about how the Addekkeans offered themselves, so these dented people seemed a foregone conclusion. But she hadn't expected all these other Rachels. *Was* that a good omen? Or the punch line to some cosmic joke?

The monocled man smiled. "Rachel. I understand your mistrust, but what makes you think we have anything to hide?"

"The fact that you're all standing around saying you *don't* have anything to hide feels like sort of a bad start, if I'm being honest."

He laughed. "Last week, we opened ourselves to the world to *share* the gifts we've cultivated here. Mark's sudden departure was a miscommunication between peoples, nothing more. If you spend time with us, you'll see. Heck, in three days, you'll see either way." He shrugged lightly. "Stay, go. Makes no difference in the end. The fog will bless us all, fellow Rachel." He put a hand to his chest. "*I* am All-Speaker Urquhart."

"Charmed," said Durwood.

"And this," he continued, "is Victoria. My beautiful raven." He scratched the raven under her chin. She chortled for him and gave Durwood a territorial look.

All-Speaker Urquhart held out a hand to the dented woman. "This is Isabella Zambrano, our Speaker of Public Health. She was a nurse at Bartrick Regional. Before."

"Pleasure," said Durwood, nodding to her.

"Guardian Rachel," said Isabella. "On behalf of myself and the other speakers here, we welcome you to New Addekkea." She sang again, and everyone behind her sang one clear "Oooooohhh" along with her.

Urquhart stepped forward. "I would be honored to show you around so you can see what we've been up to these last ten years. All you out-worlders must have so many questions." He chuckled again. His one eye moved endlessly as he spoke, roving over her body, the go-bag slung over her shoulder, her bike. It unnerved her that she could not see what the other eye was doing.

"Yeah, I have a few," she said.

"And I'm happy to answer them all. Please." He gestured for her to follow him. "My assistant Fogg will make us some tea back at my estate. We've been growing our own tea here, and it has a surprisingly sweet flavor that I think you'll enjoy. Would you care to follow?"

"Love to," said Durwood, giving him a tight smile.

Urquhart clapped his hands. Victoria the raven squawked. "Wonderful. Thank you everyone!" He addressed the crowd. "Again, *please* be hospitable to our guest. Though she may be a knifewoman of the out-world, it is good to be kind, to leave behind a legacy of kinship for whatever new life may prosper on this earth when we are gone in the fog. Be good people for this good earth, and show our guest a hearty welcome. Oh-ooh?"

"Ooh-ooh," answered the crowd, a *yes sir* en masse.

"Be free, then, and have faith in the fog. Do not forget Rachel Anne's ceremony tomorrow eve!"

They dispersed. Durwood followed after Urquhart, keeping the heel of her right hand loose on the handlebar, ready to flex out her talon at any moment as the dented bodies parted before her.

A tall man reached out of the crowd. His hand had only two fingers: thumb, forefinger. Numbly, she shook his hand against her better judgment. It felt molten and strange in her grip.

"Pleasure to meet you," he said. He squinted through cracked glasses. He was balding under thin white hair. He smiled, showing small teeth. "I'm Dr. Danforth, Speaker for the Children. You can call me Eric."

"Nice to meet you," said Durwood stiffly.

He smiled, squinting harder. "Do let me know if there's any way I can help with your investigation, Guardian Rachel. I hope Mark is alright. He was kind. And handsome." He winked.

She ran her tongue over her teeth. "Appreciate you, Dr. Danforth."

"Oh, please." He smiled squintily. "Call me Eric."

URQUHART LED DURWOOD THROUGH A TOWN OVERGROWN BY VEGE-tation. There was a movie theater, the parking lot now a vineyard. An Italian restaurant named Eddie Spaghetti's was now at the center of a cornfield. A Pancake Planet had been turned into a makeshift greenhouse, filled with herbs and spices. Overall, the topography of New Addekkea was startlingly diverse. There were patches of woods, orchards, and min-iature swamps. Everywhere, people tended to gardens, milked cows, wa-tered plants, picked root vegetables. Everywhere, dogs barked happily and cats strolled, sunned themselves, chased each other through tall grass. Everyone sang, smiling, as Urquhart passed. He waved to them all.

Victoria cawed and pushed herself into the air, keeping pace overhead. Urquhart smiled up at her. When he wasn't actively engaged in saying hello to people, he watched Victoria carefully, as if listening to her. In be-tween all the waving and these curious silences, he explained their customs to Durwood. Most of the orthodoxy was familiar to Durwood after read-ing the Gray Book, but she was curious to see how Urquhart described it:

"All of this is pig-grown," he said, gesturing to a large pumpkin patch. "Those horses tilling the field there? They're bat-grown. Look, these tomatoes were fertilized by our Speaker of Records, Edie Neglani."

"Uh-huh," said Durwood dubiously. She was not entirely convinced by Urquhart's smug explanation of magic pooping pigs and puking bats. She opted not to ask about the Botanist just yet. Instead, she'd *be smart* and listen. "So you just make a wish when you offer your flesh, and the beasts make that wish come true? You've seen this happen?"

"Indeed," said Urquhart. "Many times. We wish for whatever the community needs. Food, wool, cotton; resources such as firewood, lux-uries like monk fruit and orchids for vanilla . . . Everything we have is thanks to the beasts."

"And people offer themselves willingly for these items."

Urquhart smiled at her. "Always. We believe the more you give of yourself, the closer you are to the earth."

"Gotcha," Durwood nodded. "More stumps means more holy."

Urquhart winced. "In a way. Though that's a crass way to put it. There's our amphitheater, by the way. We're very fond of plays here in New Addekkea, as you can imagine. And farmers markets, though we employ a barter system here . . ." She only caught about half of what he was saying as she took in the parking lots converted to grazing fields, the rows of peppers along side streets, the old buildings filled with crops. She kept wringing the handlebars of her bike. All around her, the cheery ongoing chorus, "Oooooohhh."

Every so often, she caught the gleam of something far away. Distant bronze statues standing sentinel over a field, at an intersection. Blinding scarecrows under the sun. She squinted at them, but could never quite make them out.

"Everyone grows something," Urquhart explained. "Or tends to some of the animals. When the Fogmonger first came, there were some who had eaten of his beasts but not yet taken his song into their hearts. When they saw his power, though . . . they changed their tune. *Everyone* changed their tune." He smiled, surveying his kingdom with pride.

"I don't understand," said Durwood. "The Fogmonger already came?"

Urquhart nodded. "Yes. November twenty-sixth, 2009. He blessed everyone who had communed with the beasts in some way, and poisoned those who hadn't. Blackened their veins and withered their lungs. We fed their bodies to the bats." He chuckled. "Pardon me. I've a bit of déjà vu. I had this same conversation with Mark just last week. I suppose that means he really *did* vanish before he told you anything."

Who was this fucking twenty-something, talking to her like this? She felt like she was watching a child pretend to be an adult, wearing a small tie and playing Business. With his fucking monocle.

"Anyway," he explained, "that night, poor Rachel Galloway sacrificed herself to keep the fog from spreading into the rest of Renfield. If she hadn't done that, you might have choked to death on your own blood as well. Just like all the other nonbelievers." He chuckled again. Like this was a game.

"I'm grateful," Durwood grumbled. "But what happened to the Fogmonger then? Just left?"

"Vanished without a trace," said Urquhart. "Just like the story of old. But set to return very soon, to bless us even more powerfully than before."

"Uh-huh."

Urquhart waved to someone picking peaches in the turf of the football field at the high school. She waved back and offered him a fresh fruit from her basket. He accepted it with a reverent nod and held it out to Durwood. "Hungry?"

"I ate." She hadn't, but a collage of images swam in her mind. The stringy veins of the peach; the ripe, juicy human flesh that had gone into it. She winced when Urquhart bit into the fruit, the skin shriveling between his teeth.

As he chewed, he led her through many more avenues filled with produce, flowers, and trees, crowding the entire town. Always, he walked one step ahead of her, pointing and waving at everything and everyone. All the people tilling the fields, walking their cows and goats along the streets, all of them greeted him with a song, "Oooooohhh." Durwood wondered if the show was for her or Urquhart, or both.

Eventually, they approached a park. She could see the wall of the woods against the park's edge. A shrine had been set up out there, against the trees. An archway of flowers and twining roots, in a clearing surrounded by tiki torches.

Sitting at a picnic table a short ways away was a young man, perhaps a few years older than Urquhart, closer to Durwood's age. He had his legs stretched out in front of him (well, his leg and a half), and he gazed at the shrine against the woods with an unreadable, solemn expression. A long wooden walking stick stood at his side, propped against the table.

As Durwood passed, his gaze shifted toward her. His face did something she couldn't quite read. Surprise, fear, relief?

He lifted a hand in greeting. Durwood nodded in return.

Through the park and up a hill they went, until they reached a large mansion at the hilltop. A three-story affair with a tall white brick tower, covered in windows. A black iron gate spiked up from the ground at the end of its gravel drive, guarded by twin iron ravens, wings outstretched. Durwood's mind was focused on the archway and the young man in the park as they approached the estate. A loud cawing jerked her out of her reverie, and she turned, and found herself face-to-face with a gleaming metal scarecrow.

It was as tall as she was, mostly human, draped in a dirty black robe, completely neutralizing the person's sex. On its head was a kind of brass helmet, crafted into the shape of a raven-head. This head was twice the size of a normal human skull, probably ridiculously heavy. The metal eyes were wide and blank. The beak was curved dangerously sharp, but not as sharp as the scythe poised over its shoulder. A long frown of gleaming steel, curved so sharp, so perfectly sharp, the very tip of it sang in the sun. In its other hand, this raven-headed scarecrow carried a large brass birdcage. Inside was a single raven, and it was throwing itself against the bars, cawing madly.

There were, in fact, two of these scarecrows guarding the gates. Two gleaming brass helmets. Two scythes. Two caged ravens screaming at her.

"Whoa." Durwood stopped dead in her tracks, flexing her wrist, talon ready to sing out into the air.

Urquhart put out a hand between them. "No need to be afraid. This is a *ravenknight*. A protector of the community. We have little use for police here, but the knights keep watch over our home. Just in case."

The ravens settled. Durwood flicked her eyes between the brass heads, the scythes. "In case of what?"

"Well, a prepared body is a calm heart," said Urquhart. He addressed the knights. "Please."

The knights placed their cages on the ground and used their free hands to swing the black gates wide. Urquhart led the way through. Durwood remained tense as she passed the ravenknights. She could hear them breathing. Low, metal whistling. The ravens in their cages cocked their heads. Watching her.

Up close, she could see that the heads lacked orifices. How did they see? They must be suffocating in there. The breath she heard rushing through the helmets must be coming from down around the seam. They were so quiet, tracking her with their eyeless masks. She heard only their breath. *Whoo. Sniff. Whoo. Sniff . . .*

"It's elaborate, I know," said Urquhart as he led her up the driveway. "But the chorus insisted on it. They were *very* grateful that I could be here to guide them in the wake of Galloway's sacrifice."

"I'm sure they were," muttered Durwood. "And how did she sacrifice herself, exactly?" She was beyond the Gray Book now, in new dogmatic territory.

"Well, it was her who went down into the mine to blow the tunnel from beneath. To stop the fog from spreading and killing anyone else who wasn't a member of the chorus. She gave herself to the hills, and the hills offered an additional gift in return. I was there with her at the end, to accept this gift." Urquhart sighed. "Ours is a complicated story, dear Rachel. One chapter at a time."

She turned to see the knights shutting the gate behind her. As soon as their hands were off the thick iron bars, they took up their matching brass cages with matching black ravens, and turned to glare out at the road once more.

Durwood liked Urquhart even less when she saw his house up close. It was regal and lonely. She'd bet any amount of money it was the largest house in town.

"No Mrs. Urquhart, huh?" she asked.

"Aha, no," he said. "I like to keep my mind and body clear for the chorus. A clear heart sees far."

"Mmhmm."

As they approached the estate's front door, it swung open, and out stepped a tight-jawed man with a gaunt face and a red ascot tucked into a white button-down. His black jacket was sleek and sharp-cornered, bringing to mind even more ravens.

"This is my assistant Fogg," said Urquhart. "Fogg, this is our guest, Rachel, ah . . . Oh, it'll be awkward simply calling you *Rachel.*"

"Durwood," she said, wincing at giving over her full name. There were creatures in Renfield who could work powerful magic against you if they had your full name.

Fogg shook her hand. His voice was cold and flat. "Pleasure." He looked at Urquhart. "Mark?"

"Poor Mark seems to have vanished," said Urquhart. "Isn't that sad? Ms. *Durwood* here is with the Guard. She's investigating."

Fogg grunted. He flicked his eyes up and down her body with a trig-german's clinical glare.

"Please," said Urquhart. "Come in. Fogg will make us that tea. You'll love it. Fogg?"

Fogg glanced at him again, nodded to Durwood, and vanished inside.

Urquhart swung a hand toward the open hall of the mansion. "After you."

Inside, it was stuffy and smelled of hay. Surprisingly cramped for a house that occupied so much space. The foyer ran off in three directions: straight back to the kitchen, to the left a windowless den, and to her right was a grand oak room, with a wide picture window looking out over the yard. It was the sunniest, cheeriest room in sight. It was here she expected him to lead her, but instead he took her into the windowless den. Walls full of shelves, a black wooden desk in the middle of dark carpet. On the back wall, encased in glass, were two weathered composition notebooks. Both had marbled covers. The one on the left was gray, marked *Gray Book* in black Sharpie. The one on the right was yellow, and was marked, appropriately, *Yellow Book*.

As Urquhart entered the low-ceilinged room, Victoria hopped off his shoulder and settled onto a perch next to the desk, where she could remain eye level with Durwood.

"Whaddya got there?" Durwood pointed at the glass case.

"Those are the two texts that made our community what it is today," said Urquhart. "The Gray Book is filled with Galloway's visions, stories, and prayers. The Yellow is filled with her teachings and commandments. She wrote that one in secret. Not even *I* knew about it until after her sacrifice."

"They look like someone's history notebooks," said Durwood. She came around the desk and leaned close to the glass. "It even says 'History' in pencil there."

"It *was* her history notebook," said Urquhart. "Very astute. You see, this all started in history class. Rachel was just a girl before her visions began. Before the beasts. She thought she was simply *doodling*, but no . . . Oh! My fog, I almost forgot." Urquhart snapped his fingers and smacked his fist into his palm as he twirled in a full circle. "Where did I put the . . . Yes." He wagged his finger, figuring it out, and walked to a shelf on the far wall.

The shelves were filled with leatherbound volumes; old, weathered paperbacks; and various ornaments such as a daisy pressed behind glass. Two of these shelves were monochromatic. A gray shelf and a yellow shelf, packed with identical clothbound volumes. Urquhart selected a gray book and a yellow book from their respective shelves, and carried them to her in both hands, reverently.

"So you may learn our ways." He smiled.

God, she wanted to smack that smug grin right off his face, stab him in the monocle and demand answers. *What's happening in three days?!* she wanted to scream. *Did you kill my goddamn friend?!*

"Thank you," she said. She ran her thumbs over the soft covers. Twin images of Rachel Galloway with her hands outstretched, surrounded by beasts. One in gray, the other in yellow.

Durwood dropped her bag on the carpet and unzipped it, sliding the volumes inside. She zipped it back up before Urquhart could peer inside and see that she already *had* a Gray Book.

"Ahh, the tea," he said as Fogg carried in a wicker tray. Two white mugs with a silver steaming kettle and a few small bowls of leaves. Fogg placed the tray on the desk, nodded, and left.

"Sit," said Urquhart. "Please." He dropped into the chair behind his desk with a sigh and started fussing with his tea. "There's honey and cream, sugar, lemon . . . Everything we consume we grow ourselves, of course. That's a commandment from the Yellow Book."

"One must be self-sufficient," said Durwood.

"Precisely."

She helped herself to a spoonful of dried red leaves that she dropped into a strainer over her cup. She poured water over it. It smelled good, she had to admit. Like cinnamon, apples, and licorice. She waited for Urquhart to drink first.

"So," he said. "Offer me a question. Though, of course, whenever your heart is full of questions, there is no room for faith." He smiled. "That's from the Yellow Book as well."

"I'll work on it." She cleared her throat. "But first, can you tell me exactly what happened with Mark? How did he get here? Why was he 'confused'? You didn't notice anything odd before he vanished?"

"Well," said Urquhart, sipping his tea, "he seemed alarmed that we were doing so well on our own, for one. I'll admit, our faith encourages us to be wary of outworlders, as you noticed. I'm not sure how welcoming my chorus was when he arrived. That's why I made such a point of singing for your arrival. But I showed him around, shared our ceremonies with him, our miracles. And then he simply vanished."

"What miracles specifically?"

"He observed an offering to the beasts, watched a banana tree grow overnight, and"—Urquhart's eye twinkled—"he met Galloway's final gift."

Durwood's stomach flipped. She had a guess about what that final gift was. But she wanted him to say it. "You mentioned this gift before."

Urquhart sipped his tea. "Mm. That's good. This is Straus tea, by the way. Very flavorful."

"Straus is a plant?"

Urquhart laughed. "*Alan* Straus. He offered his hand to grow the first batch of those tea leaves. Go ahead, try it."

Durwood grimaced as she sniffed the mug.

Urquhart laughed. "It's not pieces *of* Alan in there. It's tea he grew. Go on." He took an encouraging sip himself.

Durwood took a tiny sip. It tasted the way it smelled: an autumn harvest of apples and leaves. It was, in fact, delicious.

"Num." She smacked her lips. "But you're dodging my question."

He eyed her over his mug, smiling steadily. "Yes. I suppose I am. This is another reason we've kept to ourselves all these years. To keep our miracles safe. Do you know the kind of uproar it would cause if people knew the Renfields had been reborn?"

Durwood sat very still, heart suddenly hammering in her ribs. "Are you saying . . . the Renfields are here? In Burnskidde."

Urquhart frowned melodramatically. "We no longer call ourselves by that cursed name. We are New Addekkea, Ms. Durwood. Pure and beautiful. Free of crime and tragedy at last. Unlike your filthy valley," he sneered.

She tried not to sneer back. *Be smart.* She unclenched her jaw and looked down into her lap. "So the Renfields are alive here in *New* Addekkea?"

Urquhart smiled. "Indeed they are."

"Could you introduce me?"

"If I do, will you *also* run off in the night and bring more outworld attention to our home? I'm thrilled to share our blessing, but I'm wary of drawing more people here who might attempt to interfere with it."

"Guard's honor," she said.

Urquhart considered. "Very well. Finish your tea and I'll take you." He sipped loudly at his mug.

Durwood stared at him for a moment before cracking back her head and swallowing her entire cup in one scalding gulp. It hurt bad, billowing heat and pain down her chest. Her eyes watered. But she held her expression firm as she clapped the mug back onto the tray.

"Aces," she said, slapping her thighs and hopping to her feet. "Let's go meet these miracles. Please," she added with her best shit-eating grin.

BURNSKIDDE, NOVEMBER 2009

Duplicate Drings

The Monday after the first offering, they sat Galloway down in Dr. Eric's office. Dr. Eric loomed in the corner, tapping his fingertips together, as Chief Pittner asked her questions. She had never seen him in the flesh. He was a haggard-looking man with a thick black mustache that almost hid his mouth completely. A face that looked accustomed to scowling.

"And how many people actually *saw* this pig?" he scowled at her.

"Everyone who was there," said Galloway. "You can ask anybody. I didn't cut off Greg's leg. They took it."

"The beasts," Pittner clarified.

"Yes. I mean, the bat, yeah," said Galloway. "The pig took Dom's hand. The bat took Greg's foot."

"Okay. Everyone saw this bat as well?"

"No . . . But the pig was there."

"And they just dined and dashed. Came out, took a bite, scampered off."

"More or less. The wounds were voluntary."

"Mmhmm." Pittner glanced at Dr. Eric. The principal was watching Galloway with fascinated, narrow eyes.

"Well, then, at the very least, this is a public health concern," said Pittner. "I could easily call mental health services and have all three of you—you, Mr. Zambrano, and Mr. Dring—actually, everyone who was *there* that night—in custody for self-endangerment and endangerment of the community. I could arrest Mr. Tolley right now for endangering minors."

"I'm sorry," said Galloway meekly.

"Did you promise them anything in exchange for this 'offering,' or were they coerced in any way?" Dr. Eric asked. "Is anyone coercing *you*?"

"No," said Galloway. "They offered."

Dr. Eric tapped his fingertips together. "Intriguing."

"Are these the same critters who've been stealing cars?" Pittner asked.

"I don't know," said Galloway. "That's not in any of my stories. You can look. Here." She pulled her notebook out of her backpack and held it out.

She let him flip through it in silence for a minute before he handed it back and said, "Looks like a bunch of doodles."

"It is; it's just a story," said Galloway, slipping the book back in her bag. "Whatever people do with it isn't my fault."

Pittner tsked. "Kinda is, though. A good story's all you need. Did you know women never shaved their armpits until Gillette decided they needed to sell more razors? They *invented* shaving your armpits. To sell *razors*. And you tell me it's just a story."

"Could I see a copy of that book?" Dr. Eric asked.

"Sure," said Galloway. "I'll, uh . . . make one."

"Excellent." Dr. Eric smiled so that his eyes almost disappeared, they squinted so hard. "I try to stay on top of current trends amongst the student body. It sounds like she had some willing participants, Chief."

"Hundreds of willing participants at Jonestown, too," Pittner grumbled. "Okay. You can go. But you make a copy of that book for me, too. And you be careful what stories you tell people. Especially my *son*. Okay?"

"Yes, sir," she mumbled. She'd never been in trouble before.

"Okay," said Pittner. He pointed out the door. "Now get your ass to class."

LAWN MOWERS, MOTORCYCLES, AC UNITS, WATER HEATERS. METAL-lic objects continued to go missing at an alarming rate. Was someone melting them down? For what?

But it wasn't just *things*. Hannah Nichols went missing from the playground in her neighborhood. Austin Tanner vanished somewhere between his home and the elementary school. Kayla Christian's mother let go of her shopping cart in the parking lot of the Fresh N Good for a moment—just a moment—and the entire cart disappeared. Groceries, three-year-old Kayla, and all.

Gone without a trace, every single one. As if the very ground had swallowed them whole.

"REMEMBER THEM." Posters with this phrase started showing up across town, plastered over the missing-pet posters and the posters asking for information on Dear's disappearance. "REMEMBER THEM," in huge letters over pictures of Abby Fetterman, Hannah Nichols, Austin Tanner. On the bus one afternoon, Galloway saw Seth Brenner stapling one to a telephone pole. A Noxboro burned between his lips as he worked.

Facebook and neighborhood forums were alive with speculation and accusation. There were angry mutterings among the adults. The police hadn't even *attempted* to stop this kidnapper/kleptomaniac. A monster was in their midst, and the police didn't even care!

On the daily news, Chief Pittner continued to argue that there was nothing he *could* do. Unless he conducted an exhaustive town-wide manhunt for a stockpile of metal and missing kids, he was at a loss. The crimewave of October 2009 was the greatest headache of his career.

Even Galloway's parents were tired of him.

"He shouldn't be wasting his time interrogating *you* when he should be looking for those people," said Nicole firmly over dinner. "Or our mailbox. Especially when *you're* the one trying to help everyone." Worry breezed over her face. "Right? That . . . offering was supposed to help, wasn't it?"

"Of course," said Keith. "She's not stealing mailboxes, Nic. Her whole project is about giving back. She didn't force those boys to do anything."

"Right," said Galloway, though she was not sure this was right. She wasn't sure anymore that she was innocent. She was only sure that something was happening beyond her control.

FRANCIS WAS IN THE CLEARING BEHIND THE PARK, JUST AS SHE'D hoped he'd be. It was a gray afternoon, the light a dull slate. Francis knelt before the pig's bounty in his long black trench coat, and smiled to himself as he slipped a raspberry off the vine. It was so beautifully ripe it slid off without resistance, and he placed it on his tongue with the utmost reverence.

"Did you plant these?" Galloway asked, standing behind him.

Francis turned, surprised. He rose to his feet, slapping dirt off his hands. "What do you mean?"

"I mean on Friday, did you come back here overnight and plant all of these?"

He looked around and spread his hands. "Where would I have gotten them?"

Galloway crossed her arms. "I don't know. Maybe you bought em in advance at the Fresh N Good. Kept em . . . maybe in a stash nearby, until—"

"Rachel, I . . . Even if I'd wanted to do that, I didn't *know* where the pig was going to lead us."

"Francis, did you shit in the woods?"

"No."

"Did you shit in these woods?!"

"No!" he wailed, like an accused child.

She glared at him, bobbing her foot. Then looked away. "Okay."

His voice rose. "What are you blaming *me* for? You said this would happen. We called the pig because of *you*."

"I didn't call anything."

"But your words. Your song. It drew them here from the woods. We sang and the beasts answered. I don't understand why you're mad at me."

She'd never seen him like this before. Infantile, indignant. She kept her arms crossed so tight she couldn't feel the blood in them anymore. She had to swallow a scared lump before she could manage to get the words out: "I *drew* them, Francis. I didn't draw them *to* us, I sketched them in class."

"And wrote their song," said Francis, stepping closer. "Told their stories. They're as much a part of this land as you are, Rachel."

"Come on."

"Renfield's blood beats through Burnskidde, sure. But so does something *else*. Something good. And it heard you call its name. It heard you call to the hair along its back, all the trees of the Shembelwoods and the

spine of the Billows. The beasts *heard* you, and came to us. We're blessed."
He laughed, took another step closer.

She stood her ground. Kept her prickling, numb arms crossed tight.
Her voice was small. "I'm just scared we're gonna be, like, implicated. I
didn't *want* anything to happen to Greg or Dom, I just . . . It's . . ." *Fuck
you, fuck you*, she told her body, as it began to tremble and leak. It made
her breath hitch, her voice wet, her eyes sting. *Don't you fucking cry.*

She gritted her teeth. Her voice shook. "I don't want anything bad to
happen."

Francis put his hands on her shoulders. "*We* are not hurting people,
Rachel. We are letting them blossom. Look." He stepped aside and gestured to the grove they'd created. It looked like a painting. So saccharine
and colorful it made Galloway ache.

"That was flesh," said Francis. "All of that was flesh, born and raised
under Renfield's curse. We turned it into good soil, gave birth to new
life. *You* did that. You should be proud, not scared. And if anyone tries to
claim we did something wrong, we have the chorus on our side. Here."

He knelt by the flowers and picked a whole bunch of them. He separated them into two handfuls of brilliant purple, copper, yellow, blue. He
presented them to her, smiling. "Have faith in the fog, Rachel. Behold the
beauty you've wrought."

She sniffed, then dipped her nose into the flowers. They smelled wonderful. She laughed, looked up at him. So handsome. His black jacket
shone darkly. His hair looked so soft.

"No one's ever gotten me flowers before," she said.

Francis smiled. He reached out and slid a tear away from her eye. So
gentle, she almost didn't feel his touch. He let the teardrop dangle off his
fingertip until it fell to the earth below.

"Every storm produces water," he said. "A seed must break for life to
grow."

She laughed again. "I should put that in the book."

"YOU ARE ALL AT THE VERY BEGINNING OF YOUR LIVES," CHIEF
Pittner said into the microphone. He gripped the podium with both

hands. "I know it might not feel that way. When you're seventeen, it feels like the world is ending all the time. But trust me, this is just a prologue. You want to lose a hand, a foot, during your *prologue*? No. This?" He held up the copy of the Gray Book Galloway had made after school (one for him and one for Dr. Eric, who accepted it from her with both hands and a greasy smile). Pittner shook the sheaf of inky paper at everyone. "*This* is something I cannot condone. If Greg Dring hadn't made it to the hospital in time that night, he could have died. Okay? Same for Dominic Zambrano," whose name he mispronounced. "There are doctors at Bartrick Regional calling me with concerns about a new trend amongst the teenagers here, and imagine their horror when I told them *adults* were involved as well."

In the bleachers of the gym, Tolley's class glanced around at each other with blank looks. It wasn't their fault adults had gotten involved. Tolley and the Drings could have stopped Greg and Dom at any time.

Pittner was practically yelling now, barking at the hundreds of teens assembled in the gym. "You think about the cost to your *families*—the medical cost, the emotional cost—before you get back in those woods and sing at a bunch of wild animals. Okay? Do not forget that we live in a dangerous part of the country. People are missing. Have you forgotten that?"

The students had not. In fact, they were tired of assemblies like this. Tired of staring apathetically at some adult standing right where Pittner was, under the cartoon gaze of Prospector Percy on the wall, yelling about how careful they all needed to be.

"Half a dozen people," Pittner went on. "Whisked into the woods without a trace just in the last three weeks. Okay? Keep that in mind when you're thinking this is just some fun new trend. Losing a hand isn't the same as getting a lip ring. This is dangerous, this can be deadly, and you need to be aware of that. Okay? And if anyone suggests to you that you 'offer' part of yourself to these animals, especially against your will? You call me immediately. Okay?"

He glared at them. They stared back, unmoved.

"Okay," he finished. He stepped away from the podium, and Dr. Eric slid into his place, chuckling amidst the awkward silence.

"Okay," he said, laughing and steepling his fingers. "Well. I hope this has been very informative. You may all return to third period. And have faith in the fog! Aha ha."

Pittner was standing, hands on hips, beside Safety Officer Wilson. When Dr. Eric said this, Wilson leaned over. "I kinda like the sound of that. Faith in the fog."

Pittner just growled.

Others glanced at Galloway as they filed slowly off the bleachers. Word was spreading. She blushed in the wake of their whispers.

"I actually do want a lip ring," said Galloway. "When you're seventeen, you can go without your parents, right? Because I don't know if my mom would be into it."

She looked at Emma. Emma was staring at the floor.

"Hey." Galloway nudged her. "You okay?"

Emma brought her head up. "Hm? Oh. Yeah. I'm okay." She frowned. "I'll tell you later. You'd look hot with a lip ring."

Emma continued to be distant and despondent over lunch. She kept eyeing the tv, where local news was interviewing Dom about receiving Greg's foot-born lamb. Dom was laughing as he led the lamb around his yard. He had a member of the American Society for the Prevention of Cruelty to Animals inspecting the lamb, reporting that it was in good health.

"The story is that a . . . creature puked this little guy up," said the ASPCA woman, holding the lamb. "I don't know if that's true, but we *have* seen some weird things around here. Animals eat all kinds of stuff. We pulled a full bike tire out of a golden retriever once. So I wouldn't be surprised, I guess. Them's the breaks." She laughed.

The feed cut to Mrs. Zambrano, smiling stiffly.

"How do you feel about all this?" the interviewer asked.

"Mixed," said Mrs. Zambrano. "I don't want my boy to lose any more limbs. But the lamb has been a blessing. She makes my sons happy." Footage of Dom's little brother, Tomas, playing with the lamb, giggling. "And I suppose she will offer us gifts. Wool and, one day, meat."

"I think it's a good omen," said Dom. "If something bad is really coming to Burnskidde on November twenty-sixth, then this is a sign that the Fogmonger and his beasts will protect us." Beaming into the camera.

Emma frowned until the news cut away to the weather. She didn't even glance at her tray of prison food.

"I'm gonna ask again just for shits and giggles," said Galloway. "Are you okay?"

"I'm fine," said Emma, still looking at the tv.

Galloway said nothing. She felt like a hurricane, everything around her beginning to swirl. And she was the eye.

"I WANT TO OFFER MYSELF," SAID ASHLEIGH.

Galloway blinked at her. "What? Why?"

"I don't know," said Ashleigh. "I want to see if the pigs like me."

"Ashleigh." Galloway was annoyed she even had to say this. "You have . . . great flesh. What are you talking about?"

"Do I?" Her voice rose. "Because I have this feeling lately like everyone's allergic to me. Jake doesn't want to talk to me anymore; he's always flirting with Emma. *You* don't want to be my friend. I don't know, I just . . . want to see. Dom says it didn't hurt that bad. And his mom is a nurse. We can invite her this time, have her ready with her, like, nurse stuff. And then maybe other adults will see it isn't dangerous, and Pittner will drop it."

"Pittner won't drop it if we get adults involved. You heard him."

"Adults are already involved," said Ashleigh. "My parents are in the same bowling league as Emma's parents, and they said the Drings can't stop talking about it. About how it's, like, a religious experience." She glanced at Tolley. "My mom doesn't even want me talking to you. She's just scared because hers was one of the cars that got stolen last week."

"Really? God, I'm sorry."

Ashleigh shook her head. "It's okay. I mean, she's fine, she's got insurance. I'm just saying it's scary how close this stuff is to us." She pointed at Galloway's notebook. "Can I . . . borrow that to show her? I think she could really use some guidance."

"It's . . . sort of the only copy I have. I could—"

"I can make a copy," Ashleigh cut her off. "After school, in the year-book office."

"You're in the yearbook?"

"I like making the layouts." Ashleigh jerked her chin at the notebook. "Bring it to the yearbook office after school. I'll make copies."

Mr. Tolley had granted them another period to work on their history projects, and their desks were all in clusters around the room. He hadn't spoken to Galloway since their conversation in the park, but he kept giving her these long, dark looks.

"You say my name?" Troy Pittner turned around in his desk.

"Yeah, we want to get your dad onboard with the chorus," said Ash-leigh. "Do you think he'd come, like, supervise if we wanted to have an-other event?"

"I think he'd insist on it," said Troy. "Could I come, too? I gotta see these pigs again."

"Sure," Ashleigh chirped. "Would you want to offer yourself?"

He shrugged. "They like thumbs, right? How many thumbs do I need?"

"I don't know," said Galloway warily. "Your dad was pretty harsh on me last time."

"He's harsh on everybody," said Troy bitterly. "He can kiss my ass. I'll tell him to back off. I'd love to see the look on his face when I grow an Xbox out of my thumbs."

Galloway did *not* want to see the look on his face. "That's not how it—"

"Pittner," said Mr. Tolley. "Hunt. Are we working or socializing?"

"Working," said Ashleigh, ducking her head.

"Good," said Tolley. He eyed Galloway, whacking his chalk against his knuckles. "Good . . ."

At the end of class, Jake caught her by the door. "Hey, I was wonder-ing. Can I do the next one, too? I heard you and Troy talking."

Galloway was reeling. "The next . . . what?"

"The next offering." He smiled. "I want to see if I can grow tomatoes. I *love* tomatoes."

IT WAS GREG'S FIRST NIGHT HOME FROM THE HOSPITAL, AND THE Drings threw a dinner party.

The Galloway twins played Russian roulette with their Nerf revolvers on the living room floor. Bobby shot himself in the temple and rolled his eyes, pretending to die. Teddy cackled.

Greg had his stump propped up on the coffee table. His cast was a labyrinth of signatures. He was the life of the party, laughing and joking around. Keith and Mr. Dring were drilling him with questions.

"It had *hands*?" Keith asked. "You felt hands grab you."

"More like little paws," said Greg.

"It's not little, though," said Dom on the other end of the couch. "That gluttonbat was *big*, yo."

"Big enough to steal a car?" asked Mr. Dring.

"Dad," Greg chided. "Beasts are friends."

Emma sat at his side, tight-lipped. Whenever Galloway asked if she was alright, she whispered automatically, "I'm fine. I'll tell you later." Causing Galloway more anxiety every time.

Just before dinner, the doorbell rang.

"Oh!" Mrs. Dring clapped. "I hope you don't mind, I invited some bowling league friends as well."

She opened the door to a short, twitchy woman with stiff hair. The woman sang, "Darlene!" They gave each other a squealing hug. The woman marched into the living room and jabbed a red-lacquered nail at Galloway. "You're Rachel. The one with the visions."

"Uh, yeah," said Galloway.

"I'm Edie, you go to school with my son." Edie spoke in short sentences that she clipped off with her teeth. "Willy Neglani. Do you have any classes with him? He's tall."

"Wait." Galloway blinked. "Wait, wait. You . . . Your son is Willy Neglani? Your name is Edie Neglani?"

"My maiden name is Pecorelli," said Edie Neglani.

Galloway's breath caught in her throat. She felt like she might cry. "Is your husband's name Edward Spaghetti?"

Eddie Spaghetti burst through the front door with a big bowl, hairier and sweatier than ever.

"I have the macaroni salad," he announced. Then his eyes landed on Galloway and he grinned. "Ahh. The artist."

"Let me find a picture of Willy," said Edie Neglani, yanking her phone out of her purse.

"That's okay, I . . . know your son," said Galloway.

Keith appeared at her side, shaking Eddie's hand. "Mr. Spaghetti."

Eddie chortled and dropped the bowl on the dining room table. He clasped Keith's hand with both of his meaty fists. "My favorite customer," he drawled.

"It's so great to have you here," said Keith. "We love your restaurant."

"And I love the money you *spend* at my restaurant." Eddie laughed.

"Anyway," said Edie, giving up on finding a picture of Willy. She chucked her phone back in her purse and said confidentially, "He's slow." She made a face. "Sorry, Willy, but it's true."

Suddenly, Nicole was there, too, introducing herself to Edie. Galloway seized the opportunity to slip away and grab Emma, clutching her arm, digging the nails into her skin.

"Ow," said Emma. "Huge ow."

"You let her invite Edward fucking Spaghettward?" Galloway hissed.

"He bowls," said Emma. "I don't know."

"You know he's my archnemesis."

"Rach, you have, like, three archnemeses."

"So?"

"If she becomes famous, I could display her art in the restaurant," Eddie Spaghetti was saying. He spread his hands. "Wow!"

"Kill me," Galloway moaned.

For dinner, everyone crowded around the table and ate burgers, bratwurst, beans, and mac salad.

"You will love my macaroni," said Eddie, spooning a massive amount onto Galloway's plate. She grimaced, and reminded herself to tell him noodles were forbidden in her world.

In the center of the table was a wildflower bouquet, picked directly from the clearing. Despite the feeling that she was swirling away, sweating amidst these laughing adults, Galloway felt a secret thrill knowing that there was a similar bouquet living in her locker. A bouquet she'd gotten from a *boy*. But the tightness in her chest outweighed that thrill by far.

Emma kept her head down for the entire meal. Eating without a word.

When the plates had been cleared away, Mrs. Dring presented them all with a pie. She placed it on the table like it was a holy relic.

"Raspberry," she said, with a gleam in her eye. She popped a metal server through its crust. Blood oozed out from within. "From our Dominic."

The pie was delicious.

"Those berries taste so *fresh*," said Keith.

"Truly, the best I've ever had," Mr. Dring agreed. "In theory, if we can get all this from one hand, imagine what we could get out of a whole arm."

"Lotsa spaghetti," said Eddie.

The adults laughed.

Greg lifted his glass of water. "To Dom. Good flesh for good earth."

"Is that your prayer?" Nicole asked.

"Yes," said Galloway. She lifted her glass, too, and everyone followed suit. "Flesh to earth. Man to beast. Have faith in the fog. And then we sing. Oooooohhh."

They all sang with her. Teddy and Bobby threw their heads back and moaned at the ceiling. The adults glanced at each other, excited and proud of their children. Nicole made a spooky, "Oooh!" Waggling her fingers.

"My grill," said Eddie. "In our backyard. Stolen!" He snapped his fingers. "We suffer just like the others."

"Mmhmm," said Edie, nodding. "That's right."

"So, tell me," Eddie turned to Galloway, "about this fog."

"ALRIGHT, WHAT THE FUCK IS GOING ON WITH YOU?" GALLOWAY demanded as soon as they were alone in Emma's room.

Emma sat on the edge of her bed with a sigh. She stared into her lap.

"Emma."

Emma shook her head, looked up. "Do you think . . . the pigs would know my mom and dad?"

"What? What do you mean?"

"Do you think they'd recognize them?" Emma asked. "Like, would they be able to tell if they were good flesh versus . . . something else?"

Galloway drifted down onto the bed next to Emma. She was light-headed. "What . . . else would they be?"

Emma rolled her eyes and gave Galloway a pointed look.

Galloway shook her head. "No. Come on. No way."

"Why not? Isn't the whole point to tell bad flesh from good?"

"Because they're *adults*, Em. They'd have to want to do it, and even if they did, Pittner really gave me shit about last time."

"People are willing. I mean, how many volunteers did you get just to-day?" Emma ticked them off on her fingers. "Ashleigh, Jake, Troy. Plus, the Neglanis seemed really excited to hear about the Fogmonger."

"Come on."

"I have a gut sense, Rach," said Emma. "I know you think I'm nuts, but they say always trust your gut, especially in Renfield. And my gut says something is *wrong* with them. Look how social they're being! I . . . I want to do another offering."

"No." Galloway shook her head. "No, everyone needs to stop. Em, the fucking *police* told me to lay off. He asked for a copy of the book, I think to make sure there's not, like, violent shit in there."

"But there isn't. You don't have anything to worry about. We'd get my parents to volunteer."

"No."

"Just like Greg and Dom."

"No!"

Emma threw up her hands. "Why won't you believe me? Why don't you even want to *see*? If the pigs don't want to eat them, doesn't that mean they're not flesh at all? And isn't that—"

"Emma, your parents aren't fucking plants!"

Silence. Emma looked gravely wounded, picking at her cuticles on the edge of her bed, staring at Galloway through deep-bagged eyes.

"Look," she said. "If your whole thing is about protecting and helping the town, then help and protect *me*. I know someone hurt my parents. So are you gonna help me or not?"

They stared at each other for a long time.

"For the record," said Galloway, "I think this is a bad idea. It's all becoming too real. We don't even know if the things that attacked Dom and Greg were *my* things."

"They didn't *attack*, Rach." Emma snorted. "And it's been real for a while. You just need to have faith in the fog."

"A PINKIE FINGER," SAID EMMA. "IT DOESN'T HAVE TO BE ANY MORE than that."

Jeff and Darlene Dring sat on the couch in their living room, staring up at their daughter with confused, surprised expressions.

"Sorry, why do you want us to do this, again?" Mr. Dring asked.

"It's important to our faith," said Emma firmly. "To prove you're good flesh."

"Why do we need to prove that, honey?" Mrs. Dring asked. She glanced at Galloway.

"She wants you to be a part of this," said Galloway. She leaned against the wall at a distance.

"Sweetie, we can be a part of your club without hurting ourselves." Mrs. Dring laughed nervously. "Can't we?"

"It didn't hurt," said Greg. He was in an armchair, stump up on the ottoman. "I mean, it does at first, but it goes away quickly."

Mr. Dring cleared his throat, adjusted his glasses. "Did someone put you up to this?"

"No, Dad," said Emma.

"Was this Rachel's idea or yours?"

"Hers," said Galloway quickly.

The Drings looked at each other, then their daughter. The look in Emma's eyes was painfully earnest and cold.

"Well," Mr. Dring sighed, patting his wife's knee. He shrugged. "One finger couldn't hurt. If it means that much for us to support all this."

"I do like being supportive." Mrs. Dring smiled. "I'll make my potato salad."

FRANCIS RENTED THE PARK AGAIN FOR THE FOLLOWING EVENING, with the caveat that Pittner and Mrs. Zambrano be in attendance.

The next day was madness. By the time Galloway woke up and came downstairs, her mother was already on the phone. When she saw Galloway, she clapped her hands.

"This is going to be so much fun tonight," she said, phone cradled against her shoulder. "You excited?"

"Totally," said Galloway.

Nicole went back to the phone: "Yeah, I'll grab the chips. I'll make my sangria, too."

"Ohh, the sangria," Keith crooned from the couch, where he was playing sudoku horizontally, socked feet in the air. He sang, "Sangria, my sweet. You're worth every heartburn to me . . ."

This scene brought a deep thunderous ache to Galloway's belly. She still couldn't silence the small part of her that wanted to yell, *Don't*.

But they were adults. They were planning a party. How dangerous could it be?

On the bus, Galloway listened to the White Stripes on her iPod. "Icky Thump" matched the excited, grinding rumble in her stomach as she stared out the window. There was Seth Brenner again, stapling posters to telephone poles. Dozens of them, all over town. "REMEMBER THEM," slapped across pictures of his son, smiling in grainy black-and-white.

Maybe a big party was exactly what this town needed. To forget, just for an evening, the elusive vise of Renfield's curse.

Her head continued to spin for the rest of the day. By the time she got her backpack from her locker, she was on autopilot.

"My dad says you made him sing a song."

Galloway jumped, twirling around and putting her back to her locker.

Willy Neglani had been standing behind her. He gaped at her with his acne scars and green braces. Much like his father, he was more bull than man. He had short blond hair that he gelled straight up. He breathed through his mouth, and was, as his mother, Edie, had said, quite tall. If he ever decided to play football, Galloway believed he could stand still and the other guys would crack their own skulls running into him.

"I didn't *make* him sing, Willy," she said. She shut her locker and hustled toward her bus. "He did it on his own. Your mom, too."

He trailed after her. "We had math together last year. We sat adjacent. Do you remember?"

"I *know*, Willy." She walked faster, and he walked faster to catch up to her, breathing hard in her ear from above.

"Is your group like church?" he asked. "I don't like church. My mom makes me do youth group."

"It's like choir practice with stories," said Galloway quickly. "I mean, yeah, I guess it's like church. But cooler. There's monsters."

"Monsters are cool. What kind?"

"Nice ones. Not the ones who took your grill. Look." She had arrived at the side door leading out to her bus. She spun around to face Willy. He skidded to a halt very close to her.

"We're having another party tonight," she said. "I'm sure your mom already told you, but if you want to be a part of our chorus instead of church, you and your folks should come."

He shook his head sadly. "I hate church."

"I know, Willy. This'll be more fun. There's pigs."

Willy brightened. "Pigs are smart!"

"They are." She darted outside.

THE TIKI TORCHES WERE RELIT. THE TABLES WERE RELAID. THE woods were dark and deep beyond Horridge Park. The wall of brambles flickered sharp bloodstained shadows onto the branches. Francis stared longingly at Horridge House, its shadowed tower looming over all.

The chorus had doubled since their last offering. More kids from school. Isabella Zambrano brought two EMTs. They stood uncertainly by the dip, chewing and flipping through copies of the Gray Book.

Greg and Dom were surrounded by people who wanted to meet the miracle lamb and ask what it was like to be partially eaten alive.

"Fucking awesome," Greg told them from his wheelchair throne.

"We're like heroes, dude," said Dom, laughing.

Ashleigh had brought her parents, as had Jake Mendez and several others. The Galloway twins were sword-fighting with unused tiki torches. Nicole was chatting with Safety Officer Wilson. No Mr. Tolley, but other teachers had come. Dr. Eric stood with them, hands in the pockets of his peacoat, shoulders hunched against the dark autumn chill.

Ashleigh was handing out slick pages of photocopied material to everyone in the park. *THE GRAY BOOK*, in big black Sharpie letters across the cover of the stapled sheaves of paper, going out into everyone's hands.

Galloway no longer worried they would laugh at her. She saw wonder and fear in their eyes as they examined her drawings of poo-pigs, glutton-bats, the Fogmonger . . .

Edie Neglani dumped a bowl onto the table next to Galloway. "Hi, Darlene," she cooed.

"Hi!" Mrs. Dring gave her a big hug. "What did you bring? You didn't have to bring anything."

"It's my macaroni salad," said Edie. "It's Willy's favorite. Ya know, I—"

"No!" Galloway sliced her hand through the air. "No fuckin noodles of any kind allowed. Haven't you read the book? The Fogmonger forbids it."

Edie and Mrs. Dring glanced at each other. Edie shrugged and said, "Well, if the Fogmonger says so, we don't have to do any pasta. I'll tell Eddie to bring the chicken cutlets out of the car instead. Do you know how much that man eats?"

Galloway slipped away. She smiled and nodded her way past throngs of people. She passed Dr. Eric standing before Ashleigh, grinning with his fingers steepled. "You're in cheer, yes? Aren't those new uniforms great? They're a bit shorter in the front . . ."

Galloway felt a little breathless. How had she managed to get all these people to indulge her? People she didn't even know. *Why?* She peered up at the branches of a nearby tree. Where was the bucket of pig's blood?

Where was the slideshow of embarrassing baby photos? Where was the other fucking *shoe*?

She felt a hand on her shoulder. She jerked away—and Francis was offering her more flowers.

"Again?" she asked. "Francis . . ." They smelled even better than before.

"They just keep growing." He grinned. "It's incredible, Rach. And look at all these people you've gathered to us. The Fogmonger's chorus is expanding *beautifully*. This should be a strong-enough group already to greet his blessing on November twenty-sixth. Imagine if we could get the entire *town* to sing with us. The Monger's breath could bless everybody!"

"That would be something," Galloway muttered, looking around at all these people, standing in the cold on a Friday night with her. She wanted badly to ask him, *Do you think this is a good idea?* But really, what would he say?

"Break a leg," said Francis, before kissing her forehead and sauntering off, and suddenly, she was on fire.

She basked in the glow of that kiss for a long moment before Willy Neglani galumphed up to her. His peach-fuzzed upper lip was stained red by Hawaiian Punch. "Where's the macaroni salad?"

"Jesus, fuck off, Willy," she snapped.

"Okay, everyone!" Nicole was clapping her hands in the middle of the party. "Let's get started! I want to thank you all for coming here tonight and bringing food. We're all really excited to share this with everyone. I'm going to turn it over to Rachel now. She's going to tell us a little bit about what we're doing here, then she'll lead us in the offering. Rach?"

She stepped aside, clapping. A smattering of applause followed Galloway as she took the patch of dirt that seemed to be center stage. She waved awkwardly at everyone. "Hello. Uh . . . Yeah. Thank you for coming. Um." She looked around. Slimy Dr. Eric with his steepled fingers and squinty eyes. Eddie Spaghetti breathing like a sweating bear.

And Francis, smiling supportively at her.

"This group started a couple weeks ago," she went on. "I want to thank everyone for supporting me and . . . not laughing at me. And thank you, Francis, for encouraging me."

Francis smiled at her and accepted his own small scattering of applause. He had his hands shoved deep in the pockets of his trench coat.

Galloway held up her gray notebook and said, "I numbered the pages in here so you can follow along with your copies. Um. I'm going to talk to you tonight about some of the main ideas this book discusses. Let's start with the pigs. Everyone, open your gospels to page three."

Galloway preached to them about the beasts, and the Fogmonger's arrival. How his breath blew away sickness and poisoned the knifemen, the nonbelievers. How he could restore every ill that had happened to their town, if only they had faith.

When she was done, there was silence. Everyone stared at her.

Teddy burped. Bobby cackled.

"Where was Addekkea again?" Edie Neglani asked, raising her hand.

"North of here," said Galloway.

"And when was this?" Edie asked.

"Sixteen hundreds," said Emma.

"Explains why I never heard of it," said Edie, crossing her arms.

"Addekkea," said Dr. Eric, peering at Galloway over his steepled fingertips. "Is that Dutch?"

"Yes," said Galloway confidently.

"And the beasts," said Keith, raising his hand. "They're . . . magical?"

"Kind of. The journals call them miracles." Galloway shrugged.

Keith nodded his approval and looked at Nicole, who gave Galloway a big thumbs-up.

"Okay." Galloway turned to the Drings. "You ready?"

"Are you sure it doesn't hurt?" Mrs. Dring asked softly.

"I don't know, Mrs. Dring. I'm sorry."

"It'll be fine," said Mr. Dring, holding her hand. "It's just a finger. And if this is what Emma needs to see that we still love her, then so be it."

"Okay," said Galloway. "Let's begin."

She led them through the brief prayer she'd bullshit just a few weeks ago. Everyone stood around in reverent silence, listening to her like this was real, like this wasn't some game she couldn't stop. She watched from outside herself as the Drings knelt at the edge of the light and slid their arms into the wall of trees together, calling into the dark: "Beasts of the woods! Accept our offering. We offer good flesh for good earth. Please hear our song, and accept our bodies. Ooooooohhh."

Gradually, the song spread across the clearing. Edie Neglani elbowed her husband to sing. Keith gave a token "Oooh." Dr. Eric was the last to open his mouth, the last to take up the call. "Oooooohhh."

They sang, and sang, and after a long time—there was a rustling in the undergrowth.

The newcomers stepped back in alarm. They glanced at each other, at Galloway. Pittner, at the edge of the clearing, unfolded his arms, hand drifting toward the gun at his hip.

Everyone held their breath. And listened.

In the silence, softly at first, then louder, came the sounds of beasts. Hot breath, snorffling and oinking.

"If these pigs are fuckin real, I'll shit a brick," Pittner muttered.

"Jeffrey," whispered Mrs. Dring. "Something is . . . sniffing me."

"Don't startle it," Mr. Dring hissed back.

The sounds of sniffing, snuffling, snorting went on for quite some time. Something in the darkness was rooting around in the thorns. Hot breath rose from the brambles, steaming about the Drings.

Then they heard the thing—sneeze. It paused. And squealed in alarm.

The twins clapped their hands to their ears. People gasped. Emma's face went paper white. The Drings looked around, panicked.

"Wait a minute," said Mrs. Dring. "What does that mean?"

The thing squealed louder. High, piercing. A crashing in the undergrowth as it dashed away from the park, screeching so loudly Galloway could barely hear Mrs. Dring shouting, "What does that mean?!"

"Bad flesh!" Emma cried, pointing at her. "Bad flesh!"

"Hold on," said Galloway. "Wait."

"Bad flesh!" Francis echoed, pointing. "The pigs rejected them!"

"Now, hold on," said Mr. Dring, struggling to his feet.

Francis and Emma started to chant, "Bad flesh, bad flesh!" And to Galloway's horror, others took up the cry as well. The children, the teenagers, all pointed and chanted, "Bad flesh, bad flesh!" The adults didn't chant. Not yet. Like Galloway, they were frozen.

"What do we do?" Mrs. Dring asked no one in particular, standing and looking all around with widened eyes. "What does this mean?!"

Galloway watched Emma's shoulders heaving, her lips curling. Emma pointed and screamed, "Bad flesh, bad flesh!"

"Emma!" her mother cried.

"Gregory, talk to her," said Mr. Dring.

"She was right," Greg breathed. "Jesus Christ. You're not human."

"Not human?" Mr. Dring spat. "What in god's name are you talking about?"

Mrs. Dring reached for her daughter. "Emma, please."

"Don't touch me." Emma jerked away from her.

The park was full of noise. People chanting, crying out. Pittner looking around wildly, trying to figure out what he should do, what was happening. The thing in the woods continued to squeal, and it occurred to Galloway only then, only when it was too late, that it wasn't just complaining.

It was raising an alarm.

"Wait," she said. "Stop. We have to stop."

But no one heard her.

"This is madness!" Mr. Dring yelled. "Emma, look at us."

The chant went on. "Bad flesh, bad flesh!"

Galloway stepped forward, but she felt a hand on her shoulder. Francis pulling her back.

"This is the way of the beasts," he said.

"They're our friends' parents."

"No," he said. "They're something else."

"Are you fucking joking?" She jerked away from his hand. "This is insane. I'm calling this off."

"Emma, please." Mrs. Dring gripped the front of her daughter's shirt. "Don't do this."

Pittner stepped up. "Alright, let's all calm down."

"Get off me!" Emma cried, shoving at Mrs. Dring's clawing hands. "Get off! You're not my mom! Not my mom!" She shoved her hard, so that Mrs. Dring landed on her back in the dirt.

"Whoa!" Pittner launched himself between Emma and Mrs. Dring, hands out, peacekeeping. Mrs. Dring stumbled to her feet, took a step forward—and something behind her burst out of the trees. It slammed into her back, gripping her shoulders. When it screamed, lit flickering from the torches all around, Galloway could see what it was, and she wanted to scream back at it in answer.

A large gargoyle beast. Red skin; wide, sharp wings; and a long, barbed tail. It had short legs; muscular, sinewy arms; and paws with three fingers each, clawed and terrible. It snarled its pug-nosed, half-bat, half-human face at the crowd, sneering and dripping drool into Mrs. Dring's hair. It raked its claws gently along her cheeks, caressing her. Flicked its tail back and forth. It spread its wings to their full extent, far larger than seemed possible, and screamed again.

This was a far cry from the adorable smiling bats she'd drawn . . . what? Weeks ago? Years? No, the gluttonbat perched on Mrs. Dring's shoulders was nightmarish. It glared at them, claiming Darlene and growling at Pittner, who had his gun out at his side, very still.

Nobody moved.

Mrs. Dring trembled. Her voice shook as the bat's tail curled about her throat. "What . . . what do I . . . What is it . . . ?"

Mr. Dring put out a hand, slowly. "Darlene. Don't. Move."

"What do I do, Jeff?" she cried. "Oh my god, what do I—"

The bat screeched, dug its hands under Mrs. Dring's armpits, and pulled. Her arms popped out of their sockets and flew through the air as the bat tossed them into the shadows. Mrs. Dring screamed. Pittner fired at the bat, *bam bam*, twice, fast. It roared at him and lifted Mrs. Dring into the air, claws buried into her open shoulders, wounds spurting dark fluid. It dropped her, then gripped her legs as she screamed, "No, please god, don't!" It grabbed one leg in each hand and tore them sideways, splitting her body like a wishbone. She was still screaming, gurgling, as the bat twisted her head off her shoulders with a sickening *crack*, and chucked it at Chief Pittner. Warm arterial spray spurted across Galloway's face, blinding her. She heard another gunshot, Mr. Dring screaming, "Oh my god!" Then more twisting, tearing. Mr. Dring's own horrible wet gasps.

She swiped the blood away and managed to see again just as the gluttonbat was flying away with Mr. Dring's limbless torso.

The clearing was still, silent. Pieces lay steaming on the ground. Chunks and pools of dark shadow.

Edie Neglani vomited on her husband's shoes. Willy stood dumbfounded, macaroni salad half-chewed in his mouth.

"Come!" Francis cried. He yanked a tiki torch out of the ground. "We have to follow the bat! It can turn ill flesh into useful meat. Greg's lamb is proof of this. Come! Oooooohhh!"

Suddenly, kids were shoving Galloway, grabbing torches, singing, following Francis into the dark. The bat screeched again overhead as the kids who had been there for the first offering tore across the park, following fast, all of them singing, "Oooooohhh."

Willy Neglani shoved past his parents, carrying another torch, eyes locked on the woods. "Oooooohhh!"

Galloway's mother was clutching at her, clawing at her face. "Oh my god, are you okay? Oh my god." Smothering her against her chest. "Oh my god, what *was* that? Jesus."

"The bats," said Galloway, muffled against her mother's bosom. "They came . . ."

The twins jumping around her, shouting, "That was awesome! Is that what was supposed to happen? Wow!" They started chanting: "Call the beasts! Call the beasts! Oooooohhh! Oooooohhh!" Jumping up and down.

"Guys, stop!" Galloway shoved past them.

Emma was smearing blood off her face, spitting it out of her mouth, when Galloway reached her.

"Are you okay?" she asked, not sure what else to say.

Nicole pushed past and started pawing at Emma's face with a towel. Isabella Zambrano was there with bandages, Pittner was shouting at people. Keith was yelling at the twins to "Stop screaming, *please*!" Pandemonium in the park. Greg hobbled over on crutches, ghastly pale.

"Emma, are you okay?" Galloway asked again.

"What can we do?" Nicole kept asking, swiping at Emma's face. "What do we do?"

"Stop," Emma gasped, choking and coughing. "Stop! Look."

But Nicole seemed broken, stuck. "Honey, what can we do? What do we do?"

"Stop!" Emma shoved her away. She blinked down at her hands, her breath coming in short, sharp stabs. She held up her palms, trembling, and Galloway could see for the first time that the gore splashed across her, across the ground—was green. Not red. No bits of sinew or muscle tissue or human bone. No strewn organs, or anything other than the dark green fluid of a severed plant.

"I told you," Emma rasped. She began to laugh, *hard*. She held up her hands for everyone to see. "I fucking told you! The pigs know! The beasts know us all!"

"We need to get you to a hospital," said Pittner, holstering his gun. "You're in shock."

"I've never been clearer in my fucking life," Emma spat at him. She stabbed a finger in his chest. "*You* did this. You never caught her. You never saved anybody. You can't protect this town. You never have. I'll tell everybody," she wheezed, still laughing. "I'm gonna tell fucking *everybody* that you never did a goddamn thing. The Botanist . . . is still out there!"

Everything that happened next happened very fast.

NEW ADDEKKEA, OCTOBER 2019

Meeting the Miracles

On the edge of town, the man-made jungle was thick, and deep-drooping willow branches brushed along the top of Durwood's head. She ducked under them while Urquhart strolled easily, letting the tendrils of the trees whisper across his face.

"They reconstructed it from memory," he explained as they walked. "I'm sure there are small details inside that aren't quite accurate, but what can you do?"

"Wow," said Durwood. She was trying to be cool, but she kept wringing her bike's handlebars.

Urquhart glanced at her. "I'd try not to look so shocked when you meet them. We've isolated ourselves from the world because, for one thing, they don't . . . know."

"Know what? That they're the centerpiece of the most famous crime in the county?"

"Yes," said Urquhart, "as far as they're concerned, it's still 1928."

"Really? So they just had a nice Christmas and woke up here?"

"That, they're not so sure about. But it was one of the first decisions the other Speakers and I made, that we would call them simply *revived*. We didn't think the mental strain would be worth it to them."

"Uh-huh. Revived through Galloway's sacrifice."

"Yes. To prove the curse had reversed itself here in the wake of the Fogmonger's blessing." Urquhart smiled into a faceful of branches.

Durwood was sweating. "But what are they . . . Like, *how*?"

Urquhart smiled dreamily. "Questions leave no room for faith, Ms. Durwood."

"I bet if I asked the right ones, they wouldn't leave a lot of room for the Botanist, either."

Urquhart stopped. He turned to her. The one eye blinked.

"Why would you say that?" he asked. "You must know that name carries a weight of fear here."

"I'm just trying to understand."

Urquhart clicked his teeth, considering.

"She died," he said. "During the blessing of '09. Poisoned, along with the rest of those who did not follow the way of the beasts. She did not *regrow* the Renfields, if that's what you're getting at."

"How do you know?" Durwood asked.

"Because I have faith," said Urquhart, losing his patience a little. "Everyone who refused the Fogmonger's song perished that day. You should have *seen* the stacks of corpses. I assume the Botanist, wherever she may have been, was no exception. We haven't had any ridiculous rumors of plant-people in our community for a decade now, and how *good* it feels to be free from that shadow. Another thing for which I am grateful to the Fogmonger." He cocked his head. "Is that really why you're here? Chasing a ghost?"

"One of her old experiments attacked me a few nights ago," said Durwood. "I thought maybe if the tunnel had been opened—"

"How did you know it was her experiment?"

"Because we have a case file that links it to her."

"Mm. But you only believe that because somebody else *told* you that. Because it was in your Shelter archive."

"So?"

"So I believe what I believe. We all believe what we are shown *first*, Ms. Durwood." He smiled. His monocle gleamed brilliantly amongst the sun and leaves. "Your faith in the Guard is as subjective as my faith in the fog. There's no reason to be so confrontational about it."

Durwood gave an unhappy grunt.

"Besides." Urquhart turned away, began walking again. "Even the

Botanist's experiments were said to have aged over time. The Renfields do not age. They were revived post-human."

"Post-human." Durwood scoffed. "So they think it's been 1928 for ten years."

Urquhart laughed lightly. "I know, can you imagine? Anyway, here we are."

They emerged from the trees to find a house sitting at the top of a tall-grass-covered hill, at the end of a winding drive similar to Urquhart's. Perhaps all New Addekkean royalty had matching gravel drives. This house also had a matching ravenknight just outside its front door. The raven cawed when it saw them, and Victoria cawed in answer.

But Durwood wasn't concerned with the ravens or the driveway. She was intimately familiar with Renfield family lore. She knew their middle names, knew what the coroner's report said about each one. She had studied all the crime scene photos many times, and she knew the objects in every inch of every frame. She had even seen some of those objects in real life. She'd met the man who bought the Renfield refrigerator at auction, and she'd seen the dark slash of Adelaide's blood across its face.

She knew every board of this home. *This* home. The one she was currently fucking looking at.

Her breath left her body as she took it all in. Just like the pictures, the house had two stories, but there was no barn in back. The walls were dark unpainted wood, but the house itself was not uninviting. Dried cornstalks and sunflowers were woven together and bent into arches around the door, surrounded by small pumpkins, orange and white, like a beautiful autumnal bouquet. There were wildflowers sprouting alongside the driveway, butterflies and bees humming and dancing amongst the sunbeams of a warm October day.

Black-and-white images flashed through her mind. Adelaide's brains scattered in shreds in the kitchen sink. May on the toilet, slumped over her knees. The mess in the crib that had been a little girl.

She turned to Urquhart. "I want to speak to them alone, if that's alright."

He faltered. It was clearly not alright. On his shoulder, Victoria grumbled, puffing out her feathers to make herself larger.

"Why?" Urquhart asked. "To cut them and see if they bleed green?"

Several snarky things came to mind at once. She swallowed all of them, digging the heel of her hand into her bike handle to ground herself. "This is a miracle, Mr. Urquhart. I want to experience it by myself. Let me experience your faith. Plus, you have an eye on me, don't you?" She nodded at the ravenknight up the hill.

Urquhart tilted his head back, regarding her with his monocle. "Can you find your way back to the estate if you—"

"Yes. Thank you."

"Well," he said. "Alright. *Don't* antagonize them. I'll check on you soon." He wandered off through the willows, Victoria flapping in his wake.

Durwood took a beat. She looked up at the house, squinting against the sun. It seemed like a mirage.

She stepped up carefully to the front door and paused. Suddenly, her heart wasn't working right, like one of its valves had sealed itself shut. It thuddered and squeeshed in an irregular rhythm that made her rub at her sternum and take a deep, shuddering breath.

She laid her bike in the grass next to the stoop, adjusted her go-bag on her shoulder. She put up a hand to knock. Hesitated. Then rapped lightly. Brushed the back of her hand off on her pants, stepped back.

She looked at the ravenknight. The giant brass hood and the raven in its cage both stared at her. The knight was missing a hand. Its birdcage swung slightly on a hook. She could hear it breathing. *Whoo. Sniff. Whoo.*

"How ya doin?" she said.

The knight did not respond.

"Cool." She glanced around. Such a nice day. All sunny and quiet, aside from the ravenknight's breathing. No cars, no motors. It was easy to see, for a flash, why people liked it here.

Muffled footsteps from within. A thick, heavy deadbolt undone, and the great click of a well-fitted door handle turning. The high whine of the door swinging inward . . .

Durwood had only ever seen two photographs of Adelaide Renfield. In one, Adelaide was surrounded by her family. This was the family portrait Lawrence had splurged on in Lillian, several weeks before they died. They all stared into the camera as one. Adelaide, the matriarch;

Henry, the young son; and Robert, the doomed four-year-old, the poor child who would end up shot in the back, sprawled in the snow, dragged into the barn, and dashed across the wall in a mockery of art. He gazed at the camera with lips slightly parted, as if the life had already breathed out of his body. Next to him, May Renfield, the sixteen-year-old daughter, whom Durwood knew admittedly little about. Then the baby, only a month old. Adelaide and Lawrence had never agreed upon a name, and Durwood always wondered if that was because he knew. Maybe Lawrence knew, far in advance, what he was going to do to them all on December 20, 1927.

For ninety-two years, the Renfields had been dead.

So then how was Adelaide Renfield, in her housedress, with her hair done up in a frizzy bun, standing in front of Durwood now, in 2019? In fucking Technicolor?

"Hello," said Adelaide. Her voice was light and a bit smoky, as if she'd been a lounge singer in another life. She was wiping her hands on a dish towel. "Can I help you?"

"Uhh," said Durwood. "I . . . Uhh."

Adelaide frowned and glanced around outside. "Did you take that bicycle all the way up here? It's a big hill."

"I walked," said Durwood stiffly.

"You must be ill," said Adelaide. "You *sound* ill, I must say."

"I'm feeling a little ill for sure . . . ma'am." Mumbling. Lips numb, heart thudding, thudding.

Adelaide squinted out at the day. "It's so hot out. Do you need water?"

"I . . . No." Durwood shook her head, snapped out of it. "I'm sorry. My name is Guardian Durwood. I'm with the County Guard." She held up her coin.

Adelaide frowned at it. "The who?"

Durwood blinked. "Right. No. I'm . . . We're police. We—"

"Ohh!" Adelaide realized something. "You know Mark. All-Speaker said we might have another outworlder coming in. How exciting. It's such a pleasure to meet you. I'm Adelaide."

"Nice to meet you," said Durwood through trembling lips. "You met Mark?"

"Only briefly. He gave us the same expression *you're* giving me."

Durwood laughed like someone had just punched her stomach. "Yeah, I hear you emerged from a mine."

Adelaide laughed, too. What a pretty laugh. She had pretty eyes, laugh lines. Durwood stared at the small pulse in the vein in her neck.

"That's right," said Adelaide. "I know it's a strange story, but we all fell asleep on Christmas and . . . woke up here, in the mine. He told us our old home was gone, the rest of the valley sealed away. Sad." She frowned. "Where is Mark now?"

"Missing, ma'am. I'm here to find him."

Adelaide nodded gravely. "I told him not to be out after nightfall. Sometimes, the beasts can be . . . aggressive in their duty to protect the town. If you haven't heard from Mark in some time, I sadly wouldn't be surprised if they hadn't . . . Well."

Durwood's heart sank. She'd had little reason to hope that Mark was still alive, and yet . . . she had anyway.

Adelaide smiled. "Why don't you come in?"

She stood aside and Durwood could see into the house. So much wood. Polished wooden floors, wooden ceiling, paneled wooden walls, wooden stairs leading up. Grandfather clock, wooden furniture. She could see the kitchen beyond. A flash in her mind: Adelaide sprawled across the kitchen floor. Her face no more than a patchy red mess, teeth blossoming outward from shattered gums, tongue lolling to the side, torn down the middle. One hand lay over her chest, the other lay in a dark crimson pool along the floor.

All this *house* inside, and none of it stained. All of it whole, pure, and filled with sun.

Durwood's breath hitched in her throat. Her voice came out small.

"Thank you," she said as she stepped over the threshold. She watched the door shut on the ravenknight behind her, tracking her with its lifeless metal eyes.

The only sound inside was the ticking of the grandfather clock in the living room. She couldn't see it, but she knew *exactly* where it was. If she thought about it, she could probably name every item in the house and its exact location. She found herself holding her breath, not wanting to disturb even the air. She felt, truly, like she'd stepped back in time, like she had the power to alter coming events, like Lawrence would be right around that corner with his shotgun, and if Durwood could say the right thing, she could stop the future, she could save her mother, save Tom and Mark, save everybo—

"Can I get you something to drink?" Adelaide asked. Her smile nearly exploded Durwood's heart. She wanted to grab this woman and shake her. *You're gonna fucking die!*

"No thank you," said Durwood brightly. "Where can we sit? I have some questions about Mark, if you don't mind."

"Of course. Here." Adelaide guided her into the living room, where Henry was sitting in an armchair, reading an old copy of *Treasure Island*.

Startled, Durwood made a guttural sound, "Whoa dafffuck."

"Henry, this is Miss Durwood," said Adelaide.

"Hello," said Henry, without looking up.

"Would you mind giving us a moment?" Adelaide asked in her sweet mother-voice.

"Mom, I'm almost at the end of the chapter," Henry whined.

"You can finish it, just finish it upstairs."

Henry sighed and closed the book around his finger. He gave Durwood a sour look before he slumped out of the room. Durwood watched him go. Watched his little knickers and his little socks with their familiar stripes. His socks were blue. She'd never guessed his socks were blue. She'd only ever seen them in black-and-white.

"Please." Adelaide gestured to the armchair he'd just vacated. "Sit."

Durwood slid uneasily onto the chair. She ran her hands over the arm-rests, all the brass buttons holding the red cushion to the frame. It was still warm. "Tell me about Mark."

"Well, he came by about a week ago," said Adelaide. "He talked with each of us for a bit, asked some questions that didn't . . . really make sense to me. I was surprised we even had someone from out of town so soon after we'd unsealed the tunnel, but I guess someone was bound to come through."

"Hm." Durwood rubbed her hands on the armrests.

Adelaide leaned forward, clutching her hands in her lap. "I'm sorry about your friend, Miss Durwood. You seem overwhelmed."

"I am sort of overwhelmed."

"*Do* you want some water?"

"Oh, I'm okay." Drinking Renfield water—even "miracle" Renfield water—seemed like a bad idea. "Is your, uh . . . Is your husband home?"

"He's in town, but he should be back soon," said Adelaide.

Durwood nodded. She hoped to be gone before Lawrence showed up. Seeing two of the Renfields alive and well was enough for one day.

"What questions did Mark ask you?" Durwood asked. "What did *he* want to know?"

"Oh, how long we'd been living here, how we ended up here . . . I told him it's not very exciting. We've lived here for about a year."

"Lotta changing seasons for one year."

Adelaide frowned and gazed distantly at the ceiling. "Yeeess. I suppose it *has* been a long year . . ." Her mouth hung open, and she gave the impression of a computer rebooting itself. "I turn thirty-eight this year."

"And you're gorgeous. But what's the last thing you remember before the mine?"

"Christmas," Adelaide whispered.

She paused.

Then blinked, and smiled. "Are you sure you don't want something to drink? We have this tea—"

A screech cut through the air. Durwood was on her feet, talon out, in less than a second.

Adelaide rose from the couch and clicked her tongue. "That's just little Robin." She ran her hands over her face and sighed. "She's been crying *so* much lately. If you could just excuse me for a moment."

"I'll come with you," said Durwood. She flexed her talon back into her arm before Adelaide could see it. She shivered. *Of course it's only the baby. It's only Lawrence upstairs bludgeoning the baby as we speak.*

"Lovely," said Adelaide. "Please. This way."

She led Durwood up the creaking wooden stairs. Durwood eyed the open bathroom door as they passed. The bathtub, the toilet. A flash: poor teenage May, slumped to the side, pouring herself out into the tub through a colony of buckshot holes.

She shivered again as they went down the short hall to the master bedroom. The bed was perfectly made. Several windows let in sun. It was an achingly cozy little room. One you could sink into for entire long afternoons.

The crib in the corner was a tall, white-painted thing. From within its wooden bars, something squalled and screamed, louder and higher pitched than any baby Durwood had ever known.

Adelaide cooed as she reached in and picked up the little girl. But upon seeing the child, Durwood was hesitant to call it a "girl." It looked only nominally human. Pink and raw. Its limbs looked welded on poorly, like chicken legs flailing oddly in their sockets. Its face protruded around the mouth and nose, as if it was growing a snout. It screamed as Adelaide lifted it to her chest and murmured, "Sweet Robin, what a sweet song. You're supposed to be napping, dear girl."

The baby screamed so horribly Durwood thought her eardrums might burst.

A door slammed downstairs. She jumped again, and Adelaide laughed. "My, you're twitchy. It's just my husband." She called out, "Darling? Is that you?"

The voice from downstairs was low and rough, and it made Durwood's blood run cold. "It's me. Whose bicycle is that?"

Durwood shot a look to Adelaide, like they were hiding. Adelaide called out, "We have that outworlder with us." Turning to Durwood, she asked, "Do you want to stay for lunch? Have you eaten? A late lunch."

"Uh," said Durwood, looking around. "I, uh . . ."

Footsteps thumping up the stairs. Coming closer, closer, and there he was. In overalls and a yellow shirt. He had a beard, that was new. It was reddish in the sun. His eyes burned beneath his mop of wild brown hair. They were green. She'd never known they were green. He was disarmingly handsome. He smiled at her. "Hello."

"Hi," she squeaked.

"This is Miss Durwood," said Adelaide. "I'm hoping she'll stay for lunch, is that alright?"

"Of course," said Lawrence. "Pleasure."

She shook his hand, feeling numb and cold. His skin was farm-rough. She withdrew her hand as quickly as possible.

"You're here about Mark, right?" he asked. "Just heard he's gone missing."

"Yes," she whispered.

"Well, I hope you find him. And you'll get to have a *true* Addekkean experience tomorrow night. Little Rachel Anne's getting offered."

"Oh, that's right!" said Adelaide, shifting the baby to her other hip. "That's exciting. You'll stay, won't you?"

They looked at her so earnestly, so human. That misshapen thing in Adelaide's hands wailed. Her hands full of veins full of blood, still pumping, warm . . .

"I'll stay," said Durwood.

"Marvelous." Lawrence clapped his hands on his stomach and grinned. "I've got a *giant* appetite."

LUNCH WAS AN ARRAY OF FRUITS, ROOT VEGETABLES, GOAT CHEESE, and cured meat, with homemade loaves of bread, butter, honey, mustard, and cornichons. Durwood watched Adelaide assemble this spread with growing disgust. Urquhart's tea gurgled uneasily in her gut. Those tea leaves had been fingers once. These pickles had been toes, this mustard had been blood.

But at the same time, Durwood was drawn to this woman. Was enthralled by every movement of her fingers.

"All-Speaker says *we* aren't allowed to offer ourselves," said Adelaide. "My family and I. Our flesh is too special, he says."

"I thought it was good flesh for good earth?" said Durwood. "If your flesh is, like, a miracle, shouldn't it be, like, the best earth?"

Adelaide shrugged cheerily. "I don't make the rules. I'm just grateful that the benevolent powers here have given my family and me a new home."

"Right." Durwood coughed. "I'm just wondering if there are any inconsistencies in Urquhart's commandments. Like, everyone sacrifices part of themselves for the community except you. Except Urquhart. Plus, the *ravenknights* all get a raven, but Urquhart's not a knight and he has fuckin Victoria. That's an inconsistency right there."

"Oh, we don't swear in this house." Adelaide wrinkled her nose. "And Victoria is the Raven-Speaker. She reports back to Urquhart what all the other ravens see. They keep us safe from knifemen and other outworlders. No offense."

"None taken." Durwood watched her put almonds in a small dish. "So you're . . . happy here."

"More than ever." Adelaide beamed as she wiped her hands on her apron. "Soup's on."

Meeting each member of the family was a fresh blow. First, Adelaide called Robert in from the field out back. When the young boy came inside, Durwood could not stop a small cry from escaping her throat. He had the same innocent, doughy look he had in the classic photograph, except he looked unnaturally wide, like he'd been smushed down to the size of a four-year-old. His stout body waddled, as if his knees had melted and condensed. He plopped himself into a chair with great difficulty.

Adelaide called up the stairs to Henry, who came bounding down them two at a time. He disregarded Durwood and reached immediately for a hunk of bread.

Adelaide swatted his hand. "Prayers first. And wait for the others!"

Henry groaned, but obeyed.

May was the strangest of all. As she came in from the backyard where she'd been chasing butterflies with Robert, she stared long at Durwood. She was just as beautiful as Adelaide, with long brown hair and a small frame. She looked haunted.

"It's nice to meet you," said Durwood, barely above a whisper.

"Likewise," said May, before reaching her hands out to her sides.

Everyone around the table held hands, including Durwood. She found herself staring at the floor, feeling Adelaide's fingers on one side, Lawrence's on the other. The Renfields spoke as one: "Thank you, beasts, for this bounty. Good flesh for good earth. Good men for good meat. And faith in the fog that another meal will come tomorrow. Ooh-oh."

Lawrence squeezed Durwood's hand and smiled at her. Durwood fought the urge to punch him in the nose and run screaming.

She sat among the dead as they ate and laughed and chatted politely. They seemed to have no issue with eating food that supposedly used to be people. Durwood, on the other hand, sniffed hesitantly at everything she was offered. Adelaide made her a slice of grainy sourdough slathered with goat cheese, topped with a large apricot in honey. Durwood nibbled at it and found it delicious, but couldn't bring herself to take full bites. She jumped every time Henry crunched into an apple slice, every time Lawrence popped an almond between his teeth.

Lawrence seemed so at peace. He got into a brief food fight with Robert, tossing chunks of bread back and forth over the table. Durwood was very tense for this exchange.

"So," said Lawrence finally. "Are you staying for the Fogmonger's return?"

"You should," said Adelaide. "Even if you don't hold with our ways, the Fogmonger comes for everyone. You'll feel his breath either way, now that the tunnel's open. But it would be fun to share it with you."

"Stay or go, it won't matter," said Henry.

"I'll definitely be staying," said Durwood, though every time they mentioned the Fogmonger, Barnaby Wroth's boxes in the bog bobbed into her brain.

Throughout the lunch, May stared wide-eyed at Durwood. She caught the girl looking at her in small moments, in between snatches of conversation. May would catch Durwood's eye, then tuck her face back down into her food, frowning.

"So what do you guys do all day?" she asked.

"I tend the house," said Adelaide. "Lawrence takes care of the tobacco in town. May is actually Speaker of Arts & Entertainment. She helps put on banquets, plays, all kinds of things."

Don't spose you do No Longer Lawrence *around here*, Durwood joked grimly to herself.

No Longer Lawrence was a popular play about the Renfield family massacre. It was written by Carter Moone, the same man who'd penned the story about Lawrence's undying heart.

Adelaide was still talking: "May helped make your welcome banner, wasn't that nice? And Henry and Robert are in the Academy."

"What kinds of things do you learn at the Academy?" Durwood asked Henry.

"Songs," he said. "For the Fogmonger and the other beasts. And about plants and stuff."

She nodded. She was sensing a real theme here. "And you all met Mark?"

A chorus of "Mmhmm" and "He was nice."

"But none of you know what happened to him," said Durwood.

"All-Speaker knows," said May.

Everyone went quiet. May bowed her head to her plate. She murmured, "He knows. He doesn't tell us everything."

"For our protection," said Lawrence, a warning in his tone.

Robert shook his head, trembling his smushed doughy jowls. "May, don't. Ravens hear."

Sure enough—there was a knock at the door.

Durwood burst out of her chair, angling her wrist and stopping herself at the last second from flicking out her talon.

Lawrence rose. "Peace, Miss Durwood." He went to the door.

She drifted back into her chair, and caught May peering at her hawk-scar. She rolled down the sleeve of her plaid shirt to cover it.

Lawrence came back into the room, beaming. "Look who it is!"

Urquhart and Victoria came into the room. On command, the Renfields all stood and offered an "Ooohh" in greeting.

"Ah!" Urquhart smiled wide at Durwood. "There she is. We were beginning to worry she got lost. But she's been here this whole time."

"She's been lovely," said Adelaide.

"Good," said Urquhart. "Ms. Durwood, we should let them rest. It's getting late."

"Alright. Thank you," said Durwood. She held out her hand for Lawrence to shake.

He frowned at her as he shook it. Jerked his chin at Urquhart. "You take care of this one. She seems a little rattled to be among so many miracles."

"I'm a little rattled all the time," said Durwood. "Thank you for the lunch. This was a pleasure." She shook Adelaide's hand, too.

Adelaide smiled warmly. "The pleasure was all ours, dear."

Lawrence and Urquhart waited by the door, chatting about the latest tobacco crop, as Durwood retrieved her go-bag from the kitchen. She slung it over her shoulder, then paused, staring out the window over the sink.

Robert had retreated to the backyard, waddling in the grass after a butterfly. Durwood watched him. Urquhart may have been hiding something, sure, but she couldn't deny that there was also a positive atmosphere here. A communal breath that drew her in, sighed her out. The Tattooist's voice, *Any cult worth its salt . . .*

"It's my fault."

Durwood turned from the window. May stood in the doorway, eyes wide. She whispered urgently, "Mark. It's my fault he's gone."

"Why is that?" Durwood whispered back.

"He tried to save me," said May, and Durwood's blood ran cold. "The last night he was here. He begged me to come with him. Tell my story. Share my notes."

"Those were yours," Durwood breathed.

"He tried to get me to come with him," May whispered, on the verge of tears. "He wanted to stop the fog but didn't know how. He tried to save me. The knights heard us talking and . . . The beasts have killed before, Miss Durwood. People who don't offer themselves are taken anyway. People who speak out or question Urquhart's ways are . . ." She glanced back down the hall. "If you're here, word got out before Mark died. That's good."

"Why?" Durwood's mouth was suddenly dry.

"Because people need to know," said May.

"Ms. Durwood?" Urquhart peered down the hall at her. On his shoulder, Victoria's head was cocked, as if she'd been listening intently. "Are you ready?"

Durwood looked back at May. The girl didn't blink.

"Yes," said Durwood, nodding at her, hoping that nod communicated some modicum of comfort. "I'm ready."

"Positive?" Urquhart gave a one-eyed, greasy grin.

"Absolutely." Durwood hefted her go-bag on her shoulder and said, with just a hint of venom, "After you, *All*-Speaker."

As she followed him into town, she looked back at the Renfields, smiling and waving in the doorway of their revived home. Always protected by their very own knight.

BURNSKIDDE, NOVEMBER 2009

The Botanist

The sundering of the Drings was the tipping point. Clearly, Burnskidde's police force couldn't police anything. Monsters were in their midst. Neighbors seemed human but weren't. People began writing letters to the town board, asking for Chief Pittner's removal. He had been on thin ice since this latest slew of disappearances began, but now, that ice had cracked irreparably.

Metal continued to go missing all over town. Parents were discovering copies of the Gray Book in their kids' rooms. They were either livid or intrigued. This was either another sign that Burnskidde's sanity was disintegrating or it was the godsend they'd been looking for, to replace their broken faith in Pittner and the town's government.

The bat who had gorged itself on the Drings regurgitated their pieces on the Drings' front lawn. Emma and Greg, hollow-eyed orphans, fed only by pizza and casserole from concerned neighbors, found themselves the proud new parents of five baby goats and four calves.

Emma stopped showing up to school, stopped coming in to work. She wouldn't return Galloway's texts or calls. She folded in on herself entirely.

For days, Galloway worried that Emma blamed her. Maybe if Galloway had been a better friend, had listened more, they would have caught the faux Drings sooner.

"She's not responding?" Francis asked one night while they were hanging out at the Planet. "That's funny, she sent me this last night."

He pulled up YouTube on his phone. Seth Brenner's latest video rant: "SPECIAL GUEST STAR."

"I just want everyone to be respectful," said Emma, seated in Seth Brenner's office/recording studio. She held two baby goats in her lap. "I know a lot is happening right now, but Rachel's beasts aren't responsible. They're trying to help. They want to guide us toward a life in which we don't have to worry about the curse anymore. A life in which people don't go missing and people say, 'Them's the breaks!'" Almost shouting.

Galloway stared at the tiny screen. Not so long ago, she and Emma had been watching these videos together, on this side of the glass. Now, Emma had been sucked inside.

Maybe this was all still a prank somehow. Maybe that bucket of pig's blood was still lurking somewhere. Because there was no way people were taking this seriously. Impossible. As fake as Galloway's doodles.

"We should be grateful," said Seth, "that these kids are doing this for *us*. Grateful that they're doing it in time to save *your* kids." Pointing at the screen. "Y'all have been ignoring the signs, but something big is coming very soon. *I* know." He tapped his temple. "I've been paying attention to what people are saying! I'm—I'm just the messenger! But I know in my heart that it's true. This isn't just some crazy lady in a shack who loves plants. This is *big*. And we need to be ready before the fog arrives on November twenty-sixth."

"She's spreading the word," said Francis. "Look at all the views."

"You guys are still texting?" Galloway asked limply.

THE GOATS WERE TOO MUCH FOR SOME PEOPLE, WHO POSTED VITRI-olic rants on Facebook about devil worship. But there were just as many people who insisted Greg's lamb meant the chorus was graced by God. Cows were sacred as well, technically speaking. The imagery was altogether confusing. It never serves to transmute the symbolism from one faith onto another, but people always try when they're afraid.

Edie Neglani wrote a letter and presented it at the next meeting of the town board, in the old event hall. Tile floor, rows of metal folding chairs. This particular meeting had the best attendance the town board had ever seen. The fervor of the chorus appalled Town Supervisor Fadden (a whining gentleman with greasy black hair).

"Unknown agents have infiltrated our way of life," Edie read off a piece of paper, standing. Next to her, Eddie Spaghetti sat with his beefy arms folded over his great chest. He nodded as his wife read. "Nowhere in Galloway's literature does she encourage or condone violence, nor does she suggest any upheaval of the town's current structure. She's not *trying* to threaten your Christian way of life. If anything, Rachel is attempting to *support* our home by taking advantage of local lore to create food and stability for a community that has been critically unstable for as long as I have lived here. In fact, we should be grateful to her for enlightening us to the fact that not everyone in Burnskidde is good flesh."

She seated herself to scattered applause and much headshaking.

Supervisor Fadden cleared his throat and addressed Dom, seated next to his mother. "Mr. Zambrano, you have more up-close experience with Galloway's gospel than anyone else here. What do you think about all this?"

Mrs. Hunt, Ashleigh's mom, shot to her feet. "He's a child, what does he know?"

"Annie, please," said Fadden patiently.

"My daughter is out of her mind with this bullcrap—"

"Annie, *please*."

"Mrs. Neglani is right," said Dom. "We're not trying to hurt anyone. We're helping."

Murmurs and more headshaking.

"It's true!" Dom insisted. "These beasts aren't, like, *beasts*. They're providing for us. Wool, milk, cheese, meat. Warmth. Sustenance. Protein. It's not *Satan*. It's nature, only different."

"That is the most *un*natural nonsense I've ever heard," cried Mr. Tolley, gripping the chair in front of him and using it to launch himself to his feet. "I can't stay silent anymore. Mr. Fadden, this is a classic example of mob mentality. I believe this entire faith is *manufactured*."

Scoffing, hissing. Shifting in seats.

Tolley turned from the town board to address the crowd. "What? You're all just as superstitious as I am. Don't make me sound like a goddamn maniac. You can't actually believe this is all true, without a doubt, when we live in a place that *feeds* on us!" He was shouting now over the others. "When the entire reason we're here is because this place *feeds* on our—"

"But you've seen it." Mrs. Zambrano stood. She had worn her scrubs as a sign that she was not insane. She was employed; she was strong; she was a fuckin nurse, and she spoke calmly with her chin raised and her hands clasped at her waist. "Mr. Tolley, you have seen this miracle. Part of my son's body is flowers now. Food. I have literally eaten of his flesh and blood. His friend Gregory has given us a gift as well. These things may not be natural, but I cannot ignore the beauty of them. Life here has been difficult, yes. But now? I eat freely from the earth." She swallowed. "And tomorrow night . . . I intend to offer myself to the beasts of the woods."

Uproar. People stood, shook her. She stood firm. Supervisor Fadden banged his gavel.

Mrs. Zambrano raised her voice over the crowd. "I have faith in the fog, Mr. Tolley."

"Come on, sit down, sit *down*!" Fadden cried.

Slowly, the crowd died down.

"Ms. Zambrano," he said, "we can't have people feeding themselves to vermin. It's endangering the local wildlife, and it's a problem for the mental stability of our entire town. If you're saying that you're a threat to yourself or—"

"I am not a threat," said Mrs. Zambrano, speaking clearly, shaking her head. "I am following the will of the Fogmonger."

"Well, if you follow that will into Horridge Park again after dark, I'm going to have to arrest you," Fadden sneered. "Do you understand that, ma'am?"

"Others will come with me," she said. "You will have to arrest us all."

"If those others are under eighteen, I can have you charged with child endangerment."

"My son is nineteen. Gregory is nineteen as well."

"That may be, but . . ." Fadden picked up a paper and squinted at it. "Ms. Ashleigh Hunt is sixteen, Mr. William Neglani is seventeen, and

Mr. Jacob Mendez is sixteen." He dropped the paper. "It would also seem that this *cult* of yours has inspired our Chief of Police's son, Troy, to offer himself as well. How do you suggest he follow his basketball scholarship to E.C. without a leg, Ms. Zambrano?"

"I have not encouraged any of them to offer themselves," she said, fingers twisting anxiously in her fists. "You may think I am the problem because I am the one here speaking to you, but that is not the case, Mr. Fadden. There are many of us."

"Well, again, if 'us' is you and a bunch of sixteen-year-olds, Ms. Zambrano, I'm gonna have you arrested." He banged his gavel, tired and annoyed. "Look, we're running over time, we gotta move on to the next agenda item. Bea, what's on the agenda here?"

The crowd muttered itself into silence. Mrs. Zambrano did not blink as she drifted slowly back down into her seat.

Tolley glared at her from several folding-chair rows ahead. He snorted, shook his head, and watched the rest of the meeting with his arms crossed.

"I WONDER IF YOU WOULDN'T MIND LEADING A SCHOOL ASSEMBLY for us," said Dr. Eric, tapping his fingertips together, squinting at her through his thick glasses. Galloway sat across from him in his office. He wore his usual pinstripe suit and blue and yellow tie. "I just want to assuage some of the doubts of the more vocal members of the P.T.A. I'm sure you're familiar with whom I'm speaking about."

Galloway was. She'd walked by them earlier today, in fact, on her way into school, holding signs in the parking lot: CULT-FREE SCHOOL. Annie Hunt was among them. She'd glared at Galloway without a word.

"I . . . I don't know."

Dr. Eric spread his hands. "We can get rid of spaghetti at lunch. I forget what commandment that is off the top of my head, but how does that sound?"

Galloway considered this. "That sounds . . . pretty good."

They shook on it.

She had become a minor celebrity. The people she passed in the halls were no more than walls of whispers: *Why did she do that, get rid of the spaghetti? Is it a religious thing? Does she have, like, a condition? I heard she has seizures. Her eyes roll back and she starts yelling in Latin. Wait, does spaghetti give you seizures?*

Galloway hunched her shoulders against all this noise as she walked down the hall. Hallways filled with bodies. Bodies with thumbs and feet and all kinds of eatable appendages. She turned a corner and Willy Neglani blocked her path.

"My mom thinks I'm dumb," he said. "I want to show her I'm good flesh."

"Get in line," she mumbled, shoving past him.

History was strange without Emma, and Tolley was cold toward her, barely glancing in her direction as he droned on about the Crusades, and how "dangerous religion can be." He practically yelled at them about church and state.

The bus ride home was surreal. Everyone kept glancing at her as she slid farther down in her seat, blasting the volume on her iPod.

When she got home, Nicole and Keith were both on the phone with different people, talking quickly.

"I mean, all they need is a finger, right?" said Nicole. She saw Galloway and turned away, lowering her voice. "I could offer *one* finger. I just don't want to bleed green, Isabella."

"Of course it's a real book," said Keith. "Well, I don't *know* the title, but she found it in the library . . ."

Galloway's cellphone buzzed in her pocket when she reached her room. She fumbled for it, and froze when she saw the screen. She held it to her ear.

"Hey," said Galloway, unsure what else to say. They hadn't spoken for a week, since she'd dropped Emma at home the night her parents died. Or, not her parents, but . . . "Are you okay?"

"We found her," said Emma, voice ragged and hoarse but deeply excited. She spoke fast, "Rach, Francis fucking found her. Her little shack. I know where it is. He put together a bunch of Seth's maps and—"

"Are you . . ." Galloway floated down onto her bed, her knees weak. "Are you talking about who I think you're talking about?"

"Hell yes," said Emma. "I *found* the Horridge Hill Botanist."

EMMA DID NOT LOOK WELL. GALLOWAY HAD ALWAYS READ ABOUT people's eyes looking "sunken" in books, but she never understood what that meant until she saw the dark bags under Emma's eyes. Greg's old Burnskidde High sweater hung loosely on her sharp shoulders. Galloway wondered what she'd eaten since her parents had . . . Since the duplicates of her parents were . . .

"Em, are you really okay?" she asked.

Emma peered through the windshield at the dark service road behind the park, gripping the wheel in both hands. She jerked her head to Galloway, then focused back on the road. Her eyes were wide and wild. "I'm awesome. I'm excited. I've been *dreaming* of this."

"Yeah, ease off the gas," said Greg from the backseat.

It was the three of them in Darlene's PT Cruiser. Emma didn't have her license, but Greg didn't have the coordination to drive with his left foot, so he offered scattered advice from the back. Galloway clutched the oh-shit handle as the car bumped along the dirt road.

They'd driven around Horridge Park to its back entrance, passing a pair of police cruisers parked outside the main gate. The cars were dark, but there were lights by the picnic tables. Maybe Pittner had set up some kind of blockade to discourage anyone else from offering themselves. Galloway didn't want to think about it. She didn't want to think about *any* of this. She wanted to stand on the roof of the school and scream, "Just kidding!" But even so, she hadn't made up the Drings. She had not doodled the Botanist in class.

They bumped farther down the service road. No lights. Big potholes. Powerlines on one side, supposedly the "service" this road was catering to.

"What are we looking for?" Galloway asked.

"Should be up ahead," said Emma, leaning over the wheel.

The car bumped hard over a crater. Greg swore. "Easy, easy. Slow down."

"There are supposedly tree-beasts around here somewhere, too," said Emma. "They're usually only seen along the county roads, but some people have posted . . . There!" She pointed to a dent in the trees that may have once been a road. She rolled the car to a stop. It was a tiny dirt road, barely wide enough to allow the car to pass through.

They stared at it. Breathing.

Emma threw on her blinker.

"Nice," said Greg. "Good job. Safety first."

"I think this whole thing is safety last," said Galloway. "I mean, we all know this is a horrible idea, right? Just, like, going in and confronting her?"

"It's the best idea I've ever had," said Emma. "Francis told me I needed to confront my demons. He said I should go alone, but . . ." She glanced at Galloway, pursed her lips. "I thought you should be here." She cranked the wheel and slid the car into the tunnel of branches.

The headlights illuminated tall weeds reaching out of twin tire divots. Branches scraped along the sides of the car as they drove in absolute silence, inch by creeping inch.

After an eternity, they emerged into a small clearing dominated by a giant weeping willow. Through the curtain of its leaves, they could see light flickering in a window, the dim outline of a shack.

"No fucking way." Greg leaned forward.

"Holy shit," Galloway whispered.

Emma put the car in park. She sat for a moment, staring through the windshield at the pinpoint of light, hidden in the drapery of leaves. She didn't look at Galloway. She remained still, hands on the wheel. Then she unbuckled her seat belt and said, "Okay."

"Well, wait," said Galloway. "We don't have to do this."

Emma whipped her head around, glaring at her. "What are you talking about? She killed my mom."

"I know."

Emma sneered. "Why would you even get in the car? Isn't this your whole *point*? We had bad flesh in our midst. I deserve to know why."

She opened the car door. Galloway felt a lurch in her stomach.

"But," she said quickly, "if she can really control, like, plants and stuff, how can we make it out of here? I mean, look at all the plants. What if she takes *us*?"

Emma leveled her gaze at Galloway. "I have faith in the fog." And she launched herself out of the car.

Galloway climbed out, legs unsteady. Greg leaned forward again and called through the open door. "Be careful, though, yeah? You're the only Dring I have left."

Emma turned to him. "Ooh-ah, Greg. Have faith."

"Ah-ooh." Greg made devil horns with his hand. "Rock on."

Together, Emma and Galloway approached the curtain of leaves. Emma put up her hands and cut through the billowing strands, gliding forward. Galloway followed her lead.

They drifted through the willow, leaves brushing over their faces, their necks, whispering over their hands, through their fingers. At last, the wooden wall appeared before them. Not very tall, maybe six feet. Slanted, crooked boards of wood. Warping and held together with rusting nails. The window was fogged; they could see nothing inside except the warm orange glow of firelight. There was a crooked door with a dark handle.

Emma swallowed. She stared at the door.

"This whole thing could be barnwood," Galloway pointed out.

"Right." Emma pulled the sleeve of her sweatshirt over her knuckles and knocked.

The door swung inward, hinges shrieking. They peered inside, skin cold and prickly.

A fireplace to their left. An armchair losing its stuffing at the seams. A window across from them, looking out over a swamp. Everything else—shelves, workbenches, the corners of the floor—covered in loose piles and stacks of stuff. Papers, notes, sketches, anatomical designs of people, creatures, plants. Jars filled with liquid, lining the shelves, dark things floating within. Tinkling bottles and jars hanging from lengths of twine nailed to the rafters overhead, filled with macabre miscellany. Filleted frogs, eyes of varying sizes and species. Worms still wriggling, a salamander struggling in fluid. All this, and much, much worse.

The girls stepped inside, standing as close to each other as they possibly could. Galloway was grateful to be this close to Emma again, despite everything.

A voice rolled out from the shadows, from a dark doorway beyond the fireplace. It scratched at their ears like an old, cracked fingernail, "What are you girls looking for? A love potion? A sleeping draught? Something stronger?"

Emma swallowed. "My name is Emma Dring. I . . . You took my parents."

Wheezing laughter. "Dring, Dring . . . Yes, that *rings* a bell." A dark, wet chuckle. "Please. Come in. I'm tending to something precarious, or I would greet you properly. Come and see."

The girls pressed even closer together. Emma's fingers dug into the crook of Galloway's arm, and Galloway was relieved that she could be useful somehow, putting a hand over Emma's as they walked deeper into the shack, nudging jars out of the way. The tinkling of glass, the crack of the fire, and the eyes all over her, from the jars, the jars.

They turned the corner into the other room, similarly cluttered but with the addition of a cot in the corner. This room was even more densely populated by jars and books and plants. A large sunflower sat in a pot by the door. It lifted its head and tracked the girls as they moved into the room, shivering in pain. Next to it, a man's head lay lopsided in a mound of dirt. His toothless jaw opened and closed silently. From every other orifice, flowers bloomed. They blossomed out of his nostrils and his ears, straight out of his eyes. The eye-flowers were white and bloodshot. As they inched closer, Galloway saw many other heads behind him. Some human, some possum, cat, dog. All of them still breathing, all riddled with greenery, sprouting from their flesh and curling up from their nostrils, roots trailing down into the dirt from their ears. Other dark, tortured shapes populated the shadows in the corners of the room.

The woman had her back to them, bent over a workbench along the far wall. She turned slightly as they approached, and they could see her gray skin. She was short and stout, wrapped all in black, and sharp dark hair shot down from the top of her head in all directions, poking into her eyes and ears, matted and unshowered. She had a wide mouth, a sharp nose. Crooked teeth cracked out of her gums. She turned back, and re-sumed scooping messy pinkish bits out of a large glass jar filled with yel-low fluid. They looked like peach pits, with strings and bits of flesh still attached. She plopped them onto a silver tray one by one.

"It's you," Galloway breathed. "It's *been* you all along."

The woman took up a scalpel and dissected one of the nuts. It squirted a bright yellow goo. Galloway swallowed a sudden uprising of bile as an acrid, rotten-apple stench filled the room. The woman smiled as she worked. "What's been me, dear?"

"The pigs and the bats. This is where they're coming from. From *you*." A pop from the fireplace made Galloway jump.

The Botanist glanced at her, frowning. She poked around inside the nut, pulling out a small twig. "Alas. I was so ready for you to accuse me of something I actually did. But I don't grow pigs and bats. I have only ever been interested in flora. Never fauna. Although *you're* a pretty pair of flowers, I'll admit."

"Then the plants," said Galloway. "The—the miracle plants. You grew those."

"I doubt it." The Botanist chuckled. And her amusement was so gen-uine that Galloway found herself believing her.

"You killed my mom," said Emma. "You did that, didn't you? Hm? And my dad?" She stepped forward. Galloway dropped back. She'd never heard Emma speak so confidently or so fiercely.

The Botanist smiled. "Why do you think so?"

"Because we cut them open, and they bled green," said Emma, voice trembling with rage.

The Botanist continued picking at her peach pit, pulling a small acorn hat out of the goo with the tip of her knife. "Well, that is strong evidence. What were their names again, Ms. Dring?"

"Jeff and Darlene."

"Ahh." The Botanist grinned. She turned to them, holding the knife. They could see pale roots writhing between her teeth. "Yess. You were the hiking ones."

Emma lunged for her. Galloway grabbed her arm, held her back, but

Emma was already yelling through her teeth, "You psycho bitch! You killed my fucking mom!"

"I've never killed anyone," said the Botanist, unmoved. She turned back to her work, slicing into another nut on her tray. "I have given new life to many things, your mother included. But rest assured, she was already dead when I discovered her. Tree-beasts haunt these woods. Yess. They'd brutalized her. Chewed her organs. I simply gave her corpse new breath. Your father, too."

"Bullshit," Emma yelled.

The Botanist tsked. "This land is full of dangers, sweet flower. Wheels within wheels, as they say. If fate exists, it's likely a vastly complicated machine, don't you think? Ahh. *There* you are," she cooed. She dipped her knife into the nut and gently lifted out a small, mewling homunculus. It looked like a miniature infant, the size of a thumbtack. It waved its little arms and wailed softly, tiny eyes squeezed shut. The Botanist shaved away the bits of nut still stuck to its skin as she went on, "I have spent years scavenging the leftovers of creatures like tree-beasts for my own purposes. So much *material* these Renfield things leave behind."

"You grew them," Emma spat. "You grew them and you tricked me."

"I have no desire to trick anyone," said the Botanist, genuinely wounded. She laid the homunculus on the tray and scraped goo off it as it writhed. "Case in point, I didn't grow whatever pigs and bats you're accusing me of. And I certainly didn't grow new Drings just to have a laugh. I was *trying* to help you." She grinned again. "Consider yourself, young Dring, a lucky component of an ongoing experiment." She laid her blade against the tiny bicep of the homunculus and pressed down. Galloway heard the pop of metal through flesh, and the infant screamed, a sound so piercing it buckled Galloway's knees.

"This experiment," said the Botanist, "has been quite some time in the making, but I do believe we're *getting* somewhere." She popped the knife through the infant's other arm. It screamed louder. "The intersection between flora and fauna changes all the time. Little baby plants, little plant-babies. Getting the world they *deserve*." She enunciated her words with every downward hack of the knife. "*Step* by step"—off came a leg—"they'll have their Earth *back*"—went the other. Glass-shattering screams tightened about Galloway's eardrums. "People are a poison, little Dring-flower. Plants are *quite* the opposite." One more *hack*, and the screams cut short.

"Emma, let's go," whispered Galloway, shaking. "She's not helping us."

"I can't go," said Emma, jaw trembling. "She's lying."

The Botanist cocked her head. She put down the scalpel and turned from the tray, wiping her hands on her robe. She swooped close to Emma, but Emma stood her ground, quaking with fury.

"My sweet flower," said the Botanist. "I wouldn't lie to you. Renfield has a complex food chain that humans are at the bottom of. I didn't kill your parents. I *used* your parents' corpses. Escorted them to a nice place where they could regrow. In fact, that was over a year ago, wasn't it? Over a year, they've been walking around, and you just now came wondering. An extra *year* you've had with them. I'd consider that a courtesy, not a trick. Wouldn't you?"

"I'd call it fucking terrorism," Emma spat.

The Botanist frowned. "Sweet flower. How can I get you to understand? I am not a murderer. Your father simply blossomed into a new version of himself. See, it's all a cycle. Even you." She ran a finger down the side of Emma's face. "You're rainwater, dear. You're dinosaur urine and mammoth fat. You're rock and pulp and dirt. All God's creatures absorb everything else. Nature connects us all." She floated even closer. "Would it comfort you, my dear, to know that you were with them when I found their bodies? That you, too, blossomed into something new that day? Technically speaking, *you're still with them.*"

She shot out her hand, grabbed Emma's wrist. In the same motion, the very same second, the Botanist shot out her other hand. Neither girl saw the blade before it sliced up, down, twice very fast, across Emma's arm. Galloway grabbed her, put herself between Emma and the woman. Emma thrashed against her.

"I'll fucking kill you!" she screamed. "I'll tear your fucking heart out, you witch! You fucking witch!"

The Botanist stood grinning, holding half a garden shear in her hand. The sharp rusted blade dripped onto the floor.

Galloway pulled Emma toward the door. The Botanist leered at them as she faded back into the jingling, jangling shadows of her jar-filled hovel. "I only grow flowers," she called from the dark. "If someone's growing pigs and bats, it isn't me . . ."

Emma held her hand tight over the slice-wounds in her arm as Galloway hustled her through the willow branches, toward the car. The curtains of leaves were swirling with a sudden wind, swiping at their cheeks, their necks. Galloway climbed into the driver's seat and shut the door, Emma hyperventilating at her side.

"Are you okay?" Galloway asked, raising her voice over the noise outside.

"What the hell happened?" Greg asked from the backseat.

Emma took great gasping breaths and did not respond.

"Hey!" Galloway grabbed her shoulder, tried to get Emma to look at her. "Emma. Are you okay?"

Emma was not okay. She was panicking, panicking. Shaking and sobbing and bleeding, she was *bleeding*. She whipped her head around, back and forth, suddenly lost. Was she in a *car*, where was she? Her eyes rolled wildly, and she finally located the dome light in the ceiling. Galloway and Greg, calling to her from somewhere far away, calling through the wind, the rushing leaves. Emma reached up with a hand shaking so badly she could barely control it, but she punched the light on, and in its dim yellow glow, she could see her arms were smeared with green. A viscous yellow-green pumping out of the two thin, deep lines running up her forearm. She swiped at it furiously, heart slamming against her sternum, wanting out, *out*, she wanted out of this body, this wasn't her body, she was bleeding green *ooze*, it was oozing out of *her*. She was trying to swipe it away and it wouldn't go away, it was coming *out* of her, she was bleeding *green*, and Galloway was yelling, yelling, somewhere far away, lost in the woods, "Oh my god, Emma! Emma, stop! *Emma!*"

But Emma just screamed and screamed and screamed.

"RACHEL'S NOT ANSWERING," SAID FRANCIS, CLAPPING HIS PHONE shut and turning to the crowd.

The park was filled with people. Some of them held signs in protest, but watched in sick fascination. Pittner and two of his deputies were there, to see what this was all about. Dom had brought Greg's foot-lamb along, on a leash. Isabella Zambrano hadn't come, for her own safety, but the Neglanis were there, the Hunts, Mr. Tolley with his arms crossed, and poor Seth Brenner with his useless cigarettes.

Kneeling by the edge of the woods: Ashleigh, Troy, Jake, and Willy.

Francis shrugged. "I guess she's busy. Oh well. I'll lead us." He lifted his arms toward the dark. "Come. Let's sing."

NEW ADDEKKEA, OCTOBER 2019

Nighttime at the Post Office

Urquhart was monologuing again. Striding one pace ahead of her as he led her back into town. He sounded more smug than ever. "Yes, we're witnesses to the making of a new biblical age here, Ms. Durwood. These are miracles we cannot fully comprehend. And why would we want to? Why not simply be *grateful* for what we've been offered?"

"Right," said Durwood. She walked alongside her bike, scanning the fields, lit brilliant gold by the setting sun.

Urquhart cleared his throat. "Well. I've given you *quite* the tour today. But it's getting late. Do you have a room at the hotel?"

She checked her watch. "Ahh, shit." She'd gotten so focused, it would be dark by the time she got her bike back through the tunnel. It wasn't far from the tunnel to her apartment, but it wasn't nothing. And she'd be biking past the diner where Mark was taken.

She shouldn't have allowed this town to eat an entire day of her time. That was stupid, but also classic Durwood. She was annoyed at herself, but not surprised.

"Where's the hotel?" she sighed.

"The Post Office," said Urquhart. "When Burnskidde was first founded, the building was an inn, tavern, post office, and police department. The old mail slots are still there behind the bar, as a novelty. We keep the rooms open, too, though they've largely been empty since we sealed ourselves away. Occasionally, we've had people stay there if they have fights at home and don't want to sleep on the couch." He chuckled. "You'll be comfortable there."

It wasn't a big deal. She had her go-bag. She just didn't love the idea of this guy knowing where she slept. But at least this would give her a chance to assess the town at night. That was what Bruce had suggested, after all.

"Alright," she relented. "Let's go . . . check my mail."

THE POST OFFICE LAY LIKE A BROWN-SHINGLED SLUG, CURLED around a gravel parking lot. The head of this worm was the bar/hotel office/jail cells now used for storage. The hotel rooms opened directly onto the lot, and each door was marked with a wicker number.

The bar itself was a low-ceilinged room with little light. Oil lamps were spaced evenly across the bar, and long white candles burned on the wooden tables scattered throughout the room, which wasn't very big. Unlabeled bottles on the shelves behind the bar. No doubt everything they served they'd grown and distilled themselves. A hive of time-warped wooden mail slots were poked into the wall next to the shelves. A stale lemon smell had sunk deep into the core of the room, fuming off the wood-paneled walls; the thin, burnt, green carpet. On the wall behind the bar, there was a massive chalk mural of Galloway and her beasts. A mirror image of the Gray Book's cover.

When the manager/bartender clinked Durwood's key down on the pinewood bar, she saw it had a wicker tag attached to it, painted with a purple 9.

The man had scraggly gray whiskers and large gaps between his crooked teeth. But his eyes were bright and his laugh lines were deep. His genuinely calming vibe was a relief after spending the day with All-Speaker Urquhart and the Renfields.

"Nine's the one straight back," he explained, pointing directly behind her. "Last one in the row."

She scraped up the key. "What is it a night?"

"We only barter here. Money wouldn't mean anything."

"Okay. So what can I barter?"

He waved a hand. "Room's on me. All-Speaker said to treat you hospitable-like."

She eyed him. Pointed the key at him. "What's your name, kind sir?"

"Barry Barr."

"You're . . . Your name is Barry Barr."

"My pa had a sense of humor."

"And you're a bartender."

He spread his hands. "Bartender Barry Barr, at your service."

"Awesome," said Durwood, swinging her key. "Barry, you must've lived in Burn . . . *Addekkea* since before the Fogmonger came, yeah?"

"Oh yeah," said Barry. "M'whole life. Started working in the mine when I was sixteen. Messed up mah teeth."

"Urquhart must have been about sixteen himself when the Fogmonger came."

"Sure, I guess so."

"So how'd he end up in charge? I mean, it's not like all the adults died."

The bags beneath Barry's eyes seemed to grow darker. "Lots of people *did* die. Lotta nonbelievers retching in the streets, skin sloughin off . . . Horrible. But Urquhart was the one who organized us all. He was the one with the miracle. Hard not to listen to a miracle."

Durwood grunted. "Well, good thing you were in the chorus, huh?"

"Oh yeah." Barry brightened. "I don't miss the old ways at all."

"Alright, well. Thanks for the key."

"Come back if you want a nightcap!" Barry called as she walked outside.

Leaving the bar, she passed another man coming in. She held the door for him and he nodded his thanks. He ducked inside and Durwood heard Barry cry cheerfully, "Oh my fog, you son of a bitch . . ."

Room 9 was surprisingly bland and midtier. Durwood had expected a headboard made of branches, maybe a quilt with pigs sewn onto it. Instead, it looked like a common hotel room, except for the oil lamp on the nightstand. The thin carpet had that old semen smell. The walls were white-paneled, wallpapered in orange, and stained in odd patterns. The crisp white bed sat facing her, against the far wall, and the door to the bathroom was beyond. A window to her right, a door to the adjoining room on the left. A black faux-wood desk sat next to the adjoining door, and a small table with peeling lacquer stood by the window.

Super-exposed sleeping conditions. Terrible feng shui.

She checked all the corners, under the bed. Rattled the doorknob to the adjoining room, then shoved the desk in front of the door. Ripped back the shower curtain, much to the dismay of a millipede who scuttled away down the drain. She peeked through the bathroom window over the toilet. Saw a bank of trees outside. She peeked out the window by the bed and saw a bit of road, more trees.

She sat on the edge of the bed, acclimating. Strange, being in a regular old shitty motel room, lit by oil lamp. She bounced. Grunted.

Time to organize.

She got up, tossed her bag on the bed, and zipped it open. She pulled out the bundle she'd adopted from Mark and placed it on the bed. She rooted around inside the bag for her notebook and sat at the table, brought the oil lamp close. She felt calm rush through her as she opened her notebook, clicked her pen. Felt good to be back at a desk by the light of a single lamp. Durwood felt more at ease, now that she had four walls around her and could see only as far as her little bubble of light.

She began writing new questions down, adding to the ones she'd had since Mark's note:

1. Renfields are alive? Used to be real. Plants!
2. Mass suicide event? Fog?
3. Urquhart has light in his office. Connection to outside/ electricity?
4. Galloway killed? Urquhart's rise to power—ravenknights not in GRAY BOOK.

She hesitated. Then, as much as it pained her, she turned the exclamation point after **plants** into a question mark.

"Mm." She dropped her pen, fanned her fingers to crack her knuckles, and got up again. She got her phone charger out of her go-bag, then stopped. "Mm." Tried plugging it into the old outlet by the bed. Her phone didn't light up. "Mmm." She unplugged it, blew into the power socket, and plugged it back in. Nothin.

"Fuuuck." She looked at the battery. Twenty-seven percent remaining. Alright. She could make that last.

Was Urquhart the only one in town with electricity? God, every question she had just led to more questions.

She brought her three books over to the table under the window and lined them up side by side. Folded her arms on the table and rested her chin on top of her wrists.

She began flipping through the Yellow Book. It was composed mostly of commandments and rules, and opened with a dedication to Rachel Galloway, "lost on the night of the fog, but never lost to our hearts."

"Ugh," said Durwood.

Below that was a dedication to the rest of the Galloways, who allegedly died in the poison gas that same night. November 26, 2009: Keith, Nicole, Theodore, Robert, and the little dog, Doofus.

"RIP Doofus," Durwood muttered as she turned the page.

There were several chapters full of aphorisms such as "Offerings are always voluntary, but refusing to volunteer hurts your community. Disobeying community rules IS volunteering."

Another: "The outworld will never understand our ways. Do not mourn the loss of them, nor lionize their barbarism."

"Noodles are against the Fogmonger's nature. Noodles of any kind will not be tolerated in the new colony."

"When the fog returns, breathe deep the great blessing and sing loud the Monger's song."

Oof. She felt like this required a drink.

She got up and shoved Mark's bundle deep under her mattress for safekeeping, in case anyone barged in while she was away.

She marched outside. Kept glancing around. Nothing stirred except the wind.

She stepped inside the bar just as Barry was saying, "By the way, your granddaughter wrote you another letter."

"Thank fog," said the man who'd entered as Durwood had been leaving. He sat wearily on one of the old cracked stools at the bar. Barry plucked a letter from a slot on the wall, and the man accepted it with a sigh.

"Dear Grandpa," the man read. "I hope the hotel is treating you well. Mom tried some of the new Straus tea today and said it was very good. Maybe we can have you over for dinner tomorrow before Rachel Anne's offering and you can try it. Hope you don't have any . . ." He squinted, pulled an oil lamp closer. "Hope you don't have any *nightmares* again. Love, Rachel Marie." He dropped the letter on the bar and pushed the lamp away. "Delightful."

"Nother beer?" Barry asked him.

"Please," said Grandpa. He rubbed the bridge of his nose and finally saw that Durwood had joined him at the bar. "Ahh. You're the knife-woman."

"Is that what people are saying?" Durwood asked, hefting herself onto a stool.

"I've heard a few people express . . . hesitation in dealing with you. Heard you were harassing our resident miracles, too."

"I thought we had a very cordial lunch."

The man raised his eyebrows and gave her an amused smile. He extended his hand. "Seth. Seth Brenner."

"Rachel," she said, shaking it.

Seth laughed. "No shit."

"None at all."

"You must feel right at home here," said Seth.

"He's kidding," Barry explained as he opened a dark bottle of beer. "Seth feels only mildly at home here. He was a professor at Edenville. Before."

"History," said Seth, sipping his beer. "I specialized in ancient religions. Ironically. My PhD thesis was on Mithraism."

"I'm not familiar," said Durwood.

"Mithras was a deity born out of a rock. I suppose anything's possible." Seth toasted the mural over the bar with a sardonic, "Ooh-ah."

"What's up?" Barry asked her. "Need towels?"

"Oh, my phone charger isn't working," said Durwood. "I was wondering if you had power anywhere."

"Geez, I haven't had a phone since '09," said Barry. "Nobody has."

"But you have service out here." She showed him her screen. "I have bars."

Barry leaned forward and squinted at her phone. "Holy fog, is that what cellphones look like now? Your screen is huge! You have so many apps!"

Durwood retracted her phone. "Sorry. Didn't mean to blow your mind. You don't have any electricity out here?"

Barry shook his head. "The sealing of the tunnel was . . . pretty final. We don't have any contact with outworld stuff."

"How do you write your granddaughter, then?" Durwood asked. "I mean, if you're all cut off, how do you have mail?"

"She's not my granddaughter," said Seth. "Rachel Marie lives up by the goat fields. It's her class's give-back project to write letters to *adopted* elders. So we don't get lonely and disgruntled."

"Give-back?" Durwood asked.

"Each class at the Academy does a project that benefits the rest of the chorus," Barry explained. "Something they build or tend to for the town. I think it's nice they write you letters, Seth."

"Yeah, that's sweet," Durwood offered.

"They didn't even ask my permission," Seth grumbled. "And I'm not an elder; I'm fucking fifty. It's just another stupid trick to keep tabs on people."

"I think local mail's a nice way to honor an old outworld tradition," said Barry. "Not everybody does it. It's like a hobby." He coughed. "Listen, I'm sorry about your phone. You want a drink?"

Durwood eyed the bottles behind him. "That's all pig whiskey?"

"Course! We have gin, too. Vodka. Beer. All good flesh for good earth," he said proudly. "I grew a little juniper myself." He held up his hand, and Durwood could see he was missing his ring finger.

"Yeahh, I had to try it," said Seth, pulling up his pant leg to reveal a huge dent in his calf. He gave Durwood a bleak but bemused look. "I grew shrooms. They worked, but I had a panic attack thinking about eating myself."

"The whiskey is our best," said Barry, pulling a bottle off the shelf. He looked at the bottom. "This is Palmer's thumbs, I think. Palmer and McLoskey."

"Mmm." Durwood narrowed her eyes at the dark liquid. She looked at Seth. "Is it worth it?"

"It is upsettingly good," said Seth, nursing his beer.

"Want a glass?" Barry asked brightly.

Durwood sucked air through her teeth. "Don't spose you have rocks."

"I'd have to go down to the ice cellar."

"Straight's fine," she said. "Double."

He poured a glass, put it in front of her. She stared at it for a moment, arms crossed on the bar.

She took a sip. *Ohh*, good. The blooming warmth. The burn in the back of her throat.

She nodded. Smacked her lips, said slowly, "Wow. Yum."

Seth snorted.

She wondered how much work went into distilling whiskey. How beleaguered were these people, really? And how ready were they for . . . whatever came next?

"So what exactly happens in a few days when the Fogmonger returns?" she asked.

"He restores our offerings," said Barry, wriggling his stumped finger. "Blows a healing balm across the town that brings new life and longevity to all. So we can continue to grow."

"But he poisons the nonbelievers in the process," she clarified.

"That was only last time," said Barry. "The second coming will be different. What happened in '09 is . . . bad memories."

"Bad memories." Seth scoffed. "Barry wasn't involved. I was there. I *helped* make this happen. I was vocal, I was supportive, I stoked the fucking fla—"

"Heyy," said Barry quickly. "You want another?"

Durwood looked at the glass in her hand. When had she finished that drink?

"Yes," she said, putting her glass back on the bar. "You sure I can't barter for it?"

Barry shook his head, pouring her another shot. "I have faith in the fog that you'll pay it forward somehow."

"Well, if you wouldn't mind answering a few more questions," said Durwood, slurring her words only a little. "Thata be great."

"Shoot," said Barry.

"Alright. You meet my buddy Mark last week?"

"Oh." Barry laughed. "Yeah. So bizarre to meet an outworlder. He didn't stay long. He, uh . . . He hit it off with May real well. Saw them talking a few times."

"No good," said Seth. "Man must have been forty, hitting on a teenage girl."

"Teenage *miracle* girl," Barry corrected. Confidentially, "He's just bitter. Lost a son to Renfield, back before."

"Ahh," said Durwood. "That's why you were vocal in turning to the way of the beasts."

"It *seemed* like a fine alternative to that whole 'no roads out' nonsense we grew up with," Seth admitted. "When Nate went missing, I was scrounging for . . . I don't know. Solid ground. Then I saw those bats, and . . ."

"And you regret it now," she said.

Seth gave her a look, then said into his beer, "Not at all. No, I'm grateful for the Monger."

"You believe in the fog?"

"I have faith in the fog, yes," said Seth lifelessly.

If Durwood had been in Burnskidde ten years ago, and she had just lost her family to Renfield, would she have fallen for the way of the beasts as well?

She wasn't sure.

"Anyway," Barry surged ahead, "Mark stayed one night in that same room you're in. Second night he was here, he went out to see May. Next thing I knew, the sirens were goin. Never saw Mark again."

Because he tried to save her, thought Durwood. *Urquhart stopped him from bringing her outside, bringing more attention to Burnskidde before the fog returns. Just like he's keeping me from the truth with his bullshit act.*

Barry shrugged. "That's all I know."

"That's more than enough. Thank you." She tipped her glass to him and slugged her drink in one gulp, clapped the glass back on the bar. "What do I say? Ooh-oh?"

Barry laughed. "Ooh-ah. You want another?"

"Noo." She stared down into her glass. "Yeahh, why not. One more."

He poured a round for all three of them, and they saluted each other, "Ooh-ah." She managed to say good night after that, which felt like a Herculean feat. Her legs were unsteady after a day of hard biking and walking. She wove across the darkened parking lot, back to Room 9. Everything was so quiet out here. The other rooms were all dark. Candles burned gently in sconces between the doors.

The room felt more cramped and uncanny than before. She kicked her shoes into the corner and lurched over to the nightstand, pulled open its one drawer. Sure as shit: another Gray Book lay inside, atop a Yellow. Galloway on the covers in stained glass, surrounded by beasts.

Voices outside. Durwood shut the drawer and went to the door. She peered out the peephole. Across the parking lot, she saw Barry closing the bar, Seth staggering back to his room. There was cawing from the road, and another ravenknight swung its angular body through the dark. The scythe glinted starlight over its shoulder as it swaggered away, holding the cage out like a lantern, swaying to and fro. On patrol.

"Comforting," Durwood murmured.

She went to the mattress, knelt, and shoved her hand underneath to retrieve May's notes.

A scream.

Durwood dropped the book and shot up, pressing herself against the wall. She leaned forward and peered outside the window.

Silence.

Another high, piercing scream. Ripping through the night.

Then silence, stillness again. Nothing but shadows and trees.

She pulled her gun from her waistband, checked the chamber, and eased open the door. The lot was empty except for her bike, perched against the outer wall. She glanced around, pulled the bike into the room, then stepped fully outside. The bar looked abandoned and lonely. There was light in Room 1. Seth, if she had to guess.

She drew her attention back to the woods and scanned the treeline for glinting eyes, tall looming shadows, anything at all.

The dark was still. It held its breath, just as she was holding hers.

She gave it one last appraising look and backed slowly inside. She locked the door, pushed a chair up against it. She sat at the desk with a sigh, glanced out the window, and looked down again at the books.

Another screech from outside, farther away.

An answering call, somewhere closer.

The beasts were on patrol.

She dug through her go-bag and found an old sandwich baggie with a smear of crusted mustard inside. She wiped away the mustard with a Kleenex, stuffed May's notes inside, and removed the lid of the toilet tank. She pushed the papers down under the water. They floated to the top. She went outside again and took a few stones from the gravel in the lot. She tossed them up and down in her palm as she went back inside. She felt very alone in this place. Like she could walk right back into the bar and have more whiskey, endless whiskey, without asking anybody.

She shoved the chair back against the door, slipped the rocks into the baggie, and dipped it into the water of the tank. She watched it drift to the bottom, nodded with satisfaction, and put the lid back on.

She lay on the bed with a sigh. Stared at the ceiling for a while, feeling her heartbeat. She took out her phone. Twenty-six percent battery. She texted Bruce: *I'm alright but staying the night. Wish me luck.*

She lay on the floor and cracked open her Yellow Book. She found a chapter called "Reconstruction," which centered on the days after the Fogmonger's initial appearance.

She was writing a note about the gluttonbats feasting on piles of heretic corpses, when her phone vibrated under her stomach.

Bruce: *Be smart!*

She snorted a laugh and sent him a thumbs-up. Then she read and made notes and reread until dawn.

This was her absolute favorite thing to do. It'd almost killed her once, a year ago. But there were still people to save, mysteries to pick at, and a foggy mass suicide event that was only two days away, which she had no goddamn idea how to stop.

A Beating in the Deep

Galloway saw her life in montage. Detached. Like this was a show she'd stumbled across on late-night tv. Nothing more than a weird nightmare. She'd wake up in the morning, and everyone would be alive and whole. But for now, she floated through a fever dream, fading in and out of consciousness on the couch. She *must* be dozing on a couch somewhere in front of a tv, because none of this was real:

Emma on the news, showing off her green-ooze blood, encouraging everyone to prove themselves as good flesh. "Technically, I should feed myself to the beasts, too! But Francis says I have greater purpose. I am here to spread the word. People: You only have a few weeks before the Fogmonger arrives on the twenty-sixth! Join us and be blessed!"

Ashleigh, Jake, Troy, and Willy: all leaving the hospital without their left hands.

When Galloway confronts Francis in the hall (how could he lead an offering without her?), he looks confused. Smiling, he says, "Isn't this what you wanted? I'm helping the chorus grow." Then he laughs and brushes her hair out of her face. "You're really cute when you're worried." She's too stunned to speak, then he's strolling away from her toward his bus, whistling the Fogmonger's song.

Galloway walking through the halls, everyone looking at her, whispering her name. She realizes it was actually cozy to drift in a crowd, surrounded by brick walls that would never change, would never remember her name. She could never have that now. She ruined that life for herself with her own art.

Her history class is half empty, most in the hospital or kept home by their parents. Tolley glaring at her from the front of the room, but teaching on. It'd be against school policy to express a political or religious opinion in class, so he doesn't say anything outright, but all the kids can tell how he feels.

Dr. Eric over the PA system: "Have a burden-free day, Burnskidde. And have faith in the fog." People glancing at her in the cafeteria, her cheeks burning. She sits by herself in the corner, flipping dazedly through the ink-heavy pages of her notebook. All the way back to the pooping happy pigs that Francis had loved.

Boys keep stabbing each other with tacks in the hallway. Nobody has bled green yet, but you can tell everybody's spooked. Everybody's waiting.

Nicole scrambling around the house, cooking for their next visit to the park. Galloway has never seen her this intently focused before. Doofus doesn't even get in her way, he just lies in the corner, ears back. The entire house stinks of onions and boiling meat. Keith and the twins watch football in the other room. Teddy and Bobby shoot awkward, wide-eyed glances at Galloway anytime she comes in the room. She tries to start conversations with Keith, but he seems distracted, quiet, elsewhere.

ASHLEIGH, JAKE, TROY, AND WILLY ALL REFUSED HOSPITAL TREATMENT. Instead, they went home with rudimentary bandages to watch over their pigs. To witness the miracle. Sitting on their lawns under the stars, stroking their bloated hairless hides and singing, "Ooooooohhh."

Chief Pittner peered through the curtains of his living room. Great steaming breaths punching into the air as Troy's pig panted and shat and oinked happily, its tusks nudging Troy's chest, tail flicking. Pittner sneered in disgust.

Ashleigh's mother, Annie, hand to mouth, watched her daughter coo at the shitting wild hog in their backyard.

"Do we call someone?" her husband asked behind her. "Like a therapist, or . . . ?"

"What if it knows we don't like it?" Annie said through her hand. "What if they, like . . ." She shook her head.

"What?" asked Mr. Hunt.

"What if Rachel fucking takes over the town, Harold?" she hissed. "And we're the ones who sent one of their choir to the asylum? How will that look?"

Harold put up his hands. "Well, what the hell, we're just gonna do nothing? She can't be hurting herself like this. And Rachel wouldn't do that, she's a nice kid. We've known her since she was eight."

Annie just shook her head. "She doesn't like Ashleigh anymore. They never hang out. Ever since Ash joined cheer, Rachel's been a little bitch toward her. You'll see. She's not our friend anymore . . ."

Willy sang, "Ooooooohhh," as he stroked his poo-pig's flank with his stump. His parents stood behind him, beaming proudly as they sang along.

Mr. and Mrs. Mendez watched their son from the porch. His arm, too, was bandaged in a stump just above the elbow. It hurt bad when the pig crunched through that joint. That was when Jake had screamed the loudest.

But it was worth it. All four kids knew it was worth it. Because all four of them gasped in awe when those spiraling leaves burst out of the ground, twisting up, up. Branches stretching in a matter of minutes, growing from the manure that was *their* manure, that *they* had given birth to, tended to and wished for. Watching those twisting vines and stretching leaves—growing so fast they could hear it all *creak* as it stretched—that was everything they needed. Like getting a tattoo for the first time. *This isn't scary, this is cool. What can I do next?*

GALLOWAY'S NIGHTMARE-MONTAGE CONTINUES WITH HER ASSEMbly in the gym: a more subdued crowd than the pep rally a few weeks before. Her fellow students stare at her in vaguely frightened silence as she greets them. "Hi everyone. My name is Rachel Galloway. Some of you I've known for a long time, others only in passing. Many of you I've *never* met. But I think most of you have heard of me at this point, which is . . . weird. To say the least."

Nighttime, in the park: Edie Neglani helps Nicole spread tablecloths over tables. Willy is lighting the torches one by one. Keith, Eddie, and Safety Officer Wilson are chatting with Pittner and a male EMT. The EMT heard about what happened last time, and he isn't so sure about this, you guys.

"Trust us," says Pittner. "She's volunteering for this." They all look over at Mrs. Zambrano, tying up her mass of dark curls. "If they want to kill themselves," Pittner sneers, "Fadden and I say fuckin let em."

Assembly: "At first," says Galloway, "I didn't understand these visions. I thought I had made them up, and I *told* people that. But my—our class-mates believed in me. And I know people are angry with me now, but I promise I was only trying to inspire a community that has historically lacked hope." She glances at Dr. Eric, his fingers steepled as always. He nods at her. She catches Francis's eye in the crowd and he nods at her, too.

The park: "I'm so nervous," Mrs. Zambrano laughs. "Will it hurt?" She wrings her hands.

"Honey, you're about to have a finger bitten off," says Nicole. "I'm positive it'll hurt."

Galloway tells the assembled high schoolers: "The creatures I've seen in my visions are no ordinary Renfield vermin. They don't want to hurt us. They only killed the Drings because those weren't the Drings at all. Look, we all grew up here. I *know* you've seen weird things. I know we were all there last fall when Stopwatch Man showed up on the roof, so I'm telling you, this is . . . It's just different."

Galloway stands in the park with her arms outstretched over Mrs. Zambrano's head. The woman kneels before the woods. Someone has constructed an archway against the trees. It could have been anyone. Galloway has lost track of reality. She hardly feels like herself when she shouts, "Beasts of the wood, hear our call!"

Everyone in the circle of torches around her yells, "Hear our call."

In the gym, Galloway licks her lips. "Look, I didn't ask for this. But somehow, I know that on Thanksgiving, the Fogmonger is coming for us. And if you don't follow his song . . . I don't know what will happen to you."

The park: "Beasts of the woods, we offer this flesh to you in return for prosperity and life," says Galloway. "This is good flesh that we hope to exchange for good earth."

"Good flesh for good earth," echo the people around her.

"We sing loud the Monger's song," says Galloway. "Hear us, please. And answer." And she begins to sing.

The gym: "We've been trading with the creatures of the woods in order to protect ourselves. To ensure the survival of this town that has always struggled to survive. We offer ourselves, and the creatures give us *life* in return. Not the death we're used to. We hope that we can get enough people to sing their song so that when the Fogmonger comes, he will bless us as his followers."

"Ooooooohhh," she sings in the park.

"Ooooooohhh," the people around her pick up the cry.

"Ooooooohhh," Mrs. Zambrano sings, loud, trembling, fingers reaching for the dark, tears pulsing down her cheeks as the undergrowth begins to rustle.

The assembly in the gym: "Like I said, I didn't believe in myself either. But this is real. Many people have *seen* how this is real, and you can, too. You, too, can sing your belief before it's too late."

"Ooooooohhh," sing the people in the park. Isabella Zambrano sings the loudest of all, practically shouting. She takes a deep breath in and bellows it out, "Ooooooohhh!"

The pig emerges from the trees. Mrs. Zambrano's voice cuts short. The pale snout snorts as the pig waddles close to her. Everyone holds their breath. The park is entirely silent. She remains still, outstretched fingers trembling. The pig sniffs at her fingertips, tusks grazing her skin. Then, fast, it lunges forward and takes three of her fingers in its mouth. Rips off her knuckles and chews, already turning back to the woods, ignoring the sinews and arteries that stretch and pop, spraying silent jets of blood across Isabella's face. She screams and holds up her hand. The EMT is at her side. Nicole and Edie are lifting her to her feet, speaking rapidly, consoling, "Keep it elevated. You did it! What did you wish for?"

But Isabella doesn't need any consoling. She's laughing, eyes wide, gaping down at her spurting stumps.

"Thank you," she sobs, laughing and crying simultaneously. "Thank you. I am flesh. Thank fog, I am good flesh!" She dissolves into happy sobbing as they haul her into the ambulance.

"Please." Galloway grips the podium in the gym with both hands, feeling dizzy, outside herself. "Have faith in the fog."

Thrum-thrum. In the morning, each of Isabella's fingers blossoms into a different tree. An apple tree, a pear tree, an orange tree—all pregnant with fruit. *Thrum-thrum*, the beating in the ground made it so. It pumped and pushed and *pulled*, draining energy from the forest, the hills, the mines. Not a miracle, but a cancer within a cancer, rooting deeper, digging faster, as it gave Francis everything he asked for. *Thrum-thrum*, take a deer and crack its bones. *Thrum-thrum*, inflate the skin, suck off its hair, shove it back up as something new. *Thrum-thrum*. Dirt grinding, squeezing, making. Veins pulsing bright and clear.

Soon, Francis would give it what it wanted. He had promised. And if he didn't, it would simply pull him under and bend him into something new.

Thrum-thrum, it took trash and corpses and fresh meat. *Thrum-thrum*, working them like taffy into new shapes. *Thrum-thrum*, there was so much material to use, when you were working underground. *Thrum-thrum*.

DOM WAS FLIPPING BURGERS ONE-HANDED. NEITHER GREG NOR Emma had reported to work since their trip to the Botanist, so Galloway and Dom mostly worked in subdued silence, serving the lone patron here and there. It was actually cozy. She could listen to her iPod as much as she wanted. But it was also achingly lonely. Emma still wouldn't even respond to her texts. She was busy tending animals, taking care of their house, spreading the good word. Galloway felt lost, like she'd created this big, exciting thing that had launched everyone far away from her.

The bell over the door chimed. She looked up, and there was Francis, beaming, in his black trench coat.

"Hey," he said.

"Hi," she answered warily.

He took a breath before he asked, "Can I show you something?"

She glanced at Dom through the kitchen window. "Where?"

"Like . . . my place?"

Galloway's stomach flipped. "What."

"Look, I know I've been a little distant lately, but there's a reason. I've been . . . caring for something. Something amazing."

"Okay," she said slowly.

"I want to show you what it is." He grinned, then seemed insecure. "If that's alright."

She glanced back at Dom again. He was intent on lifting a fryer basket and dumping out its onion ring contents with one hand.

"I'm off in half an hour," she said. "Promise me this isn't something weird."

"Don't worry," said Francis, sliding into a booth to wait. "It's gonna be miraculous."

WHEN THE BURNSKIDDE UNCONSOLIDATED MINING COMPANY FIRST moved in, the Post Office had been in the center of town, right next to the church and the mining camp. As Burnskidde grew, the Office shifted from town center toward its outskirts, and was largely forgotten. The Office still served as a hub of PO boxes for the neighborhood of modular homes in the shadow of the Billowhills. But it didn't serve much else.

Galloway had never even been to this part of town before. She lived in a cul-de-sac on the western edge. She walked silently with Francis, who was pushing his bike alongside her. She eyed the squat brown building of the Post Office, its glaring red neon OPEN sign. They walked past it, to the dim colony of modular homes. Here and there, windows were lit flickering by tvs.

Francis leaned his bike against a scraggly tree standing guard over a front yard of dead grass. Galloway gazed up at the house: a shotgun affair with a narrow porch. A light winked on as they approached. Francis dug a key out of his coat pocket and unlocked the door. It squealed badly as it opened, and Galloway almost felt bad, like the door was yelping every time someone walked through it.

She stood very still while Francis flicked on a light, then stood even more still. The light he'd turned on was an old chandelier over a dining table covered in trash. Old Pop-Tarts wrappers and Cheez-It boxes. Netflix envelopes and a handful of PS2 games rented from the video store. The couch in the living room faced a horribly mistreated coffee table and a tv on the floor. A sink dripped somewhere.

Galloway felt a tightness in her chest, a sudden flickering panic.

"Where's your mom?" she asked.

"She works late," said Francis, as cool and breezy as he said everything. "Come on, it's in my room."

Galloway didn't particularly want to go deeper into this house. It didn't feel like a house at all; it felt like a nest that contained Francis only when absolutely necessary. No wonder he'd sought solace in the woods. She had a feeling his mom didn't even exist.

He led her through the living room, picking his way over an empty pizza box. He flicked on the light to his room and revealed a small box of a space with a single blue-curtained window. There was a desk stacked with recognizable schoolbooks and a twin bed jammed in the corner, its sheets twisted badly. There were stacks of books along one wall, comics and pulp novels, and a small mountain of dirty clothes. And in the middle of all this mess was a large square thing, sitting in the center of the room with a blanket over it.

Something was alive in there.

"Um," said Galloway, stopping in the doorway.

"Here." Francis pulled a wobbling chair out from the desk. A thin-cushioned plastic perch with a missing wheel and unidentifiable stains. She sat on the edge, touching as little chair as possible.

"Such a mess, I apologize." Francis started kicking paperbacks and trash into the corners of the room, clearing space.

Galloway swiveled and gazed at the chaos of his desk. An old dirty monitor and a little spiral-bound notebook. She peered down at its open page. It held a pencil drawing of a man with a large, shining raven head.

Below the metal helmet, he wore a dark robe and carried a scythe in one hand. In the other, he held a gleaming cage. The cage held a single raven.

"What is this?" she asked.

Francis brightened when he saw what she was looking at. "Oh! I've been drawing. Yeah, just like you. Bet you didn't know I could draw, too."

"What is this," Galloway repeated.

"I call it a ravenknight," said Francis. "He keeps one of Addekkea's psychic ravens in his cage, and uses it to guide him. Like a lantern, but one that talks inside his mind. See, the helmet blocks off his senses from the world. In fact, to *become* a ravenknight, you have to blind and deafen yourself. *Give* yourself to the raven in service of the Fogmonger. It's a symbol of ultimate trust in the beasts."

Galloway stared at the sketch. The scythe, the cage. All that metal. It wasn't Addekkean. It wasn't right. "I didn't write this. My psychic ravens flew free."

"Yes, until beasts and men started working *together*," said Francis.

"But . . ." Galloway struggled.

"Look, I'm sorry again I've been distant," said Francis. "It just took me a long time to wrangle everything. That's actually why the house is such a mess, because they were flying around." He said this as an afterthought, like he had just concocted a clever lie to explain his home.

Galloway's lips were numb. So much was happening right now. "What were you . . . wrangling? Sorry, flying?"

"At first, I didn't understand. Then I realized why they came to me, instead of everyone else. It *knew* about my drawing of the ravenknights."

"Francis, what's under the sheet?"

"They didn't want to listen to me," he laughed, walking behind the blanketed crate. "They *wanted* to find their sworn companions, but I told them we weren't ready yet. Took me a *while* to get them to obey." He knelt.

"Francis, please tell me what's under the sheet."

"They just came *flying* out of the ground." He laughed again. "Right in my front yard! It must have taken a bunch of chickens or crows or something."

"Francis."

"But it doesn't matter what they *were*." He gripped the sheet, began to pull. "What matters is they're here now."

The blanket swept up over the crate just as Galloway said, "Wait."

It was a large black cage filled to the brim with ravens. Galloway had never seen one in real life. She was surprised by how large and wild they were. Scruffy and violent, they roared and fluttered and shook the cage against the sudden light. A great rush of fluttering wings. The cage rattled as they beat against each other, pecking, sending jet-black feathers flying out between the bars.

Galloway pushed herself to her feet, stepped back, pressing against Francis's desk.

He put up a hand. "They won't hurt you. They do have a will of their own, but they serve *your* will."

"I don't have a fucking will," said Galloway, gaping at the cage. "Where . . . Francis, where did you get these?"

"From the ground. Like I said." He stood. The ravens continued to squawk and bang against the sides of the cage. Scrabbling and screeching as he stepped around them, coming close to Galloway. "Don't you see? This is the kind of miracle we're dealing with. We can reshape anything." He spread his hands, laughing. "I mean, this is perfect, right?"

Galloway let out a sound that was half moan, half cry for help. She shook her head. "I don't . . . You're not gonna have a relationship with your talking fucking birds, Francis. These aren't Addekkean ravens."

"But they *are*," said Francis, whining a little. "Why don't you believe me? I wrangled these for you. For *New* Addekkea."

Galloway blinked. Took a breath. Laughed. Then rubbed her face furiously with both hands, up and down, up and down, trying to wash her face of this nightmare. She finally gave up, throwing her hands into the air and shaking them, demanding to know, "Where did you get these fucking ravens?!"

"Ask them." He stepped aside. "Here. Go ahead. Ask them where they came from."

Galloway stared into the cage. They settled, ruffling their feathers, quorking and cocking their heads at her. Narrowing their beady eyes.

She licked her lips. "Where . . ." She looked at Francis. "Don't fuck with me."

"No fucking." He put up his hands.

She blew out a shaky breath and looked into the cage. "Where . . . did you come from?"

A pause. The ravens were still.

Then a voice needled into her ear. Cold, wet, and gravelly, as if it were swallowing the words instead of speaking them: *We come from the earth. We are born for you, Rachel Galloway. We protect Burnskidde. We protect Addekkea. We protect the chorus. Protect the chorus. Protect the chorus. Protect—*

"Cover it!" she shrieked. She clapped her hands over her ears. "Please cover it!"

He threw the blanket over the cage. The voice went silent.

They stood there for a moment, Galloway's eyes squeezed shut, her hands tight over her ears.

"They were speaking to you in your head," said Francis softly. "Am I right?"

She opened her eyes. "You couldn't hear that?"

He shook his head, a smile creeping over his face. "See? They're psychic. They only talk to who they want to."

She whimpered, "Oh my god."

"So the blanket didn't make them stop; they stopped because they wanted to."

"I get it."

"Because they heard you and they respect what you have to sa—"

"Stop." She shook her head, lowered her hands. "Just stop." She was on the verge of tears. "I don't understand how this is happening. I don't understand where they're all coming from. These fucking *beasts*. 'From the earth' isn't an answer. Please. Tell me what's happening. What's really going on."

Francis looked innocent. He stared at her. She stared back.

"Okay," he said, expressionless. "Fine, I'll show you the rest of it. But you can't be scared." He pushed past her out of the room.

She scoffed. "Where are we going now?"

In the living room, he turned back, his face in shadow. "Outside. To the mine."

IT IS A CURIOUS TRAIT OF HUMANKIND TO OBSERVE VIBRATIONS about a place but to ignore vibrations we receive from people. We are so much more willing to forgive the negative vibe we get off a new friend than we are to do the same with houses or caves or antique shops. We do not excuse the behavior of buildings. We don't walk by an abandoned hospital and say, "Oh, he's not haunted, he's just having a bad paint job today." But we will go far out of our way, for years, to excuse the assholery of someone we want to believe is good. Perhaps this is because people can apologize, and buildings cannot. People can lie, but land never does.

So even though Galloway found herself standing outside the jagged, dripping entrance of Burnskidde Mine, a place she had never once entered nor had a desire to enter, she also found herself looking at Francis. Framed by rock. Her sweet, quiet friend. Her human friend. Inviting her inside.

Galloway would have been lying if she said she hadn't wriggled an X-acto knife under her skin to check the color of her blood. It's hard to pop your own skin. The body resists. But the bead of dark crimson that had welled out of her thumb was worth it.

If she jabbed Francis with a pin, what color would he bleed?

"You coming?" he called. His voice rang through the rock surrounding him. He took a small flashlight from his pocket, clicked it on, and swung it about the entryway. Leagues of dark stone in every direction. "It's beautiful in here."

Galloway saw him there, smiling and welcoming. And despite the tremor in her heart—the whisper behind her ribs saying, *Don't*—she stepped inside the bowels of the hill.

Ohh, she had so many opportunities while Francis opened the door of the shaft elevator, invited her in, clanged the door shut, and sealed them inside the cage. So many chances to run back outside. But Francis had the only flashlight. And now that they were descending, machinery grinding and squeaking, heat rising to meet them, she was stuck. The cage ground down, down, hundreds of feet per second.

"How . . . deep are we going?" she asked breathlessly.

Francis held the flashlight under his chin and smiled. "Hot, isn't it? This particular shaft is about two thousand feet deep. That's, like, the whole Empire State Building. You imagine, the Empire State Building going *down*? And then being on top of it?!"

"Awesome," said Galloway, swallowing hot, dry air.

Francis started to say something else, but the sound interrupted him.

Thrum thrum.

Thrum thrum.

He gasped and bobbed on his heels, like an excited child. "We're almost heeere."

She wanted to say, *Francis, I change my mind, I don't want to see it.* But she imagined his voice rising. Imagined the whining anger she'd glimpsed before. And she kept her mouth shut.

At last, the cage clanged to a stop at the bottom of the shaft. It lurched and rattled. The air was so warm down here; they were so much closer to the angry molten core of the planet. She had to breathe very deliberately.

Francis opened the cage door and held out a hand. "After you."

She stepped out into the tunnel, wide and dark and throbbing. A familiar sound in her chest. *Thrum thrum. Thrum thrum.* As the throbbing continued, it dawned on Galloway what she was about to see. At last, the final piece slid into place.

"Oh my god," she murmured. "You gotta be kidding me."

"You know what it is?" Francis asked, excited, bouncing. "You know where we are?"

"How did you find this?" she asked. "Does anyone else know about this?"

"No one. I used to explore down here all the time. I found it all on my own."

"Jesus," Galloway murmured, breathing hard as he led her down a tunnel, around a corner, down another tunnel. This way and that, and the beating grew louder, louder, constricting her eardrums, and finally, there it was: Lawrence Renfield's heart.

It beat in the center of a wide, tall chamber. Veins spun out from its meaty purple-red center, cracking into a thick net all over the floor, up the walls, curving up into the ceiling. With each pulse, the valves of the heart opened, closed. Light beat through its veins, a yellow firefly glow, rippling out into the earth. *Thrum thrum. Thrum thrum.*

"Francis." She was about to faint, to scream. "Did you . . . wish this all would happen? Did you wish for those pigs?"

"No," he said, wounded. "I wished you would pay attention to me. That people would pay attention to *you* and make you feel . . . like . . . how I see you. Strong. Talented." He lifted his shoulders. "I didn't know any of this would happen. I just wished . . . you would notice me."

"And the heart did everything else."

"The heart made it real. Just like in the story! It can make *anything* real."

"Francis, I *did* notice you. You didn't have to do any of this."

"Oh." He stepped closer to her. "You did?"

She stepped back. "I don't want to be down here."

"It's okay. Really, it's just like the old legend. Go ahead. Ask it. Ask anything!"

She stared down at the beating organ, nestled in the middle of its red veiny tomb. It called to her. *Thrum thrum. Thrum thrum.* She could wish for this all to go away, right? Technically speaking? But the heart would exact a price, according to the myth.

She shook her head, stepping farther back. "No, I . . . I don't want to."

Francis nodded. "Of course. I understand. Just as long as you know that the heart is beating for you. It's making all this in *your* name."

"That's not true. He doesn't care about me." She pointed at the heart, wondering if Lawrence could hear her. Wondering if Lawrence Renfield could *always* hear her. Her voice rose, "He takes things, Francis. He takes our flesh, he's *going* to take something else. He's not doing this for free. *That's* just like the story."

Francis stood straighter, and she could tell he already knew this. She could tell he knew the price, but wasn't going to share what it was.

"That's unfair," he said coldly. "The heart takes things, yes, but only to help."

"This is our fucking curse!" she shouted. In answer, the heart *thumped* harder, brighter. She took another step back, lowered her voice. "Why are you ignoring how that story ends? We *all* read that book of Carter Moone's stories in eighth grade. The heart story *ends* with people dying. Sheriff Rook killed himself down here to keep this a secret."

"I know," said Francis. "That's how I knew the story was real. I moved his bones myself last summer. But that's not the point. Look, look." He ran to a pile of things across the chamber. He picked up a large metal contraption and brought it back to her. "The heart made these for us, too. For your gospel."

The contraption appeared to be some kind of cage. It was about a foot long. Slim metal bars ran vertically between two horizontal squares. From the top square of metal hung four sharp glinting spikes. They were angled down over the sides of the cage, as if ready to swing in at the push of a button, piercing whatever lay inside. A long needle on the back of the cage was attached to a little glass vial. Opposite this needle was a small slab of metal. All of these pieces were connected with tiny wires and gears, leading to a small metal ring, dangling off one side of the cage.

"I don't know what that is," she said.

Francis held the contraption out to her. "This is for the ravenknights. It's the cage they put their heads inside to symbolize their gift to the fog. See, they give their senses to the ravens. When they pull the tab," he fingered the metal ring, "these barbs swing down into their eyes and ears. This bit grinds into their tongues. They lose all sense of the world outside of what they hear from their sworn raven. The heart and the gluttonbats have been collecting metal from across town, and it's been making these for *us*."

"But how does it do that?" Galloway asked, trembling, eyes locked on the cage. "It shouldn't be doing that."

"Who cares!" Francis threw up his hands, laughing. "Who cares how miracles work as long as they do! Look, we can have ravenknights now. Actual protectors. We can show the people of Burnskidde that our chorus is the way."

"Jesus, Francis, you want someone to put their head in that? To actually . . . ?"

"Give themselves to the fog in every sense? Of course."

"This is insane." She shook her head again. "This is fucking . . . They'll die."

Francis smirked, like this was no big deal. "They won't. I've got the key right here. See?" He pointed to the little glass vial. "That's the purest Renfield anesthetic you can buy. Allegedly invented by the mad scientist, the Edenville Butcher herself. As an aerosol spray, it's relatively weak, but still far more powerful than a typical anesthetic. A vial of it in pure liquid form, though? *That* can inspire and harden. It can twist pain into a bliss that people say is addictive. Look, straight shot to the top of the spine. They won't feel a fuckin thing."

"I didn't design this," said Galloway. "This wasn't in my book."

Francis shrugged. "Look, it'll be fine. I bought the serum from a guy in the Falls. Off Craigslist. Very cheap. We can buy more easily if we need to."

She hissed between her teeth, staring at the pile of head-cages behind him. She counted twelve glittering, barbed ages.

Then she frowned. Slowly, she asked, "Francis . . . all the metal you took from around town is going into those?"

"Yes."

She shook her head. "But the ratio isn't right. It must be making something else."

Francis didn't answer.

"Francis, it took way more metal than that. What else is the heart making?"

He stared at her. "I don't know."

She shoved him. "What *else* is it making?"

"I don't know!"

Thrum thrum. The heart beat louder. *Thrumthrum, thrumthrum, thrumthrum.* Faster, brighter, color pulsing through its veins, through the town.

Galloway breathed hard, looking around. Looking at the metal head-cage in Francis's hands. The barbs, the serum, and the little wire pull cord that they'd yank to make the contraption spring to life.

"Take me home," she said. "Take me out of here, I want to go home."

"Oh," said Francis, deflating. "I . . . thought you'd be more excited."

"Take me home," she said firmly.

He looked at the floor. His lip curled. He narrowed his eyes.

He swallowed. "Fine. We can go."

GALLOWAY TREMBLED ALL THE WAY UP THE SHAFT AS FRANCIS sulked in the corner of the cage behind her. She trembled all the way back to his house, and as she walked quickly away. He called behind her, "Have faith, Rachel! You'll see!"

She trembled all the way home. She trembled in bed, eyes on the ceiling, feeling the dirt throb beneath her, *thrum thrum. Thrum thrum.* She lay awake into the night, thinking about the heart, the missing metal. *Thrum thrum.* How much did it need? *Thrum thrum.* Could it actually produce the fog? *Thrum thrum.* Was it possible? *Thrum thrum.* Could it happen? *Thrum thrum.* How much metal and meat would it need to build a god?

NEW ADDEKKEA, OCTOBER 2019
Offerings & Obfuscations

Durwood stared at herself in the mirror. Sunlight was slipping through the bathroom window. A light blue glow on the horizon, burning through the spiderwebs of tree branches. She had a thin streak of muddy red from her mouth across her cheek. She was not surprised. She had done this before. All-nighters in college, hunched over a table in the library, picking at any piece of herself that might yield to her fingernails. A skin tag behind her ear, a scabbed zit, hangnails, cuticles, the corner of her mouth. Picking at yourself was the Durwood way, which is probably why Durwood tried so hard to find *other* things to pick at. Friends, family, the county itself. Maybe if she dug deep enough, she would find things hiding in herself, worming around her jaw. Maybe she would finally locate the humming, buzzing core of everything that made her— her. Maybe at the end, at the very last moment, Tom and Mom had seen that core in themselves—

A knock at the door.

She sprang away from the mirror and launched herself onto the bedroom floor, where May's notes were arranged in chronological order. She swept them into a loose pile and shoved them under the mattress. The second knock came just as she lifted the chair away from the door and slid up behind it. Through the peephole, she could see Fogg, with his red ascot and sharp chin. Behind him, a ravenknight. She felt those wide metal eyes on her, through the wall.

She unlocked the door and opened it a crack. Hand hidden, talon ready to flex.

"Mornin," she said.

"Did you sleep well?" asked Fogg in his cold, crisp voice.

"Yeah. Perfectly. You?"

"Yes." Fogg held up an envelope. "An invitation."

Durwood plucked it from his thick fingers. A sheet of parchment folded over and sealed with a blue blob of wax, imprinted with a raven.

"Cool. Thank you."

Fogg dipped his head and turned to go.

"Hey," she said. "You must have been here for the Fogmonger, right? I mean, everyone over ten must remember it."

He stared at her over his shoulder before answering, "I was not here before the fog. You bleed." He turned away again. The knight lingered for another moment before their raven squawked. The knight lurched away, swinging the cage out in front of themselves as they followed behind Fogg.

"Don't love how you put that, but I'll allow it," Durwood muttered as she closed the door.

She tongued the blood-smear in the corner of her mouth as she popped the wax seal and opened the letter. It was written in thick black ink with a slight purple tint at its edges. She'd read somewhere that you could make your own ink by boiling tea leaves with honey. Must be a pain in the ass. *Everything* around here must be a pain in the ass. If you needed, like, cinnamon, you had to grate it yourself. No shaky cans of spice here.

Dear Ms. Durwood,

I do hope you slept well in our modest but charming accommodations. Today, preparations begin for Clear Night, held tomorrow eve. It is to be a celebration of the last unfogged night of our time here, before the Monger returns. This morning, the Speakers and I are meeting to settle some last-minute affairs related to the organization of Clear Night festivities. I am hoping you might be willing to sit in? See how our humble community operates? Meeting the other governing voices of our chorus may help alleviate some of your suspicions about our ways.

The meeting will be held in the estate. Refreshments will be provided.

Have faith in the fog,
All-Speaker Urquhart

"Hm." Durwood folded the note and stuffed it in the back pocket of her jeans.

She knelt to her notebook, open on the floor, full of scribbled notes and questions, and added to it: Fog: Where does it come from?

That was the key. She was so used to having monsters reveal themselves, then stabbing and shooting them into submission. But the Fogmonger wouldn't reveal himself until it was too late. She'd have to go to *him* somehow. So where were these beasts coming from?

She got her phone from the nightstand. Twenty-three percent. Beautiful.

She debated, tapping the phone against her chin. She had no need to bring the go-bag along for the entire day, but she didn't love the prospect of leaving it here. She assumed someone would be rummaging through her things the moment she left this room. Probably Fogg, unless Urquhart had other cronies she hadn't met yet. Maybe he'd send one of the knights to come slash their scythe around, ribboning May's notes along with the carpet and bedspread, gouging the ceiling, wildly arcing that gleaming blade back and forth.

Eventually, she stuffed the notes in their baggie with the gravel, and dunked them back in the toilet tank. "Stay," she told them. She took an old cough drop wrapper from the bottom depths of her bag and placed it very specifically on the floor just inside the door. She bent one corner of it so that when the door opened, it was sure to slide across the carpet. She took a picture with her phone and eased the door shut.

"Fuck," she said, and went back inside to finally wash the blood off her face.

⤜⤛

IN HER NOTES TO MARK, MAY RENFIELD REMEMBERED BEING IN the park when people began offering themselves by the dozen. She remembered the police getting involved, people dying.

Durwood saw Burnskidde through May's eyes as she pedaled through the center of town. Despite the cool October breeze, she was sweating. She tried to pedal slowly so she didn't sweat to death, and so she could analyze everything around her.

May remembered Horridge Park, now rebranded as Galloway Park, in big white letters on the park sign. May remembered the old Burnskidde water tower, which serviced the entire town now that they were cut off from the county mainline. May also remembered a time when these streets were actual streets, and there were many more cars, not just the abandoned vehicles now rusting in parking lots and random driveways, filled with weeds.

Crawling over the old shell of Burnskidde were hundreds of people setting up a big fair. Canvas tents, big stoves and grills. Stages and small puppet theaters, banquet tables, booths for selling goods. The excited hum of a Carnevale was buzzing through the air, vibrating beneath the constant noise of people singing as they worked. Wordless, tuneless notes, "Ooh-ooohh! Aah-aaahh!" Beaming at each other all the while, laboring without hands or feet, skin stretched bright and tight over dents missing in shoulders, backs, faces.

Durwood watched one man with a missing cheek, half his mouth open to the daylight, drooling as he sang. His voice was strained but clear as he attempted to raise a tent with two fingerless hands.

Durwood gave up trying to weave her bike through all the people. She reached for her phone in her back pocket, then remembered Barry's reaction the night before. She didn't want to blow anyone's minds with her cheap three-year-old Android.

"Excuse me?" she asked a middle-aged woman setting out wooden dolls and toys in a booth.

The woman looked up. "Ooh-ooh?"

"Yeah, right. Ah-oh, or . . . Do you know what time it is?"

The woman leaned out over her wares and peered up at the sun. "About midmorning, I'd say. Maybe nine thirty, outworld time. We don't keep clocks."

"Right. Okay." Durwood nodded. "Thank you."

"Happy Clear Day!" the woman called as Durwood walked away.

She had three similar conversations with three similarly zealous townsfolk that morning. Everyone was so painfully cheery, and despite all the signs of mutilation, it was strangely heartwarming, watching everyone work together, free from clocks and social media. Everyone had given some piece of themselves to the community. That hit Durwood, really struck her, for the first time as she looked around and saw how *much* there was. You could shear off a hand and grow an entire tomato plant, a field of strawberries, a palm tree. She could offer herself and grow a birch clump for Bruce, to replace the one she'd smashed last year. Everyone else was doing it. Except for Urquhart and the Renfields, of course. And Fogg!

Another question for the notebook.

She paused and leaned her bike against the side of a booth. She got out her notebook and scribbled, *Who are exceptions? Why?*

"What are you writing?"

Durwood jerked her head up and almost flexed her talon when she saw Lawrence Renfield standing in the booth at her side, smiling casually with his hands in his pockets.

He chuckled. "Still jumpy, Miss Durwood? Did you sleep alright?"

"Good as I ever do," she said, relaxing. "You?"

"Oh, I always sleep like a baby." He rocked happily on the balls of his feet. He spread his hands around his booth. "Smoke?"

His booth was filled with small burlap packets of tobacco leaves. He even seemed to have different flavors. Interspersed between these packets were several intricately carved wooden pipes, long and slender, slick with lacquer. All different colors and types of wood.

"You made these?" she asked.

"Of course. I always wanted to sell tobacco and pipes, except we didn't have the climate for tobacco. Now, it's no matter with the beasts. Steenson over there has bananas, if you can believe it. So when we, ah . . .

woke up"—he chuckled—"I figured the hell with it, I should follow my dream. Carving's always been a passion of mine. See?" He held up a little wooden bear. It was beautifully detailed. Adorable, slightly cartoonish.

"Aw, his little paws" said Durwood. "I mean, expertly done," she added professionally.

"Yeah, he's a handsome fella." Lawrence put him back on the table. "Anyway, yes. These are my pipes."

"They're gorgeous," she said, lifting one gently in both hands. "What wood is this?"

"Birchwood," said Lawrence. "Nice, isn't it?"

"Beautiful," she breathed. She tilted it, watching the light shift along its length. For a moment, all her questions, her need to dig, left her. "Lawrence, I'm amazed."

"Thank you," he said. He seemed so genuinely pleased with himself that her heart broke.

"What would you trade for something like this?" she asked.

Lawrence screwed up his face, thinking. "Well. Depends on what someone has to offer. But on Clear Night? For you? I'd say just take it."

"That's way too kind," she said, lost for words.

"You can never be too kind," said Lawrence. "A good heart is good flesh."

"Right." She stared at the pipe. "Thank you."

Lawrence cleared his throat and said gently, "I can see you struggling with this place. Mark struggled, too. That's why . . ." He looked around. The closest ravenknight was supervising the erection of a dance tent several yards away. "That's why he tried to take May out of here."

"Got himself killed doing it," said Durwood.

"Probably." Lawrence nodded sadly. "Look, if your ultimate question is, Do I trust the fog? Do I trust this place? My answer is yes. Look at what it's already given me."

He was smiling at something behind her, and Durwood turned to see Robert waddling into the booth. He still looked smushed and somehow inhuman, but when Lawrence swung him up into his arms and blew raspberries on his cheeks, he laughed like a real little boy. His compressed little body kicked its stubby legs and smacked at Lawrence playfully with both pudgy hands.

Adelaide was approaching from down the street, baby Robin in her arms. Robin gaped at Durwood with vacant black eyes. Her mouth was open, and it looked even more snoutlike than before.

Maybe this family wasn't regrown by the Botanist after all. Two of them (Robin and Robert) were deformed, and none of the Botanist's alleged victims (Ariel Young, Nic Donnelly, etc.) were ever reported to be smushed or blemished. But then . . . *how?*

"Guardian Durwood." Adelaide smiled. "How are you today?"

"Good. Your husband gave me a pipe." She held up her gift.

"Ohh, that's a pretty one." Adelaide wrinkled her nose in delight. "Isn't he great?"

"Best pipe carver I've ever met," said Durwood.

Adelaide leaned in to give Lawrence a kiss. They smiled at each other, their children in their arms. Durwood wanted to stand here and watch them for a long time.

"Where's May?" she asked.

"Up at Urquhart's estate," said Adelaide.

"Big leagues," said Lawrence. "Speaker of Arts and Entertainment."

"How'd she swing that?" Durwood asked. "Do you get elected, or?"

"Informally," said Lawrence. "Each fall, we decide who speaks for what. May's a beautiful artist, and she has a good eye for plays, so we voted her in."

"We love plays," said Adelaide. "The children put on shows regularly."

"I bet," said Durwood. "No tv."

They blinked at her.

She coughed. "Well, I should skedaddle. Thank you so much, again. Lawrence."

"Ah-ooh," said Lawrence, beaming. "Blessings."

She smiled despite herself. "Ah-ooh."

She walked away, cradling the pipe in both hands. Good wood. Unhaunted wood. Gifted to her from Lawrence Renfield himself.

New Addekkea was a trippy place indeed.

⊷

THE RAVENKNIGHTS SWUNG THE BLACK GATE WIDE. THEY STARED at her with their expressionless metal bird-helmets, their scythes poised over their shoulders. Their birdcages swung unsteadily from their hook-hands as they breathed. *Whoo. Sniff. Whoo . . .*

Durwood parked her bike against the front of Urquhart's mansion and knocked on the door. Fogg answered in the same red ascot and black coat. She wondered if he had multiple pairs, or how often he did laundry.

"Everyone is upstairs," he said, stepping aside and ushering her into the estate. He gestured her toward the grand oak stairs, which creaked under her sneakers. Victoria was perched on the banister above, watching Durwood ascend. The bird cocked her head, ruffling her feathers. Durwood wondered if she was telepathically reporting her arrival to Urquhart, or if that psychic raven gag was just more control-mongering bullshit. Even if it was, the community did *seem* crime-free. So what if they all wanted to stand in the fog and sing their little hearts out? *Mass suicide event . . . I tried to save her . . .* Had Mark been wrong? No. She could feel it in her gut.

The upper floor was a wide hall with tall ceilings, filled with windows. Gray light poured in at her from every angle. All of the regal wooden doors were closed, including the double doors at the end of the hall. Fogg brushed past her and shoved those double doors open, revealing a wide, tall banquet hall. Through the windows, she could see all of New Addekkea, all the way to the Post Office and the autumn-stained wall of the Billowhills. The variety was stunning from up here. Palm fronds, lemon trees, fields of tobacco and corn. Chickens and horses and turkeys and bees . . .

She fogged up the glass, looking out at this blessed little bubble of civilization. It was only when she heard Urquhart's voice that she fully registered the rest of the room. "Ms. Durwood. Thank you for joining us."

She turned and assessed the room. Two tables, one against the far wall, laden with plates of scones and fruits and little cakes, as well as pots of coffee and tea, steaming over open flames in cauldrons. The other table was a massive dark wooden beast, several wooden chairs seated around it. At the head of this table sat All-Speaker Urquhart in his sky-blue robe. At his sides sat Dr. Eric and a meaty man with hairy arms, bright with scar tissue, stretched tight over dented flesh. He looked to be sixty years old, mouth constantly flickering between smug grin and snarl. Next to him was a skinny twitching woman, and the one-legged man from the park. He fiddled with his cane and eyed Durwood with a disgusted expression she couldn't quite decipher. Next to *him* sat Isabella Zambrano and, closest to Durwood, May Renfield.

Surrounding the perimeter of the room were eight brass-headed ravenknights. One for each Speaker, and two flanking Urquhart. Cages in one hand (or hook), scythes in the other. Breathing like mechanical bulls. The ravens in the cages cocked their heads this way and that, silently appraising Durwood as one.

Urquhart smiled at her and spread his hands. "I am *so* pleased you could make it."

She made a shaka sign with her hand, gave it a little cowabunga shake, and said, "Wouldn't miss it."

"Everyone," said Urquhart, "this is our outworlder guest. Ms. Durwood will be joining us for the great blessing. Hopefully, we can get her to have a bit more faith in the fog than she currently does." His monocle glinted mischievously.

"I feel like I currently have an appropriate amount of faith," she said.

Urquhart laughed. "Tell that to our Speaker of Faith himself, Gregory Dring."

The young man with the cane nodded to her. Out of them all, he seemed the least happy to be here. The bags under his eyes were especially dark.

"Our Speaker for the Children, you met yesterday, of course," said Urquhart, gesturing to Dr. Eric. "Isabella, too, she's the Speaker of Public Health, I think I mentioned. May, of course, you met. And this is Eddie and Edie Neglani. Speakers of Commerce and Records, respectively."

"Good to officially meet you all," said Durwood. "Are these scones up for grabs?" She realized she hadn't had dinner. Or breakfast. A hangover was poking at the backs of her eyes.

"Absolutely," said Urquhart. "I told Fogg to bring a chair for you, but . . . Ah."

Fogg had appeared behind her. "Chair," he said, placing a hardbacked wicker chair before her.

"Wow," she said, biting her tongue on a sarcastic jab about miracles.

She sat in the corner by the end of the tea table, chewing.

"Where were we?" Urquhart asked.

"We were discussing the Clear Night pageant," said Dr. Eric.

"Yes! Of course," said Urquhart.

"We do one every year," Edie added curtly to Durwood.

"Nice," said Durwood politely, mouth full. The scone was, of course, delicious.

"But this year, it'll be the actual Clear Night," said Edie. "The night before his return. Ohh!" She clapped her hands. "I'm so excited."

Eddie laughed and patted her shoulder.

"Usually, it's the same," said Dr. Eric, smiling his squinty-eyed smile. "The pageant, I mean. A variation on a theme."

"What's the theme?" Durwood asked.

"A toast to the memories of Old Burnskidde," said Dr. Eric, tapping the steepled stubs of his once-upon-a-time fingers. "A celebration of everything we've endured."

"It's skits," said Greg. "Skits based on stories from the Gray Book."

"The boys' choir is in charge of constructing the papier-mâché Fogmonger this year," said Dr. Eric, flipping through his parchment-paper notes. "Usually, a float for Clear Night celebrations is their give-back project."

"Anyone ever complain about having to give back?" Durwood asked.

"People rarely complain at all," Eddie asserted, eliciting a raspy laugh from Isabella, who nodded in agreement.

Edie tittered with excitement. "Oooh, I can't wait."

Eddie Neglani laughed and rubbed her back with a three-fingered hand. "My pious wife."

The meeting went on with surprisingly boring minutiae. For a people whose promised savior was supposedly mere days away, they certainly seemed pretty calm about it (except for Edie). She found herself tuning out, roving her eyes about the room. The ravenknights around its perimeter made her itch. She felt their cold metal stare chilling her skin, and she wondered if they viewed her as a fellow bird of prey, or just as prey.

She couldn't sit still anymore. "I have a question."

Everyone blinked at her.

"Yes?" said Urquhart, amused.

"Do you have a Speaker of Science? I mean your system is based on old Addekkea's form of government, right? Well, seems like you have all other categories covered, but according to the Gray Book, old Addekkea had a Speaker of Science as well."

"Oh." Dr. Eric frowned. "Yes, we don't . . . have one of those."

"We are a place of miracles," said Urquhart. "We don't *require* science. Our children are taught to tend the earth at the Academy. The earth is all about breath and renewal. Science isn't necessarily involved."

"Okay, well, beg to differ. All due respect. And what about a Speaker of History? You don't have one of those either. According to the 'Addekkean Journals,' Addekkea had a Speaker of History as well. They're the one who unearthed the scroll in the Addekkean archives about the way of the beasts in the first place. So." She looked up from her notes and caught Greg Dring's bemused eye. "That seems like something important to have."

Urquhart scoffed. "Edie is our Speaker of Records. She was here from the beginning, as most of us have been. She keeps the histories. Look." Urquhart cleared his throat and leaned forward over the table. He folded his hands, cracked his knuckles. "Our government was *inspired* by Addekkean ways. They had slightly different needs and priorities. I think," he addressed the group, "this is a prime example of outworlders poking at our ways. Maybe we shouldn't have opened the tunnel at all." He shrugged. "But I said this before, of course."

"It's important that we share the fog with everyone," said Greg evenly. "I've always said this. With the tunnel open, we can bless the valley as well. Even if they're not faithful, the—"

"You made your argument persuasively enough *weeks* ago," said Urquhart bitterly. "It's open, it's done." He shuffled his notes. "That's all the business we have for today, and it's a holiday anyway, so let's adjourn there. Oh-ooh?"

"Ooh-oh," the Speakers sang back in agreement.

"Ah-ooh," said Urquhart. "May your day be clear."

"And have faith in the fog," they all said together.

They began scraping back their chairs. May shot Durwood a look before darting away. They all filed out after her, giving Durwood quick smiles on their way past. The only one who didn't smile was Eddie Neglani, who growled at her as he left the room. The ravenknights swaggered out after the Speakers, and Durwood was alone with Urquhart once more.

"Well, I hope that was enlightening," he said. "You see, we don't have anything particularly nefarious to discuss at these meetings. They've only ever been about keeping the chorus happy. It's almost hard to grasp." He gazed out the windows at his domain. "The ravens announced his return just a month ago. And now it's here. The Fogmonger's great blessing." He shuddered with anticipation. "Edie's right, I have goose bumps."

"You're right," said Durwood. "I'm dubious. But I get how the community works. Taking care of each other? It's . . . admirable." She almost gagged on the word.

Urquhart smiled smugly. "Isn't it? If you had seen the chaos we clawed out of back in '09, you'd be proud of us."

"I'm sure," said Durwood. "Hey, why is it that you have light here? Downstairs. You have power when no one else in town does."

"The mansion has a generator," said Urquhart. "It runs on vegetable oil. You'll find there *are* other generators here and there. The high school gymnasium is a highly effective greenhouse these days." He clicked his teeth together. "Or would you like to disbelieve and poke holes in *that* idea as well?"

"Thought you tried to live off the land," said Durwood.

"Yes, well, not every bit of rhetoric can . . . reasonably be followed comprehensively."

"Is that why you've never offered yourself to the beasts?"

"Oh, I do so much else for the community," he said, in a perfect imitation of a politician. "I hardly have the time. Here's one for *you*: Why were you asking about our Speakers? What's the point?"

"Well, like you said." Durwood rose to her feet. "Just pokin holes."

WHEN SHE EMERGED FROM THE ESTATE, BLINKING IN THE DAY-light, Durwood found her bike bent in half. One of the wheels had been tossed into the yard; the other was badly dented and barely hanging on to its chain. The handlebars were wrapped around each other, and her little mirror was shattered.

"What the fuck," she muttered. She picked up a corner of the dented, bent mess and dropped it. It clanged sadly on the ground.

Urquhart came outside, Victoria flapping away into the sky.

"Someone fucked up my bike," said Durwood.

"Ohh, it must have been one of the other knights," he said. "They're probably feeling protective."

"Then tell them to back off," she said, losing her cool.

He shrugged. "I'm sorry. They *can* be overzealous, I'll admit. But . . ." He shrugged again.

"Stop shrugging," she snapped. "Shit, man. They broke my bike."

Urquhart tsked. "That is unfortunate. Perhaps they're encouraging you to relax. To stop poking holes." He chuckled darkly before saunter-ing off. "Have a clear day, Durwood."

She mimicked him when he was out of earshot, whining, "Have a clear day." She turned her ruin of a bike over and over, searching for telltale claw and/or bite marks. Something she could easily identify or recognize from the Shelter archives. But as far as she could tell, the bike had been pulled apart by human hands.

She caught Fogg glaring at her through a window.

"You fuck my bike?" she yelled.

He responded by slowly lowering the blinds, blocking her from view. She took that as a yes.

DURWOOD SET OUT TO FIND MAY. IF THEY COULD TALK MORE ABOUT Mark and what May remembered, some of Durwood's missing pieces might slide into place.

She walked through streets lined with booths and stages, fiddling with her birchwood pipe. She passed a tent in the parking lot of the old Pan-cake Planet. Inside was a long makeshift wicker bar and several wooden tables. A band played in one corner. Fiddles and guitars, a player piano. A large group of people were engaged in some Addekkean drinking song, arms draped over each other, swinging back and forth, wailing about "that knifeman who stole my love away." The band wasn't bad. The fid-dler had one hand and a series of leather straps holding the fiddle to his stump. The pianist had no legs. He pulled strings to work the pedals.

She saw Bartender Barry Barr slinging drinks and waved to him. He waved back cheerfully as she walked by.

A group of boys were slathering together a huge rounded knob of papier-mâché. Dr. Eric stood to one side, squinting at them. "Yes. Put your backs into it . . ."

At last, she found May overseeing another part of the pageant, a large mural that was apparently supposed to roll off- and onstage. She looked happy, talking animatedly as she painted, smiling as she added a dab of red to the Addekkean sunrise. *Red. Dead on the toilet.*

Durwood wondered what the original May had thought about, cared for, wanted to do with her life. May's 1927 diary had never been copied online, and Durwood wished badly she or anyone else in the Guard had managed to get their hands on it.

Poor girl. Strewn to pieces and scattered into rumors. And yet, here she was. Durwood couldn't help but see her in slow motion. Every movement, every vibration of her throat as she spoke. The way her eyes moved . . .

"Are you okay?" May asked her.

Durwood realized she'd been staring. "Oh. Yeah. I mean . . . Oh-oh, or whatever."

"You're bleeding."

"Hm?" Her fingers were at her mouth again. Her thumb was smeared with a thin layer of red and the corner of her mouth stung. "Oh. No, I'm fine."

"Here." May put down her palette and brush and took a handkerchief from her pocket. She pressed it against the corner of Durwood's mouth.

The cloth was cool and silky. May's eyes were bright and blue. Suddenly, they were very close.

"Were you looking for me?" May whispered.

"I saw your notes," Durwood whispered back.

"Good," said May. "Mark didn't know what to do. He said I should come with him. Avoid the fog and find shelter with your people."

"You don't trust the fog?"

"I did. Until I started to remember. Now . . ." Her eyes searched Durwood's.

"Does your family have memories?"

"No. I've pried."

Durwood grunted. "But something's wrong with them, too. Robert looks . . . melted. And that baby? How long has she been a baby?"

May got a dreamy look in her eye. "Since she was born, I suppose. I don't know what you mean."

Durwood had hit a wall with that one. There was clearly a pall over the Renfields, which kept their minds relatively sedate. Good for May, breaking through it even a little. She was strong.

"These memories you're having," Durwood said. "When did they start?"

"A month ago."

"Just out of the blue?"

May smiled. "Around here, we say out of the fog."

"Of course." Durwood suppressed an eye roll.

"Miss Durwood, I've said all I know," said May. "I wrote those notes for Mark. To get the lies *out*. He said this kind of thing has happened before."

Durwood grunted. *Barnaby Wroth's bottles in the bog.*

"There are others who have lost faith," May whispered. "When Urquhart announced the Monger's return, Greg was the one who argued for opening the tunnel. Urquhart didn't want to. Greg told him it was to spread the fog, but really it was so someone could come through and *help* us."

"Help you what? Without a lead, I don't understand what I'm looking for. I . . ."

Over May's shoulder, Durwood saw a ravenknight turn slowly toward them.

"I'm digging," she whispered, clutching the handkerchief. "But do you have any other direction? *Any* clue about how to stop the blessing?"

"May?" Dr. Eric called over. "Your expertise is required. Aha ha."

"Keep it," said May, pressing the handkerchief to Durwood's face, then turning back to the mural. Slowly, the ravenknight directed its attention elsewhere.

Durwood stared at the handkerchief. In certain circles, May Renfield's personal effects could be worth thousands of dollars.

She stuffed it in her pocket.

SHE SPENT THE AFTERNOON TROMPING THROUGH THE WOODS, TRY-ing to trace paths from Galloway Park to wherever the beasts were coming from. There were no prints, no lingering scat—nothing at all that she could track. It was as if the beasts had popped up out of the very ground. So she returned to town and began literally digging. She would kneel down, scan the area for ravenknights, and flex out her talon, pulling up the roots of various plants: peppers, berries, a plum tree.

"Don't tell, don't tell," she muttered as she jabbed a goat in the thigh. The goat bleated and jerked away from her, but it bled a normal red. She jabbed a cow, too. It, too, bled normally. She skulked away as it mooed, far gone before the closest ravenknight could glide over and investigate the noise.

She interviewed half a dozen people who all told her the same thing: They were happy here. They trusted Urquhart and the fog's power, partially because of the miracle of the Renfields. Yes, the beasts could be frightening, and their orthodoxy *was* strict about never leaving New Addekkea. But ultimately, the offerings felt no more bizarre than any other religious rite.

"I love the beasts," Isabella Zambrano said, her tongue pressing through her half cheek. "Fifteen years ago, I would've been scandalized to hear myself say that, but it's true. I like the parties. I like feeling useful.

I wouldn't go back if I could!" She rasped a laugh as she prepared fresh bandages for Rachel Anne's offering.

Little Rachel Anne expressed the same sentiments: "I want to become sugarcane. My mom says I have sweet blood."

"You're not scared about the pain?" Durwood asked her.

Rachel Anne shrugged. "My mom says birth hurts, too. What are we supposed to do? Stop giving birth?"

"I do *not* even *miss* the *noodles*," said Eddie Neglani, as he hammered tent stakes into the ground, enunciating with each swing. "The fog is *nothing* to fear. All our pain is in the *past*." Eddie paused to wipe sweat off his brow. "Oh-ooh?"

"Ooh-ooh," said Durwood, eyeing the hammer. "Do you know where I could find Greg Dring?"

BY THE TIME SHE ARRIVED AT THE OLD DRING HOUSE, THE SUN WAS beginning to set. It took so long to walk there, she was sweating again. But it stung at the small wound in the corner of her mouth in a way that grounded her.

The house was lopsided and losing its paint. No one had cared for it in a long time. She knocked, and Greg opened the door with a dour expression. He sighed. "Took you long enough. Come in."

Inside, the house was just as weathered, with peeling blue wallpaper and sad furniture. As Greg led her into the living room, he explained that he'd lived here once with his entire family.

"They're gone now," he said, limping along in front of her. "I can't keep it all up very well on my own."

"Yeah, I noticed your porch," she said, meaning the missing plank of wood outside, a gaping wound looking down into the crawlspace.

"Oh, that was Renfield wood," he said, waving a hand. "Got rid of that right before the fog came. Actually how I lost my foot. Stubbed my toe and it never healed. Offered my foot to the bats and sold the stained board to some woman up in Lillian."

They sat in his living room before the fireplace. He instructed his personal ravenknight to gather firewood. The caged raven cawed in protest, then led its sworn knight out of the room, leaving Greg and Durwood alone.

"Fog, I can't talk with her around." Greg massaged his face. He sighed. "She just stands there and breathes."

"They ever go into action?" Durwood asked.

"Rarely. The image alone is enough to deter disobedience. I don't think the knights even sleep. Always watching."

Durwood grunted. "So. May said you were the one who suggested they unseal the tunnel."

Greg sighed. "Yeah, I thought someone might come through and . . . I don't know. You haven't found anything yet?"

"I don't know where to look."

"Damn. Neither did Mark. All *I* know is that Urquhart isn't always truthful. I have a gut sense the blessing is gonna be . . . bad."

"And you didn't have that feeling before now?"

Greg shrugged. His voice was small. "Back in '09, I thought we were helping. I had faith in the fog. In all of it. But in the last month, since Urquhart announced the Fogmonger's return and May told me she remembers being someone else . . . I've had doubts, Ms. Durwood."

Durwood leaned forward. "Do you think Urquhart killed Galloway?"

Greg shook his head slowly. "I don't know. He was her friend. We all were."

"Do you have any idea who the Renfields might have been? You were there from the beginning. Who would . . . ?"

"I don't know," said Greg sadly. "They bleed red, though. Adelaide cut her finger slicing veggies at a potluck once. Everyone was like . . ." He blew his hands away from his head, indicating everyone had their minds blown. "Look, we were all shocked when they came out of the mine. Most people were *so* shocked they bowed to Urquhart immediately. Really, that gave him the clout he needed to declare himself All-Speaker. And with Galloway gone, nobody knew where else to turn."

"Alright," said Durwood. "Assuming the beasts are legitimately magical or whatever the fuck, maybe their magic brought the Renfields back? And Urquhart's an asshole, so the Fogmonger's return is probably something terrible instead of something great. But where does he come from? What's the terrible thing? How do we stop it? You see how vague this all is, Greg?"

"I know, you're tellin me."

Durwood leaned back and threw up her hands. "Then what am I doin here, man? You're the one who got Mark and me to come here. So . . . what?"

Greg sighed, long and deep. "I just . . . Sometimes I wonder if it's my fault. If I should have said something. In the beginning. I—"

The ravenknight came back into the room and dumped an armload of firewood by the fireplace. The raven cawed, and the knight stood sentinel, unmoving.

Greg sighed again, staring off into space. "I miss tv. I miss music. Kings of Leon. *Halo*. I never even got a chance to play *ODST*. You don't understand. When it started, we thought it was fun. Then Emma and Dom, they . . ." He shook his head, swallowed. "I'm sorry about your friend. I just . . ." He glanced at the ravenknight in the corner. "I didn't want to lose everything that's happened here. In Burnskidde."

The raven cawed.

Greg grunted to his feet (well, *foot*). "Rachel Anne's offering is about to begin. As a Speaker, I have to be there, but you don't—"

"I need to see it," said Durwood, standing.

Greg paused, then nodded. "Yeah. I spose you do. Follow me."

IT OCCURRED TO DURWOOD AS SHE WALKED WITH GREG (AND HIS lumbering personal knight) to the park that the only reason she was being allowed to wander around so freely was because Urquhart thought he'd already won. She had no idea what she was doing. This was usually the part of the investigation when things tried to kill her, she killed them first, she filed her report, wham bam, no thanks, ma'am, let's go get some hash browns. For all she knew, the Fogmonger wouldn't even come. *Oh sorry everyone, the ravens miscalculated.* Next *October, he'll be here.* Urquhart could pull that trick for years without losing clout. So long as he had the ravenknights by his side.

She followed the procession of people into the park, to the old harvest arch. The Speakers gathered before it in blue robes. Greg Dring leaned on his cane, looking gaunt. Eddie Neglani glared around the crowd, and Dr. Eric squinted and grinned.

Little Rachel Anne stood before them in a red dress and a crown made of daisies, twitching with nervous excitement.

When everyone had gathered, Urquhart lifted his hands and led them through a brief prayer. "Rachel Anne offers this flesh to you, O beasts. See her offering and know she is good of heart. Good flesh for good earth. Oooooohhh."

Everyone lifted their hands and sang, "Oooooohhh." Even Greg joined in, out of necessity.

Rachel Anne knelt slowly, put out her hand, singing loud, voice wavering only once, "Oooooohhh." And after a moment, out of the thorned shadows of the woods beyond the arch, came the hog. Large, bloated, and pale. Long, curved tusks. It waddled forward, sniffing closer and closer to Rachel Anne's outstretched fist. She held her hand steady as she sang, "Oooooohhh." Her voice trembling with uncertainty, "Oooooohhh."

The hog sniffed at her knuckles.

"This was the first miracle of Burnskidde," Greg whispered sardonically in Durwood's ear.

She was about to respond when the hog lashed out, clamped down on the girl's hand. Durwood heard bone crunch. Blood spurted out the sides of the pig's snout. Rachel Anne screamed as her parents clutched at each other, their faces a maddening blend of pride and pain. Around them, the town sang louder, some of them convulsing in ecstasy. "Oooooohhh."

From the branches above, dark shapes squatted and watched. Their wings twitched, their long tails flicked side to side. The gluttonbats peered down on the proceedings from the shadows, hungry and waiting.

Durwood watched them back. She couldn't look at Rachel Anne any longer, bleeding and screaming as Isabella sang and bandaged her. She couldn't watch the torchlit procession that followed the hog away.

She shivered, shaking off the spell like a wet dog. This was not a magical place. This was a bad place, and it needed to be shut down.

SETH BRENNER ACCOMPANIED HER BACK TO THE POST OFFICE. THEY walked slowly under the stars. When they were alone, he glanced around, and said, "What'd you think?"

"Nauseating," said Durwood softly.

He nodded. "Yes." He fished a cigarette and matches out of his pocket. "Hey, you don't have any Noxboros, do you? This pig tobacco isn't the same."

"Don't smoke, sorry," she said. "Can't you wish for Noxboro leaves?"

He held up a stump of a thumb. "Doesn't take. Different soil." He took a drag and winced. "God, I miss things."

"Hasn't anyone tried to escape?" Durwood asked, lowering her voice. "People must have relatives outside, or friends. Colleagues must have wondered where you went."

"We had one flight since the tunnel opened," said Seth. "Guy named Kevin Fetterman. His wife, Abby, was taken before the fog came. He was an avid supporter of the beasts, until . . . he wasn't. According to Urquhart, he 'offered himself' by trying to flee. 'Disobeying community rules *is* volunteering,' according to the Yellow Book. Bats chewed him up and spat him back out as a pair of horses."

"Jesus," said Durwood.

"So no," said Seth. "I'm not escaping."

"Why don't more people speak out against these offerings?" Durwood asked. "Especially the bullshit ones like . . . what's his name."

"Kevin? Well, people are foolish. Hungry for safety. Even the *illusion* of safety. Being willingly blind to the underbelly of Burnskidde is like eating a hot dog. You just don't want to know. You sure you don't have Noxboros?"

She patted his shoulder. "I'm sorry."

"That's alright," he sighed. "I don't think they'd do anything against this place anyway. You have a safe night, Ms. Durwood." They'd reached the hotel.

"You, too, Professor Brenner," she said.

That got a smile out of him, just before he closed his door.

She opened her door to find the cough drop wrapper moved across the carpet. Thankfully, May's notes remained where she'd hidden them, and nothing else was missing. Between this and the bike, she felt like Urquhart was just "poking holes" at her, too. The smarmy bastard.

She muttered bitterly to herself as she shut the door, never once noticing the ravenknight in the shadows beyond the parking lot. Standing utterly still, its lifeless bronze eyes always watching.

SHE TOOK A VERY LONG SHOWER. WHEN SHE CAME OUT, SHE STARED at the toilet tank. She removed the tank lid, dug out May's papers, and brought them out to the room. She sat cross-legged on the floor and spread the notes before her.

One more time: May Renfield had been a part of the town. She'd eaten at Eddie Spaghetti's, she'd gone to the high school. She was, like, a *person*. And she must have been someone close to Galloway, because many of the memories were about Galloway's early sermons. People gathered in the Dring basement, out in the park. Greg offering his leg. Durwood went over everything May remembered again, and circled the final line of the last note: *I remember that we never wanted anyone to get hurt.*

She sat on the floor, leaned back against her bed, and sighed. She put her hand on the carpet. Stared at it. She could offer all her fingers, all her toes, but it wouldn't bring Tom back. There had been a moment or two, since she'd entered New Addekkea, when she'd thought maybe . . . But no. *Stupid.*

She laid out May's handkerchief and Lawrence's pipe on the floor. That stupid asshole Urquhart. How had he made them? What was this fog? What was she missing? What did Mark *hear* that she couldn't—

A wail broke through the night.

She went rigid, listening.

Silence.

The wail again, floating through the air. Different from the patrolling beasts. A low moaning, hollow and pained.

She went to the door and pressed her ear against it. She heard it again. Like a wounded animal.

"Okay, okay," she muttered, making sure her gun was loaded, easing the door open, licking her lips, heart beating fast. "Fuck yes. Let's go, whaddya got?"

The bar was dark. The creaking of her door hinges was the only sound. She listened, head poking out of the room.

Another strangled cry. A groaning, sobbing pain. Someone sucking in a long breath and letting it out in an agonized mortal howl.

"Fuck." Durwood stepped out onto the gravel. Each step against the sea of small rocks sounded too loud. Everything so eerily still. Not even the gentlest of breezes. She was very exposed.

She turned in a careful circle, trying to pinpoint the direction of the sound. She heard it once more, coming from behind the bar. She took painfully careful steps, quiet and steady over the gravel, making as little noise as possible. She twitched at the sound of another scream. That's when she noticed Seth's door.

Open.

Slow, horribly slow, she stepped across the gravel toward the alley behind the bar. Heart drumming so fast. The gun heavy in her hands as she held it in the unique way she'd taught herself this last year: Angled toward the ground, her wrist held up along the barrel, talon ready to sling out at a moment's notice, so she was prepared to shoot or stab simultaneously.

The keening grew louder. She crept around the corner of the bar, peering into the alleyway beyond, and at last, she saw its source. Her heart sank.

Two large, pale hogs lay side by side. They looked bigger than the one who had come for Rachel Anne. Crueler somehow, too. Their skin was a mottled gray-purple, glimmering with a slick sheen of sweat. They looked ill-formed, like balloons filled with jelly. Their feet were long, soft pads caught somewhere between hoof and human hand. Steam poured from their snouts in great gusts of hot air as they panted like dogs, chests heaving with every quick breath. Their eyes were closed, tongues lolled. They looked like they'd eaten full to bursting. An overripe stench of gluttony hovered over them like flies around the dead.

But they were not the thing crying. Something wriggled underneath them.

It took her a moment to register the full picture in the dim light. First, she saw the drool spilling from their mouths. Saw the blood and shreds between their tusks. Saw the gore caked over their lips, the pools of shadow along the ground. Then she saw what they were lying on top of. Saw the arm reaching. The terrified, pain-addled eyes of Seth Brenner.

He had gouges and chunks missing all over his body. One of his legs had been chewed down to the bone and, as she stepped closer, she could see that the bone was missing dents itself, the marrow sucked out while the man still lived. His other leg was missing below the knee. Holes had been torn open in his thighs and shoulders. Bites had been taken out of his cheeks, his arms. One hand was still attached by a few tattered ribbons of tissue. The other had been bitten sideways, like a sandwich, the thumb missing entirely. *They love thumbs.*

Seth was leaking onto the pavement in great pulsing rivers of dark red. He lay completely still. Aside from his jaw, and the red froth pouring out of it as he screamed over and over, he might as well have been dead. He *should* have been dead. But still he screamed.

The hogs panted as they digested him. Too fat to move off their meal, stomachs engorged with flesh. It added insult to injury that they were lying on *top* of him, *full* of him. Durwood's mind reeled, thinking about what that must feel like.

"Help me," he cried, the words gargled and wet. "*Please.*"

A moment passed where Durwood remained absolutely still, frozen in horror. Then suddenly, blind panic surged through her body. Half fury, half maddening terror. She felt her eyes go wide, felt herself say, "Hey." Her voice was hoarse, choked, as if she were dreaming. She tried again. "Hey!"

The beasts lifted their heads. They eyed her, detached, uninterested. One yawned, tusks glinting wide. It felt like such a fuck-you that she shot it in the ear. The top half of the ear flew away, and the beast squealed in pain. It rolled off Seth's almost-corpse, sloughing off more chunks as it went. It struggled to its feet and bounded away down the alley, squealing. The other pig was slower, still kicking its legs, trying to hoist its fat ass onto its feet, when she marched up to it and stabbed it in the brain, lots of times. "Fuck *you*, fuck *you*." The beast hiccupped, spurted urine, shivered, and died. Panting, she looked up after the earless hog, but it had already vanished into the woods. She looked back down, and saw the beast bleeding red, leaking gray matter.

Seth was taking big, wheezing breaths as she knelt at his side. He was coughing blood out of a half-missing throat. Tubes and arteries mangled, sticking out.

"Seth," she said gently. "You didn't volunteer."

He twitched and blew blood bubbles, gasping, "Told you . . . Told you . . ."

Her heart hurt. She put a hand on his forehead. It was ice cold, clammy.

"It's gonna be great," she whispered, brushing his hair back. His eyebrows jerked, and she explained: "Wherever you're going. It's gonna be awesome. I can tell."

He gargled a laugh. His face twitched. Then he smiled. "Nate . . ." He choked on the word, and passed away.

She sat stroking his hair for quite some time. So long, in fact, that when she looked up, the sky had turned the dark blue of dawn.

Someone was behind her. She whirled around, spike out.

Urquhart was aghast. "You . . . you've killed a sacred pig. A beast of the woods!"

Durwood rose and glared at him. He was flanked by knights. She didn't think she'd be able to shoot or stab all of them before a scythe found her throat.

"He didn't offer himself," said Durwood. "They took him."

Urquhart sputtered. "They don't . . . He *clearly* volunteered! But *you* killed a sacred beast. An envoy of the Fogmonger himself!"

"Sacred, huh?" She put her foot on the pig and kicked it over. Its ear flopped up, its tongue lolled out. The illusion of this place had officially shattered. "Then how come I killed it so easily?"

BURNSKIDDE, NOVEMBER 2009

Rise of the Ravenknights

November 19, 2009. A week before the fog was set to arrive.

A vast dread burned beneath Galloway all the time. As if all that stolen scrap was heating up underground, boiling the entire town. She pictured the heart in the mine beating faster, hotter, *thrum thrum, thrumthrum, thrumthrum*.

In Eddie Spaghetti's, Willy led them to a special table by the window. "Best seat in the house."

"Thanks, Willy," said Nicole as he held out her chair for her.

"Ah-ooh," said Willy, saluting them with his stump. "Have faith in the fog."

"Ooooooohh!" the twins cried in unison, startling people at nearby tables.

Eddie himself delivered their meals, pointing out specific ingredients. "My son grew these mushrooms. Jake Mendez grew these tomatoes . . ."

"Oh," said Keith. He peered at his plate. "This was all . . . ?"

"On the house," said Eddie. "No noodles for the Fogmonger." He laughed, then thrust a finger at Galloway. "*This* I will make into bay leaves. Yes?" He laughed again.

SIX DAYS UNTIL THE FOG.

Galloway felt utterly untethered. She felt behind herself somehow, and the imp driving her skin would say things she only partially comprehended. "This is where the Addekkean Academy used to be," holding up a sketch of the old Addekkean colony for her history report. Just going through the motions now, half the class absent or mutilated or both. Bartrick Regional had an entire ward now under Isabella Zambrano's supervision, dedicated to people post-offering. People had asked Galloway to visit, but she couldn't do it. Didn't want to see how many of them were there.

Everything had started here, in this overheated corner room of Burnskidde High. Now, Tolley watched her give this bullshit report from behind his desk, rapping a pen against his knuckles.

"It's interesting," he said when she was done. "You did a fine job. But I can't find *any* real evidence of Addekkea, anywhere I look. I've tried googling it, but nothing comes up." He tilted his head.

"Mr. T," said Jake. He looked appalled. "That's heresy, yo."

Tolley looked around at the other kids with bandaged stumps. They outnumbered him by far.

"I see," he said. "Then I suppose you get an A, Galloway. I hope it was worth it." Sneering as he scrawled an A in his gradebook.

After school, Ashleigh spearheaded the second edition of the Gray Book. She had transformed the yearbook office into a small press. At the big table in the center of the room, other students Galloway didn't even know were tearing sheets of paper out of yearbooks.

"These are ones from last year that nobody bought," Ashleigh explained. "The idea is to stuff the copies inside these recycled hardcovers and paste the new cover on top. Are you *sure* you like the design?" She held the picture up again. A pencil drawing, like the outline of a stained-glass portrait. It depicted Galloway in the center with her mouth singing open wide, her hands outstretched, palms up. Surrounding her were the beasts of Addekkea, snarling and roaring in a monstrous corona.

"I love it," said Galloway, numb.

Ashleigh grinned. "Ooh-oh. I was *so* hoping you would. I had faith that you would. I mean I'm not as good as you, but I think it's cool, right?" She held it up again. "You look like a saint. Saint Rachel."

"Don't . . ." Galloway started. She coughed. "Thank you, Ashleigh. It's beautiful." Inhaling the warm ink and plastic scent of a dozen copiers, cranking and whirring all around the room.

FIVE DAYS LEFT UNTIL THE FOG.

Seth Brenner on street corners, gesticulating wildly with his copy of the Gray Book, chain-smoking Noxboros. On Facebook, people sharing pictures of their backyards and street corners, the lawns in front of the library and the movie theater. Plants were springing up everywhere, all kinds of things. Huge yellow squash, brilliant orange pumpkins. Peppers, spices, flowers, cucumbers and carrots and wheat, barley, potatoes. Willy Neglani had even asked to become corn.

At that week's board meeting, Town Supervisor Fadden leaned far over his bench and said, "Son, what you did technically constitutes self-harm."

"Yes, sir," said Willy blankly.

"And the only reason we haven't locked up everyone involved, out of concern for their mental health, is because of the argument that this is somehow related to your religious freedom. Frankly, I'm surprised the shock didn't make you pass out when you lost that hand."

"I was excited," said Willy. His parents sat at his side. He glanced at them, and they smiled proudly. "I *wanted* to get bit. I'm good flesh. Now I'm corn, too. Good corn! I love corn."

"Well, I hate to stand between a young man and his . . . dream to be corn," said Fadden. "But—"

Edie cut him off with a smile. "Mr. Fadden. Have a little faith in the fog, huh?" At her side, Eddie Spaghetti folded his massive meaty arms and glared Fadden into silence.

FOUR DAYS LEFT UNTIL THE FOG.

Francis began posting regularly on Facebook about the knighthood. Then Emma took up the call. She kept pulling away from Galloway, which made it hurt all the worse when Galloway saw her posts about ravenknights. "Give yourself to the fog," Emma wrote. "Meet your sworn raven and become a knight!" Galloway ached to tell her the ravenknights weren't even hers. Out of all the fake nonsense attached to Galloway's name, the knights were the most nonsensical. But that was the great irony here: Everyone was paying attention to Galloway, but nobody listened.

Emma and Francis were careful to leave out mention of the head-cages in their posts, lest they get pinged for encouraging self-harm or endangering the community. But people knew what the knighthood entailed through whisper networks offline. People knew that "giving yourself to the fog" meant relying on a fucking bird for the rest of your life.

Even so—people were eager to respond. Classmates, neighbors, adults, kids, people Galloway didn't even *know* were commenting and asking how they could get involved. Anyone could be a knight.

"Isn't that exciting?" Nicole asked over dinner. "Even I could be a knight."

"You'd have to poke out your ears, hun," said Keith. "You'd never hear music again."

"That's a good point," said Galloway. "You'd never be able to taste soup again either. The helmets eliminate *all* senses."

"Mmm." Nicole considered this as she sipped a glass of wine. "I guess. It'd be fun to protect the town, though. Wield a big scythe."

"What's a scythe?" Teddy asked.

"It's what Death has," said Bobby. He swung an imaginary scythe across the table, "Whoosh!" Shouting so loud it made Doofus jump.

"I want a scythe," said Teddy.

"Then we can scythe fight," said Bobby.

They fought with imaginary blades over the table. "Cling! Clang!"

"Alright, alright," said Keith. "You're too young to be knights. Right, Rach?"

"Well," she said slowly. Technically, Francis had put no age restriction on it. She imagined the head-cages sliding up out of the dirt in the mine, fully formed and gleaming, sharp. What went into them? A bit of car, a little snowblower?

"Anyone can be a knight," she said, her mind elsewhere.

⁓

THREE DAYS LEFT UNTIL THE FOG.

"This is out of fucking control," said Pittner, watching a dozen people lift their hands to the woods, singing.

"You see their farmers market today?" Officer Wilson asked. "All the food they've been growing? It's good. I mean, I had some fried zucchini Isabella grew, and . . ."

Pittner glared at him.

"It . . . didn't have any flavor at all," said Wilson, shaking his head. "Very, uh . . . not good. Wouldn't eat it again for sure." He cleared his throat.

"Mere weeks ago," Pittner growled, "people were afraid of these woods. So scared they took it out on *me*. They would never have communed with vermin like this. It ain't right."

"Just because it's new doesn't mean it's bad," said Wilson.

Pittner glared at him, as a dozen pigs crept out of the shadows into the park.

TWO DAYS LEFT BEFORE THE FOG.

People were terrified. They didn't know what was coming. They begged Galloway for more information, but she had none to give.

Francis stood outside the school, just off school property, swinging a birdcage in the air. "Rejoice!" he shouted at kids getting off and onto buses, at the beginning and end of each day. "The beasts have crafted gifts for us! This is where your metal has gone. Give yourself to the fog so we can protect this town together! Free it from the grip of heretics and knifemen like Chief Dickner."

Safety Officer Wilson and Dr. Eric stood in the school entryway, watching Francis with twin cool smiles.

"Oh," said Wilson, noticing Dr. Eric's missing thumb. "What'd you grow?"

"A peach tree," Dr. Eric grinned. "You?"

Wilson held up his bandaged half hand. "Eggplant," he said proudly.

Galloway felt helpless, so helpless. She didn't know what she could say or do. She was in the belly of a beast that had swallowed the entire town. Ever since she saw the heart, she had not been able to free her mind from the sound of its thumping underground. *Thrum thrum*, it was making this all happen. *Thrum thrum*, crafting it for her. *Thrum thrum*, dragging the fog ever closer.

So when Emma texted her, it was with a numb, inevitable sinking in her gut that she texted back, *Okay*.

"Dad?" she asked Keith in his den. "Can you drop me off at Emma's? They're about to swear in the knights."

KEITH CRANED HIS NECK OVER THE WHEEL TO LOOK UP THROUGH the windshield. "Certainly a more scenic drive these days."

Palm fronds drooped over the road. New colors rainbowed through the neighborhoods. Zinnias, goldenrod, carnations, daffodils. Signs with Galloway's name crossed out in big red Sharpie had been stapled over the REMEMBER THEM posters. She was shocked no one had thrown a brick through her window.

"Do you think," she started. She chewed her lip.

"What, sweetie?"

"Do you think this is all wrong?" she asked. "Just feels so out of control."

Keith cocked his head. "It's been a wild few weeks, for sure. But I think you're doin great, honey."

"Really?"

"Of course. Who cares about the naysayers? It's okay to have doubts." He smiled at her. Her dad. Her kind, warm dad. "But you're a freakin hero. I've lived in Renfield long enough to know that you don't look a premonition in the mouth. And you've raised awareness about *this* premonition as best you can. So at this point, we just have to wait and see. But you did your best, and that's what counts."

"Right," she said, staring out the window at a one-armed man feeding chickens in his front yard.

They pulled up to the Dring household. Many other cars were parked in the driveway already.

"Good luck," said Keith as she opened the door. He beamed at her. "I have faith in the fog."

"Thanks, Daddy." She slammed the car door shut.

SHE STEPPED OVER THE MISSING PLANK IN THE DRING PORCH AND knocked on the door. No one answered. She eased it open and peered inside. "Hello?"

The house seemed empty.

She went in and looked around. Fast food containers and pizza boxes everywhere. A stale, sweaty smell. And a voice.

"Emma?" she called. She walked into the living room. There was the large square cage that she'd seen in Francis's house. Leaning against it were several steel scythes. Surrounding it, a dozen brass birdcages.

She stood staring at the assembly of metal. The birds in their cage cocked their heads.

"Where?" she asked.

Downstairs, they whispered in her mind. *Our sworn companions are just downstairs, downstairs, downstairs . . .*

The basement door was open. Voices coming from *downstairs*. She crept toward the steps and saw that they were clogged with people. The person closest to her turned and smiled, and it took her a moment to register Eddie Spaghetti's huge meaty mug.

"She is here!" he announced.

Song erupted from below. People parted before her, pressing in on her from all sides as she descended, singing to her in welcome. So many voices, so much sound, "Oooooohhh."

The Dring basement was packed. Students and parents and Seth Brenner and Dr. Eric. And sitting cross-legged in a ring on the floor were twelve teenagers. Emma, Dom, Ashleigh, Jake, Willy, Troy, and six others that Galloway recognized only vaguely from school. They were all here for the gleaming metal head-cages laid out on the floor in the center of the room.

"Rachel," said Francis, standing amongst them. "We were just about to start. Do you want to lead us through the knighting?"

Galloway looked around. All these expectant faces. Emma and Ashleigh, looking up at her with hollow eyes. Mutilated because she'd *told* them to. Her mouth was so dry. "I, um . . ."

"That's okay," said Francis. "I'll lead." He thrust his hands toward the ceiling, not missing a beat. "Beasts of the wood, hear our call."

"Hear our call," echoed every single person in that basement except Galloway.

"You have been kind to us," Francis continued. "You have given us gifts. And in turn, we have fed you, cared for your kind. Tended to the gifts we have received. We are ready now to pledge these bodies to you, to solidify our kinship through unbreakable bonds. These soldiers will protect our town with their lives. Beasts of the wood, hear our call."

"Hear our call," chorused the basement once more.

Francis lifted one of the head-cages. "This represents the cage that man has kept bird inside for centuries. But tonight—" He carried the cage to Emma and slid it over her head. She closed her eyes, mouth open in rapture. "Tonight, we reverse that dynamic. We cage man so that bird may lead the way once more."

He turned a key in the side of the head-cage, locking it in place.

"Beasts of the wood," he said, "hear our call."

"Hear our call," said everyone else.

He went around the circle, sliding the helmets into place and repeating the prayer. Every time he said it, every time she heard the click of the key locking those helmets forever, Galloway flinched. The metal barbs glinted in the low light. Four of them in a corona around each cage, ready to swing down into eyes and ears. The grinding bit of metal ready to clamp tongues to the roofs of mouths. And the small vial of serum, its needle ready to pop through the spinal column at the nape of the neck.

They can't possibly survive this, Galloway thought. *They're gonna die.*

When all twelve helmets were in place, Francis looked around and asked, "Are you ready?"

Emma and Dom glanced at each other through the slim metal bars of their cages. After a moment, Emma nodded, and Dom nodded back.

"We swear to protect the colony," said Emma.

"We swear," said the others.

Francis bowed. "Then pull your pins, and give yourselves to the fog."

"Wait."

All heads turned toward Galloway. Murmurs and a shifting of feet.

Francis looked around. "Did we forget something?"

"No." Galloway shook her head. "No, it's just . . . We shouldn't be doing this."

More murmurs and shifting around. Dr. Eric tapped his fingertips together. Eddie Spaghetti snorted and crossed his arms.

Francis narrowed his eyes. "What do you mean?"

"I mean this isn't right," said Galloway. "This isn't in the gospel."

Disbelief. The kids on the floor glanced around at each other uncertainly.

Francis scoffed. "You *wrote* the gospel."

"Francis," she said, appealing to a version of him she was no longer sure existed.

He shook his head slow. "This is heresy," he said evenly. "You're speaking heresy. Just like the other day when you asked me to stop."

"Well, Francis . . ." She gave him a pleading look. "That was . . . This is hurting people."

"The world hurts people," he said. "Tomorrow, we will be blessed, but we need protection moving forward. Protection from outworlders and knifemen. Anyone who doesn't understand our ways. Heretics like Fadden and Pittner, who would strip us of our faith unless we have people like these protecting us. These *brave* souls. Giving themselves to be knights at a time when we need it the most. Their scythes and sworn ravens are ready to go. You can't say this is all wrong *now*. It's already happening."

"You know what I mean," she said, silently begging him to realize that this wasn't right, it never had been, and she knew that now, seeing Emma in a cage on the basement floor. This was actually the worst possible thing that could be happening.

"I don't," Francis warned, eyes digging into her. "Don't do this, Rachel. Don't make this mistake."

She ignored him. "Emma." She knelt before her friend, her best friend. This girl she'd played mini golf with when they were ten. This girl she knew when they both had braces and stayed up late watching cartoons on the small tv in Emma's room. "Emma, *please* don't do this." She fumbled for Emma's hands, squeezed them. Emma's fingers curled distantly around her own. "I'm telling you. *I'm* telling you." She ran her thumbs over Emma's knuckles, with as much tender care as she had ever mustered in her life. "I'm telling you don't do this."

Emma's face didn't change.

"This isn't real," Galloway whispered. "I made this all up. You *know* that, you saw me do it. Please. You know—"

"Nothing's real," said Emma. Her voice was thick. "You don't understand. You cut yourself, I know you did. What color did you bleed? Hm?" Emma shoved her away. "You don't get it. I'm a fucking plant-person. This is the only real thing I have left."

"*I'm* a real thing." Galloway's heart was hammering so hard she could barely speak. Every word dragged out of her throat in a clotted, barbed wad. But she spoke with the crystal clarity of a woman begging someone not to jump. "Emma, you still have people who know you. I don't care that you're plants; I'm your *friend*. Please. Please don't do this. It. Isn't. Real. I promise you. I made this *all* up." She looked around at the others, watching her with empty eyes. She could tell none of them would be swayed. Not even Dom or Ashleigh. They were simply waiting for the signal to trigger the clamps, the thorns, the syringe . . .

"You don't have to do this," said Galloway. "I'll find something else. You can do something else. I'll, I'll write something into the gospel. You can have a place. A *home*. But don't do *this*. Please. Please."

Emma stared at her, lips pursed. She breathed heavily through her nose. Her eyes were pained and panicked and furious. She flicked them around the room. The eleven others on the floor all met her gaze with level and vacant expressions.

"I give myself to the fog," she said. She bit down on the clamp and yanked the metal ring at the back of the head-cage. There was the chime of a grenade pin being pulled, the grind of metal gears, and the bottom of the device tightened. Its base ground up into Emma's jaw, green blood spurted from her mouth onto Galloway's face, and Emma gargled and shook as the thing ground its way through her tongue.

"*No!*" Galloway wailed.

There was a high metal *ting* and the barbs swung down. Dark emerald ooze pumped out of Emma's ears, faster than seemed possible. She gurgled and screamed. Her eyes were the last to go, which made it all worse because she had time to give Galloway one moment of absolutely wild, horrible regret, just before the barbs swung down.

So much thick, viscous ooze. The grind of the screws as they wound deeper, *deeper*, the entire cage tightening around Emma's skull. Her hands trembled, her body rocked as she gagged on arterial green. Galloway was moaning, sobbing, "Nooo! NOOO!"

The vial popped down with a small *crack*, into the top of Emma's spine. She shuddered, whined—was still.

She lifted her head slowly, strings of ooze and spit drooling off her chin. Long green lines of snot dangled from her nostrils as she took deep, rasping breaths, like a wounded animal wheezing its last. She looked at Galloway with her twin metal barbs. One of her eyes had been lodged sideways, was squeezed halfway out of its socket. She eyed Galloway with this dead glazed orb. Sniffed. Then opened her mouth, breathed a long, gargling rasp, and smiled. Grinning with green-stained teeth.

"I have faith in the fog!" Dom cried from across the room. He jammed the metal between his teeth and pulled the pin on his own head-cage. It whirred and sang and crunched. His scream came out muffled and wet as he bent forward and vomited blood onto the floor.

"I have faith in the fog!" Ashleigh cried. *Ting*, she pulled her pin.

"I have faith in the fog!" Jake yelled, voice cracking. He, too, pulled his pin, *ting*. And all around her, Galloway heard the bursts of screaming, yelling, "I have faith in the fog! I have faith in the fog!" And the room was filled with noise, wet, spattering noise. Some of them puked through the bars of their cages, chunky red globules, ruined half-tongues sloughing *slap* onto the floor. Metal pinged and whirred and ground. And Galloway could do nothing but sit there, hyperventilating, tears pulsing down her cheeks. All around her, teenagers barbed and ground themselves into numb, eternal voids.

The worst was when it was done. Galloway almost preferred the screaming. The moaning and drooling was deafening, horrible. As if she'd fallen far down into a fetid pit filled with half-corpses, writhing in pain.

She cast her eyes around the disaster of a basement. Red spreading everywhere, with streaks of Emma's green. All of the teens wore dopey lobotomized smiles. They gurgled and chirped.

"They're happy," said Francis, his voice misty, proud. "You'd have denied them that?"

"How did you convince them to do this?" she asked.

"I didn't do anything," said Francis. "It's *your* gospel."

"It isn't!" Tears stung at her eyes. "I never wanted them to do *this*. I told you the gospel was fake. I told you over and over. Why wouldn't you listen? Why?" Yelling at Emma now.

Francis stared at her. She glared back at him. Her entire body shook. "*Why?*"

For just a moment, Francis's face cracked. He wanted to tell her *why*, he really did. She could see it in him. Saw the anger, the feeling that no girl would ever want a weirdo like him. He wanted to show her how powerful he could be. Really rub it in her face, what she was missing out on. But at the same time, he was surrounded by acolytes.

Suddenly, she saw all this in him, and truly knew him for the first time.

He lifted his head. Stood straighter. Pointed a finger at her, and said, "Bad flesh."

"Francis," she gasped.

"Bad flesh," he repeated. He spoke louder, faster. "You're not Rachel Galloway. You're some other thing. Some other heretic *thing*. Bad flesh, like the Drings. Like the nonbelievers. You're *bad* flesh!"

"Bad flesh!" cried Eddie Spaghetti.

"Bad flesh!" Edie cried with him.

"Imposter!" shouted Seth Brenner.

"Heretic!" cried Mrs. Zambrano.

"Bad flesh, bad flesh, bad flesh!"

In their eternal dark cages, all twelve knights cried out in answer. Blood rolled between their teeth as they opened their mouths and rasped. They began to swing themselves to their feet, rising unsteadily, heads too heavy to hold, arms reaching, fingers groping, stumps flailing.

"Bad flesh! Bad flesh!" the crowd chanted on.

"Stop it!" Galloway sobbed.

The knights around her screeched. Eddie grabbed her from behind, pinning her arms behind her back. She thrashed and stomped on his feet, but he wouldn't budge. She could smell the hot garlic of his breath as he chanted zombie-like in her ear, "Bad flesh. Bad flesh."

"Let's get everyone upstairs," Francis called out over the chanting. "We'll make her the first example of the power of the knights."

Eddie laughed. "Yes! Pincushion her!"

"No!" Galloway screamed, thrashing harder. "No!"

The knights screamed back at her. Adults came to them and put hands on their shoulders, tenderly, still chanting, ushering them toward the stairs as Eddie dragged Galloway backward out of the basement.

He threw her onto the floor of the living room, and when she tried to scramble to her feet, he rammed a boot into the bottom of her spine, pushed her back down onto the floor, pressing her face into the carpet. It smelled like sleepovers, like microwave popcorn and nylon sleeping bag, rubbery Polly Pocket, plastic VHS. She was going to die here, on this floor she'd slept on since she was little.

The ravens in their big cage squawked and beat at the bars with their wings, sending feathers flying through the air. She heard them crying in her mind, excited, *Sworn! Our sworn friends are close! We hear them! Sworn!*

Galloway reached up and scrabbled at the clasp on the cage as Eddie laughed overhead in his thick Dracula voice, "Such unnecessary struggle." He ground his boot into her spine, making her hiss in pain. Men like Edward Neglani were just itching for an excuse to use their boots. "Your flesh will be reborn as animals, pure and miraculous. So do not worry. Have *faith* in the fog."

"Fuck your fog." She ripped back the clasp, sending ravens pouring into the air.

Eddie gasped in surprise and lifted his boot just enough that she could roll away. She scrambled to her hands and knees and looked up, saw the ravens swarming him. He swatted at them, growling.

FRIENDS! they cried. *Where are friends?!*

Galloway grabbed one of the scythes and swung it, screaming with rage. She buried the blade in Eddie's shoulder, felt the metal grate against bone. He cried out and gripped the blade in both hands as she drove him backward against the wall. They struggled, ravens swarming their heads, tangling in her hair. But she saw nothing except the blade and Edward fucking Spaghettward. She pushed that curved blade into his flesh, grinding her teeth so hard she thought they'd shatter, and then he shot up his elbow, cracking her in the nose. Something in her skull popped and her head jerked back, but she held firm to the scythe. Her face felt numb and full, and she realized he must have broken her nose. Then he grabbed the haft of the scythe, wrapping his hands over hers, and wrenched it sideways, snapping the two-foot blade in half. He jerked the haft, caught her in the knee, and she fell to the floor. She lifted herself, wobbling, just as he swung the long shaft of wood down and cracked her across the middle of her back. She dropped to the carpet once more, but the adrenaline was pumping hard now. She shoved herself back to her feet, launched forward, and ripped the blade out of his shoulder before he knew what was happening. She went to stab him straight in his fuckin throat, but he grabbed her wrist, snarled in her face. She rammed her knee into his balls, and when his legs buckled, she took off, limping fast for the front door, gripping the half-a-scythe-blade in her hand. Her fingers were slick with blood, pain pounding through her head and slicing up her wrists, but at least she had a weapon. She was outside. She was running; she was free; maybe she could survive.

Maybe.

THE KNIGHTS CAME UP THE BASEMENT STAIRS. WILLY FIRST, GUIDED by Edie. She saw her husband groaning, slumped against the wall, his shirt torn and bloodied. She left Willy to drool at the top of the stairs as she went to him.

"Baby, are you okay?" she asked.

He lifted his head, pain and anger swirling in his eyes. "We have to cleanse the town, darling. Tonight, we have to show Burnskidde that our faith . . . is the *right* faith."

FRANCIS LINGERED IN THE BASEMENT AFTER EVERYONE HAD GONE upstairs, the knights drooling and moaning as their sworn raven-friends nestled into their individual cages. Those who lacked hands were fitted with hooks, birdcages slung onto those hooks and scythes placed in the other hand. They wheezed delightedly as they were unleashed upon the world.

Down below, Francis lay on his stomach on the floor, away from the lake of blood and gore. He pressed his face to the ground and whispered, "Let's do it tonight. I don't want to wait until tomorrow. I'll do what you want. But *I* want to do it tonight."

Far under the earth, Lawrence's heart heard him through its veins.

Tonight? *Thrum-thrum.* It could do tonight. *Thrum-thrum.* It had been ready for days, *so* ready to hatch what it had been cooking. *Thrum-thrum.* It had simply been waiting for the go-ahead. *Thrum-thrum.* This was very exciting. *Thrum-thrum.* At last. *Thrum-thrum.* Time to bring the end. *Thrum-thrum.*

REVELATIONS
The Book of Metal & Mist

A child—curious and innocent—once asked of Galloway, "What is his breath, exactly? How *does* the Fogmonger breathe blessings? How are these miracles possible?"

All-Speaker Galloway looked upon this child and said, "When your heart is full of questions, there is no room for faith. The Fogmonger already arrived centuries ago. He came once for *us* already, and is destined to return. Do you question that history?"

"No," answered the child.

"Do you question history itself?"

"No," said the child.

"And do you question the miracle of the pigs and the bats?"

"No," said the child, thoroughly chastened.

"Then do not you question the machinations of heaven," said Galloway. "For when you question one miracle, you must question *all* miracles. Every moment your mouth is open in query, it could be open in song. Do not eschew the harmony of faith for the explorations of science. Science brought the knifemen and the outworlders. Faith has only ever brought us song."

"On Obedience"
F. Urquhart, the Yellow Book

BURNSKIDDE, NOVEMBER 2009

Sing Loud, the Monger's Song

"Citizens of Burnskidde!" Officer Wilson stood in the back of the Neglani pickup truck, shouting into a megaphone as Edie drove through the neighborhood at three miles per hour. "Citizens of Burnskidde, come out of your homes. Give yourselves to the fog, and it will not harm you. Come outside and sing. Do not hide before your salvation."

A pair of gluttonbats swooped overhead, large black shadows against the evening sun. They screeched out of their gnarled mouths and beat their torn, pointed wings, blowing Wilson's hair back as they flew low over the truck, dragging their knobbed bone tails along the roof of the cab.

Below, Edie ducked on reflex. She bent forward to gaze up through the windshield as the bats swooped back up into the air, crying to each other and snarling down upon the town.

"Oh, wow." She shook her head in awe. "What a day to be a member of the chorus."

"Citizens of Burnskidde." Wilson's voice was staticky and booming. "Come *out* of your homes. I know you're afraid, but I would not lie to you. You're my neighbors. My friends. I want to *help* you."

He swept his gaze over the homes they passed. Some front doors opened and people came out singing, whether they had faith or not. Some trembled in terror, singing to survive, clinging to the idea that they knew the song, they had eaten the special crops, they were safe. Others darted away from their windows, electric with fear. They'd dreaded this moment for weeks. The moment when Galloway's chorus turned its violence outward. It wasn't enough to cut off their own limbs—now they were coming for the limbs of the town.

Alongside Edie's truck marched Eddie Spaghetti, laughing. His shoulder was heavily bandaged and his chest puffed out far. He was flanked by four of the newly minted ravenknights. They'd all been fitted with black robes, shadowing their faces and anonymizing their last defining features. There would come a day soon when Francis would lead them through another ceremony. When he would clean their wounds and present them with their brass raven-headed helmets, sliding them one by one over the head-cages. But for now, the caged sores of their skulls wept openly. The Butcher's Serum was deep in their spine, pumping through their systems, and they felt no pain. Only glory, glory, blissful, zealous glory, as they felt the cage-vibrations in their hands and the croaking raven-voices in their minds: *Keep straight, keep walking. You're so brave, we're going to be such good friends. I swear myself to you. I looove youuu.*

Edie glanced at the knight by her window. She had no idea who it was. Just a hooded shape. It might even be her son. It kept its gaze straight. It rasped and wheezed as it held the cage aloft in its hooked hand, the long scythe in the other. It struggled a bit. Its muscles weren't used to holding such heavy items. It was just some *kid* under there, after all. It kept adjusting the scythe on its shoulder and hefting the cage with a grunt. But it took measured, determined steps, never breaking stride.

She leaned out the window. "Nice evening for a parade, isn't it?"

Whoever it was beneath that gore snarled and hissed at her, "Gaaahhkk!"

Edie's smile faltered. She leaned back into the truck and cleared her throat. She didn't look back at the knight. Instead, she sang, "Ooooooohhh."

"Citizens of Burnskidde!" Wilson hollered through the megaphone. "Come outside! Please! Eat of the beasts and be purified. Give yourself and be saved!"

A procession was gathering behind the truck. Dozens of people singing, "Ooooooohhh. Ooooooohhh." So deafening, the people hiding in their homes couldn't think.

Suddenly, a police cruiser screamed out of a side street, skidding to a stop across the road and blocking half of it. Chief Pittner stepped out of the driver's seat, shotgun raised. "Wilson, stop this goddamn madness *right* now."

Eddie Neglani strode up to him, a cool smile stretched across his skull. "Ahh. Dickner."

Pittner held his shotgun by the slide, pumped it, and leveled it at Eddie's face. "Ed, I'm fuckin warnin you."

Eddie wrapped one large paw around Pittner's face, smothering him. He lifted the chief off the ground by his head. The shotgun fired blindly once, *BOOM*, as Eddie lifted the man a full inch and slammed him back down. Pittner felt something pop in his neck, felt his fingers go cold. Eddie laughed and clapped his hands, stepping over Pittner without breaking stride.

Pittner lay twitching in the gutter. He could see the shotgun right there. He could see the knights passing by. One of them glanced at him.

"Troy," he gasped.

The knight snarled and lurched onward.

Pittner's eyes blurred with tears. He could barely see the smudgy shapes of bats overhead. Circling lower, lower. Like vultures.

"Sing, Burnskidde!" shouted Wilson. "Sing loud, the Monger's song!"

The Hunts were throwing things into the back of their car when the parade came through their neighborhood. Annie saw them first.

"Oh my god," she said, running to the end of the driveway.

"Annie, don't!" Harold called after her.

"Ashleigh!" Annie ran up to the knights, pushing back their hoods to see their faces. "Ashleigh, is that you? Oh my god," retching when she saw their mangled faces. "Oh my god, what the . . . Baby, where are you?!"

The knights hissed at her. The ravens in their cages cawed wildly.

"Ashleigh!" she cried, running up to all the knights in turn. "Ash!"

Harold ran after her. "Honey, she's not here, we have to *go*."

"Ashleigh, baby, please!" she sobbed, running up to the last knight in the procession. She threw back its hood, saw the shock of blond hair stained red, and she screamed, "Ashle—"

She gasped. Looked down. Down at the blade buried in her gut. She looked up at the knight. It wheezed in her face and slid the blade of its scythe deeper.

Trembling, Annie reached out for the brutalized face of her daughter. "Ash . . ."

Ashleigh gave a wet, rasping roar, and the other knights snarled in answer, breaking out of the procession to come staggering toward her.

"Annie!" Harold cried. Annie saw him running, saw one of the knights behind him hiss and swing its blade. She saw the spurt of blood, the sharp steel burst through his chest. He yelped and fell to his knees, pinned from behind. There were other knights on him then, four of them slicing their scythes across his body, puckering mouths of rent flesh along his back, his arms, through his jaw as he screamed. Annie could see his molars, the ruin of his tongue, waterfalling blood as his eyes rolled and the knights pinned him from multiple angles at once, yanking their blades back so that he *burst* at the seams and was sundered into ribbons.

Annie cried out in pain as Ashleigh ripped her blade free and wandered off to rejoin the procession.

Annie collapsed to the ground and reached limply across the grass toward her ruin of a husband.

She was still alive when the bats swooped down to feed.

GALLOWAY BURST INTO HER HOME, PANTING, HAND TREMBLING around her broken scythe blade. "Mom! Dad?"

Keith and Nicole came running out of the living room. They both had their cellphones in hand.

"What's happening?" Keith asked. "Everyone's calling . . . Oh my god, your hands."

"We just got this police alert," said Nicole. "There's some kind of raiding party on the streets? Where are the knights? Shouldn't they be stopping this?"

"We have to go," said Galloway. "Where are the twins?"

"Upstairs," said Keith.

"We have to get them. We have to go!"

"Honey, what's happening?" asked Nicole.

"Is it knifemen?" Keith asked.

"Listen to me!" Galloway yelled. "We have to go *right* now. We have to get the twins in the car and get out of Burnskidde before something really bad happens."

"But we're in the chorus," said Keith. "We ate the miracle food for *weeks*. We're safe, right?"

"Honey, *what* is going on?" Nicole asked.

"I'm going crazy," Galloway murmured, beginning to hyperventilate. "I'm going out of my mind. You can't hear me. I'm not here. You're not hearing me."

"Okay, let's take some deep breaths," said Keith, leading her to the couch.

"I'll get some bandages," said Nicole, leaving.

"Just breathe," said Keith, easing her onto a cushion.

"Don't sit down," said Galloway, struggling against her father's hands. "We can't sit down, we have to *go*."

A banging on the door. Francis shouting, "Rachel, are you in there?"

"Oh, it's Francis," said Nicole, coming back into the room with the bandages. "I'll get it."

"Mom, no!" Galloway tried to stop her, but Keith grabbed her, held her back. She started crying. "Dad, stop, please!"

Nicole opened the door, and the very moment she did so, Eddie Neglani rushed her, shoved a handkerchief against her face. She gave a muffled cry, and dropped.

"Oh my god!" Keith rushed to the entryway. He grabbed Eddie, but one of the knights hissed through the open door and swung the haft of their scythe against Keith's throat, pushing him against the wall and pinning him, the haft against his Adam's apple as he struggled and kicked. Francis shoved another handkerchief to his mouth and Keith's feet went still. His shoulders sagged, and when the knight released him, he crumpled to the floor.

Galloway stood in the living room, mere feet away, shivering. While Francis checked her father's pulse, she slipped the broken blade into her waistband, pressing it against the small of her back. She readjusted her shirt just as Francis whipped the handkerchief in his hand and came toward her. He laughed. "You really can buy anything in the Falls. And it works like a charm! I didn't think chloroform would work so fast, but—"

"Please don't do this," she gasped, severely out of breath, sweating and bleeding and cornered in her own home.

"This doesn't have to be a big deal," said Francis, coming closer. "You can come willingly. Lookit, you've already done enough damage. You took the blade out of Jake's scythe."

The knight in the doorway rasped. Indeed, his was the scythe she'd broken while fighting Eddie. But she wouldn't have been able to identify Jake Mendez under all that mess, his eyeballs half sloughed out of their sockets, popped by those twin metal barbs.

"Come on," said Francis. "Don't be difficult. I need you alive."

"I thought I was bad flesh," she said.

"You are to some," he said, stepping closer, hands outstretched, the handkerchief draped over his fingers. "But you're a gift to me."

She angled her hand behind her back, was about to grab the blade and drive it into his smug fucking face—when the ground began to rumble. The entire house shook. Galloway lost her balance, fell to one knee. There was a tremendous ripping, like the earth splitting open, explosions underground. It knocked Francis off-balance, too. He dropped the handkerchief.

She made a break for the stairs, stumbling as the ground roared. The knights in the entryway knocked against each other, against the walls. Their ravens cried out in distress.

As she dove past Francis, he caught her by the hair, yanked her back, floored her. He tried to shove the cloth against her mouth. She could feel the cold sting of chemicals in her nostrils as she shoved him away, rolled him over and pinned him to the carpet as things crashed off the shelves and tumbled to the floor all around them. She reached behind her for the blade again, her body vibrating. Windows breaking, everything shaking. As soon as she felt the blade between her fingertips, she heard it. Far overhead and booming loud, she heard a voice: *Citizensss of Buuurnskidde.*

It echoed off the walls and rattled the glass in every window. It trembled the items in Nicole's sideboard, make them sing off each other, chiming in a tinkling rain. It boomed across town, rattling the stacked plates in Eddie Spaghetti's, vibrating through the halls of the high school and the movie theater, making the few moviegoers wonder why the people in the movie weren't responding to that colossal voice as it thundered a second time, *Citizens of Buuurnskiiidde.*

Galloway did not turn around. Did not look up through the window at the thing casting its wide shadow over the town. She just gaped down at Francis's face as a crazed, vindicated smile tugged at the corners of his mouth.

"What . . . is that?" she asked.

"You know what it is," he told her, in his cool, feathery voice. "You know *exactly* what it is. The heart made it for you. Look and see."

Slowly, she turned, and through the opening of her front door, she saw a vast red underbelly. It towered over Burnskidde on four thick, elephantine legs. Its triangular head blotted out the sun. Its crimson flesh was puffy and mottled, like gobs of melted wax stuck together. Sheets of metal were stitched into its hide. She saw a length of fencing, a car door, corrugated sheets of steel. She saw the underside of its massive jaw, reptilian and hellish, its red lips hooked wide in a grin that showed off double rows of bright white teeth. Hard slabs of brilliant metal, these teeth leered down upon the town, and her heart sank because of course, she was not surprised. This nightmare was nothing like how she'd imagined, just as the smiling pigs and gleeful bats had been so much more terrible off the page. This god was a molten hodgepodge of everything Francis had stolen from Burnskidde and given to the heart. It was not her god. It glared at her from the sky with swirling yellow eyes.

"Oh my god," she breathed.

"Don't worry." Francis shoved the cloth into her mouth. "The fog is here."

She thrashed, swatting at him with both fists. As she blurred out of existence, she heard him say, "Get the twins. We're going to need them all."

Then everything went dark.

THERE WERE PEOPLE WHO WOULD NEVER FULLY BELIEVE WHAT they saw that night. People who stood below this twisted amalgam of stolen metal and meat as its gleaming iron teeth opened wide. It bellowed at them, *This . . . is your blessing.*

"Finally," said Dr. Eric. He stood before the doors of his kingdom, the high school, and spread his mutilated hands wide. "Bless me."

Other members of the chorus stopped what they were doing to lift their hands in adulation. They sang louder than they ever had before as the Fogmonger bent his head and vomited a tsunami of bright crimson gas. It rolled into the streets with a sonic *boom*. Smashed out the windows of the school, punched into the brick hallways and the gymnasium. It blasted into people's homes and the grocery store, the movie theater, billowing beneath the seats so that people gagged in the dark before they understood what was happening.

As the red fog crashed into the town, exploding through windows and staining the air, people screamed, fled the streets. So much gas roared from between the teeth of the amalgam that the world turned crimson and muddy. Before long, the entire town was drowned in a thick sulfurous rot, and only those who believed in the Fogmonger greeted it with a smile and a feeling of deep, satisfied vindication. They sang as the fog rolled over them, filling their lungs, their hearts, "Ooooohhh."

Over the next few days, the fog would dissipate, but not before everything natural in Burnskidde shriveled. The food on the shelves in the Fresh N Good became inedible. Babies were born decayed. Burnskidde's pets grew cruel, cannibalizing each other and mauling their owners. When they were caught and sliced open, their insides were blackened. All the vegetation around Burnskidde was the same. Hundreds of people coughed themselves to death, drowning in blood.

Except for those animals and plants that had grown from the heart, and the people who fed off them. They alone were spared. And eventually, one by one, down to the very last reluctant soul, the survivors gave themselves completely to the fog. Fed themselves to the beasts. Turned themselves into knights. Awaited the Fogmonger's return.

That night, the fog was so thick they could not see the amalgam as its giant teeth clanged shut. It lingered for a moment, leering down at the destruction, the crimson sea, its only purpose on this planet. When it was done, the Fogmonger took great, lumbering steps toward the tunnel, and slammed itself headfirst into the rock, smothering the tunnel and itself, and cutting Burnskidde off from the world. When that was finished, the heart pulled the pieces of machinery and flesh back inside itself. Francis had said he did not want them to be discovered. He wanted the Monger to be a wraith. It could return anytime. That idea would keep people afraid.

Francis needed the people to be afraid.

NEW ADDEKKEA, OCTOBER 2019

Reunion

"Ms. Durwood." Urquhart stood in the alley behind the Post Office, glowering at her. The dead pig lay between them. "Have we not been accommodating?"

"Very," she said.

"Have we not given you a warm welcome despite our inclination to do the exact opposite?"

"You have."

"Then why," he sneered, "do you insist on poisoning our way of life?"

Durwood's blood was electric. She eyed the knights behind Urquhart, her entire body tensed and ready to fight. "All due respect, your way of life seems a bit poisonous itself."

Urquhart looked wounded. "I invited you into the midst of our chorus. Left you alone with our earth-born miracles when I *know* you have metal under your skin. We made you a *banner*. I was showing you our ways, bringing you with us to heaven, and you *shot* our ways. Do you understand that? That pig had a bellyful of good flesh. That could have been crops! Could have been an entire field of, of corn or grain. You took food out of the mouths of our chorus."

"The man was suffering," said Durwood. "He didn't offer himself. It looked like they caught him and tortured him. In fact, my guess is that's been happening a lot more around here than you want to let on."

"What in the fog does that mean?" Urquhart scoffed.

"I see the looks on people's faces. I know people get 'offered' when they speak out or try to escape. Mark was 'offered,' wasn't he? Plus, I know the Renfields are a lie, and your Fogmonger is probably bullshit that's going to get everyone here killed. What I can't figure out is what *you* get out of it or how to stop it from happening. *That's* what in the fog I mean."

Urquhart glared at her.

"I see," he said tightly.

Durwood held her ground. The possibility of violence crackled between them like lightning. Silently, she begged him to make the first move. *Say the word. Just say it. Tell them to kill me. Tell them to fucking try. I—*

A wailing cut through the night. A hollow wooden moaning. It grew and faded, grew and faded, as if there were a tornado barreling toward them.

The ravens cawed, beating against the bars of their cages. The knights groaned. Urquhart blinked, off guard.

"Did you call someone?" he demanded.

Durwood's muscles relaxed. "What is that?"

"The knights at the perimeter," said Urquhart. "They blow the horn when they've spotted an outworlder." He stepped forward. "Who did you call?"

"They didn't blow it when I arrived."

"That was different." Urquhart stepped closer, pressing his face near. "Who. Did you. *Call?*"

She flexed out her talon. "I didn't call any—"

On cue, Durwood's phone buzzed in her pocket. She took it out.

Bruce was calling.

Of course, she thought, heart leaping. *He came for me.*

She put the phone to her ear. "Bruce, are you okay?"

No answer.

"Bruce?"

She looked at the screen. It was just turning dark, telling her *goodbye*. The battery had finally drained. She'd never felt so personally attacked by a device in her life.

"Mother*fuck*." She shoved the phone back in her pocket, then shouldered her way past Urquhart. He stumbled as she started to run, yelling something after her that she couldn't hear.

Something swooped low overhead, shrieking, as she ran. She ducked, cursing, and looked up in time to see a trinity of dark shapes beating their wings against the night. They shrieked in unison, and Durwood knew they were headed to the same place she was. *Bruce* . . .

She ran fast, faster and harder than she'd ever had to before. For the first moments, she was afraid, terrified, but then relief pumped through her limbs because she had not known she could move her body this efficiently until this very moment. She pounded her feet against the pavement, feeling alive, feeling strong, feeling the night roil around her with creatures and shadows, the alarm wailing, vibrating her skull. She raced against the sounds, blood gunning angry and hot through her veins. She gritted her teeth, sides slicing with cramps. For a moment, she even forgot why she was running; she realized this was all she'd ever wanted from the Guard. She just wanted a reason to run.

She tore around the corner of the strip mall, beelining for the square. Torches in a ring, surrounding the wall of green where she'd stood just two days before.

There was Bruce. His arms were held by a pair of knights, their gleaming curved beaks facing Fogg. She dashed into the middle of the light and threw up her hands. "Wait! Don't hurt him."

Fogg turned to face her. His voice was colder than ever. "Do you know who this is?"

"He's . . . my partner," she panted. She bent forward, feeling suddenly faint, like she might puke. She managed to lift a finger toward Bruce and say again, "He's my partner. In the Guard."

"He snuck into our community," said Fogg. "The second Guard to do so in less than two weeks. You are lucky I arrived before the beasts."

She looked up into the branches hanging over the square. Yellow eyes glinted back at her. Flickering glimpses of fangs in the firelight.

"He's here for me," she managed. "Leave him."

Fogg glared at her. She had her hands on her knees, leaning over, feeling ill. But she held his gaze. She was ready to fight everyone tonight.

"Yes. Leave him." Urquhart appeared at the edge of the light. His one eye burned with rage. Torch flames danced in his monocle. "Leave the both of them." He walked over and knelt before her. Sweat stung in her eyes, but she held his gaze. His lip curled.

"What did you tell him?" Urquhart hissed. "Why is he here?"

"If you kill us, the Guard will send more," said Bruce. "One missing Guard is an inconvenience. But when the Guards checking in on that inconvenience *also* go missing?" He laughed. "They'll come. Kick us out and we'll bring them, too."

Durwood gave Urquhart a smug grin.

He snarled in answer. "You think you're clever. You think you're doing something *good* here. But all you're doing is meddling in the Fog-monger's gifts."

She smiled. "Have faith in the fog, All-Speaker. Maybe this was supposed to happen."

He breathed hard through his nose, nostrils flaring. Then he stood, and turned toward the ravenknights holding Bruce. "Escort these *Guards*"— he spat the word—"to the Post Office, and stay outside their room tonight *in* numbers. I don't want any more unsupervised snooping. Period."

They released Bruce. He cracked his neck and smiled at Durwood. "Sorry about the fuss, Gadget. Just felt like I was missin out."

She put a hand on his shoulder. His flannel shirt was so soft. He was so warm. He was solid and human and here, he was here, she was not alone.

"Thank you," she said, before launching herself at him and surrendering to a big, sweaty hug. She held it as long as she could, until the knights prodded her back with their scythes, shoving her and Bruce toward the hotel.

BURNSKIDDE, DOOMSDAY 2009
The Fall of Old Burnskidde

Thrum.

Thrum thrum.

Thrum thrum.

In the dark, Galloway heard it. *Thrum thrum.*

Her eyes fluttered open. They were so dry, she had to blink several times before she could see. She was on her back. She saw only rock. She licked her lips, tried to roll over. Couldn't. She blinked again, and saw more rock. Felt the warmth. Saw the pulses of yellow light. Finally, she registered the chamber, the heart throbbing in the dirt—and her family at her side. All four of them bound with thick rope. All of them struggling, crying her name.

She snapped to awareness, struggling, too. Pushing hard against her bonds.

"I am sorry about this," said Francis. "But the Monger was a big ask. Half-flesh, half-machine. In order to build something as big as that, the heart wanted something big in return. It's only fair."

She couldn't see him. Kept struggling, twisting her hands back and forth. Her fingers felt something hard, sharp. She paused, jerking back. Then she realized what it was.

"But it's a shame," said Francis, somewhere behind her. "All those people killed. I wish I felt worse about it, I really do. But the truth is, I've always *hated* this place."

She slid the broken scythe blade out of her waistband and started cutting. The metal rasped against the rope and she dug harder, but the blade went rogue, slipping in her fingers, an inch too far to the left, and buried itself in the heel of her hand. She had to clench her lips between her teeth to keep from crying out.

Where was Francis? She leaned up, and finally saw him. He was kneeling before the heart. Pulses of light shimmering over his face from beneath.

"I brought them," he said softly. "Are you pleased?"

Thrum thrum, it replied. *Thrum thrum.*

If Francis wanted to talk to it, he could be her fuckin guest. But did he really think it was going to talk *back*?

"Are you pleased?" Francis asked again. *Thrum thrum.* He watched the organ intently. *Thrum thrum.*

Then—one of its valves sighed open. A whisper: "*Yeeesss.*"

Galloway flexed her fingers and tried another angle on the rope, working faster. She managed to carve a small dent into the hemp, she could tell, but she got too confident then, and in the next slice, stabbed herself deep in the base of her thumb. She dropped the blade and clenched her fingers, both hands running warm and wet. *Ow ow ow, fuck.* She was grateful she couldn't see it. This was probably the most blood she'd ever lost. She felt woozy even thinking about it. Her head dipped to the side, her eyelids fluttered. She snapped back to attention and wriggled her hands. Hot and tingling. She clenched her fists, tried to hold the wound on her thumb shut. *Fuck, this is so much harder than it looks in movies.*

"Is there anything else you need?" Francis murmured to the heart.

The heart beat for a moment, as if taking in a breath so it could speak again. The valve yawned open and, in a low moan, it said, "*Home.*"

"They have a home," said Francis, smiling. "A big house. Enough bedrooms for everyone. You can redo it any way you want."

Thrum thrum. Thrum thrum. "*Baaabyyy . . .*"

"Oh. Um . . . They have a dog. I left it with one of the knights. I wasn't sure . . ."

"*Dog . . .*" *Thrum thrum.* "*. . . Will . . .*" *Thrum thrum.* "*. . . Dooo.*"

"Okay," said Francis. "Then we're in business." He stood, reached under his coat, and pulled something from his pocket. He flicked it open and the blade glinted in the yellow light.

Panic roiled in Galloway's gut. Her chest tightened. She felt hot wet on the small of her back, and she could almost see the red stain creeping up her shirt. She was *really* fucking bleeding.

Francis walked toward Keith and stood over him. Keith looked up and shook his head.

"Don't do this," he said. "Francis, don't do this. Please. Listen to me. You're better than this. You're better than—"

Francis reached down and grabbed the back of Keith's shirt. He yanked the man forward until his chin cracked against the dirt by the nearest glowing vein. Keith lay prostrate, watching lightning pulse outward through the veins in all directions. The light beat faster now that the heart smelled meat.

Galloway wriggled her hands, slicking up the rope, slicking blood all over herself until she felt the knot around her wrists loosen just a little. She kept her face as tight as possible while she worked. Her wounds dug into the rope. Her entire arms felt like they were on fire.

But it was working.

Keith breathed puffs of dirt against the floor. He tilted his head and caught the rest of his family in his eye. Rachel stared at him, jaw set, entire body sweating.

"Rach," he said, eyes wide, desperate. "Remember. This isn't your f—"

Francis grabbed his hair, yanked his head back, and rammed the knife in. He sliced it back out, spraying dark arterial froth along the ground. Nicole screamed, the twins thrashed, and Galloway gagged, almost threw up.

Keith clenched his jaw and gurgled horribly as he splashed out upon the floor, eyes bugged and rolling.

As he convulsed, veins curled up out of the dust. They floated up toward the ripped spewing mouth of Keith Galloway's torn throat, like snakes tasting the air. They reached into the wound and burrowed up into his throat, into his mind and down into his lungs, pushing beneath his skin. He pulsed with light as Lawrence's veins wove through his DNA.

Francis dropped Keith's head and walked over to Nicole.

Galloway struggled, struggled with the rope. She needed to break free now, fucking *now*.

Francis threw Nicole forward. She gasped in pain. She sobbed, "Please don't do this. Please don't do thiiis. Francis, *please*."

Francis grabbed her hair, yanked her head back.

"No, please!" she shrieked. "Please!" She hyperventilated, locked her eyes on Rachel. "Baby, I love you. Get the boys and *ru*—"

Galloway's hearing shut off. The world went numb and ringing, because she did not hear the sound her mother made when the knife plunged into her esophagus. The terrible, wet gasp and the gargling cry as the knife sliced through. Galloway did not hear that sound. She did not hear her mom cry like that. She didn't hear it. No. *This moment doesn't exist*, she told herself. *This is some other thing. This isn't me, this isn't my life, this doesn't exist.*

As the tear across Nicole's neck pumped out upon the ground, Lawrence's veins crept inside her, too. They slid into her muscles and twisted about her tendons. They pushed *deep*, and began to rebuild.

Francis sighed and wiped the back of his hand across his forehead. He gave Galloway a sheepish look.

"I haven't killed anyone before," he chuckled, walking over to the thrashing, screeching twins. "I killed a cat once, but that's different. I mean, I shot it by accident with an air soft gun, and then I figured, it couldn't *walk*, ya know, so I put it out of its—"

Galloway's hands tore free. She screamed, high and primal, sound filling her chest with audible rage. She threw herself forward, slamming her hands into Francis's waist and sending him tumbling to the ground. The knife skittered away above his head. She panted as she scrabbled her burning, dark red hands up his shirt, her ankles still tied. He tried to twist away, reaching for the knife. But she was on top of him, she had her hands around his throat. She slammed the back of his head against the ground, hard, twice. The third time, flecks of blood flew out behind his skull and his eyes fluttered shut. He moaned, hands wavering in the air.

Wheezing, Galloway reached back for her scythe blade. She twirled around and held the blade over him just long enough for him to say,

"Stop," before she buried the thing in his stomach. She yanked it out and drove it down again. His eyes went wide. She tried to pull the blade back up, but it was stuck on something, refused to budge. She left it. He wasn't quite dead, but he was spitting out blood, making wet, plaintive sounds.

"Rach," he gasped. "What . . ." His eyes rolled. He was still breathing, but it would do.

She climbed off him and went to Teddy, the closer twin. She dug at his ropes, clawing free his ankles, then his wrists, ignoring the horrifying pain in her absolutely ruined hands.

"Get your brother," she told him, voice hoarse and wild.

Teddy scrambled fast to Bobby. Tears and snot streaked both their faces, but they weren't screaming anymore and she could hear herself think. She just needed to get them out of here.

She dug at the ropes around her own ankles, kicking herself free.

Francis had one hand floating toward the knife above his head, the other dangling over his chest. He touched the broken edge of the scythe blade and winced. Tried wrapping his fingers around the steel, but Galloway had never hurt anyone before today, and she was suddenly very curious to see how easy it all was, so she grabbed his wrist and bent his arm back. She kicked his elbow, felt it crunch. He gakked in pain, squeezing his eyes shut. She knelt and decked him across the jaw.

Best feeling she'd ever had.

He coughed blood. "Why—"

She decked him the other way. Screamed again and punched him back and forth, with both fists, the way they did in movies, only *this* was easy, *this* she could do all day. "Fuck! You! Fuck! You!"

"Rachel."

She looked up. The twins were free and on their feet. They stared at her. Bobby kept shooting glances at Mom.

Galloway huffed for a moment, then stood, swaying over Francis. She screamed once more, roaring out the pain and terror of the last few hours. She stomped her heel down onto Francis's temple and ground her shoe into his face. He groaned and cried.

"Die here," she spat.

She took the twins in her arms and shoved them toward the chamber entrance. Behind them, Francis's hands waved limply in the air, found the blade in his chest, and *pulled* . . .

His scream echoed down the mine as Galloway ran with the twins, this way and that, weaving through the tunnels toward the shaft car.

When they reached it, she ripped the cage door back and shoved the twins inside. She tumbled in after them, pulled the door shut, and punched the button. They began to ascend.

She ran her hands over the twins, smearing them with crimson. "Are you okay? Oh my god, are you okay?"

They didn't say anything, just burst into tears and threw themselves at her. She held them tight, so tight, as they sobbed into her shirt. She stared over their heads at the rock, flying past outside the cage as they rose. The car was lifting them up into another world. Up into a world where none of that had happened. A fresh world with green grass and Mom's sangria and Mrs. Dring's ziti.

But no. The car wasn't carrying them *up* anywhere. They must have been going down somehow, accidentally, even farther down than the nightmare in the heart-chamber. The car was clearly carrying them *down* into hell, she realized, because dark bloody air was curling into the seams of the cage. Galloway wheezed in great breaths, heart pounding, pounding. Gas furled into the car from above, and her breathing came harder, more ragged, more panicked. She was full-on hyperventilating when the cage rattled to a stop.

"Don't breathe," she said. The twins peeled themselves from her shirt, saw the gas, and took great big breaths, puffing out their cheeks. The car was filling with artery-red air as Galloway took one last giant breath, "*Huuup*," and rolled the door back.

Gas flooded into the cage. She lurched through it, sending waves rolling away from her, pushing the twins in front of her, one hand tight on each of their shoulders. She limped through the cave toward the blood-stained light coming from outside.

They came out of the mine to find the world stained red. She looked wildly left to right, trying to figure out where she could go. What was left? Her parents were down in the mine. Emma was a knight now. And Francis . . . *Jesus*. Was this really the end of the world? Was the entire planet like this?

The Planet. The Pancake Planet basement was full of food and belowground, maybe not yet flooded with gas. She could shut that big steel door and try to survive with the twins as long as she could. Maybe Francis wouldn't think to look there.

She shoved the twins forward. Ran blind through the thick red landscape. Bobby gasped and she clapped a hand over his mouth, kept shoving them forward, running, running, pushing in the general direction of the Planet. But everything was red, so red. She could be running in the totally wrong direction.

A scream. In the distance, muffled by smog.

She paused, listening. There were actually quite a few screams. Coming from all directions, all around them. Gunshots, crying, begging, animal shrieking, the call of ravens.

An explosion boomed. A brief, brilliant flash on the horizon. Bursts of flame here and there. Gunfire. Screams and cries and inhuman babble all around. A violent coup in full effect.

"Here," Galloway choked, pushing the twins in what she hoped was the direction of the Planet. "Go!"

The twins kept taking big breaths, trying to hold them, coughing again.

"It hurts," Bobby whined.

"I can't hold it," Teddy added.

Galloway wanted to cry, hearing them try to obey her. She pushed them along, watching the shadows of a playground fade in ahead of them. The playground was behind the church, which meant they were close, they were only a few streets away from the Planet.

"It's okay," she gasped, coughing again, wet and long. "We're almost—"

A dark shape swooped down from the sky. It slammed into them, sending Galloway sprawling into the dirt. She heard the twins screaming, something *whooshing*, and she looked up to see the blur of the bat in the gas, flying off with some writhing shape in its claws. Only then did she register there was only one twin at her side.

She pushed him up, dragged him under the playset, kneeling in the mulch. Bobby, it was Bobby, she had Bobby. The bat had taken Teddy.

Who was gonna boss Bobby around now? Who was gonna shoot him with Nerf darts?

Galloway fumbled at the empty air, clutching at handfuls of gas, groping for Teddy's shirt, but Teddy was gone, he was out there somewhere in the gas, screaming dozens of feet above the ground.

Why would it do that? Why would the bat take Teddy? Teddy knew the song, he was a good boy. Good flesh, too! Healthy! Teddy had no reason to be a threat to the town or a heretic or an offering. He was eight!

Unless someone *told* it to take him. Unless the bats were taking direct orders from Francis.

Fuck, she swore. Of *course* the bats were taking orders from Francis.

"We . . . we have to get out of the gas," she said. She clutched Bobby's shoulders and shook him. "We have to get out of the gas."

Weeping, Bobby nodded.

"What . . . ?" She swiped at one of his tears. It had a streak of red in it. She looked at him, pinched his weeping eyes open. They were remarkably bloodshot.

"We have to get out of the gas," she repeated. "Okay?"

Bobby sniffled. "Teddy."

"Okay." She grabbed his arm and launched out from under the play structure. More shapes blurred by overhead.

A car crashed into a lamppost at her right, shattering sparks across the street. The man behind the wheel threw his door open, tumbled out onto the pavement. His veins were black. He coughed and retched, vomiting brilliant chunky red. Galloway jumped back from the sparks, and recognized Fadden, the town supervisor.

Shadows boiled out of the mist. Hooded and cloaked in black, they came. Scythes over their shoulders. Floating like wraiths. The cages at their sides rattled and squawked.

"Go away!" Fadden cried, writhing on the ground. "I don't know the song! Please!" He coughed and they were on him, skewering him to the ground, swinging their weapons wide, blades biting into his rib cage.

"Oh my god!" he screamed. "Don't!" They sliced their blades through the air, pinning him over and again. *Pincushioning him*, just like Eddie Neglani wanted.

"This way," she hissed to Bobby, dragging him in the complete opposite fucking direction.

The knights all lifted their heads and laid their blinded eyes on her, ravens crying madly.

Who was under there? Was it Dom? Ashleigh? *Emma?*

She ran, feeling nothing but the cold clammy grip of Bobby's little arm in her fist. She was probably clamping down so hard it hurt, it would bruise, but at least Bobby would be with her. Bobby would be the only other Galloway left.

The Pancake Planet sign loomed out of the ruby air. She pushed toward it. So much fiberglass in her chest. Every wheezing gasp of gas hurt worse than the last. Pushing. Pushing.

Suddenly, Bobby stopped, wailing, pointing behind them. She turned, and something plowed into her, sending her flying across the gravel. She slammed hard onto the ground, pebbles digging into her arms, her neck. She rolled over and saw Bobby paralyzed just outside the Planet door.

"Bobby," she gasped.

A gluttonbat slammed down on top of her. It was huge up close. It drooled from its long fangs. She could see the gristle stuck between them, could smell the bile on its breath. Its eyes were black and swirling. It snarled and growled, and three more slammed down onto the ground behind it. Four of them, standing between her and the Planet doors.

One of them grabbed Bobby's shirt and hopped away, dragging him behind, raking him along the gravel. Galloway screamed and the other bats were on her. They thrust their faces into hers and screamed back.

BOOM. One of them flew backward, pieces of its face flying. The other three hissed in surprise, turning.

Mr. Tolley marched out of the dim. Galloway saw the shape of his head, his shoulders. Then saw the rifle against his shoulder, heard him cock it, saw the shell *ping* out of the barrel and go flying.

She had never been so relieved to see her history teacher in her life.

His hair was puffed out along his skull. Black ink snaked through his veins as he stomped forward, aiming his gun at the gluttonbats. He sneered. "Fuck off back to hell, you crazy pieces of shi—"

The bats launched themselves at him. The rifle *banged* again and one of the bat's skulls shattered, sending chunks flying into the air. Tolley roared, then he was on his back, and the bats were digging into him. They dove their faces into his flesh, feeding fast and greedy. They bit into his throat, and Galloway could hear their hands tearing, rooting around, pulling out organs, cracking bones.

So delighted were they with this feast, that Galloway realized they had forgotten her.

Bobby was crying on the ground when she scooped him up and carried him through the Planet doors. She deposited him inside and went to the closest booth, grabbed one of the bench seats. She pulled at it, but it was too heavy.

"Mommy," Bobby coughed.

"Help me," she rasped.

He stumbled over to the bench seat and helped her push. Slowly, inch by inch, they scraped it across the floor toward the door.

"Why did you make this?" he sobbed.

"What?"

"Why did you *make* this?!"

She knelt in front of him and grabbed his shoulders. "Bobby, I would never draw something this scary. I would *never* try to hurt you like this. Okay?" He sobbed. "Okay?!"

As she shook him, trying to get him to hear her, she became aware that his was not the only breathing she heard.

Someone was wheezing behind her.

She turned. There, in the middle of the Planet floor, stood a single knight. Galloway saw the green ooze dripping from its face, and knew immediately who it was.

"Emma," she breathed, nudging Bobby behind her. "Don't."

Emma didn't budge. She stood by the bar, where they had stood together so many times. Just weeks ago, they'd been standing right *there*, laughing together.

That was gone now, and it was all her fault.

"Emma, *don't*," she said again, practically yelling.

Emma took a lurching step forward. Her cage swung. Her raven chortled. Her scythe gleamed with red light. Plant blood dripped onto the floor from her smashed-roadkill face.

Galloway tensed. "Emma, *stop*."

Bobby cried louder, "Rachel, why are you doing this?!"

"She's not." Francis stepped out from the back hall, behind Emma. He looked like he was on the verge of death. The eye she'd curb-stomped was a bloody, ragged mess. He cradled one arm against his shredded gut. The other hung at his side, dripping but still holding the knife. "I'm doing this."

The bats screamed outside. More gunfire and explosions.

Francis sighed. He looked around the Planet. "I figured you'd come here. S'where it all started, after all. Poetic, that it ends here as well."

Emma took another lurching, gurgling step forward.

Galloway glanced at the bench behind her. The glass doors, the monsters beyond.

"There's nowhere left for you to go," said Francis. "The fog has come and gone. The Monger's metal is already being repurposed into cages and helmets for *more* knights. And your parents . . ."

"Don't talk about them," she snarled.

"What am I supposed to talk about? There's nothing left to say, Rachel."

She looked around wildly. Where to go, where to go. The gas roiling outside, monstrous shapes churning in its wake. Before her stood the bloodied, mangled remains of her two friends, and Emma's raven—*Oh my god, the raven*.

She licked her lips, staring at it, thinking as pointedly as she could, *Let us go*.

The raven cocked its head.

Let us go, she thought again, trying so hard to vibrate this idea from her mind into that cage. *Let. Us. Go.*

The raven cocked its head again. Then cawed loudly. *Outworlderrr*, came the coarse, rumbling voice in her skull. *Bad flesh. Baaad.*

Emma lurched forward, not stopping this time, taking several quick steps toward Galloway, who pressed herself back against the booth, clutching Bobby to her side.

"Emma, stop!" she cried. "Stop! You're my friend!"

No, thought the raven, as Emma screeched a wet, gargling cry and lifted her scythe high. *Not* your *friend. Not anymore.*

"Don't cut her too bad," said Francis. "We need the meat mostly intact. Mostly." He smiled at her, his one eye pulped beyond recognition. "She's going to be our May."

The scythe whistled as it arced through the air. And in that final moment, Rachel swore she would find a way. She didn't know how or when, but she *swore* that the day would come when she would find a way to ruin Francis and his goddamn chorus. She would find a way to get the word out about this place and what he had done to it. Even if it took her years, she would find some way to—

Emma's scythe cleaved her face in two.

FINALLY.

This was everything it had wanted. After many long decades, its family was gasping back to life on the floor of the mine. Satisfied, Lawrence's heart worked its veins like appendages and crawled across the dirt into Keith Galloway's open throat. It absorbed itself into him, pushing into his chest, pulsing light into his eyes. *Yes*, this is what it had worked so hard for. So happy it was, to have finished the task at last. To finally relinquish the power it had held—all those spiraling veins under Burnskidde—in favor of an actual body. Those veins would grow cold and lightless, and the heart would lose its power to create. But that was worth it. So worth it.

It would treat its family right this time.

Francis Urquhart collapsed to the floor, wheezing and bleeding, his vision blurred beyond repair. Emma and Jake stood over him, unsure what to do. He blew bloody bubbles between his teeth, gurgling for help, but the knights did not know how.

Then.

A voice came creeping into the chamber: "Well, well, well."

Francis tried to roll his eye to see who this was, but he couldn't. His body was too battered. He couldn't move at all.

The voice went on: "Here I was in my home, tending to my own great plan, when I felt a great rumbling in the ground. *My* ground. And imagine my surprise when I saw a creature *emerging* from the swamp. Grinning at me."

As the voice came closer, Francis tasted dirt. He smelled warm grass. He saw the dim shadows of his knights raise their scythes toward the intruder, but the voice went on: "I asked the ground what it had been harboring, and it told me *this* has been down here all along. That *you* had been enacting your own plan." The voice tutted. "What foolishness. What death. Your amalgam of flesh almost poisoned my children. But! The great plan remains viable. The plan is *always* good. After all." The face leaned close, and Francis heard the razors in its voice as it purred, "Life . . . adapts."

NEW ADDEKKEA, OCTOBER 2019

The Happy Clear Night Massacre

"Okay, so what the fuck, man?" Durwood slammed the hotel room door. She turned, hands on her hips. "You said you weren't coming."

Bruce sat sheepishly on the bed. "Look, I thought—"

"You emphatically declared you weren't gonna come."

Bruce sighed. "I thought I'd . . . I wanted to see it."

She blinked. "You wanted to see how I did on my own?"

"No, *Burnskidde*. It's not . . . It's not that I didn't trust you."

She crossed her arms.

He sighed again. "I'm sorry. I was just sittin there at home, and I . . . got itchy." He threw up his hands. "I couldn't fuckin sit still! I couldn't do it, Gadget. I'm sorry. I know you know what I mean."

She did. She understood the itch very well.

She fell onto a chair. Took a big breath. "Okay."

"You're mad," said Bruce.

"Doy. I'm pissed you didn't want to come, you gave me all this shit about it, and now you're suddenly here? That's really shitty, Bruce."

"I understand."

"You scared me."

"I know. I'm sorry."

She chewed her lip, letting him feel bad for another moment. Then rolled her eyes and sighed. "Truth be told . . . I do need a plan."

"Okay." Bruce rubbed his hands. "So whaddya got?"

"Well, ten years ago, some kind of creature emerged out of the ground and gassed the entire town. Allegedly, they sealed themselves off so it wouldn't spread to the rest of the county, but a *lot* of people died. Thank 'fog' they'd already inoculated themselves against this gas by praying to the 'beasts of the woods,'" she air-quoted. "Some cult started by *this* girl." She tossed a Gray Book at him. He caught it and frowned at the cover. "Rachel Galloway somehow communed with these creatures and knew they had a blood talent for creating life. The pigs and bats supposedly have an enzyme in their gut with a special chemical composition that . . . fuckin . . . grants wishes, I don't know. Point being, everything the town has is thanks to flesh. If they hadn't had these magic crops before the gas hit, everything and everyone here would have died."

"Sounds like a convenient excuse to mutilate people," said Bruce, flipping through the Gray Book.

"Exactly. But there's a break in the story here. Galloway sacrificed herself in the mine so the county might survive. She *allegedly* granted speaking rights to this guy Urquhart, and he came out of the mine with his own gospel in tow."

"So this was a faith, but he made it a cult," said Bruce.

"Seems like. Anyone he doesn't like, he feeds em to the beasts. He keeps everyone in line with his pseudo-pastor bullshit, and it helps that he performed a miracle right away. The day he became king, he brought the Renfields back to life."

Bruce's head shot up. "So that's true?"

"Yep."

"But you saw them in the tomb."

"Right, so whatever *he* has is a copy. Or something. They're not plant-people, I'm sorry to say."

"Do you still think she's involved?"

Durwood shrugged slowly. "The beasts and the Renfields both bleed red, so if the Botanist *is* involved somehow, it's . . . hard to say how. I still don't know how the process from flesh to plants works."

Bruce clapped the Gray Book shut. "None of this has anything to do with your mass suicide event, though."

"Well, they have little self-harm events all the time." Durwood massaged her hawk-scar. "I don't know. Maybe Fogmonger shows up, swallows them all in one bite. The ultimate beast."

"Fogmonger?"

"He's like their Comet Hale-Bopp. Promises to restore all the limbs they've offered with his miracle fog breath. He'll turn New Addekkea into a kind of foggy heaven."

"That doesn't sound too bad."

Durwood fidgeted. "It never does." She swallowed. "Ostensibly, they opened the tunnel so the Fogmonger's breath could bless the entire county, but it was a splinter cell in the town's governing committee that suggested it, in the hope that someone would come through and stop the blessing from happening. Mark heard the tunnel was open when he was on patrol, tried to bring May back to the Shelter, and was killed for it. Which . . . also doesn't support the fact that the beasts are benevolent. In fact, this fog might have the potential to wipe out everything in Renfield."

Bruce gave her a lopsided grin. "Everything in Renfield?"

She wasn't amused. "People would probably die."

"I'm kidding."

Durwood picked at her cuticles.

Bruce sighed. "So what's the plan? Where is the Fogmonger supposed to arrive from?"

"That's my problem. I don't know. The scriptures are too vague."

"Where do the other beasts come from?"

Durwood stared at the floor. "They only show up if someone calls them."

She rose and began to pace. "We could set up an offering. Scare off the pig, see where it retreats to. Hopefully, that's the Fogmonger's den or whatever."

"Okay."

Durwood thought, paced, picked at herself. "We can't call them ourselves, though. We're bad flesh. They'd tear us apart. We get someone with good flesh to call them, and . . . see where it goes from there."

"Great. Then how do we stop King Beast once we find him?"

"Standard procedure. Lots of stabbing and shooting."

"Well, if it ain't broke. But what about the . . ." Bruce indicated a large helmet around his head. "Won't they try to stop us?"

"The ravenknights?" Durwood nodded. "They're slow, but they seem strong. We should find a way to call a pig when no one else is around. Or again, get someone with good flesh to offer themselves, and then follow the pig on foot? I don't know." Fidgeting, she worked her talon in and out. "Top priority is that we make sure the county is safe. That we *save* as many people as we can."

"Including a resurrected Lawrence Renfield."

"Including anybody, Bruce. This entire cult was started by some girl whose actual story is almost lost. Her name was Rachel, and she died the same night that . . . that . . ."

She trailed off.

Bruce was flipping through the Gray Book again. He continued to do so, until he looked up and saw Durwood staring into the corner of the room with her mouth open.

He glanced over his shoulder. There was nothing in the corner. "What?"

"I'm a stupid doofus," said Durwood.

"Since when?"

"Since I *got* here." She flipped open her notebook, clicked her pen, and wrote furiously. Then thrust out her hand. "Toss me that Yellow Book."

Bruce did, and she flipped back to the dedication. Moving her head quickly between the book and her notes, she scribbled again.

She threw the pen down and leaned back in her chair. Ran her hands through her hair. "Son of a bitch."

"What?" Bruce stood up behind her. Over her shoulder, he read two columns of names:

Lawrence	Keith
Adelaide	Nicole
May	Rachel
Henry	Theodore
Robert	Robert
Baby Girl	Doofus

"Who are these?" Bruce asked.

"They're the Galloways," Durwood said. "Son of a *bitch*." She lurched to her feet, began to pace again. "I should have seen it."

"They had a kid named Doofus?" Bruce asked.

"He was their dog," said Durwood. "This *must* be it, who they were molded from. Because Robert was smushed from his eight-year-old self, and that's why the baby looks weird! Maybe they're not aging because it's, like, magical, remolded flesh."

"Magical flesh?" Bruce echoed.

"He *made* them out of the Galloways to prove he was holy." She kept pacing. "Fuck. I should have seen this."

"Stop picking at yourself."

She realized she was digging into her lip again. She shoved her hands in her pockets.

"Look, we have a plan," said Bruce. "We draw out the pigs and track them back to wherever they're coming from. We'll get someone to offer themselves. Why not May? If she's magical flesh, in theory, the beasts should love her, right? Look, this place," he said gently, "is designed to make you doubt yourself and think in circles. Renfield is just warped cells. It figures out who you are, where your cracks are, through fuckin radio waves, and then it widens those cracks. You don't need to stress yourself out.

"Let's get some rest. It's getting late, and I think we could both use some sleep before tomorrow. Promises to be a long day, if doomsday is really tomorrow night."

Durwood didn't respond.

"Right?" Bruce asked.

"Yeah," she said absently. "You need to use the bathroom? I'll take the tub."

"No, you go ahead."

She took a pillow and blanket off the bed, dragging the blanket behind her as she went into the bathroom. She said over her shoulder, "Thanks again for coming."

"Of course," said Bruce, just before she shut the door.

She didn't get any sleep. She spent the night picking at herself instead.

Clawing into the corner of her mouth. Pulling at the tender flesh around the talon-hole in her palm. Digging at herself in her mind.

She listened to Bruce snore. They had never shared a hug before tonight, and she found herself yearning for another one. She wanted him to embrace her, to smother her out of this world, into a warm tomb of soap-smell and flannel.

She ached for a parent, any parent, to tell her it was all going to be okay.

THE FOGMONGER HOVERED OVER TOWN. ITS GREAT METAL TEETH creaked open, and out came the rasping, horrible voice: "Citizens of Burnskidde. This . . . is your blessing."

Bright red bubbles spewed out of its mouth. The children oohed and ahhed.

"Don't worry!" said the woman playing Galloway. "Everybody sing the song! The song will protect us!"

She got the audience of children seated on the ground around the stage to sing with her. The young boy playing the voice of the Fogmonger, just offstage, made gargling noises. "Aghh, yeess. Sing for me!" And the children laughed.

Some of them turned to look warily at Durwood and Bruce. She got the hint and gently pulled Bruce away. Their ravenknight escort swaggered along a few steps behind them.

New Addekkea had transformed overnight. Gone was the anticipatory atmosphere, all the setup and scrambling around. Now, festivities were in full swing. People were dancing, drinking, embracing, and standing in tight clusters around the stages. The little marionette stage was filled with dancing wooden dolls meant to portray Galloway's first chorus, people and pigs on strings, bobbing as they sang. Little red ribbons pumped out of their stumps as they were bitten off. Durwood had to admit, the technical wizardry was impressive.

Jugglers and magicians, dancers and joke tellers. Vendors of all kinds: basket weavers, rug crafters, quilt makers. Durwood and Oake wove their way through all of them, ducking under tightropes and dodging packs of children. Ravenknights mere inches behind them all the while.

They passed a food tent in which the Neglanis were serving steaming piles of meat and sauce. A fiddle band played in the corner. Some dirge called "Galloway's Sacrifice." Eight long verses about Galloway's descent into the mine on November 26, to beseech the Billowhills to close the Burnskidde Tunnel against the spread of the noxious fog. It reminded Durwood of a mix between "Awesome God" and "The Wreck of the Edmund Fitzgerald."

"You want a pipe from Lawrence Renfield?" Durwood asked, pointing him out.

Bruce followed her finger to where Lawrence and Adelaide were laughing in their tent, handing out pipes and wooden figurines.

"I'll be goddamned," said Bruce. "You talked to him?"

"Of course. He's super nice."

"You're kidding."

"No, he's a sweetie. They all are."

They watched as Lawrence gave away a small pine bear.

"I never thought, despite all the weird shit I've seen, I'd see Lawrence Renfield selling wood," said Bruce.

"I know." Durwood watched Robert waddling around behind their tent. She nodded at him. "There's Robert."

"Jesus," Bruce breathed.

"See what I mean? I couldn't figure it out, but the Galloway twins were eight, which explains why Henry doesn't look doughy and Robert is smushed."

"And that's Rachel?" Bruce pointed to May, in the crowd watching the pageant unfold onstage.

"In theory," said Durwood. "Come on. Let's say hi."

She led Bruce through the crowd, stepping over children. She touched May's arm, and the girl turned, surprised. Like most of the women today, she had woven flowers through her hair.

"May, this is my friend Bruce," said Durwood. "He's the outworlder everybody got upset about last night." She smiled as amicably as she could, hoping the nearby ravens wouldn't feel the need to report anything suspicious to Victoria. They stared at her, emotionless.

"Hello," said May warily. She watched a papier-mâché gluttonbat swoop its large wings across the stage.

"Bad flesh!" cried Urquhart, played by an eight-year-old boy.

The bat roared and leapt upon Mr. Tolley, played by a ten-year-old girl.

"Help!" the girl cried, as the bat's hands pulled red ribbons from her costume in great billowing gouts. The children in the audience applauded and went, "Eww!"

"May, I have a question for you," said Durwood. She glanced around and lowered her voice. "Would you ever be interested in . . . offering yourself?"

May jerked her head back. "Why?"

Durwood stepped closer. She glanced back at their escort, who seemed to be watching the play. Even their ravens seemed intrigued. "We want to know where the beasts are coming from. If we draw out a beast and then chase it off, track it back into the woods, maybe we can find where the Fogmonger is hiding before he gets here."

"You think he's hiding somewhere?" May asked.

"Well, when he arrives, he arrives *from* somewhere, right?"

May frowned. "What if they . . . eat me?"

"We'll stop them before they hurt you," said Bruce. "I will."

"They killed Mr. Brenner, didn't they?" May asked. "The pigs. All-Speaker said Mr. Brenner offered himself, but that's not true. He talked to you and they killed him for it. Is that right?"

Durwood's shoulders sagged. "Seems like, yeah."

"Just like they killed Mark."

"Probably."

May chewed her lip. She glanced at the knights, still absorbed in the play. Slowly, she nodded. "Okay. Yes. If it means putting an end to the gospel of the fog, I'll do it."

"Alright." Durwood nodded. "Tonight, then. Dusk. Somewhere that won't attract a lot of attention."

A cheer went up behind them. Durwood turned to see a group of men standing around the drinking tent. "To Seth!" they toasted.

"Behind the drinking tent," said May. "At the edge of the wood. No one ever goes over there."

"We'll meet you there, then," said Bruce.

"Do you think this will work?" May asked.

"I do," said Durwood. "Even if it doesn't, I promise that whatever happens tonight, we will stop All-Speaker Urquhart. You're the whole reason I'm here, Rach . . ." She swallowed. "You're the whole reason I'm here, May. I *will* help you."

May turned back to the pageant. "Then it's settled. Tonight. Fuck this place."

Durwood blinked in surprise, and May gave her a small smile.

"That's the last thing Mark said to me," said May. "Fuck this place."

Durwood nodded. "Fuck this place."

May smiled. "It was lovely to meet you, Bruce."

"Really nice to meet you, Ms. Renfield," said Bruce, with a pang of sorrow.

"Goodbye!" cried Galloway onstage, half buried beneath a pile of papier-mâché rubble, holding Urquhart's hand. "Share my gospel with the colony. I've always loved you . . ."

As they walked away, Durwood's senses were alive with Clear Day. Acrobats walking tightropes over the crowd, chunks of meat cooking on iron grills, various choruses singing. Everyone singing, even the cooks and the fire-breathers, everyone around them who wasn't watching a show, or in a show, or playing an instrument of some kind sang, "Oooooohhh."

Rachel Anne sat on a tall, beautiful throne made of interlocking birch branches. She looked so happy, laughing and chatting with her friends. Someone had strapped a honeycomb to her stump, so she could nibble at it and keep her remaining hand free. Durwood stared as they passed, a disquiet deep in her soul. She could have saved that girl. She still could. But she could have saved her hand as well.

Bruce dodged a unicycling, juggling man balancing homemade gluttonbat wings on his back. "So you try this pig whiskey?"

"Of course."

"Is it good?"

"Absolutely. Have to admit, they make a hell of a spread." She watched a group of mangled teens take turns trying to cut a plank of wood in half with a scythe. Three ravenknights supervised. Their raven companions cawed in what seemed like judgment, though it was hard to tell which teen was winning.

"You want to try it?" asked Durwood.

Bruce snorted. "I'll watch *you* try it."

They found a tent where Bartender Barry Barr was serving drinks. He poured her a double shot, and they toasted to Seth Brenner, portrayed in a pencil sketch on the wall, looking professorial. New Addekkea didn't have any photography, save for the odd Polaroid, so instead, sketches commemorated those who had passed. There were quite a few of them, woven into the cloth wall of the tent. And all of them bore the same swooping signature at the bottom.

"These were all done by May?" Durwood asked.

"Every one," said Barry admiringly. "Some were too old to be offered, had a heart attack in the process and were, uh, taken by the bats. Some fell to delayed effects from the fog back in '09. And some just . . . overvolunteered." He lifted his glass. "To Seth."

"To Seth," everyone echoed. They clinked glasses and drank.

"Oh boy," said Durwood. "That's really goddamn good."

"You mean *fog*damn," said Barry, and he laughed until he cried.

IT WAS NICE TO TALK WITH BRUCE AGAIN. TO HAVE A DRINK AND work a case together. She hadn't realized just how much she'd missed him.

With their armed escort, they didn't have many options. So they returned to the hotel room to shower, take stock of their ammo. Durwood cleaned her talon and ran through a series of wrist exercises, stretching and working it in circles to make sure the talon flexed as smoothly as possible. When it was almost dusk, they sat on the bed together and ate the candy Bruce had carried with him. Skittles and 3 Musketeers, as always. They ate in silence, though the swirling mix of feelings was very loud in Durwood's chest. Dread at what might come. Joy to be here again, as Durwood and Oake.

When the sky began to darken, they slipped out the window, avoiding the gaze of the ravens stationed by the door.

Fires had burst to life all around. Drums *thrummed*. The dancers danced harder, the puppets grew strange shadows, and all around the fringes of the Carnevale, there breathed the cold air of deep autumn. Samhain brewed in the grasses and the branches. Things watched from just outside the firelight, twitching and snarling in the trees, wings shivering in the dark. Shadows in the undergrowth oinked for food.

Durwood and Oake slunk through the shadows. So much was happening that it was easy to avoid being seen. Drunken laughter, much singing, giant wooden beasts stomping around town. Before Durwood knew it, they were crouching behind Barry's drinking tent, and no alarm had sounded. The band in the tent was so loud, so many people singing along with them, that Durwood barely heard Bruce when he said, "She's here."

Durwood turned. May stood several feet behind them, at the edge of the woods. She nodded at them. Durwood nodded back. May stood for another moment, then dropped to her knees. Lifted her hands and said, "Beasts of the wood."

"We're in business," said Durwood. She crouched lower, muscles coiling, ready to spring.

"Beasts of the wood, hear my call," May said. "I offer you my flesh, though I have been instructed not to. I offer myself and ask of you to *tell* me: What kind of flesh am I?"

Durwood glanced around. No one seemed to be noticing. A group of children ran past, whacking each other with wicker scythes.

"Tell me!" May shook her fists at the trees. Her eyes were wide, desperate. "What am I?!"

The undergrowth stirred. The beasts within the shadows looked at each other. *Interesting*, they thought. They had, indeed, been instructed not to interfere with the Renfields. The beasts had their own beliefs about what had happened in Burnskidde. As far as they were concerned, the heart was *their* All-Speaker. It had given them new life, and they were endlessly loyal to it, though it had not spoken to them in a long time. Ever since it had absorbed itself into Keith Galloway's chest.

The beasts did not know what they should do now.

"I beg of you!" May cried. "*Tell* me!"

"May?" A voice, calling from beyond the tent. Durwood looked around. Adelaide appeared several yards away. "May?"

"Shit," Bruce murmured.

May turned. Durwood saw the women lock eyes.

"Darling," said Adelaide, coming closer. "I've been looking everywhere. All-Speaker says it isn't safe with the outworlders here. What are . . ." She paused, finally noticing May's outstretched hands. "What are you doing?"

"Mother, go home," said May.

"What?" Adelaide took another step closer. "May, you can't be out here. Besides, you're missing your play."

"I don't care about the play," May spat.

A raven quorked nearby. A ravenknight stepped around the corner of the tent. The great brass helmet grunted steam. Some of the people singing and swinging their beer mugs around on the street stopped and turned to watch. Murmurs spread through the crowd, and Durwood saw the ripple of attention expanding. Jugglers paused. The fiddle band faltered.

Durwood licked her lips, her body tightening further.

"May, please, come inside the light," said Adelaide. "Have some pie. I have faith in the fog that whatever you're feeling now, when he returns, you'll—"

"I have no faith," May spat.

The crowd gasped. The nearby raven cocked its head, cawing in horror. Other knights began drifting in.

"May!" Adelaide was appalled.

"Don't you see?" said May. "He lies to all of us. He lied about who we were. The Fogmonger is a lie, too! I'm sure of it!"

"You watch your tongue," said Adelaide.

May turned back to the trees. "Take my tongue! Take any part of me! I offer myself! Oooooohhh."

The crowd sang with her automatically, "Oooooohhh." They glanced around at each other, unsure what was happening. But May was a miracle—if she wanted to do this, it must be right.

Sure enough, after a moment, the undergrowth shifted.

"Again," said May. "Oooooohhh."

"Oooooohhh," sang the chorus. Adelaide stood silently in their midst, face twitching with worry.

And there came the large pale hog. Hesitant but curious. Its tusks were cracked and yellow. Its eyes were rheumy. It looked old.

"Yes," May breathed. She prepared herself. She licked her lips, suddenly frightened. "Yes."

The hog approached her cautiously. It sniffed at her hand.

"Take it," May whispered. "Come on. Take it!" She shoved her hand at the hog. It oinked in surprise.

"What're we doin here, Gadget?" Bruce whispered.

"Waiting," said Durwood.

The hog seemed increasingly uncertain. It oinked again at May as she shook her fist at it. "Take me!"

"May, calm," said Adelaide. "Please. Why are you—"

"Take me!" May cried.

The hog squealed in alarm. Three knights roared at once.

"I'm intervening," said Durwood. She rose and marched forward.

Then felt a hand on her arm. She turned.

Fogg.

"Back," he said, glaring. He pulled at her, squeezing an "Ow" out of her.

"Hey." Bruce put a hand on Fogg's shoulder.

Fogg turned sharply to him. Paused. Slowly, he swiveled his head toward the bar tent.

Victoria was perched on the edge of the tent. She stared intently at Fogg.

For a moment, he seemed to listen. Durwood watched this silent exchange with utter fascination.

Then, Fogg said, his voice colder than ever, "Yes, All-Speaker."

"What's he saying?" Durwood whispered.

"To disregard Mother's request," said Fogg, eyes still on Victoria. "I am no longer required to be cordial."

"Mother?" Bruce sneered. "The fuck does—"

Fogg whirled and cracked an elbow against Bruce's nose.

Bruce grunted. "Asshole!" He grabbed Fogg, headbutted him. They struggled, pushing and pulling.

Barry shoved forward. "Hey, cut it out. Come on! It's Clear Night."

Fogg threw the first punch. Bruce swung his augmented arm, sending Fogg stumbling back into Durwood, who fell on her ass in front of the hog. Barry pushed between the two men, trying to shove them apart. The crowd gasped. Victoria squawked loudly. The hog squealed in Durwood's ear, causing her to fling up a hand in alarm, which only startled it further. It stamped its feet and squealed louder, head back, tusks glinting in the firelight. Then it charged her, tried to trample her. It roared in her face and she flexed her talon, stabbed it in the side.

"Fuck *you*," said Durwood, stabbing it again, making it squeal and lurch away from her.

Barry caught a stray elbow from Fogg and flew onto the ground before the hog. He struggled to his knees. The knights grabbed Bruce and dragged him back. He kicked, shouted.

"Hold him," said Fogg.

"Hey!" Durwood yelled. She stood. "Stop!"

"Let go of me, what the fuck!" Bruce yelled.

"Stop shouting!" May cried. "You're scaring the pi—"

It tilted its head and its snout clamped shut around Barry's throat. It ripped its head back, washing a flood of dark crimson onto the ground. Barry's eyes and tongue shot out. His hands went up to the massive dent in his neck as he convulsed, pumping out of several severed tubes. Durwood could do nothing but gape at him as the hog chewed and grunted its way back into the woods, all *screw this*. She could see Barry's bone, his spine, poking up through the ragged canyon that had once held his windpipe.

The crowd erupted into a screaming fervor. People scattered in every direction. Adelaide pulled May to her feet. May, mouth open, dumbfounded, allowed herself to be dragged away. Everyone scattered except Barry, spasming on the ground.

Durwood darted her head between Barry, dying; Bruce, struggling with Fogg and the knights; and the woods. Fogg shoved Bruce to his knees, and a knight swung its scythe up high over his head. The hog was practically gone, squealing away into the woods.

"Fuck*dammit*." Durwood twirled and drew her revolver from her waistband in one motion. She fired at the knight standing over Bruce. The bullet pinged off its helmet and the other knights turned toward her. Fogg drew his own gun, a slim black 9mm, aimed it at Durwood, and Bruce banged him in the side of the head with his augmented arm. The metal *thonked* and Fogg's eyes rolled as he went flying. One of the other knights swung its scythe at Bruce. He deflected with his forearm, steel singing against the iron in his flesh. He grabbed another scythe as it swung at him. He ripped the weapon from the knight's hand and cracked the end of the haft into the knight's stomach. As the knight staggered back, Bruce twirled the scythe upward, slicing off the knight's hand.

Bruce dropped the scythe and ran to Durwood's side. The knights crowded around their companion, who was kneeling on the ground clutching their torn wrist. They wailed a metallic, whistling note. Their cage rolled sideways on the ground, the raven within squawking horribly.

"Come on, Gadget." Bruce yanked Durwood to her feet. "We gotta catch that pi—"

Bruce was slammed back by a large dark shape shooting out of the trees. Durwood fell, but rolled over in time to see the shape fully, and knew in an instant what it was.

The gluttonbat was larger and uglier than she expected. Its skin was dark red and leathery, and its pug snout snorted steam at her as it snarled. Fangs the size of her hand clacked together, as if it could almost taste Bruce. It snarled, reaching for him with its clawed hands. It shrieked, and pounced.

Bruce threw up his heron arm and the thing clamped down. It shook his arm in its teeth like a dog.

"Fuck off me!" Bruce cried.

Durwood sprang at the bat talon first. She drove her spike deep into its back. It screeched so ear-splitting loud she couldn't see for a second.

Its tail slammed into her side and she found the wind knocked out of her as she was looking up at a spinning night sky. Then the thing was on her. It screamed in her face and tore at her shoulder. She kept jabbing her spike upward into its underbelly, screaming as she stabbed, stabbed, stabbed.

Bruce shot it in the wing. The bat roared and sprang at Bruce, grabbing his heron arm as he put it up to defend himself. It swung Bruce around so hard he dropped his gun, his face a wide O of surprise, and before he knew it, the bat was ripping the entire arm out of its socket. The joint *crunched* apart with a sickening, wet noise. Bruce yowled in pain. The bat burst into the air with a gust of wind. Durwood screamed at it, firing blind into the dark as it flew away with Bruce's arm.

Bruce fell to his knees, stunned, clutching at the sunken pit where his shoulder used to be. Durwood was at his side, urging him to his feet. "Abort. Abort. Bruce, we gotta get back inside."

Bruce did not respond. His mouth hung open. He leaned on her as she began to drag him away.

She felt more hands on her and she twisted around, shouting, talon up. But the hands shot up, palms out, defensive, not touching her.

"Don't," whispered Greg Dring. "I want to help."

"Where's your knight?" she asked.

"Ditched her," he said. "Come on, I can get you back to my house. I'll hide you."

Durwood adjusted her grip on Bruce. She nodded. "Lead."

Shrieking and howling all around them as Greg ushered them into an alleyway. He held up his hand, making them pause. He leaned out, looked right and left.

"Bruce, stay with me," said Durwood.

Bruce was pale and sweating.

"Okay, come on," said Greg.

He led them across an empty street. The alarm started up again, wailing through the darkness.

They ran into another alley. Greg put up a hand again, leaned out to check the next street—and something cracked him on the side of the head. Durwood launched herself forward, stepping between Greg and the ravenknight who had been waiting for them. Bruce slumped against a wall.

The knight grunted and swung its scythe at her. She dodged, then threw herself forward, tackling the knight to the ground, loosing its helmet and sending it pinging across the road.

The face beneath was mangled beyond belief. The most horrible mound of pus-oozing, necrotic green meat Durwood had ever seen. The mere sight of all those metal bands and hooks cutting into green-tinged flesh and exposed bone made her gag.

The knight rasped at her, pawed at her with both hands.

She hesitated. Suddenly, she didn't want to kill this thing.

Greg was pulling her up. The knight rolled over, fumbling for its scythe. It grabbed the haft, swept at their feet with the blade, and they leapt out of the way.

"You alright?" Greg asked.

"I'm fine," said Durwood. "I—Oh shit!"

Greg turned and put up his arm on instinct. The scythe swung down, spearing itself through his forearm. The curved blade bit all the way through, the tip reaching within an inch of Greg's face. Greg gaped at it, letting out small sobs of terror and pain.

The knight held firm to the scythe and leaned close. It rasped, deep and wet.

"Emma, please," Greg pleaded. "Don't do this."

Emma Dring rasped louder and ripped her scythe back with both hands.

Greg's arm tore up the middle. Flaps of flesh bloomed around the blade as it sliced. Greg screamed again, a sound cut short by the scythe whipping back around and lodging in his gut. She lifted him into the air, swung him overhead, and slammed him down onto the ground. She wrenched the blade free and swung again, but Durwood caught it by the haft and jammed her spike in Emma's throat. Emma dropped the scythe, put her hands to her neck. Durwood retracted her talon, and the wound spurted green. Emma collapsed to her knees, hands clawing at the wound. At her side, the raven-cage rolled, the bird within beating at the bars.

Durwood had no time to wonder why this knight was bleeding green. She ushered a stumbling and broken Bruce away to the hotel. It was closer than Greg's house, and she didn't know what else to do.

She did not look back to see the Dring children reaching for each other across the cracked pavement as they bled out together.

"I'm . . . sorry," said Greg.

Emma put her hand on his, and in that final moment, he believed she was sorry, too.

DURWOOD BURST THROUGH THE HOTEL ROOM DOOR AND FLOPPED Bruce onto the bed. She locked the door, jammed the table up against it, and peeked out the window, stuffing her gun into her waistband.

"Pretty bad," said Bruce. His voice was thick.

"This is nothin," said Durwood, rushing into the bathroom for towels, shoving them against his shoulder. "Hold those."

"Can't feel my arm," said Bruce.

"Here." She sat next to him, pushed the bundle of towels against his empty shoulder. They were already soaked through with red. "You'll be fine. Look, I had service. You have service. Here." She dove into the pockets of his pants, looking for his cell.

He kept turning his head, licking his pale, sweating lips. "Won't come. Ain't time."

She put the phone to her ear. A busy signal blared at her.

"God!" She dialed again. Shook her head, put the phone to her ear. "This fuckin switchboard."

"It's okay," said Bruce. "It doesn't matter."

Busy.

"Fuck." She shook her head. "This is fine. It'll be fine. We're *getting* someone to come to this fogdamn hotel." She dialed again.

Busy.

"Fuck!" She dialed again. "Come on, come on. It's gonna be fine. It's always fine, right?" She squished the sodden towels between her fingers. "We've been through worse than this. I mean, *you* have, haven't you?"

Bruce didn't answer.

"You have, haven't you?"

Bruce did not respond.

"Bruce, haven't you?"

He didn't move. His eyes were closed.

She didn't move, either. She didn't even blink.

"Bruce?" she said quietly.

The stain on the bed crept outward, reaching for the edges of the mattress.

"Well, no," she said. She dropped his phone and put a hand on his chest, put her face close to his. She shook him. "Bruce, get up. Get up, Bruce, come on." She shook him. "Bruce! Please, Bruce, please. Bruce." Tasting his name for the final living time, her voice wet with phlegm. "Bruce, *please* get up. Please don't leave me. Bruce. Oh my god . . ." She clenched her fists against his chest. She couldn't breathe. Finally, she hitched in a great breath and screamed into his face. She sobbed. "Please don't leave me. Oh my god . . ." She bent over him, put her wet face to his chest. He was still warm. "Oh my god, please. Please, please . . ."

She cried. A lot. She cried so hard she choked. She cried until her rasping breaths turned from sobs into seething, bitter hissing through her teeth. She clenched her fists so hard her nails bit into her palms, scraping off a fine layer of skin.

She launched herself off of him and marched to the side of the bed. She pulled out her go-bag and, trembling, reloaded her gun. She stuffed handfuls of bloody iron bullets in her pockets, the revolver back in her waistband, and went quickly into the bathroom. She scrubbed the blood off her hands in the sink, revealing these rust-stained, leathery worm-creatures that used to be her fingers, fingers that trembled under the steaming, scalding water. She gripped the edges of the sink and shook with fury. She clenched the sink so hard it hurt. Her heart was beating fast, fast. She was angry, burning, godlike with wrath.

Now it was time to stab and shoot and demand some fucking answers.

NEW ADDEKKEA, OCTOBER 2019

Knifewoman

The Shelter under Bartrick Regional has an elaborate training course that Durwood has run many times. It is composed of shifting wooden boxes that you have to roll under, hop over, climb on, etc. It's randomized and impossible to predict, but she got very good at headshotting the paper cutouts that sprang out of the boxes. She prided herself on how fast she was able to sprint, duck, shoot, and stab. In fact, she'd once held the second-highest score for a month, just under Mark Wend, who never got tired of ribbing her for it.

She was grateful for that experience now, creeping through alleyways and side streets, darting from shadow to shadow as the knights and bats patrolled, screeching and cawing, calling to each other, searching for her. Alarms wailing in the distance.

She dashed up the hill to Urquhart's estate, went around the side of the fence, and hopped it, careful to avoid the black iron spikes. She allowed herself to walk, panting, to the front door. She pounded on it. Within seconds, Fogg answered. His face was badly bruised. He glowered at her. She was sweating and drenched in blood, her hair hung in her eyes, and she had her gun trained on Fogg's forehead.

"Lemme see him," she said.

"No," said Fogg.

"Lemme see him or I kill more sacred beasts."

Fogg hesitated. Then stepped aside.

He led her into the office, then stood in the corner next to the display case holding Galloway's two original notebooks. Victoria squawked from her perch when Durwood entered, and Urquhart looked up from his desk, where he'd been writing something. He threw down his feathered pen and crossed his arms.

"Well, well," he said. "You are *truly* dumb. Why on earth did you come here?"

She held the gun up with her fingers splayed, not touching the trigger. She sat slowly. "I just want to ask a question."

"Where's your friend?"

"Dead."

Urquhart tsked. "I knew I never should have let you in. Emma's raven was right, Greg spoiled this entire thing. 'Share it with the world.'" He scoffed. "We should have kept this to ourselves. Protected it against filth like you. You know, I actually thought our performance as a welcoming community wou—"

"That's great," said Durwood. "So here's my question, and I want you to answer this as honestly as possible because I'm really done fucking around: Where do the beasts come from?"

Urquhart laughed and spread his hands. "This is your big demand?"

Durwood shook her head. "Don't fuck with me. I want to know where, and I want to know what happens when the Fogmonger comes."

"We're made whole, that's what *happens*. What are you talking about?" Urquhart laughed again. He glanced at Fogg. "Fogg, you believe this?"

"No," said Fogg. He chuckled.

Durwood smiled at them, sitting very still.

Urquhart cleared his throat. He shot out his fists, straightening his sleeves, and folded his hands on top of his desk. "You think you're still playing some kind of game with me, but you're mistaken. I'm not a liar. I don't know any more about the beasts than you. As far as I know, they come out of the woods. Just like the Renfields came out of the mine. I'm sorry you don't believe the soil here is blessed, but that's not my problem."

A mad grin hooked into the corner of Durwood's mouth. Calmly, she asked, "How did you turn the Galloways into Renfields?"

Urquhart's smile dropped. He glared at her. A moment passed when she thought he might break, but his face twitched back into a grin.

"Really," he said, "I don't know what you *want* here, Ms. Durwood. This was supposed to be a beautiful evening, but shame on me, because I allowed you to ruin it. I think I'm going to give you about five minutes to see yourself to the gate before I sic the beasts and knights on you. Okay?"

Durwood smiled into her lap, then looked him dead in the eye. She took a breath, clapped her thighs, and got to her feet.

"Okay," she said. "I'm sorry about the colossal amount of trouble we've caused each other. I really am. I hope the Monger's return goes exactly how you want it to."

Urquhart rose as well. He stepped around the desk. "It would have been quite the thing to share him with you. But I suppose we just believe . . . different things."

"That's a very diplomatic way to put it." Durwood stuck out her hand. "Good game."

"Ha! Yes. Good game." Urquhart clapped his hand into hers. They stood there, shaking hands, grinning at each other.

Durwood laughed.

"What?" asked Urquhart.

She flexed her wrist and her claw shot out, burying itself in Urquhart's palm, up through his wrist. Durwood held on to him as he screamed and writhed. She drove him back against the glass box, and the back of his head cracked against it. A hairline fracture flashed through the glass. She dug her claw deeper into his arm, twisting. He screamed. There was movement all around her. Fogg on one side, drawing his 9mm, freezing because her revolver was already on him. Victoria squawking and fluttering on the other side, her own talons flexed, but hesitant to attack.

Urquhart pawed at her with his free hand, smushing the side of her face and punching her shoulder. Weak little pats she easily ignored.

This was the coolest she'd ever felt.

"Don't move," she spat at Fogg. She licked her lips and yelled, "How'd you make the Renfields?"

"I didn't," cried Urquhart. "I swear to fog!"

"Bullshit. What'd you do to the Galloways?"

"They sacrificed themselves, I swear!"

"How are you making the beasts?" She twisted her hand, digging the spike in farther. He screamed, knees buckling. Fogg took another step forward. She thrust the gun at him, "Don't."

"Please," Urquhart sobbed. "Shoot her. Kill her. Oh my god, you fucking bitch . . ."

"What aren't you telling me?" Durwood twisted her arm harder, pushing the spike deeper up the center of his arm.

Urquhart screamed in pain, "The heart! It was the heart!"

A beat.

"Whose heart?" Durwood asked.

"Lawrence's. In the mine," Urquhart whimpered. "I—I found the heart years ago and made a deal with him. *He* made the beasts in exchange for getting his family back. They—they come out of the ground. It takes other things and remakes them. Deer, kids . . . It's all the heart."

She blinked, trembling with rage. "You made a deal . . . with Lawrence's heart?"

"He was happy to. Wouldn't *you* kill to have your family back? He said it wasn't his fault. He was possessed. He told me he wanted a second chance. He'd make me *anything* for a second chance. He made the beasts. Made helmets for the knights. And I never questioned his ask in return." He grinned like a madman. "The heart wants what the heart wants."

Tears stung at Durwood's eyes. Her throat felt tight. A high whine almost escaped her mouth, but she held it down. "You fed Rachel Galloway to a fucking . . ." She pushed her spike deeper, up into his elbow. "A fucking *monster*."

Urquhart howled. "Kill her!"

Fogg launched forward, firing. She ducked and returned fire, ripping her spike from Urquhart's arm, sending him flying, blood arcing across the glass box. Fogg's shoulder popped back, and behind him, a bright yellow mess spattered over the display case just before the bullet shattered the glass, sending the notebooks inside tumbling to the floor.

Fogg faltered for a half second, glancing down. "Shot," he said, in that dumb, cold voice. Then he looked up at her, jaw set, taking another step forward, and she shot him again, straight through the dome. His head snapped back, the base of his skull exploded in a grand flower of an exit wound, and he stumbled, a thick yellow ooze pulsing from the smoking hole above his left eye. He crumpled to the ground on his back, and was still.

Nothing moved. Durwood gaped at the yellow on the wall, the inhuman goo seeping from the man's skull.

Urquhart lurched toward the door. She had the gun on him. "Don't budge."

He put up his hands, fingers trembling, blood seeping from the angry red eye in his palm. He retreated against the wall. Victoria flew to him, perching on his shoulder.

Durwood kept the gun trained on him as she looked back at Fogg's body. A steady beat of fluid wormed from his head. Shaking, she stepped toward him. She toed at the original Yellow Book on the floor, and saw that its pages were all blank. "I knew it." She kicked it away, sneering at Urquhart. "You're endless bullshit."

He glared at her, cradling his arm.

She knelt over Fogg, gun still on the All-Speaker. She reached out and poked at the wound in Fogg's head with her talon. She rubbed two fingers together, frowning at the ooze smeared between them. Viscous yellow stuff. She sniffed it. Smelled like dead leaves.

Gently, she turned Fogg over to examine the exit wound, a wide, ragged hole through his skull. As she turned him, a slop of yellow ichor and chunks slid out. She pulled back, then began to sift through the gunk with one hand, the other still holding the gun, trained always on Urquhart. She raked through the fluid and discovered that these chunks were actually dead leaves and twigs and acorns. A mess of forest detritus, submerged in the goo that had been sloshing around the cavity of his brainless skull. She wiped her hand on the front of his shirt, swiping off her talon, suddenly desperate to have this shit off her skin.

She looked slowly up at Urquhart. "What . . . the fuck."

He yanked a Yellow Book off the shelf behind him and whipped it at her. She threw up an elbow to block it, fired blind. Urquhart bolted. The bullet slammed into the wall over his head, poofing plaster dust into the air. Suddenly, Victoria was in Durwood's face, scratching at her cheeks, cawing loud. She fired at the bird and Victoria fell back, flapping after Urquhart. Durwood scrambled to her feet and fired again down the hall. The bullet punched through a light fixture, shooting sparks and darkening everything as Urquhart ducked, hands over his head, vanishing around a corner.

Durwood sprinted down the hall, emerging into the kitchen just as the back door slammed open against the wall.

"Urquhart!" she roared. She shouldered her way out the swinging door onto the back porch. She caught a flash of blue robe moving quickly away from her, toward the trees beyond the backyard.

She hopped down the four porch steps in a single leap, grunting and stumbling as she landed weirdly on her knee. She gritted her teeth and ran. She pounded after his retreating shadow, past the bubble of light on the porch. She brought the gun up and was about to fire again at his back—when she tripped and flew face-first into the dirt. She crashed into dead leaves, cracking her chin, snapping her teeth together at an angle that sent a jolt up through her jaw, down her neck. She rolled and gripped her shin, ears ringing in pain. She took a moment to cuss and throb, then realized she was outside, at night, in *Renfield*, and she was on one knee, gun swinging wildly.

No beasts. No Urquhart. No other sounds, except the distant siren.

"Fuck," she spat. She lowered the gun and held her breath, listening for any snap of branch or crunch of leaf.

Nothing.

She reloaded as she looked back at where she'd tripped. A wide space of leaves had been disturbed by her fall. Even in the dim far light of the porch, she could see it wasn't dirt that had been hiding beneath.

She took out her flashlight and shone it on the patch of ground.

A padlock glistened in the light.

She got to her feet. The knee she'd landed on throbbed with pain. She limped to the padlock, kicked away the remaining dead leaves surrounding it, and revealed a hatch. A wide metal service hatch, relatively new-looking (or at least, not rusted and seemingly abandoned). In yellow spray paint: *Maintenance Hatch, Urq. Est.*

She lowered herself, wincing, to her knees. She popped her talon and slid it into the loop of the padlock, twisting her arm until the metal wrenched free. She ripped the lock away and tossed it aside.

She looked around at the woods once more. She didn't sense movement or sound, so she gripped the handle of the hatch door and swung it up, quickly pointing her gun downward.

A red metal ladder. A concrete chute going down, down, fantastically down. Light, way below.

"What the fuck," she muttered, swiping sweat off her forehead and glancing around again.

No sounds, no movement.

Her heart was beating so fast. She took a moment to appreciate just what a long day it had been, how it was still going, and who *knew* how long it could drag on for now. She'd put on these socks at, what? Eight a.m.? It was eight p.m. now; that was twelve hours she'd been wearing these socks. Twelve hours her feet hadn't been able to breathe, she couldn't breathe.

She put a hand to her chest and massaged her sternum, keeping her gun trained on the hatch. The pressure of her fingers made her blood flow more easily, but her heart did not slow down. It punched at her like a speed bag, *barroom barroom barroom*. She blew out a long breath. "Okay. Come on, come on . . ."

The underground beckoned.

She swallowed and moved around the hatch, gazing inside. She peered in from every angle. She couldn't see anything more than a small square of distant light.

She took several more breaths before she finally jammed her gun into the back of her jeans, ran her hands over her face, and began to descend the ladder.

It took her eons of hand-under-hand climbing, staring at the blank wall behind the ladder, trying hard to control her breathing. Eventually, she reached the bottom without incident, and drew Bruce's gun the second her sneakers hit concrete.

It was a small closet. Shelves filled with ubiquitous janitorial supplies:

rolls of toilet paper, plastic sacs of hand soap, rolls of garbage bags. There was also a door.

She scanned the shelves, but saw nothing remarkable, except that the toilet paper was triple-ply, very fancy. She considered stuffing a roll or two in her bag, but she didn't have a bag and she didn't need any toilet paper right now. That was an old synapse firing. Her brain was short-circuiting.

She shook her head, trying to blink the present mission back into focus.

The door had a small, meshed window. She peered outside. She was at the end of a very long hall, like a giant concrete tube. Spartan and industrial.

She eased the door open. Thankfully, it didn't squeak or rasp. It whispered outward at her touch, and she stepped out into the artificial cool of the hall. She closed the door behind her with a small click. Scanned the corners of the hall for security cameras, didn't see any. No lidless black eyes gaping down at her. No raven-spies either, for that matter.

She crept forward. Blue metal doors lined the walls. Anyone could waltz out of any of these rooms, at any moment, and see her standing here, like a mouse in a wide-open field.

Still breathing hard, mind still threatening to over-oxygenate and fuzz out at any moment, she glanced inside the window of each door as she snuck past.

In one room, a large hog in a standing harness, atop a table. It struggled and squealed as men in lab coats poked at it with silver tools. In the next room, they had a gluttonbat tacked to the back wall, its wings pinned up to their full length and its insides split open, flaps of flesh spread apart for a full autopsy. Men were unspooling the thing's intestines. Its wingtips twitched and it moved its mouth slowly. It was still alive as they cracked apart its miracle ribs.

She glanced back to see if anyone had left the rooms behind her. No. She kept moving forward, silent and steady.

Then she paused. Frowned.

She backtracked, peering into the gluttonbat room again.

The "men" in lab coats weren't men. They were Fogg. All three of them wore his stern face, his tight, square jaw. Their ascots weren't all red, like the Fogg she was familiar with. They were orange, blue, yellow—their only distinguishing characteristic. But they were all exact copies of the empty-skulled man she'd just shot aboveground.

She passed more doors, her popped knee hitching with every other step. Sure enough, these rooms were filled with Fogg-clones as well. Foggs in lab coats, removing the tusks of a poo-pig as it squealed. Foggs cataloging shelves of small glass vials filled with swirling white fluid. So many Foggs in so many rooms, she eventually lost count.

At the end of the hall, there was an open doorway to her left, a sliding metal door to her right. A black box in the wall next to the door blinked red, and she figured she might need a keycard or something to get through there. So she turned left, and crept forward.

A massive, cavernous control room. Several banks of computers. Monitors and blinking maps, read-outs, all kinds of equipment. A bafflingly high ceiling and many other doors leading off who-knows-where. Foggs manned the controls, typing and taking notes, monitoring all kinds of things.

But dominating the room . . . The entire wall to Durwood's right was a fluid-filled glass tank. The liquid bubbling inside was a dark blue. She couldn't see the contents of the tank fully, but she saw the four mammoth limbs bobbing gently. The elephantine skin and the dull claws. Murky, silver tendrils of fog swirled in the fluid. The great pale swell of a furry belly. She had to crane her head back, looking up, up, to see the curve of its snout. It must have been five stories tall.

The realization yawned deep in her chest and she forgot where she was for a second, forgot she was on high alert. She stared into the tank and the only thought in her head was, *Oh my god. It's him.*

A whirring from the far side of the room. She ducked behind a bank of monitors and pressed herself to the floor. She peered around the corner to watch one of the Foggs say, in that familiar cold voice, "She is here."

"She is early," said another Fogg. "Should we be alarmed?"

"No. She has said everything above is on track. The outworlder has not disturbed the plan."

"That is good."

"The plan is always good."

"I see the abovers are gathered in their town hall."

"They are alarmed. It is fine."

"Is the outworlder alive?"

"We do not know."

"That was what she wanted, yes? To keep the outworlder alive?"

"Yes. But it does not matter now."

"Of course. She cannot stop the plan. We are in its climactic moments."

"The plan is good."

"Brother. The plan . . . is *always* good."

There was an elevator *ding*, and a door slid open. Out walked a woman with her hands clasped behind her back. A woman with sharp black hair, draped in raggedy black robes. Durwood knew her immediately. Knew that *this* is what she'd been digging for all along.

"Children," said the Botanist, addressing the roomful of Foggs.

They stood at attention, hands behind their backs. As one, they said, "Mother."

"Look alive, sweet flowers. This is the night you've been dreaming of. Ever since your days in the jar."

The Foggs stood straighter, puffed their chests out higher.

"Now, I understand," said the Botanist as she strolled into the center of the room, "that the variable of this second outworlder has *concerned* some of you. I asked Urquhart to keep her calm and alive, considering the fact that our first visitor's demise only drew further attention. However, the *All*-Speaker"—her tone conveying she did not respect Urquhart at all—"and I have withdrawn our courtesy to her, in the wake of certain events. Irritating, yes, but there is no cause for alarm. This outworld girl is nothing. The beasts and knights will track her down, rest assured. Meanwhile, life adapts! The plan remains intact."

"The plan is good," said the Foggs as one.

"Yeeess," the Botanist croaked, grinning with blackened teeth as she admired the giant blue tank. "The plan . . . is *always* good."

NEW ADDEKKEA, OCTOBER 2019
The Fogmonger Cometh

After Tom Durwood was cremated, his sister carried the plastic bag of his ashes to the top of a hiking trail in the Billows. High up, where she could see the deep gray bowl of the entire valley. Her home.

She put her back to that bowl and threw Tom into the air, toward the rest of the world. Then the wind picked up, ushering that cloud of ash back over the county line. Back into Renfield.

It broke Durwood's soul. Even after death, Renfield still had a hold on you.

She thought of Tom now as she lay on the cold floor underground, listening to the Botanist lecture her creations. *Even after I die here—because I feel like I'm probably, definitely gonna die here—will this place still keep me in its claws?* And for the first time since she'd arrived in New Addekkea, Rachel Durwood was truly, really scared.

"Your brethren have assured me," said the Botanist, "that we've worked out all the kinks in the latest cluster. I recognize that the first few trials were . . . discouraging. But I personally oversaw Batch X9, and I feel quite confident about it. In fact . . ." She slid a key from inside her black robe. "We could probably pop the cork right now." She unlocked a transparent plastic box on one of the consoles. It popped open, revealing a large blue button.

The woman's hand hovered over it, fingers twitching. "No need to delay any longer. We've been ready for weeks, haven't we?" Her long, pale fingers caressed the surface of the button. "My sweetest flower. We should really let you *breathe*."

"Don't!" Durwood launched herself to her feet, gun in both hands, aimed at the back of the Botanist's skull. "Stop." Blood rushed to her head and she had to blink for a second while the sudden static cleared.

It gave the Botanist time to slowly raise her hands and turn to face Durwood. She grinned.

"The knifewoman," she purred. "I was worried we wouldn't have the chance to meet."

"Step away from the button," said Durwood.

The Botanist lifted her eyebrows. "But of course." She stepped to the side.

"Wait," said Durwood. "Lock it first, then toss me the key."

"Mm." The Botanist chuckled. "Yes, ma'am."

The Foggs watched with blank expressions as she did as she was told. For a split second, as the key sailed through the air, Durwood worried it would clatter to the floor, giving the Botanist an opening to take the gun from her. But she caught the key and stuffed it into the back pocket of her jeans, relieved.

"Is that the only one?" she asked.

"Urquhart has the original," said the Botanist, hands in the air again. "I don't know how many copies there may be."

"Okay." Durwood jerked the gun at the tank. "And is that who I think it is?"

"In a way." The Botanist grinned again. "I know you. Durwood. The family who likes to *dig*. You all dig into yourselves until there's nothing left."

Durwood twitched. "No."

"What, you thought you'd be a stranger to me? Dear flower." She leveled her eyes at Durwood. "The roots tell me everything. When your body's in the earth, it doesn't belong to you anymore. It belongs to the ground."

"Shut the fuck up," Durwood whispered. Her eyes were suddenly wet.

"Don't be embarrassed," said the Botanist. "You know me, too. Am *I* embarrassed?"

"You should be." Durwood blinked back her tears, got a grip again. "You killed kids."

"Ohh." The Botanist frowned at Durwood like she was an adorable puppy. "I *regrew* kids. Used them to build this place. It was an administration office for the mine, but when the fog shut everything down, I adopted it. Rebranded it. I finished my life's work here. My *plan*. You think I've spent decades puttering around alone in some hut in a *bog*? I'd look like a goddamn fool. Noo, I've *built* something here!" She thrust her arms into the air. "Something glorious! You can't stand in the way of that."

"I'm certainly gonna give it a shot." Durwood adjusted her grip on the gun, hands sweating. "In the name of the Renfield County Guard, I'm ordering you to shut this down."

"Shut it down?" the Botanist echoed. "What makes you think it matters what you order? What makes you think *I'm* actually here? I could have my own copies. The true Botanist could be somewhere else entirely, safe as could be. The body before you could be nothing more than a walking flower. You could shoot me and it wouldn't matter at all."

Durwood looked around at the Foggs, watching her with cold glares.

"They all plants, too?" she asked.

"Of course," said the Botanist. "Even the Fogmonger himself. Look more closely."

Durwood squinted up into the tank. It was true. The sinuous flesh of the Monger wasn't covered in hair. It writhed with giant leaves and ivy. In fact, he wasn't even flesh at all, but an amalgamation of flora woven together. Vines and branches and twisting, coiling vegetation.

"You grew this," said Durwood.

"Yeeesss." The Botanist gazed proudly into the tank. "Isn't he marvelous?"

"What was your deal?" asked Durwood. "Urquhart made a deal with Lawrence's heart to regrow the Renfields in exchange for beasts, but what about you? Once the heart got what it wanted, what deal did *you* make Urquhart?"

"He gave my plan a shape," said the Botanist, gazing at the tank. "A much more creative, beautiful shape than I'd intended. And we agreed to leave each other be. He wouldn't try to poison my home again, and I wouldn't interfere with his plaything of a cult."

Durwood felt sweat going down her back. Her heart was beating so fast. She licked her lips. "What's it do?"

The Botanist cocked her head.

"The fog," Durwood clarified. "When that thing wakes up and breathes the fog, what happens? What's your plan?"

Slowly, the Botanist grinned again. "Ohh, sweet flower. You sorely misunderstand what's happening here. It isn't fog at all. It's *spores*."

The elevator whirred. Durwood glanced at it. The Foggs all tensed.

"Who's coming down?" Durwood asked.

"Urquhart, I assume," said the Botanist, edging away. "Come to hit the button himself."

Durwood jerked the gun at her. "Stop moving."

The Botanist lifted her hands higher. "So rude. But fine. I have no need to move." Quickly, she thrust her palms into the air, summoning. "Fogg!"

The plant-men burst into action. Before Durwood understood what was happening, they were piling on top of her. Dozens of them. An unblinking, blank-faced dogpile of clones. Clawing at her. Tumbling over each other to reach for her as she toppled to the floor.

She panicked. Flexed her talon, stabbed one in the chest, pulled back. Yellow ooze bubbled out, and that broke the spell. They were just pod-dudes, not actual guys. She could stab and shoot as much as she needed to without staining her conscience.

She stabbed liberally then, slicing one Fogg across the throat, puncturing another in the jaw. She kept hacking her way through them, but more and more of them jumped onto the pile. She couldn't breathe, couldn't see anything except Fogg's cold, dead eyes, glaring at her from every direction.

Something burrowed through the pile and hooked into Durwood's shirt. It pulled her out from under the bodies and threw her across the floor. She landed hard on her back and looked up at the black robes of a ravenknight. Its hook hand swung down at her, and she rolled again. She saw Urquhart standing by the elevator with a second knight, cradling his red-weeping arm and screaming, "Somebody fucking end her!"

She started shooting. Supine on the floor, she shot the closest raven-knight three times in the chest. It fell backward, grunting, its raven scrambling in the cage. She pulled the trigger at the other knight, but the gun clicked.

The Foggs pounced, trying to wrestle the gun from her hand, gripping her limbs. She wrenched free, stabbed one through the eye. Another, she sliced across the belly, sending a cascade of goo and leaves splashing to the floor. More Foggs slipped in the mess, tripping over each other, reaching for her. As they struggled, Durwood felt something bite into her side. She looked down and found the Botanist digging half a garden shear into her ribs. Cold slid into her body like a winter wind.

"I've been curious to see how you bleed," the Botanist snarled, twisting the blade deep. She stank of dirt and decay.

Durwood roared and elbowed her in the throat, sending the Botanist reeling, gagging.

Durwood knelt, quickly emptying the chamber of her gun and slipping fresh bullets inside. Something *whooshed* overhead. She ducked and looked up to see the remaining ravenknight lifting its scythe once more. She jerked the revolver, slapping the chamber in place, jammed her gun under the knight's helmet, and fired twice. Flashes of light illuminated the bottom of the metal head. Blood poured from beneath, and the knight stumbled back, falling at last.

"Punch it!" the Botanist choked. "Let him breathe!"

"No!" Durwood cried.

She'd fucked up. She hadn't been watching.

Urquhart was at the button. He popped the plastic lid and punched the big blue button fast, before Durwood could even blink.

Red lights twirled about the control center. The remaining Foggs froze, looking around like startled birds. Alarms blared.

The Botanist laughed, clutching her throat. A gargling, maddening sound. "You should have had faith in the fog, Guard."

The ground began to shake. The entire facility was trembling. Parts of the ceiling, the walls, cracked. A low moan bellowed throughout the facility: *Oooooohhhh.*

"Yeeess," the Botanist gurgled. "Awake!"

The tank fractured. Cracks spiderwebbed across its surface. Fluid sprayed out between the hairlines. Another great, rumbling roar.

Durwood was breathless, clutching at the wound in her side. Cold pain sang through her chest, inching toward her gut. She grabbed the front of the Botanist's robe and jammed the barrel of her gun against the woman's throat. "What kind of spores?"

The Botanist gargled laughter.

Oooooohhhh. Chunks of thick glass fell away from the tank. Fluid poured out, sloshing against Durwood's sneakers. Inside, the vines of the Fogmonger writhed.

Durwood punched her gun against the Botanist's throat. "What're the fucking spores?!"

The Botanist grinned. Yellow blood stained her teeth. *Yellow. Holy shit, she wasn't kidding. She's not even here. I'm interrogating a fucking plant copy.*

Another roar shook the facility, made her skull vibrate. A massive chunk of ceiling cracked apart and landed a few feet away.

"Your ride's leaving," rasped the Botanist.

Durwood turned. Urquhart was in the elevator, punching a button, glancing up at her.

"Shit." Durwood dropped the Botanist and dashed for the elevator, stumbling over Fogg bodies and huge chunks of ceiling. She slipped through the elevator doors just as they were closing, and slammed against the far wall of the small metal box.

She looked out to see rock falling all around, splashing in the fluid coursing out of the tank, shattering sparks out of consoles as the control room cracked apart.

The Botanist lay in the center of it all. The elevator doors shut on the image of her cackling and shouting into the chaos, "Yes! Awake! Awake!"

She was still laughing when the ceiling finally collapsed and crushed her out of existence.

Durwood took a moment to slump against the wall and breathe as the elevator shook and ascended unevenly. She could not tell where they were going, but at least she wasn't buried under rubble.

"I pity you," said Urquhart.

She looked up at him. He cradled his arm, stained by fluid and blood and dirt. Victoria was perched on his shoulder. He smiled at her. "This miracle is for *all* of us."

"Shut the fuck up."

"But you're still too blind to see that. Don't you want to witness the great blessing, rather than hinder it? Isn't this what you've always wanted? As a child in Renfield's cold, lonely, embrace, didn't you wish for a cure? I did. And we made it happen. Her and me." He laughed. "All we wanted was to heal the earth. Our means may not have been entirely agreeable to you, but . . . the *ends*."

"Fuck your ends," said Durwood.

The elevator dinged. Urquhart took a satisfied breath. "Good. We're here."

"THE ALL-SPEAKER SHOULD BE HERE ANY MOMENT," SAID DR. ERIC, squinting and smarmy as ever. He could no longer steeple his fingers, his past favorite thing. But he smiled at everyone gathered before him in the town hall and held up his stumps in what he hoped was a calming gesture. "When he comes, he will instruct everyone on what we're supposed to be doing. Oh-ooh?"

"You have to keep your heads, you fools," Eddie Neglani added at his side. "Come, come. We have survived worse."

The New Addekkeans were *not* keeping their heads. The tragedy at Clear Night had shaken them badly. The sirens, wailing for the second night in a row, didn't help. Nor did whatever was making the ground shake, the chandeliers swing, the windows vibrate.

As the New Addekkeans gathered in the town hall, following emergency protocol, whispers rippled throughout the crowd: *Is that him? Is he coming now? Is it more outworlders? Tanks, it could be an army of tanks. Yes, but it* could *be him . . .*

"Please do not spread gossip," Dr. Eric tried again. "Remember: 'Gossip is a useless song, discordant and rhymeless.' That's Yellow Book, Chapter XII, Verse 18."

The Renfields were in the front row of folding chairs. Adelaide clung protectively to May. She'd barraged the girl with questions, "What were you *thinking?*" But May didn't answer. Just stared blankly into the middle distance, feeling like she'd done so little, done nothing except get two people killed. Was it all over? Had she lost? It couldn't be over. *Please.*

Dr. Eric opened his mouth once more to calm them—

Ooooooohhhh.

Dead silence. Everyone sat in the vibrating shell of the hall, listening. Booming, gut-punching, doomsday-loud: *Ooooooohhhh.*

"My fog," whispered Edie Neglani. "It's him. He's here. He's here!"

The hall burst into life. People scrambling for the windows, the door. Desperate to see.

"Come!" cried Isabella Zambrano. "Everyone into the streets!"

They poured out onto the main street of New Addekkea, boiling with anticipation and a rush of exhilarating fear. In their bones, they felt the roar of the Monger as he burst out of the ground in the park, splitting the old archway in half. Dirt and roots and chunks of concrete geysered into the sky. Even from a mile away, they saw the large white paws punching through the earth, reaching up, up.

"Oh, he's beautiful," said Edie Neglani, looping her hand through her husband's arm.

"Sing!" Eddie cried. "Ooooooohhhh!"

Everyone took up the cry. The Renfields sang loud, joyous and trusting. May's heart was beating fast, fear needling through her blood. But her mother clasped her shoulders tight, and she didn't feel like she could afford *not* to sing, though it made her throat hurt.

Her father squeezed her hand. He was on the verge of tears. "I'm so happy we got these extra years together. All that work was worth it. So worth it." And then he sang, hot tears pulsing down his cheeks.

Everyone sang as the mammoth-sized snout slid straight up out of the earth, like a whale breaching the surface of the ocean. Thick, white ivy-hair covered its belly. Fog rolled off its vegetated hide in dense, milky sheets.

"Oooooohhh," sang the chorus of New Addekkea. The Speakers, the Renfields, all the townspeople. People who had been there since the beginning. Even the ravenknights felt the vibrations of the emergence through their feet, and rejoiced. Their sworn raven-friends cried, *He is come. He is come. He is come!* Jake Mendez, Ashleigh Hunt, Troy Pittner, Dom and his little brother Tomas, Safety Officer Wilson, and all the rest stood tall and proud behind the chorus as it sang, "Oooooohhh."

The front legs of the Fogmonger braced against the ground, straining as he wriggled his way out of the dirt. His body stretched so high they couldn't see the top of his snout as he rose, rose, titanic legs swinging through the clouds of fog coursing out of his flesh. He roared into the sky, great blankets of white billowing out of his chainsaw-toothed jaws.

A blanket of snowy erasure swept through the streets, flooding out farther and farther, sweeping over the chorus with a physical *boom* that almost knocked them off their feet. It blew Eddie Neglani's hair back and he laughed, breathing deep. Edie sucked at the air through her nostrils. Isabella Zambrano drew hissing breaths through her dented jaw. Dr. Eric licked his lips, tasting the heavy, wet, cool. So icy and fresh, *ahh*, he breathed as if for the very first time.

"Oooooohhh," they sang as the fog surged through them in thick, blinding waves.

"Oooooohhh," they sang as it punched into their mouths, up their nostrils.

"Oooooohhh," they sang as fog smothered them completely.

NEW ADDEKKEA, DOOMSDAY 2019

The Great Blessing

The elevator led directly to Urquhart's estate. He swung open the windows of the second-floor chamber, where Durwood could see the entire town.

"Best seat in the colony," said Urquhart. "Look. The greatest miracle the world has ever seen." He pointed at the roiling white shadow of the Fogmonger, stomping toward the center of New Addekkea.

They could see Main Street from here. Could see all the people gathered together, arms looped around each other. Children jumping with excitement. They sang as one, the largest and most joyful chorus ever seen. The Fogmonger shook his gargantuan head and roared, long and low, pouring ever more fog from his white throat.

Durwood watched him, numb. It would take a *lot* of stabbing and shooting to fell that thing.

"He's beautiful," said Urquhart, still cradling his wounded hand. "You should be honored, outworlder. I should be down there with them. But I'm here with you, at the end." He turned to Victoria on his shoulder, smiled at her, and she nuzzled into his cheek. "A drink, I think. To celebrate." He went to a cabinet on the far wall, knelt, and began rooting around inside.

Durwood watched the townsfolk swallowed by the fog, saw it unfurling over the buildings, piling closer, closer to the edges of the windows. The Fogmonger let out another bellow, and Durwood realized she could hear the wall of blue-white fog approaching, too. Rolling like a tsunami.

Her shoulders sagged. She was tired. So tired. *God, please let there still be a way. Let me get down there and find that those people aren't dead yet. Please. I just want this to be okay. I just want to save one. Just one . . .*

She looked back. Urquhart was cinching a gas mask to his face.

"You bastard," said Durwood.

"What did you say before?" Urquhart asked, voice muffled. "Endless bullshit?"

She whipped around, had the gun on him. "Gimme the mask."

"You think I'd coordinate all this just to *give* you the mask?" He walked toward her. "You think I'd put in all that effort with the Botanist just to give up now? When she approached me after the Fogmonger's arrival, she *told* me she was always going to enact her plan, regardless of what I did. So I simply gave her a shape for it. Bought myself a back door."

Durwood pointed out the window. "That's her plan?"

"Sure," said Urquhart. "Return the valley to the plants, once and for all."

"And you were happy to just let that happen?"

"Happy is a strong word," said Urquhart, stepping ever closer. "But this was amenable to her, and it afforded me sanctuary, so . . . I gladly sang along."

"You never gave a shit about this town, did you?"

"Why should I? It never gave a shit about me until I *forced* it to." He dove for her, groping for the gun. They wrestled back and forth, slamming against the conference table and falling to the floor. Durwood managed to roll on top of him, but he kneed her in the groin, rolled away, Victoria cawing and clawing at the back of her head the entire time. She swept her talon blindly at the bird, Victoria flapping just out of reach. Urquhart grabbed her from behind and she thrust herself backward, slamming him into the wall by the window. She twirled, grabbed Urquhart's shirt, and threw him onto the floor. His head hung over the edge of the open window.

Fog swallowed the iron fence below, coming closer. Rising, rising.

"Taking that mask," Durwood growled. She clawed at its straps.

Urquhart punched the wound in her side hard, twice. She cried out as pain lashed through her ribs.

Tendrils of fog licked close. Curling into the open windows.

Durwood ripped the mask off Urquhart's head and scrambled backward, kicking at him.

"Knife-bitch!" he roared as he tried to stand. She kicked him square in the sternum. His eyes went wide, his arms windmilled, and he toppled backward out of the window, out of sight. Victoria dove after him.

Then the fog. It surged upward, and Durwood was knocked sideways by the force of it. It was cold, very cold, and wet; she could feel water droplets forming on her skin. All she could hear was her own breath, rushing through the mask as she tightened it against her skull just in time.

There was a moment of pure, white silence. Durwood breathed. Nothing moved.

Then screaming. A symphony of screams from below.

She looked out the windows. She could see nothing except fog. Pure, white death.

Spores. The Botanist had called it *spores.*

DOWN BELOW, THE NEW ADDEKKEANS WENT SILENT AS THEY breathed heaven in. Feeling the cool beauty wash up their nostrils and down into their throats. *Ahh.*

Eddie Spaghetti squeezed his wife's hand. "Oh, my dear. Isn't it *beautiful?*"

She grinned at him. Then tilted her head, wrapped her lips around his throat, and chewed out his Adam's apple.

The chorus erupted into chaos.

YOU GOTTA MOVE, DURWOOD TOLD HERSELF, TIGHTENING THE mask. *Come on, Rach, you gotta goddamn move.*

She stumbled out of the room, down the stairs, through the house. It was difficult to see where she was going; everything was drenched in moist white.

She found the front door, a mere shape in a labyrinth of pale blurs. She threw it open and stumbled outside. Screams all around her. Everything white.

Keep moving, she told herself as she limped toward the iron gate, fuzzing into view several feet away. She clutched the wound at her side. *Just get to the Shelter. Call in a Code: Absolute Red. Make sure the spores don't—*

Something smacked into the back of her head. She fell forward, fire bursting through her side as her wound hit the ground.

She flopped onto her back, the fight gone out of her. So tired. Just wanted to go home. Wanted to go back to the hotel and lie next to Bruce's body until they were both cold and decayed and full of spores.

Urquhart stood there wheezing, his body broken. His stabbed arm hung limp at his side, flopping as he lurched toward her. In his other hand, he held a rock. Victoria, as always, was perched on his shoulder. His monocle was cracked, his one visible eye entirely smoked out, as white as the fog itself. "You ruined it," he wheezed, breathing in great, rattling lungfuls of fog. "You . . . ruined it!" He fell on her, teeth gnashing, swinging his hand back to whack her again with the rock.

She shot at him, clipping Victoria's wing instead. Victoria screamed and dove for her. Durwood put up her knife-hand, her hawk-hand, and pulled from the bottom of her stomach, deep within her soul, a voice she hadn't known she'd possessed until this very moment, as she appealed to Victoria, bird to bird.

"**GO**," she commanded.

Victoria hovered, flapping hard, dropping feathers. Then flew away, squawking in panic.

Durwood wouldn't know this, of course, but Victoria lived a free life in Crumdugger Forest after that. She was a psychic raven in a land of normal crows. A miracle, born a hen, transformed by the earth itself. For a time, there were many creatures who considered her the god-queen of Crumdugger Forest.

"My bird!" Urquhart threw himself at Durwood, toppling her to the ground, clutching her shoulders and shaking her. "My bird! My bird!" He grabbed her head and slammed it against the ground.

She got her spike in his side, once, twice, punching in and out, until he let go. She rolled over on him and put her talon to his throat.

He gargled a laugh. Glared at her with that one pure white eye.

"Do it," he wheezed. "It doesn't matter. All of this happened before, in a different color. All of it will happen again. Stab me again, it won't matter. I've been stabbed before. All of this is just—"

"Stop . . ." She slid her talon slowly into his monocle, up to the hilt. ". . . talking." The glass cracked satisfactorily. She felt shards grind into him. He sputtered, spat up blood.

And was still.

Durwood sat there, listening to her breath in the mask, surrounded by fog, watching him bleed. Making sure he didn't get up.

He didn't. But after a minute, small green vines began to twist out of his nostrils, his ears, out of the corners of his remaining eye and the broken socket, germinating from within his brain.

She wanted badly to stay. To see what, exactly, these spores could do.

But there were so many screams.

Eventually, she got up and hobbled down the hill into town.

PANIC IN THE STREETS. THE FOG HAD DROWNED EVERYONE'S MINDS. They were flinging themselves at each other, biting, tearing each other to shreds. Poo-pigs ran loose, squealing and headbutting each other. Gluttonbats crashed and tussled overhead. People dove for Durwood and she shot them without thinking, breath coming in sharp, painful rasps in the mask.

Dr. Eric blindsided her in front of the high school. All of a sudden, *whoom*, he had his hands on her. Shoving his finger stumps under the straps of her mask, trying to pry it off her face.

"Sing! *Sing!*" he cried. Grinning and squinting through his cracked glasses, until Durwood rammed her spike in his kidney and ripped up.

She limped onward, leaving him gurgling on the ground. Vines twisted from the mouth of torn flesh on Eric's side as Durwood went deeper, deeper into the white.

She hobbled blind, clutching uselessly at the wound in her own side, her knee swelling badly. Yeahh, she wasn't going to make it to the Shelter. She accepted that now. She was just limping along through the apocalypse, waiting for the right moment to remove her mask and breathe in, call it a night. At intervals in the distance, she heard the Fog-monger roar as New Addekkea tore itself apart.

A shape emerged out of the fog. She trained her gun on it, but it didn't attack. It stood there, grunting at her, twitching. Durwood hobbled closer. When she came close enough that she could see who it was, her heart sank irreparably.

"Don't," said Durwood. Exhausted, pleading. "Please don't."

May Renfield stood still, rasping, drooling, zombified. Rachel Galloway, bent into something else, then warped even further beyond that.

"I'm sorry," said Durwood. "I'm so sorry."

Galloway/May hissed at her. And started sprinting.

It wasn't until Durwood felt her talon punch through Galloway's chest that she felt, officially, like she had failed. Or perhaps she had been too late to do anything, about *any* of this, from the beginning. Perhaps it wasn't her fault because there was nothing she *ever* could have done to fix it. Perhaps it had been broken long before she'd arrived. This town, this county, this world. All of it. All of this was beyond her control. It had never been her burden to be the savior of the broken, the beaten, *or* the damned. She'd only thought it was. But it had never been on her shoulders in the first place.

There is a small comfort to be had in that idea. That the world, cruel and fogged, is beyond our control.

"I tried to save you," she murmured as she held Galloway in her arms, feeling the life throb out of her, brushing her hair out of her whitewashed eyes. "I tried to save you. I tried. I tried . . ."

INTO THE FOG

Fog sweeps across the town, slithering through the walls of greenery in tendrils of brilliant white, licking at the edge of Burnskidde Tunnel. Every living thing in its wake is frothing at the mouth. Coughing up ivy and chewing at their neighbors.

"Isn't it glorious?"

High up on an outcropping behind Galloway Park, the Botanist (the true Botanist) watches her plan unfold. She breathes in the fog, immune through remedies of her own making. She clutches a jar to her chest. In the jar, a small homunculus with Fogg's face, naked and shivering. He whimpers at the screaming. Explosions, laughter, bursts of flame, across the entire drowned colony.

"Ohh, it's alright, wee one," coos the Botanist, petting the lid of the jar. "There's no need to mourn. This soil has been rotting for a long time. It *deserves* new life. All those experiments and sacrifices and deals . . . It was all worth it, sweet flower. See? This land belongs to the plants now, once more. It belongs to *you*. I told you," she purrs, "the plan was always good . . ."

Down in New Addekkea, new life doesn't seem possible to Rachel Durwood. It seems like there won't be any life anywhere ever again. But still, she lays Galloway's corpse on the ground, gently, and stands as best as she can. She needs to push just a little further. It's the least she can do, the least she ever could have done. *Push* just a little bit more.

A gluttonbat soars overhead, crying as it rides the cold air of the Monger's fog. She watches it go by, and wonders if she can climb up on a roof, or the back of the Fogmonger himself, and jump onto the back of that bat as it flies by. She'll ride it into the lightning with Muriel Gnash, rain lashing in their faces, driving their hair into their eyes as they stab at the beast together.

The bat flies away over the Monger, and Durwood's eyes fall once more onto his mountainous looming shadow. It sways as he moves his head from house to house, moaning low and long in that deafening tone, sending more and more waves of frigid white rolling out of his throat.

Durwood ducks her head and braces herself against the tightening cold. Her skin goes taut and bumpy, and she shivers uncontrollably. Her breath howls in her ears inside the mask. She lifts her head against the gale and glares up at the colossal bulk of the Monger. He glares straight down the street, right back at her. And though she can only see his large fog-dripping lower jaw, she feels his eyes lock on hers.

In the future, they will build statues of this moment. In the future, people will spray graffiti on those statues and make out on them after dark. In the future, Rachel Durwood's name will erode, but young women will look up into her birdshit-encrusted furious glare, and they will think to themselves—in a future drowned in pale blue fog, they will hold secretly to their hearts—*I have metal in me, too.*

Durwood imagines them all, flesh going on ash, many more of their names forgotten than remembered. She imagines the seasons bleaching her marbled face, and all the marbled faces of the women who follow her. She imagines the women who fight monsters and men, across all of time—and she takes another step. She walks unsteadily, blood pattering the ground below her, behind. Her hand shakes as she lifts it and rolls her wrist, flexing out her claw. She holds it up for the Monger to see.

That vast mouth, half-hidden in pale blue nothing, sneers at her.

She takes a stumbling step forward. Her side stabs at her again, and she puts a hand to it to clamp down on the bleeding. She takes another step, talon raised high, pointed straight at the Fogmonger's skull. He growls deep, and takes a step forward himself, *boom*, shaking the earth, making Durwood lose her footing. She can't balance with her hand clamped to her side, and she realizes then that it doesn't matter. She can lose all the blood she has to.

She takes her hand off her side and begins to run. She feels the muscles in her side tear, but it's okay. She only needs them once. She feels things pull and snap over her ribs, but her legs are carrying her, carrying her, pumping long and strong as she runs hard and fast down the street. The Monger is coming to meet her, taking steps faster and faster, too, legs pounding, sending a world-ending thunder throughout town.

They're both running now, running straight for each other. Rachel pulls her hand back, crouches, and springs off the ground. The Monger lunges forward, jaws spread wide, head tilted sideways to catch her as she jumps, and for a moment, she sees the Monger's eye. A massive yellow goat-thing, bloodshot and glaring at her, and she sees herself perfectly reflected there, bloody and bold. Just like she's always wanted to be.

Rachel roars and the Fogmonger roars in answer, engulfing her in pure blinding white as she swings out her arm, hooking her talon into the thing's viny flesh, burying it up to her wrist, just before those large curved teeth close around her.

She remains suspended there, in marble, forever.

Acknowledgments

Most stories begin for me as a swirl of images and scenes that I hold in my head for a long time. Months, years. I turn them over and over in my mind, telling myself stories while I'm falling asleep at night. I almost prefer stories in this stage because they're just mine. Once I start writing the plot that connects these scenes, all of a sudden, my nighttime reveries feel like work, and I have trouble sleeping; I have to move on to new images.

The key images for *Galloway's Gospel* lived in my head for a comfortable decade before they became this book:

A girl in a basement is preaching to her teenage friends about some faith she believes she's made up. Until a creepy boy presents her with a miniature creature he has made for her, based upon her sermons. This creature cannot be real.

Then: This same girl is running through the fog, trying to escape the cult she accidentally began in that basement. The boy catches up to her, and stabs her when no one is looking.

A lone detective is spending the night in a small-town hotel room as beasts wail outside in the dark. This detective must navigate a strange celebration in order to solve a missing-persons case.

That same detective discovers a vast underground lab, where all the small town's secrets are unraveled . . .

In the summer of 2017, I had these images in my head as I played the video game *Outlast 2*, in which you assume the role of an investigative journalist trying desperately to survive a townful of masochistic cultists. As you sneak and sprint through this town, with no weapons to defend yourself except a small camcorder, you discover journal entries, letters, pieces of scripture, etc. Much of *Outlast*'s story is told through these found documents, and may I just say that writers can (and should!) learn a lot from storytelling in video games? Games trust their players to connect dots and discover clues on their own, for the sake of experiencing a sprawling storyworld. To wit, highly perceptive readers can revisit *Edenville* to discover the subtle yet grisly fate of Jake Mendez's cousin Chelsea. Of course, there are numerous connections between *Galloway* and *The Poorly Made* as well.

Anyway, it occurred to me as I was picking up all these documents in *Outlast 2* that faith can be horribly contagious. What if I brought these gospels out into the world and the cult wasn't stopped, but *spread*? Truly, my prerogative should be burning these documents, not preserving them.

I was captivated by this idea of an outbreak of faith, so I paused the game at one point and made a note on my phone. It read only: GALLOWAY'S GOSPEL, because I'm a sucker for alliteration. For years, this book existed only as that vague note and the images in my head.

It's odd and bittersweet to have finally transmuted this all onto the page, so that these images and these characters live in *your* mind now. Keeping you company as you drift off to sleep.

Soo many people helped this happen. So let's start with a big freakin THANK-YOU to the kind and generous and painfully honest folks who offered this a full beta-read: Bridget D. Brave, P. L. McMillan, Clay McLeod Chapman, Allison Rassmann, and Hannah Peterson. Another huge thank-you to my core writing group, my Shelleys, who read pieces of this: Jonathan Lees, Carol Gyzander, Teel James Glenn, Meghan Arcuri-Moran, Joe Borrelli, and Kathleen Scheiner. And a shout-out to Ashley Pecorelli who started reading this, until I said I'd send her an updated draft. I never did, oops!

Thank you, Dayle Rebelein, best mom in the world, for reading multiple drafts of this and laughing your ass off when the pig pooped in the woods. I love you most and frafr.

Thank you a million times over to my amazing agent, Claire Freakin Harris. Your patience and gentle guiding hand mean everything to me. Thank you to *everyone* on the P.S. Literary team. Y'all rock!

Speaking of teams who rock, thank you to everyone at William Morrow for believing in this one. I know it wasn't easy! But Ariana Sinclair, editor extraordinaire, you helped this one fly. Again! Who knew those early drafts had so much deadweight??

Thank you to the entire badass WM team: production editor Amanda Hong, copyeditor Ana Deboo, cover designer Yeon Kim, interior designer Leah Carlson-Stanisic, proofreaders Carol Burrell and Susan Schwartz, Emily Bierman in content management, and my marketing and publicity heroes Jen McGuire and Kelly Cronin, and James Fosdike for that kickass cover.

THANK YOU:

Stacy Fass and My Chemical Romance for letting us use that lyric.

Taryn Fagerness and Alec and Debbie at IAG for embracing this world.

Ken Greller for seeing the sparkle in *Edenville*.

Mark Harris and Stanza Books for being *beyond* supportive!

My grandmother, Catherine Bell, for "supporting the arts."

My father, Robert Rebelein, for literally pushing me out of my comfort zone.

Ryan LaDuke for speaking to me about mines in New York. Any stupidities I've committed regarding the Burnskidde Salt Mine are my own. I also borrowed some details from the Stratavator at the Carnegie Museum of Natural History in Pittsburgh.

I didn't do any specific research on cults. Sorry! But I've spent my entire adult life being fascinated by them. Amanda Montell's book *Cultish*, as well as the documentaries *Wild, Wild Country* and *Prophet's Prey*, helped craft Urquhart's rhetoric and New Addekkea. Glynn Washington's podcast *Heaven's Gate* was helpful regarding mass suicides.

There are other various influences here, of course: Dr. Eric is my version of Billy Lee Tuttle from *True Detective*. Emma Dring's arc is a reimagining of R.L. Stine's iconic *Stay Out of the Basement*. The films *Midsommar*, *Men in Black*, and *The Wolf of Snow Hollow* are all ingredients here. Burnskidde High is based on my alma mater, Arlington High School (go Admirals).

Overall, *Galloway's Gospel* is half a story about cults and half a story about incurable loss. I began writing this book in June 2023 and finished the final round of edits in October 2024. During that time, my beloved Goddard College shut down. My two sweet pups passed away: Shadow & Truman, handsome little boys right up until the end. My friend and neighbor, Cindy Wheeler, passed away somewhat suddenly. She was part of the inspiration for my gleeful portrayal of creepy librarians in *Edenville*. She loved being a part of that book.

I also said goodbye this year to my number one writing friend and confidant: Jamie Sheffield. I miss you, brother. I really wish you could have read this one.

So in this year of global tumult and personal loss, please allow me to remind you, fellow reader, that you have metal in you, too. Tomorrow may look dreary and terrifying—it's hard to see what's coming through the fog. But I have faith that light will follow. So long as we, like my dear Rachel Durwood, continue to fight.

December 30, 2024

About the Author

Sam Rebelein is the Bram Stoker Award–nominated author of *Edenville*, which also received a Wonderland Book Award for Best Novel. He holds an MFA in creative writing from Goddard College, with a focus on memoir and short fiction. His work has appeared in *PseudoPod*, *Bourbon Penn*, *Gamut*, *The Deadlands*, Ellen Datlow's *Best Horror of the Year*, and elsewhere. He lives and teaches in Poughkeepsie, New York.